Love Across Time

by

Ronny Whitman

Love is two hearts connected as one, a soul-to-soul bond,

gifted by God

Prologue

Have you ever imagined what is out there? Do you believe in God, angels, also known as spirit guides, heaven, the spirit realm, karma, spirits (entities), and paranormal? What if these things exist? What if they do not? Would you like to know if they do – was true?

I found it interesting at the possibilities to the questions asked above, and after extensive research, I decided to incorporate these possibilities in this story, and I will leave it to you to decide for yourself, what is true and what is not.

To feel and be loved, is to feel great power, a power that binds us through our hearts and souls. To find a love so powerful – for two people to share their hearts, as if they were one, is rare. When you can be so lucky to find this love, you want to hold onto it with all your might. And if you are real lucky, this love will follow you from lifetime to lifetime, looking to reconnect, as if a string was pulling, drawing you back together, reattaching each other, as if they were never apart. A feeling, as if you have always known each other. In all and all, you have. This love comes from the highest power above – God. To be blessed once is beautiful. To be blessed twice – no, multiple times – now that is a true blessing, a great power, a miracle given by God. How do you know this is true? That this is real? You just do. Your heart and soul tells you so.

To feel the power of the purest love, which even now surrounds us. How do you know when you feel God's love? It's as if a wave of emotions consumes you, an overwhelming feeling of love and happiness, which practically brings you to your knees, without understanding why. This is God's love.

There are those who believe there is more out there, but does not believe in God. That's okay, because from what I learned, God is the name people of Earth gave him, but to those above – in people believe to be Heaven, is known to be the source of all power, who each and every one of us is connected to, whether you believe it or not.

The spiritual world is an unknown world we all seek to understand. What is out there? Who is out there? Is God looking out for us? If so, how? We are guided and protected from the moment of our birth – no, from even before. We are never alone or unloved. We are loved whether we know it or not.

So, read this story and decide for yourself what you believe.

For Robert and Elizabeth to find a special kind of love, a love most believe could only happen – exist in one lifetime, then to discover it is not true. A love so pure and powerful can carry on, existing lifetime after lifetime. A love since the first time it flourished, can continue even after death. Two souls searching, seeking to rekindle this love. A love forgotten until now. A love, to be told and remembered, in the hopes that one day, this love can be found once again. Here and now, in this lifetime. A love buried and forgotten due to their tragic ending from their life before. We need to know and believe that there is a love so powerful, that not even time itself can stand in its way. A love from God and remembered because of God, and with his help, will allow them to remember this love, and allow them to connect from a time before. With God's love, and through him, they can find their love from long ago.

These two souls are destined to find this love, in this lifetime, in the twenty-first century. So, allow me to tell you a story, one even to this day amazes me. To live the life I lived and still be alive, when most to have endured what I have been through, would have committed suicide long ago, or destroyed themselves little by little, through the use of drugs and alcohol. To learn later in life, how life as we know it, isn't what we believe it to be – it's not what it seems. How I learned that certain events, places, and people, were road maps guiding me, leading me to what and who I am today. This is why I think the song by Rascal Flatts, *Bless the Broken Roads*, resonates so strongly with me. The events I am about to share with you, I understand now, I was in preparation, being tested, preparing me to go through a transition, an awakening into the world of spirituality. In doing this, it put me in a place to learn about a life before.

As I look back on those days, knowing what I know now, these gifts I have, a gift that has grown beyond my expectations, were always there, although I couldn't see it. With what I was going through then, it blinded me, not allowing me to see what was happening. In the life I chose, they knew they had to slowly ease me into what they call an *awakening*.

It was best to give me only bits and pieces, until the day came when all would be revealed. Only those memories that would be important later – stuck. Until the time was right, only then would they resurface, allowing me to remember all.

When I think back on this knowledge, if I experienced these things before I was able to recognize and understand them, would I have understood what they were? What did they mean? No, I think they would have driven me mad. Like so many today, I would have been one of those children placed into a psychiatric home and medicated.

Let me ask you, do you believe in miracles, in the possibility there is something out there, greater than yourself, man or woman? Well, I didn't, not really. I hoped and prayed, wanting it to be so, and I remember wishing for a miracle, proof that God existed. Who would know that in 2011 that miracle would present itself. No, not right away, but in time. I've learned since, that everything in my life was a miracle. From the moment of my conception to the very moment this story had risen – no, even now, to this very moment, at this very instant I am typing, I continue to experience the miracle of God.

You know what's funny, someone recently told me after allowing them to read my introduction said, "this book sounds more of a religious book, not one of romance." And I told this person, "Yes and no." God is not one of religious belief – people of Christianity, but one of all of us. Each, and every part of us, whether we believe it or not, we are a part of God. This love story stems from that knowledge of a love so powerful; it could only come from one place, a place of pure love – God. So, if you view this as a religious story, that's okay, but if you can look deeper, you can see it's far more than that.

My name is Rebecca Daniels, and I was born in a small town north of Sacramento, California. When I first picked up a pen and started writing my story, I was forty-five, and now two years later, a few days before my forty-seventh birthday, so many things have changed. When everything came into perspective, and the first wave of memories started, I was forty-three, and I've nearly lived half a century. Here is my story.

Chapter 1

"God, what is happening?" This was a constant question I had during this time of my childhood, along through my adulthood. I have always had faith with a belief in God, although I was unsure if God truly existed. But there was this feeling, one I did not understand, telling me he did. I often wondered if I had a purpose on this earth. If there was, I wondered what it might be. Never in my deepest dreams could I have imagined this was to be my life, my purpose. I had to have a reason for being, that there was someone who loved and wanted me. Someone who could make me happy, in fulfilling my life, as I am to make him happy, in fulfilling his life. Take our feelings of loneliness and replace them with love. Not just any love, a great and powerful love. A gift from God.

<u>Phoenix, AZ – Summer 2017</u>

I am standing in his office facing the window, staring out to the sky above, trying to find a way to answer his questions, *"How do you know this man? How did you come to have the information you gave me? You have details…which is why I wonder, what exactly can I do to help you?"* What do I say? How am I to explain? I take a deep breath, then push away from the window, and I turn back to face him.

"Mr. Davenport," which is funny, considering what I've learned about my past life, but I am no longer surprised. It seems since I've learned what I know, these little signs have always been there – everything happens for a reason. "Do you believe in miracles? Things that happen, but you cannot explain. A knowing…a feeling?

I can see him looking at me with that, *lord, I have a real one here*, look.

He asked, "Are you referring to psychic abilities?"

For a long moment, I could only stare at him, then I thought, *do I continue or back out, and give up this idea?* Well, after taking a deep breath, I decided why the hell not. What could I lose in doing so?

"In a way, yes." How do I explain what happened to me? What is still happening to me? "Mr. Davenport, in 2013, after visiting Cheshire, England, something happened to me after my return. I even thought I was going mad, until after seeing a phycologist, and through her a psychic medium with thirty-plus years' experience, who is also a licensed phycologist, who also at one time worked with law enforcement. With my phycologist, after putting me under hypnosis, along with the psychic medium, confirmed I was not crazy. What I was remembering through dreams and visions, were real."

I was unable to look at him during my explanation, so when I glanced up to meet his eyes, he looked just as I figured, as if I am crazy. But it appears he is listening to every word I am saying, so I continue. "This man Marco, that I want you to find…well, he is a man I have been dreaming about, along with the visions. We…shared a past life together in the 1500s —" I stopped, as I was finding it difficult to explain, but I didn't want to give up, so I let out a breath and continued. "Maybe you don't need to know all the details, but I feel I need to explain, so you will understand where all this is coming from. By me telling you this, you will work to convince me…prove to me…he is real or not. Everything I have learned up to today told me he is."

After I finished, I carefully watched Mr. Davenport, looking for any sign of what he was thinking, or what he will do about my confession.

Then he says, "Ms. Daniels, please continue."

Relieved, I went on. "Thank you, Mr. Davenport. The information I gave you is from the dreams and visions I had, along with the messages I received from Marco's grandmother, who died in September of 2015. I need to know if he is real. Can you do this for me? Can you help me prove one way or the other?"

"I am here to help you, regardless of how you came to have the information. To me, this is of no matter. If you hire me to investigate this man, then I will."

I sighed with relief. I know this was a considerable risk, a chance of being laughed right out of his office, but it had to be done.

"Thank you, Mr. Davenport. I do wish to hire you, and I will accept whatever information you learn." At this, I wrote him a check and left his office.

As I was walking down the hall, I started thinking about everything that's happened in my life since this whole thing started. How it took me back to my childhood, that from the very beginning, there were signs, with bits and pieces guiding me, wanting me to know and learn what I now understand to be the truth. Even during the time when I wanted to move to England, then eventually did. I had no idea how truly close I was. To learn and know the things I learned without knowing it. I often wondered how I could remember specific points in my life in complete detail and not others. There were reasons, signs leading to this day, to him.

Rebecca Daniels is my married name, but I was born Rebecca Dahli, in a small-town north of Sacramento, California, and this is our story.

<u>Verona, Italy</u>
"Come with me. I want to speak with you, Marco?" Maria said.

Maria takes Marco by the hand and guides him to a beautiful open clearing near their family restaurant in Verona, Italy. When they arrived at the place, they sat on a fallen log near a young and beautiful lushes' tree.

"Sit here, Marco," Maria said, pointing to a spot on the log, "Beside me."

Marco sat next to his grandmother, wondering what she wanted to talk to him about. After all, he was only ten years old.

However, at ten, Maria had already noticed the intelligence and maturity in the boy, far beyond a boy of ten should be. Although this was so, it made Maria think of his life before, the one she is to reveal to him today. He was also ten when he learned of his fate, and in those times, children had to behave like mini adults. So maybe, some of his life then is already a part of him now.

Maria is wearing a blue top with white pants. She has long, beautiful wavy blond hair with crisp blue eyes. Maria looks at the amazing boy sitting next to her, as he's watching her with that sweet smile on his face. *He is a handsome boy with his thick dark curls*, she thought, causing her to laugh, knowing how much he hates them. He wore his favorite red and black stripe shirt and his black shorts. Maria smiles again, in the way Marco is sitting so patiently with his hands in his lap.

"How are things at home with your momma and papa, Marco?"

"They are well, nõnna," he said as he rubs an itch on his nose, causing his face to scrunch up.

Maria laughs before grabbing Marco's hand and pulls it away from his nose. She reaches in her pocket and pulls out a hanky, then hands it to him for him to blow his nose. Marco takes the hanky and blows his nose like a blow horn, causing Maria to laugh again. *Ah, bellissima*

"I am glad to hear this, Marco. Now, I have a story to tell you. You like stories, don't you?" Maria said, although she already knows the answer.

"Oh yes, nõnna, I do," Marco said, with a large smile, as he was filled with excitement. He loves his grandmother's stories, since she tells the most amazing ones. Marco sat up straight, placing his hands in his lap, ready to hear his grandmother's story.

"Well, the story I am going to tell you takes place in the 1500s, which was a very long time ago. There was a young boy, right around your age, and a young girl only a year younger than you. These two young people were thrown together by chance. A sister helping another sister who she loved very much, and who was being forced to marry this boy —"

Marco interrupts his grandmother. "Nõnna, why are they going to get married? They are only ten years old? I am ten, and I do not want to get married," Marco asked, "I don't even like girls," he said, as he wrinkled his nose in disgust, looking at his grandmother with confusion.

Maria laughs, "Well, times are different now. Let me continue," Maria said.

"Okay, nõnna."

"When they become of age, which in those days was seventeen, and in some cases, much younger —"

Marco says, "Oh."

Maria smiles at her nipõte and continues without stopping. "Because these two young people were thrown together by chance, they found they had a great deal in common, as they both loved the outdoors. In this love, they formed a strong bond, a friendship between a boy and a girl, which was rare in those days. Until one day, when something changed, and they found a pure love. A love so pure it connected their hearts and souls in a way, if they were away from each other, it felt as if someone was ripping their hearts right from their chest, wanting desperately to be reunited."

Marco looked at his grandmother, not understanding what she was saying. To him, it was mushy. Maria could see this, so she tried to explain it differently.

"Marco, have you played tug a war?" Marco nodded yes. "Well, you are pulling really hard, wanting the rope to be yours, but with the other side pulling, wanting to yank it from you, but you resist," Maria said.

"Yes, nõnna, I think I understand."

Maria smiled, still seeing the confusion on Marco's face, but she ignored it and continued. "This love was given to them by God, and they loved each other with all their hearts and souls. They believed their love could carry them through time; searching, seeking, wanting their hearts to one day reunite. My dear Marco, this is to happen here and now, in this lifetime."

Just then, Maria has a feeling – a sudden urge, a need to see what was happening, not understanding what it was, only that she must go, and now. Maria closes her eyes, and when she does, without delay, her spirit is whisked from her body, taken to a place where she sees a young girl with dark brown or black hair. As she is watching this girl, she gasps, she immediately knows who she is. *This is her, isn't it?* She could not believe it. This girl she sees; is the girl she was just telling Marco about. Without notice, Maria is immediately pulled back, and her spirit returns to her body.

Marco sees his grandmother suddenly go very still, and it scares him. He started calling to her, "nõnna, what is wrong!" he yelled, as he shakes his grandmother's arm.

Then suddenly, Maria was back. When she lifted her head and saw the concern and fear on her nipõte's face —

"Oh Marco, I am so sorry. I just had a thought, a feeling. I am sorry," she said, then grabs and embraces her nipõte. "I am back now. Shall I continue, or shall we go in?" Maria asked.

Marco let out a breath and relaxed, he was relieved that his grandmother was alright. "Nõnna, you scared me. I thought something bad happened to you, and I didn't know what to do."

"I am sorry, Marco," Maria said. "Now, my nipõte, shall I finish the story, or shall we return?" she said, pushing Marco away so she can look at him.

"No nõnna…I mean, yes, please finish the story."

"This girl and boy I am telling you about from so long ago…is…my nipõte…you are the boy from that time. You are here to find this girl you loved with all your heart and soul, here in this time. Oh, my dear nipõte," Maria said, putting her arms around Marco, "You have waited a long time for this to happen. Your hearts were torn apart, broken for many lifetimes. But now, here with me as your nõnna, you have another chance to be with her…your love. But my nipõte, I am afraid she is very far away. With my help, you will find each other again. This is why you were born into my family, so I can make right the wrong I did then."

Marco was confused. He didn't understand anything his grandmother was saying, but he was worried – he did not like to think his grandmother did something wrong, as he couldn't imagine his grandmother doing anything bad.

"Nõnna, what did you do wrong?" he asked. But when he saw the smile on his grandmother's face, he believed she was joshing him. "Oh nõnna, that is not real. You are playing with me."

Shaking her head, Maria said, "No Marco, I tell you the truth. You are destined to find a great love, the greatest love given to you by God. What I did, well, that I will tell you when you are older."

Marco, such a young boy does not understand his grandmother, but he loves her very much, and she seems to know things, things he could never understand.

"Nõnna, how? How am I to know? I am only a boy," he said, shaking his head in confusion.

"Yes, Marco, you are but a boy, but you will grow to be a man, and she a woman. This is when you will meet."

"What does she look like?" Marco asked, feeling a bit curious.

"Well, she is very young, but she has dark hair and tan skin, and she is very beautiful. I will tell you more as you get older. Marco, you must keep this between us. You must never tell your mamma or your papa, as they will never understand, especially your mamma. Promise me, Marco; this will be a secret between you and me?"

"I promise, nõnna."

Marco and Maria remain outdoors for a while longer, enjoying the beautiful spring day, before returning to the restaurant. Maria looks down at her nipõte and remembers the day she first saw him after he was born.

Maria was born with great psychic powers, and her abilities helped her with what she needed to do. When Marco, as Robert from the 1500s was born into her family – the first moment she saw him, she knew what she needed to do. And once she touched his hand, there were flashes of her life from that time, along with a girl and boy. To see her nipõte Marco, she knew the boy in her vision was him. The girl, she wasn't sure who she was, but she felt there was something very familiar about her. When she opened her eyes, not realizing she had closed them, she saw her nipõte staring up at her, as if he recognized her as well.

Maria smiles at the lovely memory.

After telling Marco the story, and then being pulled to the girl, she instantly knew the girl was the one from the vision, when she first touched Marco after he was born.

Since Marco's birth, Maria dreamed every night of her life from the 1500s. This is when she realized who they – she was. Maria was Grace, Elizabeth's sister, and Marco was the boy her sister fell in love with, after she forced them together. She also remembered the horror of what happened because of a decision she made. A decision that caused her to lose her entire family. It was her fault. In this, she had no doubts. Now, Maria had a second chance to make right the wrong she did then. To cleanse her soul of the karma she'd been carrying since that day. She needed to help Marco find the girl, to give them a chance to have the love they had then. To make right the wrong she's done, not only by her, but by them as well.

Throughout Marco's youth and teenage years, on to his adulthood, Maria continued to tell him about this girl, who now is a woman, of their past lives together. During the time she checked on the girl, Maria learned her name to be Rebecca. The older Marco became, the more she revealed of the life they had before and the love they shared, along with the tragedy they all suffered.

For a very long time, Marco lived with hope in his heart that one day this woman, whom his grandmother has been telling him about, will come into his life. He even found himself looking at every woman who seemed to have the characteristics of the woman his grandmother described to him. She has long dark brown hair or maybe black. She seems to change the color often. She has brown eyes, dark skin – she's of Hindu descent.

Every woman Marco met with those qualities; he would pursue. At times, there was a feeling as if he found her, but then, his grandmother would tell him he did not. There were also times when he was so sure he did, he refused to listen to his grandmother, then later learn the hard way, his grandmother was right; it was not her. Doing this caused him great pain, sorrow, and heartache, to the point he started believing, just maybe, she didn't truly exist. That instead, she was a fantasy he created from his grandmother's stories. And this, even after his grandmother assured him she existed. Marco was tired of living in a fantasy world about a woman who may or may not exist or come into his life. After a time, he became bitter and a womanizer.

California

The family I was born into was not rich, but a poor one. I was born to a mother who had no care or interest in wanting me. She did everything during her pregnancy to rid herself of me, but through the grace of God, she failed. I never knew about this until I was in my thirties, when everything was revealed to me through my sister, and through her, my aunt. And to my surprise, my mother confirmed this.

When I learned this, I looked back at my childhood, and it made sense, since I grew up miserable and unhappy. My thoughts were then, *how can I continue with this life when nothing is going right? No one cares or loves me.* Not once do I recall receiving any love or affection from my mother or my father. Well, actually, let me reframe that. Surprisingly, as I think back, there was a time I do remember my father showing me love and affection, but most of my life my father seemed to hate me, and I didn't know or understand why at the time.

Our house was out in the country, made with a mixture of brick and wood. It was a small three-bedroom house, with only one bathroom. Now, you can imagine what that was like with a family of six; two boys and two girls. Yep, gross. And the worse part of this, the bathroom was in the master bedroom. You wonder what bozo thought that was a clever idea? You got me.

We lived down a small road, with our house being the seventh house down the street. We had a long wide driveway that leads to a massive backyard. Beyond the backyard, was the water house and one acre of walnut trees. When you enter from the front door, you enter directly into the living room. The living room was a large wide room, with a brick fireplace and wood floors. There were two large windows on each side of the room facing the front of the house. To the right of the living room use to be the garage, but my parents converted it into an additional bedroom. Straight through the living room, towards the back of the house, was the dining area and kitchen combo. It wasn't a bad size, enough for a table and six chairs. To the kitchen's left was another bedroom, and to the right, and directly ahead was another, and to the left of that, was the master bedroom, then of course, was the only *little* bathroom for a family of six. Yikes.

The room on the left of the kitchen was not only a bedroom but a closed-in porch that was turned into a bedroom, but you can say it was a multipurpose room. I say this, because at one point it was a laundry room, then a bedroom, and then a bedroom and laundry room. I don't think my mother knew what she wanted to do with that room, but whoever had the room, also had a backdoor, allowing them to come and go as they pleased. Well, maybe not as they pleased, but it was very convenient, if you know what I mean, wink-wink. And yes, that room was once mine.

Now, coming back into the kitchen, through the dining area to the second bedroom, then left through the master bedroom, was another large closed-in screen porch, that was situated at the back of the house. For many years this was the laundry room, and when it rained, there was only one way in – an entrance in the back of the house. So, to keep from getting soaked down to our toes, we would use the window in the master bedroom that went directly to the room. Beyond the room was the large backyard and walnut orchard, and every summer we were all forced, of course when we were old enough, to pick walnuts, and yes, I hated it. However, we did get a small pay, and I did like that. So, I guess you can say it wasn't so bad.

I am the second born out of four children, with an older sister by two years, a brother two years younger than me, and a baby brother six years younger. You know what is odd, I'm sure a few of you cannot say this, but as I look back on my childhood, I do not recall a great deal, only bits and pieces. There is one thing I do recall that is very clear, was how miserable and unhappy I was. I felt there was something in me, telling me I didn't belong. I had always wondered if I was truly my mother's daughter. To be honest, I hoped and prayed I was not. Why? I didn't know.

There was a time – now, I do not recall how old I was exactly, but I think I was around nine or ten. Every night, or shall I say, every morning I would wake up after dreaming I was falling off a cliff, and right before I hit the rocks below, still feeling the fear and sensation of falling.

<u>Spiritual Realm</u>

"Look at her? She is starting to remember, and so young. Her abilities are strong in this life, for her to already start to remember. Should she be remembering now?"

"It is early, I agree. I feel though, for her to begin her memories now, it can only help her. For what she has already suffered and is still to suffer. Her past can save her."

"Then what do we do, Jesus?"

"Well, Joseph, I ask if you will remain with Rebecca. Watch over her and protect her. Keep her safe even from herself. If you feel her life is in danger, then call on me, and I will come."

"Yes, it will be my honor to watch over and guide Rebecca. I will do all I can to help her through her struggles and the pain she will endure."

"Thank you, Joseph. I know you are the right one to watch over Rebecca. Remember, call on me if I am needed. Otherwise, Rebecca is in good hands," Jesus said as he looked through the doorway between the human and spiritual realm to Rebecca sitting up in her bed.

"I will, thank you, Jesus."

<u>Rebecca</u>

Although I do not recall a great deal of my childhood, I do recall feeling how horrible my life was, how I wanted to die. To leave a world I didn't belong in. Growing up in this family where I felt unhappy and unloved, how does a child so young handle that? Well, she doesn't.

There was a time when I was unable to show or express love, I even believed I was incapable of it. Why? I didn't know. I remember a time, now I cannot say how old I was, but our family dog, who everyone loved was hit by a car and killed. As everyone else was upset and crying, I was standing in front of a wall, and for some reason, I started laughing. However, as I think back to that time, I believe my laughter was because I believed they loved the dog more than they loved me. To cry was to show sadness for the loss of the dog, when in reality, I was glad he was dead.

To know a dog received more love than I did, was painful. Laughter was my only comfort. With this, my mother felt there was evil within me and decided to take me to a phycologist. I only recall one visit, what happen after that, or why I didn't continue, I don't know, not even to this day. I was made to feel as if I was a burden, a child born unwanted. A nuisance. So, why am I here? Why was I brought into this life, if I am not wanted or loved by anyone?

There was a day, this I remember clearly, I was ten years old, and at my grandmother's Bebe's – this was the Indian name for mother. We were supposed to call her Bebe Gee, but it was easier to call her Bebe – house, my father's mother. I was in her bedroom staring at the bottles of pills sitting on her dresser, wondering why I was here? What is my reason? I could not think of any reason why I should stay in this world, and so, maybe it was time for me to leave by ending my life.

My grandmother's bottles of pills were enticing and calling to me, and I thought, *I can put a little of each bottle in my hand and take them. Then I will just fall asleep and wake up in heaven if that is where I will go.* There was a glass of water that she always kept on her dresser to take her pills. *If I take a little, who will notice, and who will care? No one.*

<u>Spiritual Realm</u>

"This cannot be happening. Not again. She cannot do this again. We need Jesus. Jesus, I call for you to come. We need your help."

"Joseph, I am here. What is happening?"

"Look, Rebecca's going to do it again. She is going to take her life. Do I have your permission to intervene?"

"Wait, I will ask God." Jesus leaves for what is only seconds, and when he returns, he says, "Yes Joseph, you may intervene. Go to her grandmother and send her to Rebecca. Quickly."

Joseph goes to Rebecca's grandmother, who was working outside and whispers in her ear, *you must go inside right now and check on Rebecca.*

<u>Rebecca</u>

Rebecca's grandmother does not understand why, but she goes into the house to check on Rebecca. When she finds Rebecca in her room holding a hand full of pills and a glass of water, and just as Rebecca was about to take the pills, her grandmother quickly slapped her hand, causing the pills to fall to the floor.

"What are you doing?" her grandmother yelled.

I didn't know what to say. What could I say? There was nothing I could say that would have helped me. All I could do was lower my head and cry hysterically.

My grandmother was the one who saved my life that day, but at the time, I wished she hadn't.

Shortly after, my grandmother called my mother and told her what I tried to do. When my mother picked me up, and while we were in the car on the way home, all she could do was yell and scream at me, insulting me, belittle me, swearing such obscene words. "What the fuck were you doing! What the fuck were you thinking! Are you fucking crazy!" This went on and on all the way home. The only thing I could do was turn my head away and rest it on the passenger window, looking out to the orchards and fields as we passed them by, wishing I'd been successful in ending my life.

How could I live this life with such a hateful mother? Who should have taken her daughter and hugged her instead of yelling at her. She should have tried to understand why I wanted to die, instead of yelling and screaming at me, as if I just broke a window, not of a person, a daughter, who just tried to take her own life.

I never understood why I never tried to take my life again. As I said before, I have little memory of that time in my life. And in this, I had always found strange, having this be my only memory, when most children can remember a great deal more when they were ten years old.

Spiritual Realm

"Jesus, what are we going to do? The way Rebecca is feeling right now, she is going to try to take her life again. If she succeeds, she will never have what she seeks."

"You are right Joseph, we must do something, and I think I know what. In the meantime, we will ensure she has no memory of this time in her life, of this incident, until the time is right for her to remember. You stay with her and stay close. I am also going to send her Victoria and Michael. They will help watch and protect Rebecca. As there is a great more to come, and we must ensure she does not follow the same path of her previous lives, by taking her own life. This life has to be the one she succeeds in."

"Thank you, Jesus. She has a very good soul. She is such a wonderful and blessed child of God's."

"Yes, she is, as well as all God's children, but I understand what you mean, Joseph."

Verona, Italy

Maria feels a sense of urgency, a fear which overwhelms her, of the girl Marco is to find and reconnect with. She stops what she's doing and allows her spirit to travel to Rebecca. When Maria's spirit leaves her body, she travels to California where Rebecca lives. When she arrives, the only thing she sees is Rebecca being yelled at by her mother. Something about *how could you attempt to take your own life!* Maria is shocked, then without warning, a powerful force forces Maria's spirit back into her body, with a feeling as if she was not allowed to be there. To see or witness what was happening.

When Maria returns to her body, she takes a moment to gather herself before she speaks to God.

"Dear God, please tell me Marco won't lose her before he has a chance to find her?" Maria pleads. She's afraid there is nothing she can do to help Rebecca. Without delay, Maria receives her answer in her mind. *Do not worry, Maria. She is well protected. She will endure a great deal, but there are many here to help and protect Rebecca. So, there is no need to worry.*

To hear this, a tremendous relief washes over Maria. "May I check in on her every now and then?" Maria asked. *Yes, Maria, you may. We will let you know when you can.* "Oh, thank you. They must find each other again. I cannot allow them to lose this opportunity, not after these last few hundred years," shaking her head, "And because of what I did," she said, with a feeling of great shame.

California

The funny thing is, when I look back to those days, after failing to kill myself, it also seemed my dreams of falling stopped. Then again, maybe not. It's hard to say, since I cannot recall much of that time in my life.

Although, I do not recall how old I was when this happened, there was a time I believed I was not the biological daughter of my parents, since I never felt I belonged, nor did I believe I was accepted as a daughter, until one day that fantasy – bubble was burst, when my sister showed me a younger picture of my mother, and to my shock and horror, yep, I looked just like my mother when she was young. Here is when most children – daughters would have felt relief, but for me, I only felt heartbroken and disappointment to learn it was true.

If I was not my parent's biological daughter, it would have explained everything – why I felt so disconnected towards these people, the ones I call family, if they were not. I think I stared at that picture of my mother for a long time, and found I could no longer deny the truth, I am my mother's daughter. If you can even say that, as I did not – do not feel I am, even to this very day, although I have a better understanding of why.

In the years growing up with these people, nothing changed to the disconnection I felt with them, and even to this day, has changed nothing. I recall this need to escape, to run away and find where I belonged, but I had no idea where, or with who. Who was my actual family? These were questions I had no answers to. I wanted so desperately to be away from these people, that I started questioning the reason for my own existence, to why I was born into this world, and into this family. Unfortunately, I never found these answers, until now. But, I am going to stop, as I am getting ahead of myself. Why did I have to endure such pain and sorrow, with feelings of being an outcast?

Chapter 2

Throughout my childhood, I struggled with everything, school, friends, siblings, and my parents. I was allowed to join the school band in sixth grade, and I selected to play the flute. To my surprise, I turned out to be pretty good, and for me to find something I was good at, when it seemed I wasn't good at anything, was a wonderful and happy surprise.

After I learned to play the flute, I also – when my baby brother decided to learn to play the trumpet – one day, being curious, I picked up his trumpet, his instruction book, and music sheet, and to my wonderful amazement, that same night I learned and played *when the sings come marching in*. I could not believe it. I did it. For some reason, reading music and playing musical instruments came easy to me, and when I was in sixth grade, our school went to Woodleaf, as they do every year. They did this to allow the children to experience nature in its natural habitat. We would spend a week in the mountains to learn and understand nature and life.

There were cabins for girls and boys, which I believe could accommodate up to ten girls and boys. I remember how much I loved it. I would wake up every morning and open the back door, and stand on the deck outside, taking in the fresh mountain air, enjoying the feel of the cold on my skin, along with the beauty of the forest beyond. If felt like home to me. As if this is where I belonged. This was my home. No, not Woodleaf itself, but the forest and nature that surrounded it. It gets cold in Northern California, but I cannot think of a time; I enjoyed the cold as I did at Woodleaf.

Each night after dinner, there was entertainment that anyone could choose to participate in. So, I decided to play my flute, in doing this was a considerable risk. You see, in those days, I was extremely shy. So, for me to get up on stage in front of a large group of people by myself was extremely out of character. Not to mention the risk in the music I chose to play, as it was a very difficult piece, especially to one who was still learning. Why did I do this? I guess you can say, in a way, I wanted to show my classmates, that although I was this shy girl, there was something extraordinary about me, something that I could do. Something they couldn't make fun of. The song I chose was Good King Whistles. If you know this song, you understand it is not an easy piece to play, especially for someone so new. I made sure to practice every night until it was time for me to perform. When I was up on that stage, I was so nervous, I was shaking so bad, I was afraid I would not be able to perform in front of my classmates, teachers, and strangers. But somehow, I managed to gather the strength and courage I needed to pull it off, and for that one night, I was someone important. I was appreciated. I was a part of something special.

One day while we were hiking up a mountain to a place high on a cliff – once on top, you can see far and across the forest and the world below. However, as I approached the edge, I felt such fear, as if, if I did not leave, I would fall to my death below. Was this the first time I learned of my fear of heights? I don't know. My mother suffers from a severe case of fear of heights, and when I realized I also have a fear of heights, I believed it stemmed from her.

When camp was over, so was the person I became – a person who felt free to do and be who I wanted to be, along with how I was treated. Now, I was back to the way things really were, of a life of misery. At school, I had no friends, no one I could talk to or trust. I was so gullible. I would do practically anything to get attention from my classmates. The kids saw this, and they didn't have any problems in taking advantage of me. In a way, I felt a need to prove something to someone – to everyone. So, when I was called out to fight, I never backed away. Why was I called out to fight? Honestly, I have no idea. However, in doing this, I had hoped that if I just won one, I would earn some type of respect – acceptance.

The funny thing about this, this all changed once my parents, along with the support of the school principal, allowed me to move to another school.

Yes, that's how bad things became. For me to go to this school, I had to move in with my grandmother, which ended up being a great move for me. It took me away from my parents and siblings. It was not only the kids from school but my brothers and sister as well. With this change, I became confident in myself. I even started wearing makeup, and for the first time in my young life, I had friends. It was not just one or two friends, but a large group of friends, and the popular group at that. I had friends. I was finally happy. I did not have the constant belittling and teasing as I once had from my classmates, parents, and brothers and sister. I had people who liked and accepted me. So yes, I was very happy.

I only lived with my grandmother until I graduated eighth grade, then moved back in with my parents to attend High School. However, with this newfound life, I did not revert to the way I was before. In starting High School, I had friends and made new friends as time went on. It turned out to be a wonderful time for me.

My changes continued to expand as my confidence grew, so much so, my old classmates were shocked at my new attitude. I no longer allowed anyone to walk all over me, and I lost a lot of weight. However, as I looked back, you know, I really was not that fat, but it was enough to fuel my family with daily insults. I went from size ten girls to a size three-five teen. There was no question; I dropped half the size I was. Maybe it was because I was finally happy.

During my sophomore year, our house started receiving prank calls. A man with a Hindu accent would call our house nonstop and talk dirty when either my sister or myself answered the phone. He would say, "you want fucky-fucky? Ah yeah, you want fucky-fucky." This was daily, and when we were home alone. How did he know we were home alone? This I cannot say? I wish I could say it remained only phone calls, but it did not. He graduated to stalker status. He started stalking *me*. We learned this when he called and talked about how he was following and watching me.

This was discovered when I stayed at a friend's house to go to a Halloween party. When I was in her bedroom, there was a large picture window with no curtains, and I recall looking out her side window and seeing a red car. Although I thought it was odd, I didn't put too much into it, as it could have been anyone parked there. At the time, I could not see there was anyone in the car, not until later. I remember looking, maybe a few minutes later, and the car was gone.

The following day I received a call from my sister, and she told me the man called bragging about how he saw her, thinking my sister was me on the phone. After hearing this, I called the sheriff's department, where at the time I was working as a cadet. Why is a teenager working as a cadet you ask? Well, let's just say, an incident involving my father and a car, and me on a bicycle. We will leave it at that. I talked to the sheriff's deputy who recruited me (without choice, mind you) into the cadet program, and told me there was nothing they could do since nothing happened. You see, this was before stalking laws were inexistent. It left me with the unknown and feeling scared, to what this person might do if tempted.

Another time when he called, he told my sister that he saw me in a car with my boyfriend when we were parking. He was watching us. We all know what teenagers do when they are parking and who are sexually active. You know it. This started when I was sixteen, and needless to say, it freaked me out. He talked about how he was following us on the main street in town. Now I was terrified, because for some reason, he targeted me, and I didn't know why. Since there was nothing I could do, and he didn't do anything that would be considered a criminal act, it did eventually stop. My teens were one of the few wonderful times in my life that I had. I had friends and a boyfriend who loved me. How much better could it have been.

Also, around this time, or shall I say before, when I turned seventeen, I had enough of my family not caring. It didn't seem to matter how much I changed, they were always going to see that gullible shy girl, and I am afraid to say this, they still do not see the woman I am today. It's as if I am frozen in time, as far as they are concern. So, when I was seventeen, I moved out of my parents' house and moved in with my best friend and her boyfriend. Once I was on my own, I felt so different, oh so very different. I felt free. I finally had love and happiness. What else could a girl want, right?

This man I came to love, and who loved me, his name is Richard. Our meeting was an interesting one too. You see, we met one night during a Saturday night cruise – no, not a boat cruise, but a car cruise. Back in the time when there was cruising, when you would go to a particular part of town and drive around in a large circle, and when seeing your friends, you would honk at them, or even those you found attractive. It was a lot of fun.

There was no doubt, Richard was someone I cared for very much – loved. After dating Richard for six months, he decided to break up with me right out of the blue. I was devastated when this happened. At the time, it made no sense to me, since I knew how much he cared about me – loved me.

Apparently, one of his male friends felt he was spending too much time with me, calling him pussy whipped. The night Richard broke up with me, we were at his friend's apartment, and shortly after, his friend was right there to comfort me, then that bastard tried to kiss me. Can you believe it? The bastard made a pass at me, and while Richard was still there. What fucking nerve, right?

I mentioned this to Richard, "Richard, Jeff just hit on me! He tried to kiss me! And he was the one to convince you to break up with me! For what, so he can have a chance with me? Are you that much of a fool!" I yelled. I was angry and hurt.

But it didn't matter what I said, because he said, "You are lying! Jeff would never do that!" Unbelievable, right?

"Well, he did, and you are a fool to listen to him!" Richard refused to believe me, feeling I was just saying this out of anger and hurt because he broke up with me. Bastard!

Yes, I was angry, and I was scared. For me to go from never feeling love, to finally find love, to only lose it – to have it taken away – ripped from me – yes, it was one of the hardest things I had to endure in my life. I didn't want to give it up, and I found I couldn't let it go, not when I knew how Richard felt about me. I knew he was making a big mistake.

For me to finally feel love, and to know what love was, in my desperation to keep it, I did things I was not proud of. I became an obsessive ex-girlfriend. I called him relentlessly, going to his work (his second job) to wait for him to get off, or I would go inside the video store (where he worked), to stare at him, pleading with him to speak to me, to come back to me. Yes, I was a psycho ex-girlfriend.

Other times I would call him relentlessly, at his home and at his second job. I was crazy obsessive. When I could talk to him, I would beg and plead with him to take me back. I would tell him over and over, of how much of a mistake he made. It took several months before he finally relented, and we got back together. The love I felt for him, to me, was the greatest love I ever had. You know how they say, *love is blind*, how true that is. However, being only seventeen, how did I really know what love was. I was desperate for love, I needed love, and when I found it, I could not, nor did I want to let it go. So, I refused to see the truth. I was truly blind.

When I met Richard, he was my hope. To finally find that part of me I'd been missing my whole life. Instead, he turned out to be my downfall. Taking me down a path of pain and suffering, so much suffering, I contemplated more than once, in taking my own life.

There were so many ups and downs. When I was down, I felt lost, unwanted, and unloved – again. I started thinking and questioning, *why am I here? To only live a life of heartbreak and pain.* Sometimes I wondered, why I didn't take my life. I know I wanted to, desperately. So why, why didn't I? These were questions I had no answers to.

<u>Spiritual Realm</u>
"Joseph, how is Rebecca doing?" Jesus asked.

"She seems to be doing well after Richard took her back, and she looks happy. I am concern about what is to come though," Joseph said.

"Yes, Joseph, this is the beginning of her path, and the pain and sorrow she is still to suffer."

"She has more than once thought about taking her own life. What if she tries again?"

"I am afraid this will not end, and there will be more than one occasion she will think about taking her life. But, there will be something more powerful and stronger that will prevent her from doing so."

"What will that be?"

"Although Rebecca will suffer great, she will have a love so powerful, that it will keep her on her path."

"What powerful love? God's love is the greatest power."

"Ah, Joseph, this is true. On earth, the greatest power is a mother's love." Joseph nodded in understanding. "After Rebecca follows Richard to England, God is going to give her what she's desperately wanted and prayed for. A child. But not only one, two daughters – twins, for her to care for and love."

"Twin daughters, how wonderful!"

"Her love for her daughters will give her the strength to fight."

"She lost her child when she took her life as Elizabeth, and again as Mary in her life prior to this one."

"Yes, this is a chance for her to correct two wrongs she has done. These daughters will give Rebecca the power and the strength she needs to do what must be done, which will allow her to find the love she seeks. This will take time, as it will be several earth years before she will be ready. In this time, she will be tested and endure more pain and suffering…and heartbreak. More than one should ever have to suffer. This is to happen, in order for her to prove that her heart and soul will be open and ready for the love she seeks, of the love she once had. If she follows the path we have set for her, it will allow her to make the right decisions, and succeed in this life, that she has failed in so many lives before. She must be successful in this life. God has great plans for Rebecca, more than she could have ever dreamed of. God is giving her this chance, and it will be up to her to succeed."

"Watching Rebecca all this time, I know she can do this, and I will be there to help her, as Victoria and Michael will be."

"Yes. I am also sending Angela as well, along with many others, as time continues. She will need many to help her, since I will not be able to remain with her as much as I could in the beginning."

"Yes, you are right. We will do what we can to help Rebecca, to guide her down the path she has chosen. If it means she must go through great pain and suffering for her to remain on her path."

California

In 1988 I was devastated when I learned Richard was being transferred to England. It struck me like a knife piercing my heart. I waited so long to find this love and happiness, for it to only be ripped away from me – again. It hurt more than you know. Since Richard was the first one I ever expressed or said the words *I love you* to, how can I let him go, of the one person I first opened my heart to? It didn't matter what I said or did; he had to go to England. When the military orders you somewhere, you must go. I tried to move on with my life, but found it was too difficult. I felt lost and alone. Yes, I went out with my friends and met other men, but nothing seemed to compare to what I believed I had with Richard.

The times Richard and I talked on the phone, it was clear he missed me, as much as I missed him. We even talked about me moving to England, so we could get married. The thing was, I had always wanted to go to England, and there were times, when it felt as if it was more of a need than a want. I remember watching shows and movies that took place in England, and when I saw the beautiful landscape of the English countryside, I felt a pulling, a longing, a need, and a desire to go, and I had always hoped I would get my chance one day. So, in a way, I looked at this as an opportunity to live out a dream to visit England, and at the same time, renew – continue the love I found with Richard, and escape a family I desperately wanted to get away from. So, when we talked again, we decided I would go to England, and we would get married. I was so happy and excited, and I worked hard to save the money I would need by taking a second job, and within a few months I bought a redeye ticket to England.

When the day came to leave for England, I was nervous, as it was my first time flying, and to my luck, my seat was next to an English couple. Thank God for them, because if they were not there, I would have been lost going through Heathrow Airport. If you ever flew into Heathrow, it was – is a crazy maze, especially for someone who had no understanding of such a place. If it wasn't for them, I think I would have ended up lost.

After Arriving in London, an old family friend met me at the airport and allowed me to stay a few days at their London home, before I boarded a train bound for RAF Alconbury. RAF Alconbury is near Huntington, which is about two hours north of London. Once I arrived at RAF

Alconbury, the gate security had to find Richard to let him know I have arrived, for him to vouch for me on base. To see Richard after so long, I was a bunch of nerves. Even with my nerves, I felt wonderful knowing I was going to see him again. When Richard finally showed up at the gate, and when I first saw him, I noticed there was something wrong. He didn't seem to be as happy to see me as I was to see him.

After I settled into his dorm room, I laid down on his bed to take a nap, and ended up having a strange dream that felt real. I dreamed Richard was with this other woman, and he gave her the gold chain necklace I gave him before he left California to remember me by. When I woke up, I felt such fear, as if the dream was real, and there was truth to it.

So, you can imagine what I did when Richard returned – damn right, I asked him about the chain. "Richard, where is the gold chain I gave you?" He seemed shocked that I would ask about the chain. This worried me, and I thought, *God, is it true? Could my dream be true?* Well, what do you think I did? Yep, I asked him again, since the bastard still hadn't answered me. But this time, with more firmness, as if I already knew the answer. "Where is the necklace I gave you?" He still looked stunned by me asking the question.

With resistance, he finally gave me an answer. "I gave it to a lady to wear."

I was furious, "Why would you give the necklace I gave you to another woman! How could you! That was something I gave you to remember me by! And you so easily gave it to another woman! Did it mean nothing to you!"

With hesitation, he went on to explain how it happened. "We were at the NCO (noncommission officer) Club, and she asked to wear it, so I let her."

"You what! Oh, so I meant so little to you that it was that easy to give another woman the necklace I gave you!" At this, I broke down crying, feeling as if I made a big mistake in coming to England.

Then, as if to hurt me even more, he went on to say, "I wished you didn't come. If you hadn't already bought your ticket, I would have told you not to. I met this woman, and she made me feel…I was finally getting over you."

You can imagine what I did. What would any woman do? Absolutely, I exploded and demanded he get the necklace back from this woman. To my surprise, there was no argument, and he agreed. However, when he tried to get the chain back, he told me she lost it.

"She what!" I yelled, eyeing him with such hatred and pain. You can imagine what I did. Yep, I went ape shit on him. I was so pissed, but I was more hurt than anything, and I demanded she pay for it. I was still making payments on the chain, and there was no damn way I was going to continue paying for something she lost. Without argument, he did as I asked, and she did agree to make payments, which allowed me to pay off the chain.

You would think after this, things would have continued going downhill, and I would be planning my flight back to California. Believe it or not, we did get over this hump, and went back to the way things were before Richard left California. We managed to have a wonderful time together. We did all the normal things one of youth did, when they were nineteen-twenty. Yep, you guessed it, Pub Crawl! It was a lot of fun.

Chapter 3

One night, after the guys heard of a record store in London, a group of us drove to London so the guys could check out this store. To make the long drive worth the trip, we decided to make an entire day out of it, so we could see what else London had to offer. I scarcely remember everything that happened that night, but I remember one incident clearly and in complete detail as if it happened yesterday. For some reason, although I didn't understand it at the time, this incident never left me.

As we were checking out the London scene, and of course, a few pubs – oh come on, who could resist going to a pub or two, we were in our twenties after all. However, after we left a pub, and before we headed to the record store, which was the reason we went to London after all, but we ended up stopping at a few shops and bazaars we saw on the way there.

By the time we headed for the record store, it was past dark, and the record store was down an alley. A dark alley. Go figure, right. As we headed down the alley, we saw this crazy man; he was hanging from a chained fence lined across the building next to the record store. He was shaking it ferociously, as he was yelling and screaming words I could not understand. It sounded like he was speaking in a different language.

"What is wrong with that man?" I asked, as I held on tight to Richard's arm.

"I don't know. Let's just keep walking, and quickly make it into the record store where we will be safe," Richard said.

"I'm sure he will be gone by the time we leave," said one of the men in our group.

Although I was feeling afraid, I couldn't help but look at this man, and see there was something special about him. What it was, I didn't know at the time. For some reason though, I felt sadness for him. I felt the need to reach out to him, wanting to put my arms around him and comfort him. It was as if I could understand what he was going through. As if I could feel his pain. I wanted desperately to go to him and ease the pain he was suffering. Yes, I know it's crazy, but there was something about him, something that called to me. I never understood it at the time, and eventually I put it behind me, or did I? I was twenty, and now today, I am forty-six. So why do I still remember this incident? This *one* man, as clearly today, as I did then?

It astonishes me today; when I think about this man, I remembered what he wore and what he looked like. No, not his face, as I could not see that, but what he was wearing that night. It was a white dress shirt and dark pants, and he had dark wavy hair. Although I could not see his face, for some reason, I believed him to be handsome. I remember wondering what happened to him. What caused him to behave in the way he did. The others in my group said it was because he was drunk and angry. Yes, he was angry, but something was telling me that he was more hurt than angry. Why did I want to know? Why did it matter to me? He was none of my business. But I could not stop thinking there was something more. There was just something about him that touched me. That touched my heart.

When we finished our business at the record store and headed out the door, to my – our relief, the man was gone. In a way, there was an ache in my heart that I didn't recognize, nor did I understand. We put the incident behind us and continued taking in the English culture, going to different pubs, in and around Huntington, along with restaurants and shops.

However, although we were having a great time and a lot of fun, all would change after welcoming in the New Year of 1991. At the end of January, I discovered I was pregnant. I know. I know. It was insane. What did I do? I did what most young girls of twenty did when they became pregnant. I freaked out! I was in a panic, and I didn't know what I was going to do. Yes, Richard and I were together, but the talk of marriage we had before I joined him in England was mute. I was scared to death at the idea of being pregnant. I didn't know what to do. I had to tell him, but I was afraid to. So, I chose the best way I knew how, knowing it was the chicken way out. Needless to say, it was the best way for me. Not to mention, I didn't have the time for the multiple questions I knew he was going to have, since I had to be at work.

I barged in his dorm room and woke him up, then yelled I was pregnant, sat the EPT test on his nightstand with the instructions, then ran out the door and went directly to work. Later that day, he called me at work and asked if this was a joke or if it was for real.

I told him, "Did you read the test and the instructions?"

He said, "Yes, I did, but are you sure?"

Well, of course, I was sure. How could I not be? The test was clear. Man, I remember when I took that test, it was supposed to take two minutes to get the results according to the instructions. In my case, it went to line one on the first box, then without stopping, to the second box within mere seconds. There was no denying it – I was pregnant. Apparently, Richard was going through his own denial, not wanting to believe I was pregnant. Could I blame him? No.

Did Richard ask me to marry him? Yes, he did. It was on Valentine's Day. He gave me a card, and in the card, he asked me to marry him, and of course, I said yes. It was what I had always wanted, and now, I finally had it. By the way, be careful of what you wish for! It may not always be what you want.

It's spring of 1991, and Richard and I are married. We married at the register's office in Huntington. It was the way things are done in the United Kingdom. You can marry at the register's office first, then have your elaborate wedding. Another option, you could have the register representative at your wedding ceremony, then after signing your registration, therefore, completing your marriage.

The wedding was not much. I had to find a gown in the base BX (Building Exchange), that would fit an already growing stomach, which was surprising since I was only four months pregnant. I did manage to find one, but it barely fit. My mother did send me a dress from the states, but it didn't arrive in time, and the following day when I was able to pick up the dress – it would have been much nicer than the one I ended up wearing, but it just was not meant to be.

<u>London 1991</u>

Maria checks in on Rebecca, as she has since she learned about who she was. Today though, turned out to be a somber day for her. When she looked in on Rebecca, she was pleased to see she was still in England, until Maria noticed Rebecca was getting married and was very pregnant.

To see this broke Maria's heart and she thought, *if Rebecca marries, the chances of her and Marco finding each other, with a chance for them to be together will be over.* "How can I tell him…the woman he's destine to be with…is pregnant and about to marry another man?" she said aloud.

When she first learned Rebecca was in England, Maria was very excited, and to know how close she was to where Marco lives.

Maria immediately called Marco to tell him the woman he seeks is in England, and where she will be on a particular night. She sees Rebecca going to London with a group of men, and one of those men, she is in a relationship with. Maria also noticed how much shorter Rebecca's hair was than the last time she looked in on her.

"Who is this man she's with?" Maria says aloud.

Maria is pleased to receive an answer in her mind. "The man you see is what you call her boyfriend. A man she plans to marry. This is why she is in England. She is here to be with him."

Maria was unsure what to think of this. "How can this be? No, this cannot be. How do I tell Marco?"

The voice answers her, "Maria, there is still a chance. Do not see this as the end," the voice said, then was gone.

Maria thinks about this, this is my chance, my chance to help Marco and Rebecca find each other. I must call Marco and tell him.

"Marco, if you are going to find her, you must know she is in England, because of the man she's been dating. He is in the American Air Force, and she is here to be with him. What I see, she is with a group of men. She is with the man she is dating and their friends. She will be wearing pants and a long black coat. The man she is dating is not very tall and has very short blond hair and blue eyes. I see them going down an alley to a record store. I do not know where. I am sorry. Now Marco, you must understand…she

feels she is in love with this man. If you are to approach her, you must do so with caution."

"Nõnna, are you sure? It has been a long time since you told me of her."

"Marco…I know it has been hard for you to believe in what I have told you. My nipõte, this is your chance to see what I say is true. Are you willing to take that chance?"

Marco takes a moment to think about this. Would it be so wrong to give in and try? If it is not her, and I feel nothing, then it will be proof nõnna was wrong, he thought. "Very well, nõnna, I will try. I think I know the place you saw."

"Thank you, Marco. Remember what I told you, on how you will know it is her, your heart will tell you. Listen to your heart. I wish you well, and I will pray now is the time for you both. Unfortunately, I cannot say for sure," Maria said with great regret.

"I remember what you said…I am not so sure…but I will try. Nõnna…I…I do want this to be true," he said, although the admission was difficult for him. "I have thought about this love you talked about…something inside me…I don't know how to explain it…I do want this," he said, sighing in resignation. He wants it yes, but does he honestly believe it? This, he does not know. Will this prove to him one way or the other? Thus, the reason he will go. "I want this love. I feel I need it. Not that you haven't shown me love, or my mother and father…but…" frustrated, he exhaled sharply.

"My dear Marco, you need not say more. I know what you are saying. I love you and pray this will be your time."

"Thank you, nõnna."

Marco goes to London on the day he knows Rebecca was to be there. To calm his nerves, he spends his day in a pub, as

he waits for nightfall before going to the record store he believes she will be at. While at the pub, Marco sees a woman and a group of men walk in. At hearing their voices, he knows they are Americans, and the woman has dark hair and is wearing a dark long coat, she is also with a blond-haired man. Marco raised his eyebrows, surprised, as he wonders, could this be her? What he feels in his chest...he places his hand directly over his heart, which he believes is telling him it's her. This is what his grandmother said would happen – he would know – his heart will tell him so, when their souls connected. Unbelievable! My heart...nõnna...could it be true, is my heart speaking to me, just as you said it would be? He never truly believed. He wanted to, but he had always doubted. But now, here in this pub, was the sign – that could possibly convince him that his grandmother was right. Marco, as he watched the group, noticed Rebecca look at him, and he thought, is she looking at me? She looks as if she knows me. Does she? Is it possible? He watches Rebecca, waiting and hoping something will happen, hoping she will come to him, but nothing, nothing happens. Why would she, when she is with him, he thought with disgust.

Marco just sits there drinking his beer as he watches Rebecca – watching them. She loves him, he thought. For Marco to see this, it hurts him more than he knew or believed was possible. To see how much she loves this man – no, Marco does not know her, but his heart does. To see what he sees, to his surprise, breaks his heart. He thought, but the look she gave me...it's as if – It seemed as if there was hope for Marco, but to see Rebecca with this man, No! I am wrong! I only saw what I wanted to see! he thought. Marco, feeling disappointed, gets up from his chair and shoves it away. I can't do this. I can't stay and watch, he thought. At this, he downs his pint of beer, then after tossing some money on the table, he quickly leaves the pub.

Marco only makes it a small way down the sidewalk when he stops. What am I to do? he thought as he turns back to the pub. Do I go back to the pub and approach them? Shaking his head, no, if I did, what would I say? Hello, my name is Marco, and I am destined to be with your girlfriend? Right. Bullocks. He turns back to the direction he was heading, away from the record store, contemplating on getting in his car and leaving. It is what I should do, just walk out of here and her life forever – shaking his head again. "I need to call Nõnna," he whispers. Marco sees a red phone box and walks over to call his grandmother. "I need her advice."

"Hi nõnna, I think I found her," Marco says with sadness in his voice. "I was sitting in a pub when a group of Americans came in, and in this group was a woman just as you described, and she was with a blond hair man. Nõnna, she looks like…she loves him very much. There was a moment…I thought maybe…when her eyes rested on me…that, just that moment…but then… I do not think I can do anything. I have already lost her, haven't I?" he said with a sigh. No, he doesn't want to give up, but after what he saw, how can he not.

Maria hears the pain in Marco's voice, and it breaks her heart to know how affected he was at his first encounter with Rebecca. "Marco, my nipõte…no, you have not lost her. There is still time. Take this opportunity to meet them…her. You can do this, Marco," she said with encouragement.

But Marco feels he has already lost. "I don't know, nõnna. I don't think I can." Just then, Marco sees the group leaving the pub and starts walking down the street towards the record store he believes they are going to visit.

"Nõnna, they are leaving the pub. What do I do?" he said, feeling frantic at the possibility of losing his only chance.

With excitement, and a little emotional at the joy of Marco wanting to speak to her, she says, as her voice breaks, "Go! Follow them. Find an opportunity to speak to them," she said, but then something in Marco's voice concerned her. "Marco, have you been drinking?"

Bullocks! What do I say? I cannot lie to her, she will know. Resigned, he says, "Okay...yes, a lot," he said with shame in his voice.

Maria shakes her head as she thought, Oh Marco...you should not have. "Marco, maybe tonight is not the best time," Maria said gently.

"No, I will be fine. I must go," he said, and before his grandmother could say another word, he hangs up the phone and starts after Rebecca and her group. He slowly and carefully follows them as he watches and listens, trying to hear what they were saying, especially with Rebecca and her boyfriend.

As he watches Rebecca with her boyfriend, his anger grows, revealing his strong Italian temper. As he's watching, he notices their next stop will be at the record store, the one he believes they are going to. He decides to go ahead of them, and once he walks into the alley, he stands with his back to the brick wall, waiting for the group to arrive.

Maybe I can say hello, and when they return the hello, I will notice they are Americans and asked them what military base they are at, he thought. It was a great plan, an excellent opportunity to speak to the group in whole. But, as he was standing there waiting, he kept thinking about what he saw, the looks Rebecca was giving her boyfriend. Seeing the love in her eyes for him – it should be for me! he thought, as he slammed his fist on his thigh, allowing his anger to consume him. He begins cursing God aloud. After a few moments, he is screaming at the top of his lungs. At times in English, then French, Spanish, and finally Italian. As his anger grows, he begins climbing a chain fence stretched along the wall he was standing against, climbing high, as if, if he climbed high enough, he could reach God.

"God, why have you done this to me! To allow me to find her, only to know I cannot have her! I have waited so long! Loved her for so long, for as long as I can remember!" Marco doesn't realize that some of the words he says are words and feelings he had from his life before. "To see her, and to feel what I felt when I saw her! Why! God, why! Tell me why this is! How can I make her see me as she sees him! I hate you! I hate you! For what you've done to me! Why did you allow me to learn of her? Bring me to her and allow me to feel her if I cannot be with her! Tell...tell me why!" He was lost, not understanding what was happening.

It seemed like an eternity before Marco finally calmed down. As he climbed down the chain fence, he sees Rebecca and her group walking into the store just as the door closed behind them. Oh, God – there was no doubt, with the realization, knowing they saw him. She saw me. How I must have looked. Lowering his head as he began walking out of the alley. "God, tell me I didn't?" he whispered. I have to get out of here, he thought as he looked around to make sure no one else could see him. I cannot allow her to see me like this, not again. Worse, I don't want her to look at me...if she looked at me with...no-no-no, I am sure I already scared her. It's over, and before it began. She must have been so frightened to see a mad man screaming and shaking the fence while hanging from it. I would have thought myself mad. Shaking his head again while picking up his pace. I couldn't bear for her to see me, a crazy drunk man.

Marco made quick haste as he left the alley. He headed for his car, and then to his hotel. Once he was in his room, as he was looking at the phone, he contemplated on calling his grandmother.

"Should I call nõnna and tell her what happened?" Shaking his head, "No. Don't be a fool. She will know what happened. I will wait until morning once I've sobered up and have a clear head."

The following morning when Marco woke up, it hit him like a ton of bricks. He was horrified at the memory of what happened – what he did, and how he behaved. After having coffee, he did what he'd been avoiding all morning – he called his grandmother.

"Nõnna, I know what you are going to say, so please don't. I am sorry."

"Oh, Marco…I will not say what I should, but there is no way you can try again, and take a chance one of them will remember you."

"Yes…I know. Is it over then?" he asked with regret.

"Marco…there is always a chance. So long as she is still in England…yes, there is always a chance for another opportunity. Have faith. I will pray for you. You should go to church and pray to God. One, ask God for his forgiveness for your behavior last night. Two, ask God if he will grant you another opportunity."

"Yes, nõnna…I will. I love you. Thank you…for everything."

After Maria hangs up the phone with Marco, she tries to see if there will be another opportunity, but she sees nothing, and Maria's heart breaks for Marco.

Coming back to the present, Maria cannot help but wonder about the memory, with Marco's behavior, "How can I tell him, after what he felt that night? After what he did. God, I ask for your guidance on what to do?" Maria hears the voice in her head, *Maria, it is best to leave things the way they are for now.* Maria looks up when she heard the voice. In receiving her answer, she nods and says, "I understand. He needs more time." The voice responds to her statement. *Maria, have faith.*

As you know, everything happens for a reason. It was not their time, not yet. This was more for Marco to see, to know what you have told him to be true. It is up to him. Rebecca has a path, just as Marco does, but their paths are not the same. Eventually, their paths will meet, bringing them together, but only when they are both ready.

Suddenly, Maria's thoughts turn to Rebecca, of her being pregnant, wondering what she will have when she gives birth – *two daughters,* said the voice. "Grazie. Mio Mia…Two? Bellissimo." As Maria sits thinking about this, *I wish it would be Marco to give her a child. Maybe he still can, once they are together.* The voice speaks, *Maria, Rebecca and Marco will not have children.* "This saddens me. Then, is Marco to have children with another woman?" she asked the voice. *No Maria. We are sorry.* To hear this breaks Maria's heart. *No-no.* Shaking her head, *I had always hoped Marco would have children, preferably with Rebecca, but this…* "No great-grandchildren," she said aloud. *You will have great-grandchildren Maria. Your granddaughter will give you great-grandchildren.* "Oh yes, you are right. Grazie." At this, Maria sat the rest of the time in her room in silent contemplation. When the time is right, she will tell Marco what she learned.

Chapter 4

<u>Rebecca</u>

After Richard and I were married, for a short time I lived in Richard's dorm room, although I wasn't allowed. Where else was I going to stay. It was strange how my stomach was growing at a rapid rate. It made no sense. However, a lady I worked with at the BX, who had twins, told me she believed I was pregnant with twins. I told her I couldn't be, although I knew it was possible since my grandfather was a twin on my mother's side, and his mother had five sets of twins. Unfortunately, they didn't all survive. Keep in mind, this was during the late 1800s and early 1900s since my grandfather was born at the turn of the century, 1900.

Richard had only two years of his overseas tour and was about to return to the states, but instead, he decided, and I agreed, he would extend his overseas tour. In doing this, they sent us to RAF Mildenhall, in Bury Saint Edmunds. It was also near RAF Lakenheath, in Lakenheathshire in Suffolk, which was further north of where we were, about an hour away. Before we relocated to RAF Mildenhall, we were given leave to return to the states for two weeks to visit family and friends. Once we returned, we settled into temporary base housing. By this time, I was very large. It turned out I was indeed having twins, and I will never forget the day we found out either. I still smile at the memory, as it was a happy and funny one.

We were sent to the local hospital to get my first ultrasound since the military hospital does not offer them. While we were sitting in the waiting room, waiting to be called back, there were pictures of ultrasounds, some with one baby and some with two. It was funny, before I was called back for my ultrasound, I told Richard of my concerns about the possibility of carrying twins. I went as far as talking to the base doctor, and when he checked for multiple heartbeats, he only found one.

I was finally called in for my ultrasound while Richard waited in the waiting room. The woman technician asked me, "Do you have twins in your family?"

I hesitantly said, "Yes, why?"

The technician looked at me and said, "Because you have two here."

I started laughing, remembering the look of fear on Richard's face when he saw the ultrasound with two heads. At this, the technician requested for Richard to come in, and when he was told, he nearly collapsed on the floor. I, of course, started laughing again. They had to get Richard a chair to set on. God, I will never forget. It still makes me laugh to this day.

Once we were on our way back to the base, Richard started getting angry. He was freaking out about the idea of having two babies versus one. He was yelling about the cost and all those things that we will need, since we were now having two versus one, if you know what I mean. Well, how did I know at the time, that it was the beginning of the worse to come, then a man in the moment of shock was going through. What I, or anyone would say was a normal reaction.

During my pregnancy, I blew up like a balloon. I was placed on bed rest at twenty-eight weeks, and during this time I gained fifty pounds in water weight. I was large, and now I was an embarrassment to Richard. He was ashamed to be with me, and he wouldn't – he refused to hold my hand as if he didn't want people to know we were together. It hurt more than you know. There are those women who glow and are radiant when they are pregnant. I even knew a lady who was. For me, well, I was no beauty. I was fat and ugly, and Richard had no problems making me feel so every day, by making snarl remarks. It was my family, all over again.

More than once, Richard made it clear he was not happy about my being pregnant. At one point, early on in my pregnancy, when I thought I might be having a miscarriage, and as he was driving me to the base hospital – he was supposed to drive slowly and carefully, instead, he drove over and made sure he hit each, and every bump and pothole on the road. This, in hopes I would miscarry. However, it came to nothing, as I did not miscarry. Then, while we were in temporary housing, when I was supposed to be on bed rest, Richard went looking for a house for us, but I couldn't trust he would choose the right one, since the one's he was looking at would have caused me to have an accident in the condition I was in. So, I decided to go with him on this one time, and again, he hit every bump and pothole in the road, but this time, at the stage of my pregnancy, I went into premature labor. Thanks to the doctors, they were able to stop the contractions, and I received a good lecture on how important it was for me to stay in bed.

At the seventh month of my pregnancy, I was diagnosed with toxemia. Toxemia is a very serious condition that usually occurs in women's first pregnancy and when their iron is low. My doctor decided to admit me into the hospital, so they could closely monitor my condition. At first, I was placed in a room with five or six other women. It was like a dorm room, with the only source of privacy being the screen curtain that surrounds our beds. We had one television, so the one who was lucky enough to have the remote control, was the one who controlled what everyone watched.

It really didn't matter to me, as I was asleep more than I was awake. Although sleeping was good for me, it wasn't for my bedmates. The funny thing was, at this stage in my pregnancy, with the amount of weight I had gained, I developed this horrible – and I do mean horrible snoring. It was so bad; they ended up putting me in my own room, with my own television. So, thank you snoring, because now I have my own private room. Yay-yay-yay!

The night I went into labor, I had been in the hospital for a week. Every night when I was asleep the nurses came around to periodically check my vital signs and monitor my blood pressure to make sure it didn't go above a certain point. However, this one night, it was extremely high, and it wasn't going down, even when I laid on my left side. However, I must admit, I did not stay on my left side, since it was very uncomfortable. So, as soon as the nurse left, I rolled back over to my right side, and with this, my blood pressure rose to an alarming rate. The nurses called the doctor, and shortly after, around three in the morning, I was wheeled into labor and delivery so they can induce labor. They called Richard, and I believe it was an hour by the time he arrived at the hospital. Since I was considered high risk, I was given the option to have an epidermal. You see, being overseas, the military hospitals did not offer this unless you were high risk. It was a relief, as I could hear the lady next door screaming her head off. For me, I just laid there relaxing while waiting for the contractions to come and go without notice.

After I was given the epidermal, my contractions slowed down, and the doctor decided to wait, to allow the numbness to wear off a bit, but since it was taking too long, the doctor, nurses, anesthesiologist, and other members of the delivery room decided to have lunch except – now I cannot be sure, but I believe the one person that remained was the anesthesiologist, and of course, this is when everything started to happen – it was time to have these babies, so the anesthesiologist called everyone back to the delivery room.

Sara was born at one thirty-three in the afternoon, and with no rest in sight, the doctor encouraged me to continue pushing, as there was no time to waste. They needed to get Tiffany out right away; if not, they risked losing her and me. To help with this process, they used a suction cup on her head and pulled while I was pushing. With this, Richard seemed very caring and concern for me, and then Tiffany was born at one thirty-nine in the afternoon.

Right after the girls were born, I was given a quick glimpse of them, before they took me to another room, so they could work on me. With what happened, I almost died. Once they finished, I was wheeled down to ICU, where I remained for three days. They brought the girls in for me to see and hold during this time, but I didn't remember this happening. I only learned this after seeing the video Richard took. This was when I learned that I was holding and feeding Sara. I had no idea, no recollection of this happening. When the nurse came into the room to check on me, I told her I didn't remember the girls coming to see me. This concerned her, so she began asking me questions of other things that happened after I was brought into ICU, and I didn't remember those either.

After being in the ICU for three days, I was finally moved to the maternity ward, where I was able to shower for the first time after giving birth, and it was AMAZING. Once I was settled in my private room – this time it was because I had twins, not for the snoring, as that was no longer an issue. They had me try to breastfeed, and at first, it seemed to be going well, until Tiffany started struggling, so they ended up placing a tube through her nose and down her throat. Then, she ended up with yellow jaundice and was placed under a heat lamp to clear it.

It was a week later when we were finally released to go home, but before we could be discharged as new parents, we had to be instructed on bathing and caring for our newborn daughters. However, Richard continually refused, by finding all kinds of excuses to why he didn't need to be there. However, the nurse made it very clear – by this point, she was very irritated with Richard, and if he did not partake, they would not discharge the girls into our care. Richard was a stubborn man. Since I became pregnant, this type of behavior became more common. The nurse was so furious with Richard, she ended up having a few choice words with him, then after a little more, he finally took part, and we were able to leave.

I would like to say the miracle of giving birth to our daughter's changed the way things were between Richard and myself, but it didn't. We settled into a routine, and I took advantage of their sleeping hours and rested as much as I could.

One night while Richard attempted to take care of Sara and Tiffany while I was resting, he became frustrated and ended up shaking Sara. It seemed no matter what he did; she wouldn't stop crying. When I learned this, I was upset with Richard for what he did, since he could have harmed if not killed Sara.

I woke up to the crying and immediately went downstairs to see what was happening, and this was when I learned what he did, so I said, "What were you thinking? If you couldn't handle the girls, then you should have woke me up." This didn't help any; instead, all it did was piss him off even further. I then asked, "Did you try rocking her in the rocking chair upstairs?"

He said, "No."

So, I took Sara from his arms and carried her upstairs, then sat in the rocking chair and rocked her until she fell right to sleep. It wasn't just the rocking; it was my calmness as well. Once Sara was asleep, I placed her in the crib next to her sister and went downstairs to have a word with Richard, and once I was done, I made it clear, "Next time, wake me up no matter what."

The following week, since we were new parents of twins, the hospital decided to send out a nurse every week to check in on us and help if needed. On this visit, Richard told the nurse he shook Sara, and she took this as a cry for help, and did what she had to do, she reported it to the base, who ordered Richard to take anger management. However, instead of this helping, it only angered him even more. And things between us escalated to unmanageable proportions. To a point, we were ordered to take marriage counseling. Now, when your counselor tells you, "There is nothing we can do to help him," you know you are doomed. The marriage was over.

In 1993, I finally had enough. After suffering from verbal, and at times, physical abuse – some were minor, with him throwing the girls toys at me, and at times, throwing them so hard it would cut my face. But the one that sticks out the most around this time, was a day when we were arguing in the kitchen and Richard shoved me so hard that the back of my head slammed into the corner of the wall, and I collapsed on the floor, unable to move or get up. Richard was yelling at me to get up, saying I was faking it when I was not. When I finally managed to move, I made it to the neighbors and called his first sergeant (boss). I told him what happened, what Richard did. Now, you are wondering why I called his boss instead of the SP (base police); honestly, I don't know. It would have been the wiser decision to call the SP, but I didn't.

The next thing I did, it still astonishes me today, how I managed in the state I was in, to walk across the street to the main base, RAF Lakenheath, and then to the hospital. Although I made it to the hospital, I was never seen by a doctor. Richard's boss showed up at the hospital, and we ended up in a room where he talked to us. The next thing I knew it, I was going home with Richard.

With the head injury I suffered, I should have been seen by a doctor and not allowed Richard's boss to talk me into going home instead. So, the next day I decided to go back to the hospital and have my head examined. They found I had a huge black and blue bruise on the back of my head. It was a severe injury, one that should not have been neglected. You can say, I was fortunate.

Richard's abuse towards me became more consistent, with no sign of letting up. Therefore, I made my decision – while Richard was TDY (temporary duty), I took the girls and left England, and returned to California.

You know the funny thing about all of this; I left California thinking I would have my freedom, but most of all, a man I believed loved me. I had neither. I saw England as an adventure, to be able to see a part of the world I never thought I'd ever see, and I ended up not seeing it. I spent four years in England, but I was trapped. When I wanted to do something, like take a tour of France, I was not allowed to. If it wasn't what Richard wanted to do, then we, nor I on my own, was allowed to do it. This was when I learned Richard was a very controlling man.

In all of this, I felt the strongest – I believed I found my purpose, my reason for being born. Why was I alive in this world? It was my daughters; they were my reason. Well, it's what I believed at the time. As I mentioned earlier, I didn't believe I had a purpose, but these girls – these two beautiful daughters of mine, did. I also believed if I loved them as I knew they needed to be loved, to give them the love I never received from my mother, they'd love me in return – unconditionally. I wouldn't need anything or anyone else. I know now, in having my daughters, it did the one thing that nothing else could; it prevented me from ever wanting to take my life again, as I had more than myself to think about. I had these two beautiful small people to think about, and who needed me, as no one ever needed me before.

I was twenty-three when I left England, and my daughters were only fifteen months old. I had successfully lost all the weight I gained from my pregnancy, and I was back to wearing a size five. I started working out at the gym, taking aerobics classes, and working in the weight room. I ended up in better shape than before I was pregnant.

<u>Cheshire, England</u>

After Rebecca returned to California with her daughters, Maria told Marco what happened and what her guides told her. Marco was devastated. He felt it was his fault because of what he did that night. Maria did everything to reassure him, it would not have mattered what he did, it wasn't the right time for him and Rebecca. But this did not matter, he continued blaming himself for losing Rebecca to another man. Knowing Rebecca married and had two – twin daughters broke his heart. Yes, there was some joy knowing she was separated from her husband, but then he thought, *what does it matter, since Rebecca is no longer in England. So, now what? What do I do?*

From the first night Marco saw Rebecca, there were so many times he was adamant he saw her, until it turned out it wasn't her. With this happening over, and over again, broke his heart ten times over. He often wondered, *was I seeing what I wanted to see?*

Marco would see her face in every dark-haired woman he came across, who had the same features Rebecca did. When this happened, he thought, *am I losing my mind.* He felt as if all hope was lost, but what he failed to see, was these were signs, a reminder not to give up. Instead, he was too blinded by his own guilt and pain to understand what was happening. He would think about what his grandmother said, *nõnna tried, tried so hard.* She'd say, *"Don't give up, it's not over."* Isn't it, though?

Chapter 5

From 1993 and up to 1995, I spent my time with friends going to clubs and working out at the base gym since it was free, and I was working at the local mall. This was the time when my life took a drastic change.

Since I was working thirty minutes from where I lived, I was grateful to my mother for watching my daughters since I could not afford daycare. The one good thing about this, at least my mother loved my daughters, and it seemed she loved them more than she ever loved me. This was also the time when, *the strange and unusual* things started to happen that couldn't be explained.

During this time, I went to the local bars and the clubs in Sacramento and San Francisco. I loved dancing, and yes, I was damn good at it too. No, this is not me bragging…okay, maybe a little bragging. It seems no matter where I went, I was recognized and received compliments. I appreciated the compliments; at the same time, it was irritating.

One night at our local bar, I saw this very good-looking bouncer. However, I never thought much of him, as I believed he would not be interested in me. Not until this one night, when I noticed him watching me, in the way he looked at me, I was sure I saw interest. Later I learned he was in the Air Force, and this was a second job. This was not unusual for military members, as most ended up working a second job. Since high school, it never failed the way I was drawn and attracted to Air Force men. I cannot explain why, except, the only thing I could think of, was because they were older – more mature.

You see, in high school I met this girl Sam, who became my very best friend. It was her who was into military guys, and of course, she got be hooked as well. They weren't that much older, only by five years. We remained best friends until the early nineties, as she had a slight problem – she was a compulsive liar.

Yes, I became one of those girls who hung out at the military base, but not one who had sex with all the men I met. You see, I was a virgin up until I met Richard. And yes, if the man I met was not military, I didn't give him a second thought.

During my time at the local bar, I met this woman who was in her thirties, and through her, I learned the man – the bouncer was a Master Sergeant in the Air Force, named Frank. Frank is six feet tall with a well-defined muscular body, cut just in the right places. He was so handsome; you know that rough-looking type. And yes, I did like those types – the tough, strong, and protective type.

For a long time, this guy and I only watched each other until a day I decided to do something daring and brave. I decided to stand in the spot he usually stood when the bar was busy, which is directly in front of the counter. I wanted to see what he would do. My friend Sam thought this idea was crazy, as she didn't believe he was watching me. Most of the time when I went to the bar, he was busy, but this time, since we arrived early, it was pretty much empty, except for Sam and I, along with a blond woman sitting to the right of me.

After getting our drinks, Sam and I turned to face the dance floor. I looked around trying to figure out where Frank went, and when I looked up, there, there he was on the balcony looking over the railing, and it appeared he was looking directly at me, and I mentioned this to Sam.

"Sam, look, he's looking at me."

"No, I think he's looking at the blond sitting next to you. Look at her dress?" she said, looking over at the woman.

Okay, yes, the blond was sitting there, and she was wearing a very tight dress with open holes on the side, but still —

"No, I don't think so." Well, Sam still did not believe me, so I told her, "Fine. It's easy to prove. I will go stand by the dance floor and we will see what he does." Without waiting for a response, I did just that.

As I stood at the edge of the dance floor waiting to see what he would do, to my wonderful surprise, he came down and we started talking.

He said, "Hi, how are you tonight?" At this, my stomach was swimming with butterflies. But without waiting, he then said, "You are here early tonight."

I was surprised, yet pleased he noticed. There was no doubt, he was watching me. When I finally answered, I was so full of nerves, "I'm good. Oh well…since I'm the designated driver, we decided to come early so I have time to drink."

"Oh, that's great. I'm glad you don't drink and drive. I'm Frank, by the way."

"I'm Rebecca. Yeah. I don't believe in drinking and driving, and my friend Sam…well…" I looked over at Sam, who was sitting on her stool drinking her beer looking irritated. In my opinion, she was pissed off because I was right. "…likes to drink a lot, so I have to be the one to drive home."

"Well, I'm glad to hear that. Very smart."

His compliment made me feel warm inside, and I said, "Thank you."

As we talked, I couldn't help admiring his delicious body and his strong handsome face. Now, I cannot speak for Frank, but I felt he enjoyed our time talking just as much as I did. He told me about how he worked in the Air Force, and of course, this was his part-time job.

Since that night, Frank and I formed a friendship. Every night I went to the bar, he always seemed pleased to see me, as I was to see him. I found myself making an effort to go to that bar as much as possible, just to be able to spend a few moments talking with him.

He became so comfortable with me, and I with him, so when I arrived at the bar I'd go directly to him, and he would pick me up and I'd wrap my legs around his waist, and we hugged. It seemed each time this happened, he would add something new: first a hug, then a kiss on the cheek, and each time he did this, I would do the same. What I believe was happening, he was feeling me out, trying to determine if I was interested in him as much as he was interested in me. So, when the day came when he kissed me on the lips, well, it was actually a peck, and of course I returned the kiss, his lips felt soft, and sent a tingling sensation through my body.

I am not sure what triggered it or what reasons, but I started dreaming about Frank. In some cases, they would come true. I didn't know what to think about this, as it was all so strange and unfamiliar to me.

I was at the bar with Frank, and we were on the dance floor dancing. Then, he suddenly started pushing me backward until the wall was at my back, and placed his hands on the wall, blocking me in – he kissed me. The long awaiting kiss, and it was an amazing kiss too. Then I woke up. "Awe! No! How fair is that? Come on!"

Well, I cannot say when exactly – maybe it was a few weeks after the dream, when it came true, with a slight difference. After he kissed me, he took a few steps back as he was staring at me, then said, "Wow-wow," and that was it. And all I could do was smile. It was a WOW of a kiss. It literally left me stunned. The rest of the night we were inseparable. Now, I would like to say after that night we were a couple; unfortunately, we were not. However, it did not stop there. I had another dream about Frank.

We were at a house where Frank and I were walking around as if he was giving me a guided tour, and during our tour we ended up in his bedroom, where he pulled me against his hard chest and kissed me. As we were kissing, he slowly walked me backwards until my back hit the wall. Then we were naked, and my legs were wrapped around his waist, and we were having the most unbelievable, mind-blowing, and passionate sex. A passion I have never felt before. We made love. There was nothing casual about it.

Reality: Everything about the event took place. You see, he had a housewarming party, and one of Frank's friends called my new best friend Catrina and invited her, which she in turn invited me. When we arrived, to my wonderful surprise, Frank was there, and to my disappointment, he had a girlfriend. I concluded this, since she was sitting on his lap with his arms wrapped around her. So, instead of Frank giving me the tour, it was his friend Bob. He took Catrina and I and showed us around the house, and we ended our tour where we began, in their closed-in porch which was also their home gym.

While we were standing in the room talking, I looked over at the window and saw Frank. He was standing at the table on the other side of the window watching me. Catrina also saw this, and she later told me he looked disappointed, that it wasn't him showing me the house. Which I believe explains why he came in and asked to give me a tour, and of course I said yes. So again, I toured the house, and this time we ended our tour in his bedroom, and there on the floor was a purse, a reminder he had a girlfriend. Other than that, everything else was similar. Everything about the room was exactly as it was in my dream, except for the mind-blowing sex of course. That, I'm sorry to say, did not happen, but I think…he wished it was different, as he seemed to be disappointed as well.

Since he was dating another woman, that lovely sexual fantasy I had, well, it had to remain just that, a fantasy. Was I disappointed? Yes, of course I was. The thought saddened me that he was with another woman, but there was nothing to indicate there was anything between us, except for that one moment we had on the dance floor.

Yes, there were many times I often wondered why, but what could I do, he was dating another, which to me seemed like a strong relationship. Actually, as I think back to that night at the bar, I think I know what happened. You see, after he kissed me, it was as if we were an item. Every time he tried to grab me around the waist and pull me to him, I stopped him. I think he took this as a sign that I wasn't as interested in him as he thought. But I was. The issue was, I was bloated, and I didn't want him to feel my puffy stomach. How could I tell him that? So, maybe there was regret to what we could have had. I guess I will never truly know.

Now, keep in mind, these were only two events that took place, which could not be explained. It seemed I had some abilities, but what they were, and why they were happening now, I didn't know.

For the rest of 1993, I had a wonderful time reconnecting with old friends and making new ones. I dated a few men during my separation, but nothing that turned into a relationship. One old friend I reconnected with was a guy I knew from high school. Apparently, he was just released from prison after serving time for manslaughter. I couldn't believe it. Apparently, one night when he was driving after he'd been drinking, he crashed his car into another, killing the driver of the car. We did exchange phone numbers, and it turned out he worked at the same retail store I did, but down in the basement as a stocker. He made several attempts to ask me out, but I had no interest in dating him. I only wanted to be friends. He eventually got tired of my continuous refusal and made it clear on his last attempt how angry he was with me.

It was interesting though, because shortly after that, I started receiving prank phone calls. The first one was when I was sleeping, and when the phone rang, since it was one of those old phones, with that loud, unavoidable ring tone, I couldn't just ignore it.

When I answered the phone, I was half awake and half asleep.

I said, "Hello," in a groggy voice. It was a man on the phone, and to me, at first it sounded like a man I knew. One, I dated briefly.

He said, "How are you?"

Of course, I said, "I'm okay. How are you?"

Then he said, "I'm good. What are you wearing?"

Now I thought this was an odd question, so I asked him, "What do you mean…what am I wearing? I'm in bed," I said, figuring he'd get the picture that I was wearing whatever a person usually wore to bed. Apparently, that didn't deter him, because he asked the question again.

"Yeah, so…what are you wearing?"

My thoughts at the time were, *really?* Now, why I did what I did next, I cannot say for certain; maybe it was because I thought I knew who it was, and we had once been intimate.

"I'm not wearing anything but my panties," I said.

Then, to my surprise, he said, "Take them off."

At this, it became clear what was happening. "No! What the fuck are you doing?" I yelled. At this, he hung up. At first, I was angry, but then I decided to let it go, because I thought I knew who it was, since we were intimate once.

Later that afternoon, I cannot say why, but it started bothering me, and I began to wonder why he would call and ask such questions, and the further I thought about it, I became outraged. Why didn't he explain himself? If he had, I would have told him that phone sex was not my thing, nor would I consider doing it – okay, maybe I would have, but the thing was, we hadn't spoken for a while, and the way we last left it…well, let's just say it didn't go well. So, this didn't make any sense to me, and the further I thought about it, the more it bothered me, and I decided to confront him on it.

I picked up the phone and called him, and I didn't waste time getting to the point. "What the fuck we're you doing this morning? Why did you call and talk to me like that?" I demanded.

From the background noise, it sounded as if he had friends over watching a game. He says, "What do you mean? I didn't call you."

Well, I didn't believe him, so I said, "Yeah, right!" Then I said, "Don't do it again!" And I slammed the phone down.

Later that afternoon, I am not sure exactly the time, but I received another call from the man who called me earlier that morning, and this time when I heard his voice, I knew it wasn't the man I believed it to be.

The funny thing was, although I spoke to him the way I did, John called back to check on me.

"Are you alright?" he asked.

I said, "Yes, I'm fine?" However, I wanted to be sure, so I asked, "Why did you call me this morning and talk to me the way you did?"

He proceeded to say, "It wasn't me."

As I listened to his voice, I realized he was right; it wasn't him. So, I said, "I'm sorry for calling you. I didn't mean to accuse you…it's just this person…he sounded so much like you. After I talked to you earlier, I received another call from this man, and after hearing his voice, and now yours again, I am sure it wasn't you. Again, I am very sorry."

John said, "It's okay. I just wanted to make sure you are alright."

"Yes, thank you. Again, I am very sorry." Then we ended the call, and that was the last time we ever spoke.

The prank calls became overwhelming, and I thought it was time to call the police and report them. An officer arrived, and after he took a report, he had a tracer placed on my phone. However, it was almost as if the man knew my phone was bugged, because he never called again.

A great deal later, I learned from a co-worker that the person who was harassing me was the guy I knew from high school. He must have heard me talking about the tap, so he never called me again. It amazed me, that he went through all of this because I refused to go on a date with him. Needless to say, I was pissed. I did confront him, and of course, he denied it. I guess you can say, there was one good thing that came out of this; he finally left me alone.

Chapter 6

Several months later, Catrina and I decided to become roommates and rented a house together. She had a teenage son and daughter that were both in high school at the time. The house we rented was a spacious three-bedroom, two-bath house with an open spacious living room and a large kitchen, a two-car garage, and a large front and backyard.

After we settled into our house, we had a housewarming party and I invited Frank, and to my wonderful surprise, he showed up. We spent a great deal of time talking and getting to know each other, and it was obvious, that we were both still very much attracted to one another, and although I knew he was dating someone else, I just couldn't resist him.

We were standing in the driveway in front of his 1950s truck talking, when he suddenly kissed me. This time it was longer and deeper – he was AMAZING, probably the best kisser I've ever had, and I wanted more. I couldn't get enough. I wanted him with all the passion in me, and just when I was going to take him to my room, Catrina came out to remind me it was time to go to the club in Sacramento. I wanted to say no and stay with Frank, but I couldn't do that since our housewarming party was right around my birthday, thus the reason we were going to the club.

That night goes down as one of the many regrets I have in my life.

During my time at the house, I suffered a severe head injury – a concussion from my own ignorance, to the point I could not function on my own, nor could I work since I worked retail. Therefore, I was forced to seek Richard's help. He had returned to the states and was now stationed at Travis Air Force Base, which was over an hour away. Since we were still married, I still qualified for military medical benefits; thus, we ended up getting back together.

I know exactly what you are thinking, and you are not wrong – it was a big mistake. However, allow me to continue.

Richard was not living on base, but instead, he was living in an apartment in Vacaville, which was about five or ten minutes from the base. I lived with Richard for a short time, and to my surprise, he took care of me. You see, there was very little I could do on my own, with the dizzy spells I was suffering. Yes, it did seem as if he had changed. Since I could not work, Richard was there to help me, and I began to feel, to think, that maybe I made a mistake in giving up on Richard. That maybe, for our daughters, I should give our marriage a second chance. This was also the time when the unexplained things started happening.

<u>Verona, Italy</u>

In what Marco recently learned about Rebecca, it was his final straw. To learn Rebecca reconciled with her husband *– first, she was separated, now they are back together. Will there ever be a chance?* "This is mad…I cannot! I will not do this anymore!" he yelled aloud while sitting at his desk in his cottage.

With this latest information, Marco decided to give up on ever being with Rebecca, and for his own sanity, he decided to forget she ever existed. *This great love nõnna talks about…if I am not to have…then I shall find another love.* At this, Marco began dating other women – many women. He didn't believe he was choosy, but he was. The only women he dated were those who resembled Rebecca in size and looks. At least from what he could remember. It didn't matter how hard he tried to find – to feel what he felt when he saw Rebecca – he would fail over, and over again. In doing this, it caused him to become bitter towards himself and to women in general. But more so to the women he dated.

However, on rare occasions, when he was so sure he found her, without thinking – that one, she was not in Europe, and two, the woman's name was not Rebecca, nor did she have an American accent. It was as if he was in denial, not realizing what he was doing. Yes, he may have felt something in his heart, but not to the extent of what he felt with the *true* Rebecca.

You see, there are times in life when we connect with someone through our heart, which is due to a past life connection, someone we consider family, or a true *soulmate*. No, not in the sense you think. We have many soulmates, people's *souls* we knew from previous lives. When our heart recognizes someone who was close and dear to us, you feel it in your heart. What Marco felt that night with Rebecca was stronger and more powerful, a recognition of a soul of the heart. Not a family soul, but a true soul-to-soul connection – what we believe to be true love.

When Marco believed he found Rebecca, he would take her to meet his grandmother, and when he did, he told himself he was doing it to prove to his grandmother, that regardless of what she said, he found the woman he was meant to be with, especially when his grandmother told him it wasn't her. In this, he would go to Verona, Italy, wanting to prove to his grandmother she was wrong. But more so, to prove to himself he was right. That he was not mistaken, although he never wanted to admit it, his grandmother knew things, had insight – knowledge he could never understand. So, deep down, he knew if she said it was not Rebecca, then it wasn't. But Marco didn't want to believe it. He wanted this love so much; he would convince himself it was. He had no understanding of the desperate need in him to have this love, nor, why it was so important for him to find it.

When Maria met these women, she knew right away they were not Rebecca. But trying to convince Marco of this, was another thing altogether. She would ask, "Marco, this woman you bring…is she not like the other women you've dated?"

Marco hesitated before answering his grandmother, thinking better of it, however, she would not relent until he did. "Yes, why? Is she not beautiful?" Marco said, as he put a pastry in his mouth. His grandmother always made the best pastries.

"Marco…yes, she is very beautiful. Marco…do you not see…see…" Maria tried to say the woman looks like Rebecca, knowing she was not her. But how does she? She doesn't want to hurt her nipõte, and at the same time, he needed to know the truth.

Marco, so blinded to what was happening, was unsure of his grandmother's meaning. "See what?" he asked, refusing to meet his grandmother's eyes.

Although it was difficult for Maria to explain, she knew she must. "How much…they look like her?"

Marco stiffened. He knew who his grandmother was talking about, but he refused to acknowledge it. "Like who?"

Feeling a bit irritated, Maria decided to spell it out for him, "Like Rebecca."

Marco froze, as he was about to take a drink of water from the glass he just poured, when he heard Rebecca's name. "No, she is…no." *It's not possible.* Marco turned to look at Jane, who was sitting in the dining room, which was a good distance away from where they were standing in the kitchen. *She is wrong.* He turned back to look at his grandmother, then down at the glass of water in his hand and started circling the rim with his finger.

Maria watched Marco as he looked at Jane. Just for a moment, she thought she saw the realization on his face. There was no choice; she knew she had to point it out to Marco as if he were a child.

"Marco…look at her…see how…" Maria paused for a moment, then went on. "…Jane has dark brown hair and brown eyes. Look at the shape of her face —"

Not wanting to hear anymore, Marco stopped her. "So, there are a lot of women who have brown hair and brown eyes. What does it matter? And many women have the same features as well."

Maria can sense Marco's anger growing, and so, as gently as she could, she tries again. "Marco, she —" She tried to say, *she looks like Rebecca* when Marco interrupted her again.

Marco stopped his grandmother when he slammed his glass on the counter. He knows what she's going to say, and he doesn't want to hear it. "Nõnna, stop! Please…you know I love you. Are you not willing to give Jane a chance? Not even for me? This love…this woman from the past…I am sorry…but I cannot believe…if I do…I just cannot. Please, nõnna…don't trouble me with this again." It pained Marco to speak to his grandmother as he did, but he had no choice. Without another word, he leaves his grandmother standing in the kitchen and goes to be with Jane.

Maria walks over to her kitchen window and looks out to her beautiful garden, to the different array of colorful flowers and the tall lushes' green trees and speaks to God. *God, what am I to do?* She receives her answer. *Do not give up,* is all the voice said, and Maria nodded in agreement.

For the remaining time, Maria tries to help Marco see the truth, but when she tries, he refuses to listen. This upsets Maria, causing her to become frustrated. *Does he not see…she is a part of him…his heart and soul will not allow him to forget her. He wants her so bad…he is dating women that look like her.*

California

When I told Catrina and our friend Monica that I was reconciling with Richard, I felt I was being put through an intervention. I was at Catrina's house, which use to be our house, sitting on the sofa with Catrina and Monica sitting across from me. They were doing everything they could to convince me I was making a mistake.

"You cannot go back with him. You told me how he was to you. Do you really think he has changed?" Catrina asked.

"He seems so different. What am I going to do? I have no money and no job. I cannot support myself," I said.

"Well, I can help you with that," said Monica. "You can work for me," she explained.

You see, Monica had her own business and was wealthy in her own right.

"How can I do that? You live and work in Liveoak. My car is out of commission, so I would not be able to make it."

"Then I will pay to get your car fixed, and you can pay me back out of the money you make from me," she said.

"I can't do that. How can I? If something goes wrong and I am unable to pay you back, then where will we be?"

"Don't worry about that. We will work it out."

"I don't know…I just don't know."

I wanted to take advantage of this, but I was scared to accept Monica's offer for some reason, a reason I cannot explain, so I continued to give reasons why I couldn't.

"And what about the girls? This is a chance for them to have a relationship with their father. Richard has been great with me. He really does seem as if he's changed."

This argument continued for a little longer, but I did not take Monica's offer, later though, I wish I had, if I foresaw what was to come. This will be another one of the many regrets I will have in my life.

Between 1994 and 1995, after reconciling with Richard, we moved into a townhouse on Travis Air Force Base. They were recently refurbished and looked brand new. It was a three-bedroom townhouse with two and a half baths, a large kitchen with a breakfast nook, a dining area, and a living room. Sara and Tiffany shared a room, as they didn't like being apart. There was a small outdoor patio, and just beyond the patio, in between a group of townhouses, was a large grass area. It was a great place for kids in the neighborhood to safely play and run free.

Once we were settled in the new house, it didn't take Richard long to show his true colors – he was not the man he pretended to be. To me, it felt as if he thought, *I got what I wanted. Now I don't have to keep pretending.* His control had worsened, and he was crueler than he was in England. I felt he was doing this to get back at me for what I did to him when I left England. I couldn't do anything without his knowledge or permission, and I was not allowed to have money to buy makeup or anything else I felt I needed outside of necessities. If I spent money without his knowledge, he would go off on me, and his anger was fierce. He would demand I return what I bought. If I refused, he would take his first finger and jam it hard in the center of my chest, over, and over again. The pain was so severe that to this very day, that spot is very tender.

I mentioned this to Catrina, and she told me Monica's offer was still there if I wanted it. But, by this time, for me, I felt it was too late. At least in my mind it was, since the girls were older and more connected to their father than before. How could I tear them away from him because of me? Was I to be so selfish once again? No, I had already taken them from him once, and to do so again – well, maybe not again, but this time, to rip them away from their father – no, I could not. I wouldn't do it, not again.

The worst thing about all of this, I thought his abuse in England was bad; I was wrong. It escalated to the point of him threatening to harm me, and then after a time, I felt trapped. The girls were three, and they loved him very much. Sometimes I would think, *if I never reconciled with Richard, it wouldn't have been so bad. Yes, they would have their father and still love him, but it would have been part-time, not 24/7.* It would have been normal for them since they were only fifteen months old when I separated from Richard. What was done was done, and there is no turning back. It's what I believed then, but now, as I look back, I was an utter fool.

One day, while Richard was getting ready for work, I went in the bathroom for something, what it was, I don't recall, or what caused Richard to react the way he did, but he first threatened to push me into the bathtub, and the next thing I knew it, I was falling – hitting my head against the shower wall, and Richard was walking out of the bathroom.

Another time while he was finishing getting ready for work, we were arguing once again. What about, I don't recall, but this time, this time he threatened to push me down the stairs. It turned out, although I recall the action, I have no recollection of the cause – what words were said – what the trigger was. From what a therapist once told me, this was normal with victims who suffered from abuse, that the reasons were inconsequential.

I'd like to say this was the first time he threatens to push me down the stairs, but it was not. This time though, this time our attached neighbors heard him threatening me.

He said, "If I wanted to, I could push you down the stairs.

I looked at him with shock, then started yelling, "You are threatening to push me down the stairs! Are you serious?" I did this, since I knew the neighbors could hear through the thin walls.

As these threats and abuse continued, I became fearful for my own safety, and in turn, for my daughter's. No, he hadn't done anything to the girls yet, but I felt if he continued the way he was going, he would, and I started thinking about what I was going to do? Where would I go? I was still unable to work, as I was still suffering from a concussion, and I felt stuck – trapped.

Chapter 7

When I look back to this time, with everything I endured from the abuse, I turned in on myself – losing who I was – my confidence and my strength. I felt miserable, worthless, and unhappy. I was lost and confused. The girls loved their father; how could I take them away from him, and at the same time, how could I stay and continue to endure this abuse. What if he turned his anger on the girls? Unfortunately, this answer came sooner than I expected – he did just as I feared.

It was a day – I believe the girls were doing something that angered Richard, what it was, I cannot say, but he took one of those cable cords and started hitting the girls with it. In doing this, he left welts on their legs. When he finally left to go to work, I took several pictures of the welts to show proof of his abuse, if it ever came to that. What was I to do? I didn't know. It wasn't just me now; it was also the girls. I didn't want to go back to the way things were, nor did I want to return to my parents' house. I didn't trust them, and this is why: when Richard first returned from England, my parents allowed him to stay at their house, the same place I was staying. You would think after what happened between Richard and me, my parents would have done everything to protect their daughter from such a man, but instead, through their actions, they accepted him. It was a shock, and it said more to me than words ever could.

You wonder why my parents would do this? Well, their thinking was, "Well…we figure if he's here, you two will get back together…reconcile for the girls." Seriously! Did they not listen – believe anything I told them about what Richard did to me? I could not believe this. Thank God for my grandmother, who was living with my parents at the time, due to the decline in her health, was the only one who saw the truth. But then, didn't I do exactly what they hoped would happen? Well, I can only blame myself, now can't I.

So, what was I going to do with my situation? I had no money since I wasn't able to work, and the feeling of being trapped intensified. I had no one to turn to. No one to talk to. What was I going to do? Yes, I could call Catrina, but once again, my pride got in the way. Damn that pride!

Our arguments continued to escalate, and I made sure we were loud enough for our neighbors to hear, and they did; they heard everything. One night when we were yelling, our neighbors felt the need to call the base MP (military police). We were not aware of this until there was a knock at the door. I believe I was the one who opened the door. Once I did, they immediately inquired about my health and safety. I didn't want to say anything. For some reason, I didn't want to get Richard in trouble, so I ensured them everything was fine. Once they were satisfied, they left. I know what you are thinking. But what was I going to do? Send him to jail? If I did, how would the girls feel?

Of course, as I am sure you already realized, I came to regret that decision. You see, before that night, Richard and I were lying in bed and he wanted to have sex, but I refused. This did not deter him. He was not taking no for an answer, but I continued to resist. When he realized, I wasn't going to give in, he started kicking the hell out of me, and all I could do was turn away from him and curl up in a ball as I silently cried.

Our fighting and arguing only continued to escalate. So, when the neighbors called the MP's again, I decided to be brave, and told them what was going on. The arguing, the threats, everything.

The MP at the door said, "Ms., do you feel safe?"

I said, "No…no, I don't." I then proceeded to tell them what's been happening, and with that, they took Richard into custody. As we walked out of the house, I saw my neighbors next door, and the wife mouthed, "Are you okay?" All I could do was nod yes, with a look of thank you.

Here were the positive and the negative of the situation. Richard was only placed in temporary housing for a week before they allowed him to return home. You can imagine what happened. Yep, for a short time, he was better, but of course it didn't last long.

Yes, we still had our ups and downs, but somehow, someway, I managed to get through them all. I was never a religious person, nor am I now. I did and still believe in God, and prayed when I felt the need to. Though, I was never sure if God was really listening. With the two dreams that came true, I knew something was happening to me, but I didn't understand, nor did I recognize what it was, not until after my grandmother died – my father's mother, in 1995, this was when everything changed.

My grandmother passed away right after Thanksgiving, and I was supposed to visit her in the hospital that night, but I was unable to. After we left my parents' house, Richard was tired, as was I, and we wanted to get home. However, I still wanted to visit her, but Richard argued against it. Regardless of my persistence, in the end, since Richard was driving, I never had the chance to say goodbye.

She passed away shortly after that night. Without understanding the reasons, it seemed after her death, was when everything started. Looking back on everything, I believe it was in preparation for what was to happen in the future, that brought me to where I am today. I could feel my grandmother all around me, and with her presence, strange and unusual things started happening around the house.

During my time in England, I bought a heavy brass cross that was hanging on a wall in the living room. One day when I was vacuuming, for some reason, it started swaying back and forth. I know what you are thinking, there must have been a gush of wind or something that caused it to move. Well, there wasn't. For as long as I owned that cross, it remained stationary and never moved on its own.

Another time when I was vacuuming, I saw a white silhouette from the corner of my eye, and I believed – I felt it was my grandmother's spirit. With this, I did speak to Richard about it, but he thought I was crazy. Then, one night while I was at a neighbor's house, I told them what was happening, and they convinced me there was something paranormal going on. Again, I had no real understanding or explanation, but they didn't make me feel as if I was crazy. They believed and supported me. However, I didn't tell them I believed it was my grandmother. It was funny, because one night as everyone was sitting around the table, they were trying to find a reason or an explanation for who it was and why, and if the entity was good or bad? This was great. To have people support me, unlike Richard, was reassuring.

One night, as I was lying on my stomach in bed, being unable to sleep, I felt a hand rubbing my back, just as my grandmother use to do when I was a child and couldn't sleep. Did this freak me out? No, it was reassuring, comforting, soothing, and calming. It made me feel safe.

Once I finally fell asleep, I dreamed I was in our spare bedroom, which was the brightest room in the house, since it was located on the west side. I was standing next to the window, and the bright sun filled the room, but not just the sun; there was more, a bright white light that didn't seem – feel it was from the sun. At first, I was alone in the room, when in the next second in that same spot, stood my grandmother.

She was standing right in front of me, dressed in pure white Indian garments – pant and top, ones she normally wore. She said, with her broken English, "Why did you not visit me in the hospital before I died?"

Her words struck me like a knife – piercing my heart. What could I say? I said the only thing I could, "I'm sorry. We were supposed to visit you after Thanksgiving dinner, but we were…all so tired, and Richard wanted to drive straight home…I'm sorry," I said as I was staring down at the floor, feeling so much guilt. The next thing I knew it, I was on my knees, pleading for my grandmother's forgiveness. I then said, "I love you. I meant to visit you before..." and just as quickly as she appeared she disappeared, and I was left standing there – yes standing, not kneeling, and I thought, *was this what she needed to hear…is this why she left.* Then I woke up.

I never could forget that dream. It's as clear to me today as it was then. I am not sure how long after the dream, when I was watching The Leeza Show, a daytime talk show, where one of her guests was talking about the spiritual realm – heaven. The lady said, "When those we love are in heaven, there is a place they can go and speak to those they left behind. This is an enclosed space, with what looks to be a well in the center of the room. There is a bright light flowing up and down in the well. If you put your hand into the light while you are thinking of a loved one you left behind, in entering this light, they are limited, having only a few minutes to communicate, as they are tapping into their dream. They appear to you to be surrounded by a bright white light that engulfs the space you are in." My mouth dropped open when I heard this, so you can imagine my shock. What she described was exactly what happened to me.

Keep in mind; these things would only happen periodically as I was going through the most difficult times in my life with Richard. As I write these words, in thinking back to that time, it is strange, with what I know now, it was as if someone was trying to tell me something, wanting me to know I was not alone.

On another evening, when Richard and I were arguing, I attempted to get away from him – I grabbed the car keys and left the house. I wanted to go somewhere, anywhere, so long as it was away from him. Unfortunately, I only made it to the driver's seat of our car. After sitting there for a moment, I started crying uncontrollably, at the same time trying to figure out what I was going to do.

<u>Spiritual Realm</u>

"Victoria, what can we do for Rebecca?" asked Joseph.

"Joseph, all we can do is observe Rebecca, and nothing more, not without God's permission."

"I know you are right. Michael, is there anything you can do?"

"I, too, am unable to intervene without God's permission. Why don't we call Jesus and see what he can do to help?"

"Yes, I think you are right. Jesus, we need you, please come?" Joseph called.

"I am here, Joseph. Hello Victoria and Michael. What is happening?"

"Look at Rebecca…she is so upset. Her husband has been treating her badly, and she is feeling so lost, unwanted, and unloved. Is there anything you can do? Is there something you can do to help her, that will bring her peace?"

"Yes." Without another word, Jesus goes directly to Rebecca and sits in the seat next to her. As he watches Rebecca crying, he allows himself to be seen by her, then slowly and gently places his hand on her shoulder and says, "Everything is going to be okay." At this, she immediately calms. This was done to show God is with her and loves her.

"Joseph, Victoria, and Michael, for now, that is all I can do. Continue watching over Rebecca. Call on me again if I am needed," Jesus said, then he was gone.

But then, as quickly as he vanished, he reappeared. "Joseph, God was observing what happened with Rebecca, and has agreed, with as low as Rebecca is feeling, she requires more help. She needs to know there are family who cares and loves her. God has asked Rebecca's grandmother, who's already been visiting her, and her grandfather to help her. If they sense they are needed, they are to go to her and give her the peace she needs."

Joseph is so relieved to hear this. "Thank you, Jesus," he said.

"To be a part of Rebecca's life, since the beginning, then to see her suffer, even as an angel, has broken my heart, and I have no heart. To see her feeling so lost, especially with the way her family is to her, now her husband…she needs to know that she is loved…by many," Joseph said, with sadness. "Jesus, forgive me. I know this life was what she chose for herself when she was to be reborn, but even to an angel, it's still hard to watch, knowing I cannot do anything to help."

"Joseph, there is no need to ask for forgiveness, as there is nothing to forgive. I, as much as God, understand love. It is not wrong for you to care and love Rebecca. To be part of God, who loves all he has created, and Joseph, you are part of God," Jesus said as he placed his hand on his shoulder.

Letting out a sigh of relief, Joseph turns to Jesus and says, "Thank you." Then returns his attention back to Rebecca.

When, from the corner of my eye, I saw a person. This person appeared to be in a white robe, sitting right in the front passenger seat, and to my surprise, the person appeared to be Jesus. Then I saw his arm move, placing his hand on my shoulder. With his touch, I instantly felt calm, then heard these words in my mind: *everything is going to be okay.* With this, I immediately stopped crying, as if I was wrapped in a bubble of peace and calm. I cannot say how long I stayed sitting in the car, but I remember that I did not want to leave a place where I felt peace, safe – my safe-haven.

I cannot say how long after this event when I had another strange dream. I dreamed I was falling from the sky when an angel flew down and caught me in its arms. Next, I was in my dark bedroom, standing next to my closet door, with my grandfather standing in front of me. Now keep in mind, my grandfather – my mother's father, passed away a week before my daughters were born. Now he was standing in front of me in my bedroom. He was wearing what he normally wore, jean overalls, and he looked at me with no emotions on his face, and his expressions were of a man very serious, with a purpose that should not be ignored.

He said, "Why did you summon me?"

I looked at him, not understanding his question, but said, "I did not summon you."

Ignoring me, he proceeded to ask again, "Why did you summon me?" Without an answer, he then said,

"Everything is going to be okay. Everything is going to be okay." Then he was gone, and I woke up, with a feeling and a knowing, although I am going through a rough time right now, somehow, everything is going to be okay. That there is someone watching over me. I knew in time; I would be okay.

You know what is strange about telling my story, is how I was – I am being watched and looked after, and the amount of help I received – I am still receiving.

Do you know what's funny? As I'm reliving these memories with you, I had no idea of the love and support I had during the time this took place. No, they were not of anyone here on Earth, but of those who already passed, telling me we are here. You are loved. You are protected. You have never been alone. What is even funnier, I am still receiving these messages to this very day. If you ever feel lost, I learned to look to God, to Jesus, and to those we loved, who is no longer a part of this world. Although gone from this world, they are never gone from our lives and hearts. They still love and care for us. Never did I believe you can receive love and help from those loved ones who passed. Along with God, they are always there watching over us, even before we are born. We are given those who will help guide and protect us through all the good and the bad we will endure throughout our life.

One of my most memorable occurrence that is still clear today as it was the day it happened; was the day I drove to my doctor's office. I had to take the freeway, and once I took the off-ramp and was sitting waiting for the light to turn green, I saw a man standing at the corner. He looked to be an ordinary man. He was clean and dressed in blue jeans, with a button-down jean shirt, and a white t-shirt underneath. He seemed to be somewhat tall, maybe about six feet, with salt and pepper curly hair. He approached my car and asked me for money. Apparently, he ran out of gas and had no money to buy more. I only had twenty-five dollars in cash with me, and I needed the twenty for my doctor's co-pay, so I ended up giving the man five dollars. When he took the money he said, "Thank you, and God bless you." At hearing this, I looked up and met his eyes. What I saw pierced my heart, giving me a feeling – I am not sure, even to this day, I can describe it adequately, but it felt as if my body was filled with the purest of love. His eyes were of a blue, one I had never seen before – they looked angelic. As the man backed away from my car, I was unable to take my eyes off him. It felt as if I was looking directly into the eyes of God. There was never a day that went by, I forgot about the man I saw on the corner. He left me feeling as if I looked into the eyes of God. Those blue eyes were nothing like I had ever seen before. As you can see, this has stayed with me as strong today as it was then.

Chapter 8

So many things happened in 1995 – so many unexplainable things. My daughters were even experiencing certain events and activities. In a way, it was good to know I wasn't the only one, but then again, it also concerned me.

My daughters were playing in their room as they usually did, but on this particular day, they ran downstairs and said, "Mommy-mommy. There are three ladies dressed in black playing with us under our bed. Mommy, they are scaring us."

"Honey, what do you mean, three ladies? And why are they scaring you?"

"I don't know, mommy, but they are."

"Okay, honey, I will go and see what is going on. You wait here, okay?"

"Okay, mommy."

It was strange, because at first, Sara and Tiffany seemed to be playing with these ladies, but something happened to cause them to feel as if something was not right, which caused them to become afraid. They must have realized these were not real ladies, as they believe them to be. So, when they realized something was not right, they came running down scared.

I headed for their room, and on my way there, I felt these ladies were not bad, but good. Now, how did I know? I cannot say. I just knew. It was a feeling inside me, telling me they were safe. So, I decided to speak to them.

"I know you are here, and I know who you are." I knew. Something in me said, *they are guardian angels. Sara and Tiffany's angels.* "But my daughters are confused and don't understand. So, I ask you…if you will please…do not show yourself to them again. They are feeling scared, as they do not understand who or what you are. Thank you."

Once I did this, Sara and Tiffany never mentioned them appearing in their room again, at least not to my knowledge.

There was another occasion when Sara and Tiffany saw an old man standing in their room next to their television. From their explanation, I believe the man to be Richard's grandfather – his father's father. He was a tall man, about six feet, and was very thin, with a receding hairline. The skin on his face was loose and saggy, as it gets when you get to be eighty years old. You see, he passed away shortly after the girls were born, and one day when I was home alone, the television in their room kept turning on. When I went up to their room to see what was going on, it felt as if something was not right. As if someone was there in the room with me. As I slowly walked over to their television, I scanned the room expecting to see something, but there was nothing. But I felt there was something there – in their room. Once I turned off the television, I went back downstairs to the living room and resumed my seat to watch my favorite soap opera, and it seemed right as I sat down the television in their room went on again, and then again, and again, until I marched up those stairs determined this was going to be the last time.

It was funny though, as I think back to that time, it was if the spirit was having fun with me, because each time I turned off the television and returned to the living room – just as I was about to set down – yep, you guessed it – *damn.* It went on again. It did this a few times before I marched up those stairs and stomped into that room, and this time when I turned off the television I said, "Okay already! Enough is enough! Okay, I get it! You are here!

And I acknowledge you! You have my full attention! Could you please…stop turning the television on! I am sick and tired of going up and down these stairs. Please, do not turn this," pointing to the television, "on again, thank you!"

Did it work? Yes, it did. It seemed that once I acknowledged they were there, the incident never occurred again. What I've learned since, is when things like this happen, it's because they are trying to get your attention. Once you've acknowledged them, and showed them respect, they will in turn show you respect by ceasing their activity.

My marriage was showing no signs of improvement, so I decided it was time – I could no longer stay married to Richard. It was time to make a plan and find a way to get as far away from this man as I could. It turned out, with the base closures, Richard was given the opportunity to take an early out from the Air Force. In doing this, he would receive a large sum of money.

After a great deal of thought, with the fact Richard could not make his next rank, he decided to take the early out. His plan was to move back to the east coast and spend the next ten years working as a reserve, which would give him his full twenty years, allowing him to still receive a pension when he turned sixty-five. So, I thought, okay, this is a perfect opportunity. I will not leave California and he will move back to the east coast. The problem with this thought, I had to figure out how I was going to leave without Richard discovering my plan, thus keeping me from leaving.

That summer, Richard decided to send Sarah and Tiffany to visit his parents in North Carolina for the whole summer. He did this to allow time for us to prepare for the move, and at the same time, it would allow me time to figure out what I was going to do. At first, it wasn't a big deal since the girls would return before he planned on leaving, which was when I planned to take the girls and leave. However, nothing ever goes the way you plan it, does it.

The next time Richard talked to his father, he asked if his father and stepmother would be willing to keep the girls until we moved to the east coast. They, of course said yes. I only learned about this when I asked, "When are we picking up the girls?"

He said, "We aren't. The girls will remain with my father and Stella until we move there."

I was shocked. I couldn't believe what I just heard. My plans were shot to hell, and I wondered, *what am I going to do now?* I knew there was no choice, I had to tell Richard about my plans of leaving – divorcing him, and that the girls were staying with me.

I prepared myself for the reaction I was sure to receive when I told Richard my plan. "Richard, I am not going with you, and neither are the girls. I am going to file for a divorce, and…the girls…are going to stay with me."

Well, as I expected, this did not go over well. He said, "Well, you can stay, but…I'm leaving. I'm not picking up the girls. They will remain with my dad and Stella until I get there. You can stay, but the girls are staying with my father."

I was livid, and yelled, "No! I don't think so! We need to go get them and bring them home!" I demanded. I knew in saying this that he wasn't going to listen.

"No!" he said firmly. "What are you going to do about it? You can stay, or you can go! I don't care! But the girls are staying with my father."

There was no doubt, he had me right where he wanted me – submissive to him, and I wondered, *did he figure out I had no intention of going.* Was this why he did what he did? Even to this day, I cannot say. Well, there was no question, once again, I was stuck. What else could I do? I did what any mother would do to protect her daughters. I moved with him to the east coast. There was no way in hell I was leaving my daughters with a man such as him.

He ended up choosing South Carolina, where Charleston Air Force Base was located and only a state away from where his father and Stella lived. This was where Richard would perform his reserve duty for the next ten years. With Richard knowing how I felt about our marriage, and how I wanted a divorce, the way he treated me in California was minor compared to how I was treated in South Carolina. It became so bad, I truly feared for my life and for the life of my daughter's, and I don't mean this lightly – it was horrific. To think that every day I was with Richard, I would fear for my life. I would hope and pray he wouldn't turn on the girls as he turned on me. No, I didn't believe he would hurt our daughters, but, with the way he was changing, I couldn't be sure.

Although Richard was working reserve duty, it was only part-time, so he took a part-time job at a restaurant working as a waiter. Since he started working this second job, he was rarely home. Yes, you would think this would be a good thing, but it wasn't. When he wasn't working, he spent his time with his newfound friends – his coworkers, that he rarely came home. If he did, it wouldn't be until the early morning hours. The times Richard stayed out all night, he didn't call to let me know. Why did it matter if he was leaving me alone? Well, for one, he had the only vehicle, so if there was anything I needed, I was stranded. It's not like I can walk with the girls in the summer heat. We would die from heatstroke. I didn't know anyone well enough to get a ride to the store from. I guess he felt he owed me nothing since our marriage was pretty much over. But, what about his daughters?

If you have ever been to South Carolina, you understand the summer months are one of the hottest ones in the state, with the high humidity. It makes you feel sticky, just from a few moments outside, or when you walk out the door and say, "Damn, it's too fucking hot!" Then slam the door, deciding to forget about going out for the day, not unless you really had to.

It seemed as if Richard had given up on his family, not just me, but all of us. To do what he was doing affected our daughters as well. For me, I got it, but our daughters – no, it made no sense. Our daughters should have been his main priority. However, his clear priority was to party with his friends, as if he had no other obligations or responsibilities. As if he was single again. Well, if that was the case, the bastard should have left us in California. But, for Richard, it was all about control.

One day I received a call from Richard's stepmother, and although I never said anything before, I felt this was too important to ignore. So, I explained to her what was happening, and they agreed to talk to Richard. Well, let's just say it didn't go very well. It didn't have the effect I'd hoped it would. All it did was anger him even further, and now, he hated me even more – he started screaming at me.

"What the fuck we're you doing telling my father and Stella about my business! What happens here is none of their fucking business! You fucking bitch! Do it again, and I swear…I will fucking kill you! I can hide your body where no one will find it!" he yelled.

You can imagine what happened after that. Well, I had no one to turn to. I had no life, nothing that could get me out of my situation. I can say, if it wasn't for Sara and

Tiffany, I don't think I would have made it as far as I did. I am sure I would not be here today.

Richard's threat on my life became a regular occurrence, to the point when he didn't come home, I feared he would send someone to our apartment to kill me. With this fear, I started latching the top lock. If he gave someone our apartment key, they wouldn't be able to get in, not without making a great deal of noise. With these fears, I found it difficult to sleep at night. If I did fall asleep, it was light, so I could keep an open ear to any noise. I always wondered, *will tonight be the night?* But then I would try to rationalize it – *no, he wouldn't do that, not with the girls in the apartment.* But I couldn't be a hundred percent sure. So, I struggled every night, always wondering would tonight be the night? I didn't think he was a man who would do this himself, but have someone else do it for him. My reason for these thoughts, although he was in the reserves, he was still a part of the Air Force, and I didn't believe he would do anything to risk his pension. Or would he?

It was a day of great joy, not to mention relief when Richard received orders to go TDY to Italy – *thank you. Please go.* To have a time of relief from the daily and endless torture, I was sure he knew I was going through. I felt, although it was short, I would be safe. Boy, how wrong and naïve I was. How could I have been so foolish to think I was safe. Yes, he was out of the country, but it didn't matter. Never let your guard down. Always think and plan for the worse.

The dumb ass was pulling cash out of the ATM in Italy, not considering the exchange rate, nor that I was still in the states taking care of the household bills and our daughter's, in buying food, etc. He was pulling more than he believed was in the bank, and at the same time I was writing checks to pay our bills and buy food. He thought I was taking the money and doing whatever I wanted with it. I had no idea of this, not until I received his threatening phone call.

"You fucking bitch! What the fuck did you do with my money!" he yelled.

"What are you talking about? I used the money to buy food and pay bills. What do you think I did with the money?" I asked. Seriously, did he not realize I had to pay the bills, buy food, and do what was needed.

"I don't fucking believe you! You fucked me before!"

Oh right! I fucked him before – hum, the time I left England, and had to withdraw money from our account, knowing he would be completely reimbursed, per what I learned from the military. You see, when a military's family member uses their own money to return to the states, the military member only has to submit a voucher and would receive full reimbursement, and I know he did.

"I didn't fucking do anything to you! I am here, having to care for our daughters…buying food and paying our bills! You should not have been taking money out of the account without talking to me first!"

After this, he continued yelling and threatening me, so I hung up the phone. This wasn't good enough for Richard. Oh no, the bastard called my parent's house and left a message on their answering machine threatening me. "You better get your daughter in check, or she is going to lose her life!" When I heard this message, I completely lost it. There was no choice; I had to call his dad and stepmom. It was time they knew everything. It was time to tell them what's been happening. And I mean everything. They knew we were fighting, but not to the extent of it, and I had proof. Since my parents were still using those old cassette tape answering machines, they sent me the tape, and to this day, I still have it. Although, I no longer feel I need it.

After I got his parents on the phone, I had them listen to the message themselves. They were shocked. They couldn't believe what he did and what he said. They said they would talk to Richard. Yes, this was good, but after the last time they tried talking to him, not even realizing the extent of our situation, it did no good, nor will it do any good this time either, but they tried anyway, and of course, I was right.

The only thing Richard was thinking about while he was in Italy, was having too much fun spending money on whatever he wanted and without letting me know. Nor did he inquire on what I was spending money on. Our account became so overdrawn, it wasn't funny. So, you know what happened to all that lovely extra money he made? Yep, it cleared our negative balance. Dummy!

Several months after we moved to South Carolina, my baby brother George decided to visit, as he was considering moving to South Carolina. In a way, I was relieved. I believed while he was here, I would be safe. To my surprise, he managed to get a job shortly after he arrived.

George later told me that Richard asked if he brought any weed with him. You see, my brother is no goody. He did drugs, among other unsavory things. I was shocked, and I couldn't believe he would be so stupid to bring weed, and so I asked, "George, you didn't?" He started laughing, proof that he did. That bastard! I said, "With the girls here! That is not smart! What if they went into your bag and found it!"

He said, "Shit, I didn't think of that."

Of course not, I thought, shaking my head, and then I said, "Apparently not! Get rid of it!" He didn't like that answer and started arguing about the amount of money he spent on it, and I said, "I don't give a fuck! What's more important, the money you will lose, or the girl's welfare?"

Well, whatever he did with it, it was out of the apartment and away from the girls. I didn't want to know, nor did I care, so long as it was out of my apartment.

On George's days off he hung out with Richard, and this is when I finally learned what was going on with him during his time away from home. Apparently, the group of friends Richard was hanging out with – he was doing drugs with them, and it wasn't only weed.

George said, "It's not the only thing he was doing…he's also doing cocaine."

I could not believe it and said, "Are you fucking serious?" *How could he do this? Did he have no care for his own daughters?* "What the fuck is he thinking?" And I repeated my thought aloud, "Does he have no care for his daughters?" All my brother could do was laugh, and I looked at him, "You're not helping George." He was still laughing.

However, this did explain Richard's odd behavior. At the same time, I couldn't believe he would risk his pension with the military by doing drugs. Apparently, I was wrong.

Things did not work out for my brother, so he left South Carolina and returned to California. In way, I was relieved since George was not a good influence, nor was he helping Richard. But, after George was gone, I no longer felt safe. With what I learned about Richard, in how severe things were, I didn't know what I was going to do, and I felt as if I lost everything. I had already lost myself, and again I felt trapped and scared, like a lost child who was trying to hide in an adult body, when in reality, there was no place to hide. My thoughts were at the time, *if I can't save myself, how can I save my daughters.* I felt there was no hope. No one who could help me. No one I felt I could trust. Who was going to save me from this man? If I left, how would I survive? Where would I go? Can I survive on my own and care for my daughters? These were questions, questions I had no answers to.

Yes, I did leave Richard before in England. But this time, this time was different. Then, I was stronger, and I hadn't lost myself or hope. But now, now I had. I didn't know who I was anymore. I felt helpless. I lost all confidence in myself, and felt as if I was no one, no one who mattered to anyone but me. How can I help my daughters if I can't even help myself? Although I had a job, working in a call center did not pay much, not enough to leave Richard and care for two small children.

Chapter 9

One day when I was working at the call center, something strange happened – I was sitting at my desk waiting for a call to come through when I started scribbling the name *Joe* or *Joseph* on my notepad. This name was flooding my mind, forcing me to write it down over and over again, and I filled my notepad with it, but I didn't understand why. Then, there was a feeling, something inside telling me Joe/Joseph is my guardian angel, and for some reason, I knew it was true, but why? Well, later I learned Joseph is one of many guardian angel's watching over and protecting me.

Joseph was always there for me, and at times I found myself talking to him. At this point in my life, he was the only one I could talk to who understood me. I know what you're thinking, she's crazy to be talking to a fictitious person named Joseph. But, if you believe in guardian angels, also known as spirit guides, then it's not so unusual – crazy, is it.

Now, as I look back, Joseph was there to let me know I wasn't alone, and that I am cared for. I am loved. I am protected. Trust in him and in God, and all will be well. I had no idea at the time that I was never alone. I was never unprotected. I was – I am loved. Unless we understand what is happening, we are blind and in complete denial. We allow our emotions and fears to rule us, keeping us from seeing what was – is right there in front of us – keeping us from hearing and seeing the truth. Joseph's name continued repeating in my mind all day, every day as if he wanted to ensure I knew he was always there. He made me feel, if for any reason I needed him, I only had to call on him – to say his name, and he will be there. I did. I called on Joseph many times, and he was always there, telling me everything was going to be alright, and reminding me that I was loved and cared for. Telling me not to give up and have faith in God, and he will be there for me.

One afternoon when it was time for Richard to go to work – by this time, he was leaving me the vehicle, but he would be the one to drive, then I would take the car. I guess something his parents said did work. However, there was no doubt, he wanted to be sure I understood he was still in control. You see, when it was time to turn into the parking lot where he worked, he turned extremely slow, crossing the double right lane, then he'd punch the gas right before the oncoming car was close enough to hit us.

He'd look at me and say, "See now…I could have killed you…and made it look like an accident."

I stared at him for a long moment, shocked, and in disbelief in what he just did and said. There was no doubt; the man wanted me dead. He's been contemplating on how to kill me and get away with it, and without any blame to himself. I knew if I didn't do something soon, I would forfeit my life, and in turn, my daughters. This, I had no doubt of. If something terrible happened to me, what would he eventually do to our daughters. What's even scarier, the girls were in the car with us when he did this, and I remember thinking, *what am I going to do? I am way on the other side of the country…I have no money to take the girls and go back to California.* With this, I felt so alone and lost.

<u>Verona, Italy</u>

Maria was in her kitchen preparing dinner when she felt a need to check on Rebecca.

"Mia Mio – I-E-E-E!"

Maria knows when this feeling hits her, it cannot be ignored. She stops what she's doing and turns off the stove, then goes to her bedroom. To check on Rebecca, Maria prepares to travel – astral project, sending her spirit to where Rebecca is.

Maria sits in her chair next to her French doors and begins meditating, allowing her body to fully relax, focusing her mind, heart, and soul on Rebecca. When she connects with her soul, Maria's spirit is pulled from her body and taken directly to Rebecca's.

When she arrives in the place where Rebecca is, she found herself in a vehicle, in a new and unfamiliar place, and saw Rebecca with her husband, and hears her husband tell Rebecca how he could kill her and make it look like an accident. Her heart stopped, and she could feel Rebecca's fear – *Mia Mio…what is happening? Why is her husband talking about killing her?* Maria focuses on Rebecca and attempts to send her energy, wanting her to know she is loved. That someone cares for her, and she is very much wanted, and hopes it helps. Maria wanted so much to help Rebecca, but there was nothing she can do, and she fears – worries that something horrible is going to happen to her, and there was nothing she can do but pray.

Maria returns to her body, "Mia Mio…what do I do." Does she tell Marco or not? Should she wait for the right time – *will there be a right time? If I do nothing, and something happens —*

Maria's guides feel her anguish and respond to her question. *Maria, do not fear for Rebecca. She is well taken care of. There are many who are watching and protecting her. We will not allow Rebecca to come to any harm.* To hear this, Maria feels great relief. "Oh…bellissima! Grazie!" After this, Maria goes back to her cooking, trying not to let what she heard and saw bother her, and thought, *Rebecca is in God's good hands.*

<u>South Carolina</u>

After being in South Carolina for a year, Richard came to a decision – regardless of what I had to say about it, he decided to move to Florida. Do you want to know why? Get this, it's because he wanted to be closer to one of his friends he's known since he was stationed at the Air Force Base in California. When he made his intentions known to me, I couldn't believe it, and I let him know how I felt.

"Unbelievable! Are you seriously thinking about moving to Florida? What about your reserve duty? And…you are doing this…because of your friend, regardless of what anyone else has to say about it?"

What an ass! Oh right, there is his uncle and grandmother who lives there. He could have said, 'I'm moving there to be closer to my grandmother, who doesn't have much time left' but n-o-o-o it's because of his friend! Seriously! Where are his priorities?

At the time, I wish I had the balls to say this to his face, but I didn't. Instead, I said, "What about the girls? We just moved them here, and now you want to move them again to another state?"

"The girls will be fine. They will adjust fine. Look…I am going regardless. If you want to come…fine. Otherwise, I don't care what you do. Whatever you do…the girls are coming with me."

Unbelievable ass… "Fuck you!" I yelled. The look he gave me…so I said, "Whatever! There is no way in hell I am leaving the girls with you." Let's just say…he didn't like that very much.

Here we go again! Forced to move, regardless of what I thought or how I felt. Richard left me with little choice.

There was no way in hell I was leaving the girls with him. For that to happen, it would be over my dead body. Not like that wasn't far from his mind. Regardless, he would have to go through with what he had been threatening, and I would fight like hell until I was dead.

A few months later we packed up and headed to Florida. After finding an apartment, we no longer shared the same bed or room as we did in South Carolina. What was the point. I slept in the living room on the sofa bed, and he slept in the bedroom. We moved into a two-bedroom, two-bath apartment with a kitchen that had a long narrow window. There was a pass-through into the dining/living room area. There was a closed-in porch with a view of a small lake, one of many on the property.

When Richard and I were looking for a job, I was looking at collection agencies since I had three years of experience in the field. With his ten years in the Air Force, as a crew chief for the KC-10, Richard could easily get a job working at an airport. Was that what he did, oh no-o-o-o, it was not what he "tested for." Idiot. So, he started looking for work in customer service, since it's what he scored high on from a test when he first entered the Air Force. What the idiot didn't know, your pay depends on your amount of experience. When he finally found a job, he was making six to seven dollars an hour, when he could have been making forty thousand dollars a year. Hum, you would think that would have been the smarter choice – not.

After Richard received a job offer for a customer service position at a security company, he told me they were also hiring collection agents in their collection department. Well, with his uncle's help preparing me for my interview, I got the job making eight dollars and fifty cents an hour. During my training, the lady who interviewed me was the manager of the accounting department, and she ended up pulling me out of training to ask me, "I have a position in my cash and receipt department, and I feel you would be a great fit."

I was surprised and pleased I made such an impression that she wanted to hire me for her cash and receipts department, and I saw this as a great opportunity to learn a new skill.

So of course, I said, "Yes." I would have been a fool not to. I also asked, "Would I still be able to keep the hours and the pay I negotiated?"

She said, "Yes."

So, I immediately began training in her department and was making more money than Richard. It was a great company, and I would not have known about it if it wasn't for Richard. "Thank you, Richard," I said to myself with a broad smile.

There were times my job required me to work overtime, including weekends, and in doing this, I made a great deal of money. Although, this didn't make Richard happy, since he had to take the responsibility of taking care of Sara and Tiffany. With this, Richard became very bitter about the opportunity given to me, as he didn't think I deserved it.

Apparently, to Richard, it appeared he didn't make a wise choice in his position. With the fact that I was making more money than he was, well, that was like adding fuel to an already burning fire. It wasn't just the money, but the fact he had to take care of *our* daughters, especially over the weekend, it only fueled his already growing anger, and with it, his hatred towards me. He felt it was a burden. What, are you kidding me? A burden to watch and care for his own daughters? What the fuck?

You see, watching his daughters hampered him from being able to hang out with his friends – do drugs, I say – allowing him to do whatever he wanted. I know, unbelievable. It was easier to say these things now, but then, I had no voice, I am ashamed to say. When one loses oneself, it's hard for that person to protect themselves and those around them. What I have to – no, need to say to all of those who feel this way, get out! Get out before you ever get to that point.

There was a weekend when Richard wanted to go to a ball game in Tampa, but since he had to stay home to watch the girls because I had to work, it pissed him off. So much so, he called his dad and stepmom to complain about it. However, he did not get the response he expected.

From what I learned, his father and Stella were on the phone and his father said, "Well, if she's working and making money, then it's your responsibility as a father to take care of Sara and Tiffany."

Then Stella said, "Richard, you are no longer a young man without responsibility. So, grow up and get over it."

I would like to say this helped, but it did not. All it did was add more fuel to his already growing anger towards me.

Richard was behaving as if his daughters were crippling him, instead of seeing it as spending quality time with his daughters. I remember when I confronted Richard about this, we were standing in the small front entryway, facing each other when I said, "All you care about is what you want and what you can do! You don't want the responsibility of being a father, do you?"

To my surprise, he actually admitted it. "No, I don't!" Unbelievable.

He wanted to be a single man again, and to be able do what he wanted without responsibilities. I cannot say for a hundred percent, but this seemed to have started after he reconnected with his friend, and from this, he longed to be single again. This didn't make any sense, since his friend was in a relationship. I remember thinking, *unbelievable, that he would rather party than be a responsible father.* Jackass!

There was a night – I cannot say when exactly, but one thing I know for sure, it was shortly after we moved into our apartment, because I had the hammer on the table from hanging pictures earlier that day. As I was about to go to bed, Richard, in a weird and scary way, approached me. Why? I didn't know, nor did I ask, but the look in his eyes was of a man ready to kill. For some reason, I felt the need to protect myself, so I picked up the hammer. But then something didn't feel right, and that voice in my mind I've become so familiar with, was telling me to put it down, so I did. But once I did, to my horror, Richard picked it up, and with that look in his eyes, I truly feared for my life and for the life of my daughter's.

So, I did what I had to, to prevent Richard from hurting me, and in turn, our daughters. I started talking to him, trying everything I could to find the right words that would tap into his conscience – his fears, by telling him, "If you kill me…you will lose everything. Your freedom, your career in the military." I did this…to play on his fears of incarceration, how it would be for him to be among criminals that were more vicious than he was. Also, if he were to have any criminal charges, he would be dishonorably discharged from the Air Force and lose his pension. "If you go to prison…you know…you wouldn't be able to handle it. You will not survive." I was trying to get him to see the dangers of a man such as he (weak), would become an unwilling victim in prison. Then, I returned my focus to his career with the military and the future of his retirement. Whatever did it, to my relief, he slowly put down the hammer and returned to his room, leaving me safe, at least for that night. For how long? I didn't know.

I am not sure how many days after that night when we returned home from the grocery store, and as we were putting away the groceries, for some reason, I don't know why, Richard took one of those plastic grocery bags and wrapped it around my neck and pulled it tight – he was strangling me.

Spiritual Realm

"What are we going to do? He is going to kill her," said Veronica.

"I don't know. We are not allowed to intervene. All we can do is observe," said Virginia.

"Should we call Joseph or Jesus to help?"

"Let's call Joseph first and see what he says. Joseph, please come?"

"I am here. I know what is happening. Unfortunately, this is not something we can call Jesus for. But I have an idea. Gather everyone who has been assigned to help Rebecca, including her family who is still here."

Once all the spirits from Rebecca's family, along with God's angels were gathered, they surrounded Rebecca and Richard in an unbroken circle. This is to send Rebecca the power of God's love, so it will give her the strength she needs to fight back. They speak to her spirit, asking it to leave her body. This was done to protect her. With her spirit standing outside her body, it allowed her to see what was happening. Then just as suddenly, her spirit returns and starts fighting Richard's hold on her.

Rebecca

I found myself standing outside my body – watching what was happening to me. When out of nowhere, I found the strength to force Richard backwards. Once his back was to the kitchen window, I started slamming him into it, to force him to release me. When he did, he was laughing, as if it was a big joke to him. I cannot explain what happened, but it was as if there was a surge of power – strength that took over, allowing me to force Richard to free me.

When Richard released the tight hold on the bag he had wrapped around my neck, and once I was free, I started coughing as I was trying to breathe. Then, when I glanced up, I saw my daughter Tiffany standing on the sofa crying and screaming. She watched the whole thing, of the horror of what her father was doing to her mother. After getting myself together, I went directly to Tiffany and took her in my arms, letting her know I was alright.

Anyone who's been through such trauma can never forget – never. You may be able to put it behind you, but you can never forget. My throat was so sore, and my voice was horsed, making it difficult to speak or swallow. From that moment on, I could not wear anything that felt constraining around my neck: turtlenecks, high crew neck shirts, short or choker-like necklaces, or even a scarf. No one could touch me on or near my throat. If anyone were to reach around me from behind, to pull me to them, or try to put a necklace around my neck, I would suffer tremendous anxiety – panic attacks.

There were times when my daughters would put their hands near my throat – obviously not understanding the severity of this action – would cause me to flinch. It sent me into a panic attack along with the anxiety and fear, to where I had to quickly push them off me.

In time, they did come to understand, because they would say, "I'm sorry, mommy." For this to happen, it was hard. When it did, I tried not to allow it to bother me, but it didn't always work. So, Sara and Tiffany learned to be cautious around my neck. I also knew when I did this; it would remind Tiffany of what happened to me, in what she saw. She too, suffered great trauma from this, as well as other things.

Today, I am happy to say I am a great deal better and stronger than I was then. That feeling of anxiety I once had, no longer bothers me as it did. Yes, there are still times, and thank God, they are rare now, where I still suffer from anxiety. When it happened, or how, I cannot say. It wasn't until one day, without thinking about it, I put on a crew neck t-shirt. It wasn't until a great deal later when I realized it wasn't bothering me as it once had. I did not suffer the anxiety – panic attacks as I once did. With this, I decided to try on a short necklace, one I hadn't worn in years, and to my happy surprise, I didn't suffer any anxiety. I was astonished by this. It had been so long, and to now, after all these years be able to wear shorter necklaces, scarfs, and at times, chokers, it was amazing. Yes, there are rare times the anxiety returns, but more not, then so.

As I stated earlier, I wasn't the only one that came out of this marriage with traumatic scars. You see, another incident occurred involving both Tiffany and Sara, but more so with Tiffany, and unfortunately, I am unable to say how long after Richard tried to strangle me when this incident happened.

I was in the shower, and as I was rinsing out my hair, I thought I heard screaming. I turned off the water, and when I did, I definitely heard screaming. I quickly grabbed a towel and wrapped it around me, then ran out of the master bathroom, past the living room and into the kitchen. What I saw, I could not believe. To my horror – it was one I had prayed would never happen, was happening. Richard had Tiffany bent over the kitchen counter with her pants down and her bottom bared, and he was beating her with a wooden spoon. I quickly went over and grabbed the spoon out of his hand. Once I had Tiffany safe, without hesitation, he went directly into the girl's room to go after Sara. Without thought, I ran and stood directly in front of Sara, preventing Richard from attacking her, as he did to Tiffany. I was determined to do whatever was necessary to protect Sara, since I was unable to protect Tiffany.

I yelled, "If you want Sara, you will have to go through me first!" Whatever it was that did it, he stopped and backed off. I was determined, no matter what happens to me, I would not allow Richard to harm my daughters.

However, in this, for many years after, the one thing Tiffany could remember was how I saved her sister and not her. Yes, in time she understood, but it hurt me more than you can know. To hear your daughter tell you, "Why did you safe Sara and not me?" It crushed me more than you know. It would crush any mother. I thought, *I did this. This was my fault. If I had left, none of this would have happened.* But I didn't, and I had to suffer the shame of that every day of my life since.

This was the event that finally gave me the balls to leave. My worst fears had finally come to fruition. It wasn't only me anymore. For myself, I believed I could endure anything, but once Richard touched my daughter, I knew it was time, and I had to do everything in my power to leave Richard and Florida. With my daughters in danger, this is what gave me the courage and strength to leave.

The positive aspect of this, I was making good money, enough to take the girls and leave. To go as far away from this man as I could. It was time to return to California and as quickly as possible. It's strange now, knowing what I needed to help me escape, I finally received it.

After the event with Tiffany, I contacted Amtrak with Richard in the room, and made our reservation to take a train from Florida back to California. Now, you wonder how I managed this? Honestly, I don't know. Maybe it was Richard's way of giving me a sense of security – safety, and then boom, the bomb would drop. Whatever the reason was, Richard didn't stop me, and I booked three one-way first-class tickets that included a compartment with two bunk beds with a shared bathroom. It wasn't as bad as I expected it to be. Once I booked the reservation, I called my parents to tell them what happened, and the girls and I were returning to California.

After this was done, there was something Richard wanted me to do before he allowed me to leave. He asked me to wait until after he returned from his two-week reserve duty. Without hesitation, I quickly agreed. But what he didn't know, I had no intention of keeping that agreement. I knew he was going to try to prevent me from going. So, once I was alone, I called Amtrak and made a second reservation to leave on the first Saturday he was gone. There was this feeling as if something was telling me, *if you don't leave then, you know he will not let you go. You cannot allow him to stop you.* And so, when I felt secure enough, I canceled the first reservation I made.

My boss and co-workers were aware of what happened when Richard tried to strangle me, since my throat was sore, and it was hard for me to speak, I told them what happened. They were so understanding and supportive of me. So, when I informed them that I made reservations to leave, they allowed me to work extra hours so I could make the extra money I would need. Although I managed to gather most of the money, I was still short and was left with no choice; I had to call my parents and ask for their help. To my surprise, they managed to gather the rest of the money I needed, and I secured our tickets.

It wasn't long after I made our reservations, when I received a call at work from the principal at Sara and Tiffany's school. He told me about a conversation a teacher overheard between Sara and Tiffany. Tiffany was talking to Sara about what their father did to Tiffany the other night.

The principal said, "When the teacher heard this, she asked the girls to go with her to see the nurse. The nurse examined Tiffany but was unable to find any marks. From the conversation, she felt it was necessary to inform me and asked that I talk to the girls. So, they were brought to my office, and from what I learned, I felt I needed to call you and tell you what happened."

In hearing this, I was shocked and afraid, that this incident would prevent me from taking the girls out of Florida. So, I said, "Thank you. I want you to know that I have a train reservation for the girls and me…I am taking them back to California this Saturday."

You could hear a sigh of relief in his voice, then he said, "I am glad to hear this. Because if not, I would've had no choice but to call the authorities and report this incident. In doing so, it would've prevented you from leaving, and…you need to leave." He was *firm* in this last statement.

In hearing this, I was in tears. Even now, writing about this event, I feel the tears wanting to weld up. It's unbelievable that after all these years, I can still be affected by such an event.

He continued, "I am glad you are going somewhere safe and away from your husband."

To hear this brought tremendous relief to me, and I said, "Thank you. You have no idea…how grateful I am in allowing me this opportunity to leave."

With this, we ended the call, and I broke down crying. The fear, the relief – so many emotions, and I knew I made the right decision. My co-workers notice I was upset and were very supportive, including my boss.

The journey back to California was an adventure for the girls. Our tickets included breakfast and dinner, which was a good thing, since I didn't have much spending money, only enough for small items; bottled water, chips, things like that. The girls loved the train, as it allowed them to forget everything that happened before. What was nice, there was an observation area on the train. A whole section of the train that was made of windows from one side and across the ceiling to the other side. It allowed you a great view while traveling across the country. Downstairs, just below the observation room, was a children's playroom. The girls would go back and forth between the observation area and the playroom. They had a great time. It was nice to see them happy and having so much fun with the other children on the train. By the time we arrived in California, it was very late at night, or should I say, early in the morning. Catrina offered to pick us up from the train station and drive us to my parents' house. After we arrived in California – home, I was finally able to breathe with a sigh of relief. We were safe.

Chapter 10

<u>Verona, Italy</u>

Maria felt it was time to tell Marco everything she learned about Rebecca, but Maria was afraid, because in doing so will break Marco's heart. But what she feared the most, when she told him, he will give up and turn away from Rebecca forever. This, she could not allow. She put her faith in God, and every time she went to church, she lit a candle for Marco and Rebecca, sending up a prayer in asking God to help her. To help them find their way back to each other.

"God…what is happening to Rebecca? I feel something is very wrong. I don't want to go to her…unless…it is allowed. I feel…her life…is her life in danger? If something has happened to her…I could not bear…please…please tell me. Help me understand what I am feeling?" Maria said as she looked to God for the answers she sought.

It was only a few moments when Maria received her answer. *Maria, do not fear. If you wish to go to Rebecca, you may…she is safe. Rebecca was in danger, but she is no longer.*

Maria let out a sigh of relief, then asked, "Can you tell me what happened to her?"

All we can tell you is her husband tried to strangle her but failed. Rebecca left her husband and is returning to her family in California. Rebecca's heart and soul are severely scarred.

To hear this broke Maria's heart. "I-e-e-e…No! Will…she survive…this?" she asked gently.

In time, and with our help, she will. Maria, with what Rebecca went through, it will be years before she can love again. We cannot say, but when she is ready, Marco will know…his heart will tell him so.

Maria's thoughts went to Marco, concerned of what he will think or do when he hears of this. *And he must know. I must tell Marco, but how? How can I tell him…this grievous news? He is already doubting, and to hear this, will he give up altogether? I couldn't tell him when I heard Rebecca's husband threaten to kill her, and now…I must tell him both. There is no way around it, he must be told.*

Maria telephones Marco and tells him he needs to come to Italy at once. After Marco arrives in Italy, Maria sits him down and tells him everything she's learned about Rebecca.

"I am sorry, Marco," Maria said, seeing the pain and heartbreak in her nipõte's eyes.

"Nõnna…what am I to do? How could she…how did she end up with such a man?" Marco said, dropping his shoulders as he lowers his head, with a feeling of defeat…*what am I to do?*

Maria reaches for her nipõte and places her hand on his back trying to give him the comfort he needs.

"Marco, sometimes there are those…who end up with a person, whether they are good or bad, will take them down the path they are meant to go down. This man, who hurt Rebecca…yes…he is bad…but he did bring her to England…allowing you to see her. To allow your souls, for the first time to connect, did it not?"

"Yes…but…I was aware of her…she was not aware of me."

"Yes. How do you know she was not aware of you? Can you be certain? Now…no, there is nothing you can do but wait. When the time is right, and when she is ready, you will know. Your heart will tell you so."

"Well…I…I guess I don't… there's no way of knowing when?" he said, but then anger took hold of him. Marco pulls and turns away from his grandmother before he lashes out. Not at her, but at the situation, to something he doesn't understand. "My bloody heart! My heart has failed me this far! How can I trust this," he said, turning back to face his grandmother, thrusting his finger strongly at the center of his chest, directly over his heart. "To tell me anything of truth?" He was angry, hurt, and demanded to understand things that he has no understanding of.

"No Marco, there isn't. It can be many years, or it…I can't bear to think of this…but…if she does not recover…it may never happen," Maria said. She stands and places her hand over his heart. "Marco, your heart has not failed you. You think your heart tells you what you want it to, but, your heart, when it's time, it will feel different. A part of your heart that is empty, will fill and become complete. There will be an overwhelming pain, but not a hurtful pain, a good and wonderful one. This is when you will know. Can you tell me…have you felt this with any of these women you've been with?" she asked. But Marco says nothing, he only shakes his head no. "Believe me, my nipõte…don't ask me how I know, I just do."

"Nõnna, what…no…" shaking his head, "This cannot be. Maybe…this is not to be…in this life either," he said, still shaking his head. "You told me after that life, where we took our own lives, and have failed to find each other in our other lives. How is this life different from all the others? Can you tell me that?"

For a moment, Maria only smiles at Marco, then says, "Marco," grabbing his chin and pulls it towards her, forcing him to look at her. "My nipõte, this time is different because you have me. I was Elizabeth's sister. I asked to be born in this life to help you and Rebecca, to correct the wrong I did then. You were born into my family, my nipõte, to allow me this chance to help you. Why do you think I was given this gift? This gift allowed me to recognize your soul after you were born, and at the same time, allow me to remember my life as Grace, and yours as Robert, and Rebecca's as Elizabeth's, who was my beloved sister? No Marco," shaking her head, "This life, I know in my heart," placing her other hand over her heart, "You are to be together. When I first learned of Rebecca, was when I first told you the love story of your life from before…do you remember?"

Marco listens intently to his grandmother, then only says, "Yes."

"Later, they told me in this life, she would suffer great hardship and pain. In this, it will take her down a path…the path she's meant to go. So, my nipõte, please do not give up. Hang on tight, as there is still hope."

"Nõnna…after all these years, how can I still have hope?" Shaking his head, "I don't know…I don't think I can. I don't have faith in this as you do. I just don't know. How can I? I am now in my mid-twenties, and at this point in my life, I should have someone to share my life with. To have a child or two with. In my…allowing your story of this love to affect me, of a life from before, how can I feel love for a woman I don't know or even met. But God help me," reaching for his grandmother's hand, "I have not been able to let it…her go, of this love you've spoke of. What is wrong with me? To hope…for this love, of this woman, who now after all this time, and after what she's been through…she may never be in my life." Looking directly in his grandmother's eyes, "How can I hope for something that may never happen? And what about mother? Lord knows, she has tried hard to get me married off. Wanting me to marry a woman born an heiress. But…because of Rebecca… how…" shaking his head, I cannot do this."

At this admission, Marco stands up, feeling frustrated, "This…this dream, a dream that is not to be. "I know. I cannot deny it any longer! I have been dating women, women I believed to be her, but are not!" He is angry, so angry at himself for falling for a false dream. A fairytale. A story. "You knew…you knew all along I could not forget her," he said, raising his voice, "But…now, now I must!" he said, then lowers his voice in resignation.

He is so confused. He does not want to be angry at his grandmother, but he is. He feels, if she hadn't spoke of this love since he was a child, he would not have allowed it to rule his life, and his decisions with the women he's met.

"I think…I think it's time. It's time to do what my mother wants, and marry another, and forget about Rebecca." Marco sits down with his face in his hands.

Maria reaches for her nipõte and takes him in her arms, holding him, wanting to bring him comfort, as she can feel his pain and sadness, along with his loss of hope. *God, please help me. Help Marco.*

Inside, Maria grieves for her nipõte, but on the outside, she needs to be strong and confident in what she has to say. "Marco, I am so sorry. I won't tell you not to do this, but I ask you to search your heart and ask yourself, is this right. What will you do when she is finally ready, and you are no longer available?" she said, then realized she made a grave mistake.

"Well then, it will be her turn to wait, won't it?" he said in a firm voice, irritated by her question.

"Marco, forgive me? I did not say this to hurt you, or to make you feel guilty, nor make you feel that you haven't done enough in your sacrifice. But think of this, my nipõte, you've had a good life. A rich life. Rebecca…she had a poor and unloving life. Then to have a husband she thought loved her, to only hurt her. When the time comes for her to discover you, and when she does, to learn she's already lost you. What do you think this will do to her? Although she does not know it, her heart aches for the love you both shared. She needs you, Marco, more than you can ever know." Then she realizes she cannot stop her nipõte from moving on. "I am sorry Marco, I should not say this. You are right. You should not have to wait. You must do what you need to do. Whatever that is, I will support your decision," she said with sadness in her voice.

Listening to his grandmother, it hurts Marco to see her in such distress. Does he want to do what he says? No, but he feels he has no choice. What else can he do?

"Nõnna, oh nõnna…my heart screams for this to be. Right now, I feel such pain in my chest, as if my heart's being torn apart. I wish…I want so much to be what she needs. To be able to comfort her and bring her the love and peace she seeks, as I know her love for me will bring. To give her security, a life of ease and comfort. But," shaking his head, "I'm sorry, I cannot do this anymore, not if I am to remain sane," he said. It does pain Marco to do this, but what else can he do? He's known about Rebecca since he was ten, and now he's in his twenties. Hasn't he waited long enough?

"Marco, look deep inside yourself, into your heart and soul. There, you shall find the answers. They are there. They have always been there. When you are ready, you will receive the answer you seek. This pain you feel," Maria said, laying her hand over Marco's heart, "You feel it here, when you connected with her that night in the pub. Your heart longs, needs…is seeking to reconnect with her heart…making them one once again." Maria places her hands on Marco's face. "Marco…she loves you…she just doesn't know it yet. She has her own path…she must follow, and in this path, it will prepare her, give her what she needs when it's time to find you. If she does not do this, she will never be ready. Do what you feel you must, but please, do not give up on Rebecca, and the love you had, and will have again," she said, then took a moment before she continued. This love I have told you about, Marco, it's worth waiting for."

Maria wishes she can share the memories she has from that life, of what she saw, of the times Robert and Elizabeth were together and the love they shared. How Grace wished one day, she too will find a love as her sister did. Who knew it would take her hundreds of years, and not until she was born in this life, to find her true love. Yes, she found love when she was Grace, but it's not the love she found here, in this life.

"I wanted this for you when I learned who you were and when I found Rebecca."

Marco lays his head against his grandmother's shoulder and allows her to pull him into her arms, as she did when he was a boy. After a few moments, Marco says, "I want to believe you, I really do. But I just…I don't know if I can anymore. I am sorry. All I can say is, I will try. I will try not to give up. As you know, mother has been relentless in trying to get me to marry, and she's already chosen a woman she wants me to consider…" he pauses, unsure if he should say the next… "Maybe now is the time I should."

"Marco…I don't want this. These women your mother wants you to consider..." Maria stops what she was going to say… "I should not say…I am sorry."

"No, nõnna, please speak your mind," Marco said.

There's one thing he's never doubted, is his grandmother's accuracy of the women he's dated in the past. He's learned to trust what she says, whether at the time he chooses to believe it or not.

Maria smiles up at her nipõte and says, "These women will not bring you the happiness or the love you seek. Your heart and soul will not allow it. There is only one love it will recognize, and that is Rebecca's. You have suffered this…the lack of love in your previous lives. But God has seen that now is the time…for you and Rebecca, in this life, to have the love you both seek. The love you both lost. Marco…you will never be happy…if you do this. And when Rebecca is ready…it will cause you great pain, anger, and regret. When this happens, I'm afraid you will grow to resent your mother and the woman you chose, blaming them for your pain, at the loss of your one true love…your heart. Please, think more on this?" Maria said as she places her hand on Marco's arm.

"Nõnna, I am so lost, I don't know what to do? I am a grown man," he said, shaking his head as he moves away from his grandmother. "With this, I feel helpless, like a lost child. This love you say I am to have…it pains me to think of it. It hurts more…to think and feel…what I believe, I will never have. I feel I must find a replacement, someone else to take my mind away from what I am feeling for her. In doing this, it will help me forget what I feel…of her." Marco said, unable to say, Rebecca. He no longer wants her to be real. "Maybe what you say is true. Maybe this will happen. But, how can I think of that now, when there is no time, no answer to when this will happen."

"Marco, this is true, there is no time of knowing," placing her hand over his heart again. "Your heart knows, and it will tell you when. What's important, is that you are loved by me, by your mother, your father, and your sister, most of all…by God. The power of his love is beyond any human love. He gave you his love…but also his love through her. Trust that God knows what he's doing. In all the other lives you lived, not once did you get this close to having the love you seek. To have her. This life is different. It's allowed God to connect you and Rebecca, to give you a chance to find each other and have the love you once had. Marco, God is telling you…now is the time, here in this life. Open your heart and soul to him, allow him to direct you, to guide you to this love…to Rebecca. Promise me Marco, before you decide, search your heart and soul by opening your heart, and allow it to speak to you. It will tell you what to do."

Maria is so desperate for Marco not to give up, she slumps slightly, resigned to support Marco no matter what he decides.

"I will support you no matter what, Marco. If I learn any more about Rebecca, do you want me to tell you?"

"I will do what I can, but I will not promise you, nõnna. You have always been there for me, and I love you very much. I don't know what I would do without you. If it wasn't for you…I don't know if I would be the man I am today. If you feel what you learn about Rebecca is something I should know, then yes, tell me."

Although he's prepared to walk away and find another, there's still a part of him that doesn't want to completely give up.

Marco did what his grandmother asked him to do. He opened his heart and waited for an answer. After several days of trying, he did receive an answer, but did he recognize it? Marco knew he had to wait for Rebecca, and in waiting, he decided to allow his mother to introduce him to women she chose, but his heart was never in it. His heart would not allow him to forget Rebecca. No matter what he did or who he was with, she was always there, as if her spirit was a part of him, surrounding him with a constant reminder she existed. What Marco failed to realize, that these were the signs he was looking for – his heart was screaming at him to listen.

After ignoring the signs Marco was receiving, he woke up one morning realizing he could no longer ignore what was happening, and how he feels about Rebecca. So, he ended his relationship with the woman he was currently seeing and decided to dedicate his time in building his career and strengthening his financial stability outside of his family's fortune. He believed if he focused his mind on business and family, he could put aside everything else while he waited for Rebecca to be ready. With the knowledge – the belief that his heart will tell him when the time was right.

Did he give up women altogether? No, he could not. He was a man with needs and desires, ones he found he could not do without. So, Marco started dating again but refused to commit to anyone woman.

Marco's grandmother lost her husband when he was a child, then later, when he was a man, was when he decided to dedicate his time helping his grandmother manage his grandfather's business. With Marco doing this, it angered his mother. She didn't like him splitting his time between her and their family business. She never liked Maria – she hated her since Marco's mother started dating his father. She realized early on; Maria knew things, and more than Marco's mother ever wanted anyone to know. Marco's mother hated the love he had for his grandmother, and no matter how much she argued with Marco about this, he'd ignore her so-called disagreement. Nothing his mother could do or say would force him to abandon his grandmother.

Although Marco chose to date women while he waited for Rebecca, his mother's persistence –pressure, became unbearable to ignore. Since there was no way to tell when Rebecca would be ready, he gave into his mother's persistence, even though he was determined not to marry. He thought it was best to give his mother what she wanted, at the same time, getting her off his back. However, this too proved to be a mistake. He began to feel nothing he did was right or good enough for anyone, and decided that too much time had passed, and gave up on Rebecca altogether. In doing this, he ignored his grandmother's concerns in his decision.

From all the women Marco dated, they proved to be nothing but fakes. Oh yes, this has been something he's known about, but for some reason, these women seemed to be worse than the ones he dated in the past. These women were only interested in his money, his status in society, and who his family is. In dating Marco, they'd hope to either improve or gain their own status in society. When Marco learned about this, he became even more bitter towards women than he was before, and he was tired of being used by these so-called women – fakes. They saw Marco as their ticket into high society and nothing more. Although he gave up on Rebecca, there was still hope that one of these women could love him for himself. He wanted so much to love and be loved, and then to learn these women only wanted to use him, was too much for Marco. With his bitterness and anger, he came to a decision; if these women were going to use him, he in turn will also use them. Sex was his only priority when it came to these women. When he was done or became bored with them, he would dismiss them as if he was dismissing a servant without any care or a second thought.

In what Marco was doing, it was to conceal his pain by closing off his heart. He was barely living. He was living a numb life – unfeeling to anything or anyone around him. He was so lost and alone, without the love he sought. The love he needed. No one to love him and make him feel. Yes, he had his mother, sister, father, and grandmother, but their love was different, not one of the heart, but one of the soul, for which he craved. What was he to do?

One night, after a long day at work, Marco was lying in bed thinking about his previous relationship with women, how miserable he felt, knowing how these women treated him, it left him feeling of anger, as well as sadness. With feeling so alone, lost in not finding the one woman – the love he was seeking. When he finally falls asleep, he dreams.

Marco is aware it's just a dream – he's dreaming of his life from before, sometime in the 1500s, the one his grandmother told him about.

"It is I...I am Robert Davenport." He is astonished at the realization. He is with a girl, no, a woman, "Heaven help me, she is so beautiful. But wait, she is familiar. I know her. How do I know her?"

This woman who has captivated him, there is something else, something he feels in his heart – love. He places his hand over his heart, the pain – no, not pain. His heart is filled with so much emotions – of love. He never in his life believed he could have.

Looking at this woman who is smiling before him, "It is her. She is the one making my heart feel this way. She is the one, the one nõnna has told me about. Is it possible...is she Rebecca, the one I am to be with?"

He thinks on this as he stares at the woman before him. She reaches for his hand, and when he takes hers, the sting he feels triggers memories of the love they shared. A love so powerful and pure. One that can never be taken away, nor forgotten.

"But I did…I had forgotten. Why?"

The passion between him and this woman is beyond any he's ever known. Beyond anything he thought possible. This woman standing before Marco – Robert, has shaken him to his core.

When Marco wakes, his heart is racing, still reeling from the love and passion he was feeling from the man in his dream. *Was this a memory? Can it be?* he thought. "I have to call nõnna. She will know." He throws off his covers and races to the phone to call his grandmother.

"Nõnna, I must speak with you. Do you have a moment?" Marco asked, but it sounded more like a plea.

It concerned Maria when she heard the desperation in Marco's voice. It was filled with great emotion and anguish. *What could it be?* she thought.

"Yes, of course, Marco. You know I always have time for you. What is it? What is wrong?"

"Nõnna, I had a dream this morning. It seemed to have taken place sometime in the 1500s. There was a man…he was me, and the woman, she…I believe is…was Rebecca. Oh God, nõnna, what I felt…in the love we shared…my heart…it was as you said. They…we were so much in love. A great and powerful love," he said, shaking his head. "How could I have forgotten? But I did. I forgot it all. Why?"

As Maria listened to Marco, she was filled with great joy. This was the sign he's been waiting for, proof of what she's told him all these years. Maria chose not to interrupt Marco, wanting to allow him to continue.

"When I woke, my heart…I could still feel what I was feeling in the dream, as if I was there, experiencing what he was feeling. A memory, but not. It was, wasn't it? It was a memory? I realized the stories you told me…tell me, is it true? Was the dream…a memory?"

Maria was ecstatic. She wanted to jump up and down with joy, but decided to keep her excitement under control, and asked Marco questions before she answered his. "I will see if it is true. First, before I do, let me ask you a question? What were you doing before you went to sleep last night?"

Do I tell her the truth? With resignation, he knows he must, if he is to know the answer to his question. "I was angry, very angry at not finding the love I've been searching for. At the same time, I was feeling alone. So very alone," he said, with sadness in his voice. "Nõnna, these women I've been dating, they are horrible! They only care about my money and my family status! They have no care for love!" he said, with such anger and bitterness in his voice. "All they want and care about is what I can give them! They don't care about me, nor do they want to know the man inside this body," he motioned with his hand, although he knows his grandmother cannot see him. "Nothing more! I was feeling lost, wishing I had more," he finally said.

Maria's heart breaks for her nipõte, but she also feels happiness at the revelation of what he's learned. *Blessed be.* "Oh Marco, this is good news…" She said with excitement, more than she meant to show.

Taken back, Marco became upset and confused at his grandmother's reaction, "What, how could this be —"

Maria cut Marco off before he could finish. "Wait, let me explain before you get upset."

Resigned, Marco agreed to allow his grandmother to explain. "Alright."

"This dream came to you for a reason. It was a memory of your life before, the one from the stories I have told you about, this you know. Of the great and powerful love you once shared and can still have. Do you know what this dream also means?" Maria asked.

"No," he said.

"Marco, oh my dear Marco, it means Rebecca is on the path of being ready," Maria said, with great joy in her voice.

Feeling confused, he asked, "What are you telling me?" Then something hit him with sudden excitement. "Is it possible? Could it really be…but when? Do you know? Can you see this?" Marco asked with excitement. Anxious to have a timeframe to when this will happen. He knows if Rebecca is ready, he could finally have a love – a powerful love that he's been needing, and he will no longer have to deal with these other women.

Maria, not wanting to take away Marco's excitement and joy, but she knew there was no choice, she had to tell him the truth.

"I cannot say…" Maria started to say, when she hears Marco let out a breath, knowing he's feeling frustrated. "But my nipõte, you will know. Until now, you only had this one dream and the stories I've told you about of this love from long ago. You never really believed, did you?" Maria asked, not expecting an answer.

"No. No, I did not," Marco said, feeling ashamed.

"It's alright, Marco. I do not blame you. It's hard to truly believe when you've only heard stories. To you, that's all they were. You had no knowledge or feelings of the past, not until now. Now, you have remembered and felt the love I told you of. Now you know the truth. This is the sign you have been waiting for. God has given you this gift, a memory from your past life, and the love you had and can still have. Don't you see? They've been waiting for you and Rebecca to be ready. Whatever has happened, you both are finally on the path. You are on your way to each other.

This is something to be joyful about." With this, Maria was unable to hide her joy and excitement. "It is finally happening!" she burst out with joy.

Marco wants so much to feel his grandmother's excitement and joy, but his technical mind causes him to hesitate.

"I don't know what to think. I want to believe, but how can I, and then again, how can I not, especially after this dream, and how the dream made me feel. What my heartfelt," he said.

Marco felt so confused about what was happening. Yes, he wants to believe, but there's a fear – he's afraid to hope.

Maria can sense this, and hears it in his voice. "Marco, open your heart and soul. This dream is your proof. It's what you've been looking for, of what you had, and what you can still have. This is real. This dream you had was a gift. They want you to know the truth. To believe and not give up. They want you to know, to remember the love…a great love, you once had. A powerful love, of your love for her, and hers for you."

God, I want to believe. How can I not? Not after what I felt in that dream. What I am still feeling. Although fading, it is still there, he thought.

"Nõnna…what I felt in this dream was a love beyond reality. A love so powerful and strong…God, can it be true? Is it possible to have such a love? This love I felt…in my dream…in this life?"

"Yes, and yes, you can. Would you like me to tell you what I've learned about Rebecca?"

Yes, yes, I do! But he does not say so. He reigns in his excitement, and instead says, "I don't know…okay…yes, please?"

This pleases Maria. Finally, she can give him some good news. "Rebecca divorced her husband," she started to say when she hears Marco gasp over the phone, which makes her smile. "She left California and has started a new life away from her family. She will be taking her daughters and move to Arizona," she said, feeling giddy like a young schoolgirl. "She is doing much better than she was. Marco, she has reopened her heart to allow love back into her life." Unsure how to say the next, but she knows she must. "Now, Marco, what I am to say next, do not react, just listen to what I have to say first?"

Marco hesitated for a moment, but he agrees, "Alright."

"There will be a man she will be dating…" Maria hears Marco gasp again, but she must continue. "She will believe she loves him. Now, I know what you are thinking, but stop and listen to what I have to say." With no response, she continues. "This is not to be. Marco, this is the path I told you about, the one she must go down before she will be completely ready for you.

This man she will be with, he is the one who will open her heart and allow her gifts to open and flourish fully. To allow her to know her gifts and knowledge…that what she will feel is real. So, when both of your heart and souls connect…reconnect, she will know it's real. When it's time for her to learn the truth and know who you are, she will understand that what she is feeling is real. This man, what she will experience with him, will tell her so. This will take time, Marco. But take in the knowledge this is happening now.

Rebecca is following the path she's been sent on before her birth. The path that is to lead her to you, yes, it has taken time, but there is a great deal she must know and learn to prepare her…so she will be ready for you," she said. This was easy compared to what she must say now. At first, she hesitates, but knows it must be said. "Marco, there is much both of you have to atone for, from your lives before. Can you wait? I don't feel it will be much longer," Maria asked, with anticipation of what Marco will say after what he's just learned.

"Nõnna, I don't know. This is too much right now." *What am I saying? Again, I am allowing her to pull me into this fantasy. No! I cannot. Should not.* "No, I am sorry, nõnna, I don't think I can. I am a ma…" Marco wanted to say, I am a man, and a man has needs. But this, this he could not say to his grandmother. "As we do not know how long it will take. I can say this, I will keep myself open for it, for when she is ready."

Maria laughs inside as she understands what he means. "Marco, it is true. There is no saying when this will happen. If you can be open to it, then this is all we can ask.

"Thank you, nõnna."

At this, Maria remembers the woman he was seeing and wants to know what his plans are for her. "Are you still seeing Amy? Is that her name?"

Not for much longer though, he thought. "Yes, it is. And yes, I am. It doesn't matter since she doesn't matter to me. I am using her, as she is using me. She only cares and wants what I can give her. Now, I will continue as it has been. Please don't think bad of me?" Marco said, concerned of what his grandmother might think of him. After all, she is a very strong Catholic woman.

However, to his surprise, Maria laughs. "That is your decision, Marco. I will let you know if I learn anything new. I do not and could never think bad of you."

Relieved, he says, "Thank you, nõnna."

Marco does continue his relationship with Amy for another six months before he decides enough is enough, and ends their relationship. After this, he decides to give the single (celibate) life a go; however, it only ends up lasting a year before he meets another woman, who again resembles Rebecca, and begins dating her.

Chapter 11

<u>California</u>

After returning to California, I moved into my parent's guest house, and within a short time, I found a job and did what I could to move on with my life. I tried to file for a divorce without the assistance of an attorney since I could not afford one. My first court hearing didn't turn out the way I hoped. When our case was called, I was approaching the front table to face the judge, when I learned that Richard's family in Florida helped him hire an attorney, not just in Florida, but in California as well. Needless to say, I was shocked and scared shitless.

I could not believe what I heard next, "Your honor, my client, Mr. Daniels, request his wife and daughters return to Florida."

I heard this as I approached the table, and I started shaking vigorously and dropped my purse. After picking it up and setting it on the table, in a shaky voice, I said, "No…I can't…he tried to strangle me…" at this, I started crying. "I cannot return…my…daughters, and I will not be safe. Please, I cannot return," I pleaded with the judge.

At this, the judge said, "You will not have to return to Florida, but you need to get an attorney."

I was so relieved to hear this. From my reaction, the judge could clearly see and hear the fear I felt at the idea of returning to Florida. I felt some relief, but I was still crying. As I was leaving, a few other attorneys who were there for other cases approached me and showed me sympathy, including Richard's attorney. Again, I was given advice to find an attorney.

I was so afraid that I didn't know what I was going to do. I didn't have the money to hire an attorney, but my friend Catrina thought I should talk to another close friend of ours who had the money to help. After speaking to him, to my relief, he offered his help, and I did find a great attorney who did an excellent job. There were a great many obstacles, but after a year of negotiations, I finally received my divorce. Although I didn't receive the papers until December 31, 1999, the official stamp with the judge's signature was on December 24, 1999. So, in actuality, I was a free woman on Christmas Eve. To receive my divorce papers on New Year's Eve was a wonderful surprise, and it allowed me to celebrate the new millennium as a free woman.

I remember going to the store and bought a large bottle of champagne, and when I arrived at Catrina's house, I sat the papers and the bottle of champagne on the table and told her we had more to celebrate than just the new millennium.

That night, I slept over at Catrina's house, and when I woke the following day, I felt so different, as if a heavyweight had been lifted off my shoulders, with a feeling – a sense of freedom. I remember standing at the living room window staring out, looking at the world outside, seeing it in a different light, and thinking, *I am free. Thank you.* It was a world as I've never seen it before. It was my new beginning.

For the next few years, I enjoyed life as it was. I didn't think at this point, anything could possibly go wrong to rain on my happy parade, but it did. I cannot recall exactly when this happened, but one day my father had a male friend over to their house to visit, and I learned this was the man who gave my parents the money they sent me that allowed me to leave Florida. When my father introduced the man to me, and upon hearing his voice, I could not believe my ears – *no! It cannot be! This was the man I am to thank for helping bring us back! No! I cannot!* But what was I going to do? Could I be sure he is the man? No. Yet, I was. That voice, to hear it, one could never forget it.

No, there was no doubt; he was the same man from all those years ago who called and made all those prank calls. The one who stalked me when I was seventeen. To learn this, I was angry. Furious. When my brother's and my sister heard about this, they too were just as angry. Although I was the one he followed, I wasn't the only one who endured this man's harassment. In the multitude of phone calls, and the voice behind the calls, in the words he spoke – apparently, not one of us could forget that man, nor his voice, and it didn't matter how many years had passed. That voice was embedded in our brain, to never be forgotten. I remember how all of us tried to tell our father, but he refused to listen. He would not believe this man he called friend was the man who stalked me. Who made all those phone calls, and who said those dirty, filthy words to my sister and me.

In 2003, I decided to move from California to Arizona. In order to do this, I had to move back in with my parents, so I could save as much money as possible. I had already arranged for the girls to visit their grandmother, as they normally did every summer when I started receiving those prank phone calls again from that same man. I couldn't believe it. This time though, he asked about my daughters, wanting to know if they were with me or had already left for Arizona. I of course, refused to answer and hung up the phone. However, it didn't work. The man just as before, continued to call back, until he finally gave up.

After this, I was so glad my daughters were already in Arizona. I couldn't help but think, *what if they were still here? What was this man doing before they left?* These thoughts frightened me. So, I went and closed the curtains in the living room that faced the road and the orchard beyond. I was afraid he was out there watching. Then, it infuriated me. I could not believe this was happening again! I was outraged at my father. It was clear he was telling this man about our business. This man who was my stalker. This man who talked dirty to my sister and to me.

Then I got even angrier. "This fucking pervert!" Yes, I was fucking angry! My fucking father was telling this pervert everything about us! Did he think so little of us, to not care that the man he was associating with; in knowing what he did to his daughters, to now allow this man to inquire about his granddaughters? What the fuck! I immediately called my brothers and told them what happened. They were just as outraged as I was, and they called our father and yelled at him for doing so, but the bastard didn't seem to care. He still refused to believe this man – his friend, was the one all those years ago, the one who harassed us – stalked me. All four of us told him it was true, but it didn't matter what we said; he still refused to believe it was his friend. What kind of father does that?

When my father returned home from work, and there was nowhere to escape, I went off on him. I didn't care he was my father. I was a mother protecting her daughters from a man who clearly wanted them. I told him, "What the fuck is wrong with you! Do you not care about what this man did to me! Well, if you didn't, and you don't care about me, then you damn well better care about your granddaughters! Because that bastard is after them now! The fucker called to inquire about my daughters! Your granddaughters!"

Do you know what my fucking father did? The bastard just waved his hand as if I was crazy, then acted as if he had no idea what I was talking about. No man of his culture, his religion, could possibly do something in what I was claiming this man did. It was my father's fucking ignorance that refused to see that a man he knows – known all these years, was the man who stalked me and called the house, making all those prank calls. For me, this was the final draw. I grew up expecting this kind of behavior for me, but my daughters – no, never! For him to have behaved in this way, I was done…done with my father.

Well, shortly after I left, I learned this man – his friend, who my father believed was a good man, was arrested. What for you ask? Hum, what could it be – yep, for fucking molesting a thirteen-year-old girl! My father, even with this, would not believe it. He still refused to see the truth, and I could never understand why, and it was funny and scary at the same time. I was relieved to be in Arizona, and I no longer had to worry about this man. However, although I didn't have to worry about him, I still felt the fear of being watched. Even to this day, it still bothers me. Maybe not as bad, but nevertheless, it is still there.

When I left California, I was grateful my uncle offered to help drive the moving truck to Arizona, especially after a tire blew on the road, and to our relief, being an experienced mechanic, he was the one driving at the time, managed to drive the truck off the road and to an out of nowhere station that by luck sold tires. Thank goodness I bought insurance on the truck, because it covered the replacement tire and the damage a piece did to my car we were towing.

After thirteen hours on the road, it was dark by the time we arrived in Prescott, Arizona, where the girl's grandmother lived. We spent the night at her house before heading for Scottsdale on the following morning, which turned out to be an interesting trip down the mountain. You see, we kept passing one car accident after another. Apparently, Arizona is well known for auto accidents, and after living here for over thirteen years, this is an understatement.

On the way down the mountain, I drove my car and my uncle drove the moving truck. After arriving in the valley – Phoenix, we pulled off to have lunch. This was also the time my car decided to overheat. My uncle looked at it but couldn't find anything wrong. Later, it was determined that my car was not equipped with a certain part (I don't recall what it was) that helped adjust the temperature when in excessive heat, preventing the car from overheating. No, I didn't have to buy the part, because my car ended up adapting to the heat. I say this because I didn't have any further issues after that one time.

We moved to a nice apartment in Northeast Scottsdale, where the schools were great, but, well, they were in a very rich area. Eventually, I learned Scottsdale was known as Snobsdale. The first time I went to the girl's new school for parent orientation, I was the only one without a Luis Vuitton purse, and I felt so out of place. I was not rich, but normal, average – I was barely making it. So, after my year lease was up, we moved from Scottsdale to Mesa, Arizona. The area was more affordable, not to mention the taxes were less, and I didn't have to feel as if I had to be something I wasn't.

Though, it was a bit harder for Sara and Tiffany. I remember them saying, "Mom," with the eye and attitude of snootiness, "The lockers are dirty and nasty," giving a look of disgust.

Being in Scottsdale and associating with the friends they had, they were already turning into snobs. So, I said, "Well, honey…this is how the real people live. We don't have the money for that type of society. This school may be less taken care of, but it's down to earth…normal. I don't like how you are becoming snobs. So, deal with it?"

They looked at me, then rolled their eyes. Well, after a time, they settled into their new school and environment, and the snobbishness was gone.

Moving to Arizona turned out to be a great deal more than just a change, along with the feeling of safety. It was also the time when my gifts became clear. In learning I had a guardian angel named Joseph, and what happened with my dreams in the past, they seemed to be premonitions, especially after my grandmother's death. With Richards grandfather, my grandfather, and the three ladies in black (angels), and with Jesus visiting me twice; one time in my car and again on the road as a solid person. Then finally my divorce. Wow, to think how so much had happened in such a little time, that I wasn't sure what to think.

Now, how can someone not look back on their life and say wow? How was this possible? To endure what I did, to say it was shocking is an understatement. You would think that would have been enough, right? Well, not exactly. In my time living in Arizona, I realized the extent of what was happening to me. You know, when I think back, knowing what I now know about Arizona, was this where they wanted me to be? Hum, I'll let you decide for yourself.

If I was in denial before – well, after what happened, there was no way, not this time, that I could remain in denial. Although I had moments here and there of premonitions, these strange unexplained feelings – before, it was easy to blow them off. However, in Arizona, I realized I was truly given a gift. A gift of sight and knowledge, allowing me to see things that no one else could see. Through dreams and visions, I would see places and people, along with feelings I did not understand, not until after it happened, and they came true.

After discovering these special gifts – abilities; the strange thing was, somehow, someway, I knew they were always there. As the visions continued, I discovered I could make predictions that came true. There was a knowing, a feeling about people. Why? And why now? That was the question. Can I say I trusted what was happening? No. I'd question the validity of what I saw and felt. It was so confusing to me, and it didn't make any sense, until it proved to be true.

In 2005 everything changed. I started dating Joe. He was the first man I dated after my divorce, and when I first met him, I resisted. He was not the type of man I would be interested in, nor was he single. However, in time with his persistence, I eventually gave in. It turned out there was something about him, a strong connection between us. One I could not explain. It felt as if he was the one, my soulmate – true love.

We went from friendship to love within months, and something about him changed everything. Those few feelings and predictions I'd made in the past intensified with him, to a shocking and surprising – they were eerily accurate. They were true. So much so, Joe turned from a non-believer into a believer.

How do I explain this? Well, let me try. You see, when Joe and I were not together, I could feel him. I could feel him thinking about me. When this happened, I'd have a vision, and I was able to see him and what he was doing. It was like a vivid dream.

When it happened, it was a powerful feeling, a sensation running through my body, like static electricity going from head to toe. I remember wondering, *what's happening?* These visions weren't of a past or a future event but of the here and now.

Some of the visions were of Joe sitting on his sofa watching television, or a time he was lying on his bed, and I could feel him thinking about me. There was another time I recall in explicit detail: I was home taking a nap on my sofa, when I had a very clear and vivid dream, I was making love to Joe, and when I woke up, it felt as if it actually happened. It was the strangest and oddest thing – feeling. Later, when I talked to Joe about it, I learned he had a similar dream during his nap. Was it possible we somehow connected in our dream?

What I didn't like about my gifts was the times I felt Joe questioning our relationship and wanting to end it. This, I did not like. It felt as if I was engulfed with an overwhelming amount of fear, regardless if it was good or bad. When these feelings and visions hit me, the next time I was with Joe, I would ask him, "What's going on, because I feel as if you are pulling away from me?" In my asking this question, he would confirm what I felt – believed to be true. It was only after his confirmation when I told him of the feelings I had.

Now, if it was good, I'd ask Joe what he was doing at the time I had the vision, and when he told me, he would confirm the vision I had was true, and then I would tell him about the vision. On the bad ones though, I was careful in my inquiry of what was happening at the time. When he would refuse to answer, I'd force the issue, and at times, I wish I hadn't, as those too were true. When he learned of my visions and feelings, I was having about him, it stunned and shocked him.

However, after time, with the frequency of my visions and feelings, and each time proving to be accurate, Joe came to believe that I indeed knew things. That I could see and know what he was feeling for me, even his doubts about our relationship. There was nothing he could hide from me, and at first, it disturbed him. I know it would have disturbed me. He knew he wouldn't be able to hide anything from me, and so he didn't. Now, was this a good or a bad thing? All I can say, yes and no.

Once the shock wore off, Joe decided to test me. He wanted to see how good I really was. The problem though, when it happened, I wasn't trying. Now, I was being asked to do it on a whim – on command, and I wasn't sure I could, but if I did, then it would prove I had a gift, and it would be all the proof he needed, not only to him, but to myself as well.

At times when these vision and feelings hit me, it felt as if something or someone was pulling at my soul. As if my soul was trying to separate from my body, wanting to go to the place in the future. I believe this happened to allow me to see what I needed to see. At times, the energy was so strong I felt as if I was going to pass out, losing all control of my body and my strength. At other times, there was a feeling in my chest, as if something was pulling at my heart, trying to force me to see. This was to let me know that what I was seeing was true. This occurred more when it was personal, and when it affected me directly, it would affect my heart.

More times than not, I was astonished by the accuracy of these feelings and visions. There were times these visions and feelings would happen in the most awkward situations. Like hum, I don't know – like when I was in the bloody bathroom! Really? Yes, really! Bloody hell! There is nothing worse than peeing and having a vision, and these visions were stronger than the others, but I cannot deny their truth. In the beginning it shocked me, to the accuracy of these visions, even down to the very details. It's funny to think when I first met Joe, he didn't believe in this stuff, but after, due to the multitude of times I was accurate, he became a believer.

There was a day when Joe mentioned he was thinking about moving out of Arizona to somewhere in the northeast. He felt so strongly about this that he began applying for jobs in Montana and Michigan. He eventually received a call from a company that was interested in his skills. After receiving this call, he wanted to know what his chances were if he were to pursue this position, so he had a few questions for me.

"Will this be a good move for me? Will I get the job? When will I hear back from them? If I do get the job, how much will they offer me?"

Geez, really – well, I was very pleased that Joe had that much faith in my predictions – abilities. I said, "I need time. I cannot just pull the answers out of the air. I need time to allow them to come to me. As soon as I know, you will know."

He accepted this answer and said, "Okay, call me as soon as you have the answers."

"I will."

On my way home from work that day, I focused on his questions, trying to get the answers, and to my surprise, I received them quickly and easily. I waited until the next morning before I called Joe to let him know, since I wanted to be sure what I was receiving was correct.

The next morning, I called Joe on my way to work, and when I received his voice mail, I left him this message, "Hey, it's me. I have your answers. Call me as soon as you can."

It was a couple of hours before he finally called me back. When he did, I was at work and unable to answer the phone. So, on my first break, I returned Joe's call.

When I reached him, I said, "Hey, I received your message. Sorry I couldn't call you back sooner, but I had to wait for my first break. Are you ready for the answers?"

"Yeah. Tell me," he said anxiously.

"Okay. Well, I see you getting the job, and I feel you will be very happy there. You will hear from them with an offer by either Thursday or Friday of next week. They will end up offering you fifty-five thousand a year, but you will negotiate and end up receiving sixty thousand a year."

Well, the following week, Joe did hear from the company on Thursday. The first question, check. They offered him the job, first at fifty-five thousand a year, but he negotiated and received sixty thousand a year. Question two, check. It would have been a good move for him if he took the job, but he didn't. To my relief. In the end, he decided it was best for him to remain in Arizona. For me, I was happy with this decision, as I wasn't ready to let him go. So, there was no way of knowing if that part would have come true or not. Apparently, with these questions, along with the answers convinced Joe my abilities were real.

Because I had been right so many times, Joe started taking advantage of me, which really pissed me off. Allow me to share a particular event: Joe was getting ready to go on his yearly bear hunting trip and he wanted to know how he would do. After a time, this is what I told him I saw. "I see you standing on a grassy hill, with the shining bright sun to your back. You are aiming your bow, getting ready to shoot the bear. I see the arrow flying through the air, when it hit the back of the bear. The bear is near a stone structure when you hit it."

Well, you can say I was right again. However, in the way I learned this, I was not pleased. I received a frantic call from Joe yelling and screaming at me. "Fuck! Tell me where it is! Where is the bear!"

I was baffled at what he was talking about, as he was just yelling at me, expecting me to know what he was referring to. As if I foresaw he was going to call with this issue.

So, I asked, "What are you talking about? The bear? Wh…oh, that bear," I said, comprehending the situation.

The cocky little bastard said, "Yeah, that fucking bear! Where the fuck is it?" he demanded, still yelling at me.

I said, "I don't know where the fucking bear is! How do you fucking expect me to know?" I yelled back. He was seriously pissing me off.

It made no difference. He only ignored what I was saying and went on to say, "Just fucking tell me! Where the fucking bear went!" he yelled. "I can't find it! Fuck!" he continued cursing.

"What the fuck do you want me to do? I don't know where it is!"

"You know…find the bear! Fuck! Hurry before I lose it!"

"Are you fucking kidding me! It doesn't work that way…on command!" I yelled.

Then he said, "Fuck-fuck-fuck!"

"Fine! You have to give me a minute. I can't call up my gift on demand!" I firmly said.

So, in feeling I had no choice, I sat at the edge of my bed and closed my eyes, then tried to see if I could see what happened to the bear.

As I was attempting to do this, he said, "Hurry…I'm going to lose it! Fuck!"

I was getting more and more pissed off at his demands. Not to mention the pressure he was putting me under. It wasn't that I didn't appreciate the confidence he had in me, but seriously?

"You want me to help you, then fucking back off, and allow me to focus! Putting pressure on me isn't helping!"

He finally said, "Fine!"

Well, I managed to see something, and this is what I told him. "I see the bear…it seems…after being hit…he ran off. It looks like he went to the right from where he was hit. I can see him…he's laying somewhere near…in a bush. He's well-hidden…surrounded by tall grass." Joe was walking in the direction I mentioned, but he could not find the bear. It wasn't as if I can jump through the phone and show him exactly where the bear was located. All I could do was try, by doing the best I could in explaining to Joe what I was seeing and hope it would help him find the bear.

He felt frustrated and therefore lashed out at me. "What the fuck! You are causing me to lose the bear! Fucking tell me where he is! What the fuck are you doing! Tell me where the fucking bear went! I can't find it!" he demanded, which turned into threatening.

At this, I was fed up, not to mention extremely pissed off, so I told him, "Fuck you! And go to hell! You can find the fucking bear on your own! I'm done!" I yelled and hung up the phone.

Geez. I appreciate he had such confidence and believed in my abilities, but I was no miracle worker. I could only do what I could. But to him, it wasn't enough.

Later that evening on Joe's way home he called to apologize. "Hey…I'm sorry. I didn't mean to yell at you like that. I know it wasn't your fault, and I'm sorry. I never did find the bear. Shit, I hope someone else doesn't find it. What a waste. It was…what you said… everything was exactly how you described it, so I panicked and became desperate. I needed to find the bear. I fucked up when I shot it and missed. As soon as I shot the arrow, the bear moved, and the arrow hit him in the rear."

"Look…I get it. I really do, but…you can't expect me to give you information on demand. The pressure…it's not easy when you put me under that much pressure. This can never, ever happen again. If you ever call me as you did, I won't listen. I will just hang up the phone."

There was no argument, as Joe agreed, and that was the end of it.

Since Joe decided to remain in Arizona, he was ready to move forward with his career with another company and started looking within the Phoenix area. One of the positions Joe applied for called him in for an interview. When this happened, he immediately called me and wanted to know how his interview would go, and if he will receive an offer. I agreed, so long as he understood how it would work, and he did.

He asked, "Can you tell me if I will get the job?"

I asked, "When is your interview? I will need time to see if I get anything."

"It's in a week," he said.

"Okay, good. As soon as I get any information, I will let you know."

A few days after this conversation, I finally received the answers, and of course, the answers came to me in the most inconvenient place and time – in the bathroom at work. The vision I received was a strong and powerful one, stronger than the ones I've had in the past.

After work, I called Joe and let him know what I saw. "Well, I see you…you are wearing khaki pants, with a red or rust color shirt, walking into a large, tall building, with tall double glass doors. You are sitting in a chair in what looks to be the reception area, which looks to be a wide-open space. The floor looks shiny with black tiles, and you are sitting in a chair waiting for your interview.

A lady greets you and shakes your hand, then directs you to a conference room where your interview is to be held. When you walk in, you are directly in front of a large table, with a panel of five people waiting to interview you. I see you directed to a chair at the front of this table. From what I could see, the interview goes well. After you leave, I see them talking about how they were very impressed with you and are going to offer you the job. That's not all. I also saw you walking into the that same building as an older man with gray hair. This tells me, this is where you will retire."

Needless to say, he was very happy and excited about what I told him.

You are wondering if what I predicted came true? Yep. It happened exactly as I described it, outside the older man part. As far as I know, he is still with the company. After this, I could no longer deny these gifts.

Shortly after this, things changed in our relationship. It continued as an on-and-off relationship until I finally made a complete break in 2010. It was after coming to the realization that Joe was not the man for me. He became too needy, so insecure with himself, and a man who was that needy, with the need of continuous daily reassurance – it was enough. I had enough. It was no longer a relationship, but instead, I became his therapist, with the constant need for reassurance – saying things like, "No, they are not ignoring you. Do you watch sports?" When the question was, Why the men he worked with never included him in their sports conversations, and to my question, he answered (which I already knew his answer), "Well, no."

How did I end up with a man who was such an idiot? One who worried so much about what others thought about him. I ended up saying, "Then why would you expect them to associate with you. If you want to get to know your male coworkers, find something you have in common. Go for drinks after work. You don't have to drink, but…just a *let's get to know each other*. I can't help you. You need to help yourself." Geez, enough was enough.

When I look back on this, I cannot believe the connection we had, thinking he was the one, when all along, he was not. I remember when I noticed the change, when a friend once told me, *maybe he was in your life to show you, you can love again*. At the time, who knew how right she was. I believe he was in my life to open my heart to love again, for when it *truly* comes, I will know how to recognize it. You see, after my divorce, I lived in fear, thinking Richard would have me killed. Then, when that passed, I felt anger and hatred towards men, and this occupied my mind for many years.

After further examination of our relationship, I believe he was placed in my life to not only open my heart to love again, but to help me accept the gifts I was apparently given. To give me validity to the visions and feelings I was having. This, so when *he* came into my life, I would recognize what was happening and what it was, to not ignore them, that they are true.

You know, when I think back, I recall a time shortly after I returned to California and started working, I had this vision of Tiffany walking across a busy road and was hit by a white car. I was so freaked out – filled with such fear, I started praying, pleading with God to protect my daughter until the fear subsided, and I felt Tiffany was safe. I believed what I felt was from a mother's fear, due to living near a busy road, but I rationalized it by thinking, *they are with my parents and are safe.* But when I arrived home, I asked, "Did you girls go across the road today to your friend's house on your own?" Of course, they both said no. But, to ensure this wasn't a prediction of something to come, I told my parents to keep a closer eye on the girls.

Well, I would learn many years later when Sara, Tiffany, and I were talking about the times we were living in my parent's guest house, and Tiffany told me about an incident that happened while I was at work.

Well, Tiffany told me what really happened that day. Apparently, Tiffany did cross the road on her own. She said before she crossed, she did as she was taught to do and looked both ways. Once she saw there were no cars coming, she attempted to cross the road. However, as she was crossing, she looked again to her right, and there, right in front of her, was a white car. It had stopped mere inches from hitting her. Tiffany said she didn't understand where the car came from, since when she looked, the road was empty.

I wasn't surprised to hear this. As it happens, cars drive very fast on this road. One moment it could be clear, and the next, there is a car. She said when she saw the car, it stopped mere inches from her. Tiffany didn't even hear the car or hear it stop – it was just there. I was stunned. What I saw and felt – it was true. I believe my prayers to God helped, and he sent his angels down to stop the car from hitting Tiffany, in turn saving her life. It was a true miracle. This still astonishes me, even to this very day.

How could I have known then, what I was experiencing would grow – manifest to the great power it is today. A power, I have always had, but was unaware of. Since Tiffany confirmed what happened, anytime I felt that kind of fear (although it didn't really stop before I learned the truth), I would begin praying to God, asking him to protect my daughters. I would repeat this over, and over again until I was sure the feeling of fear was gone, and I knew they were safe. The power of prayer really does work.

For many years I lived with a constant fear that something was going to happen to my daughters, and I would lose them forever. How little did I understand why, until now – eventually, I decided to send up a prayer, asking God to always keep them protected throughout my daughter's life, preventing any harm to come to them. As of today, my daughters are safe and living their own lives. For me, I no longer have that fear. They are happy, and so I am happy.

In 2010, a great many things happened to me, to where I was in jeopardy of losing my job due to the company deciding to close its doors. At the same time, I was dealing with my landlord after they allowed their house to go into foreclosure but was still taking my rent money. We had absolutely no warning, until I arrived home from work and saw the auction notice on the garage door. With all this, the stress was too much for me, causing my asthma to flare up, something I didn't have until I moved to Arizona, and this time it came back with vengeance. How can one person endure so much? With the knowledge that I was going to lose my job, my home, and then to have your health be affected, was just too much, and to think, my health turned out to be more of my downfall than the company closing its doors.

To lose my job with the health problems I was having, was the worst thing that could happen to me. I ended up on disability, which placed me in severe financial hardship, to the point of putting my daughter's and me in danger of becoming homeless. In the past, no matter how hard things became, being a single mother, not once did I place us in such hardship. Now, I have, as our once secured life was now in danger.

In all of this, something unexpected happened – memories from when I was five years old revealed a deep family secret. I'm not sure how or why it started. All I can say, is that it increased my already out of control stress, and in doing so, increased the number of asthma attacks I suffered. How do I begin to tell this little tidbit of my life? Well, it's not so little, but here it goes —

It all started when I was standing at the kitchen sink washing dishes, when a vision – a memory, is what it really felt like. I saw myself as a child, of about five, I believe:

My grandmother was standing at the kitchen sink in her house, with the lower cabinet's doors wide open. Looking inside, I saw a brown box with that old marking, you know the one, the red skull and crossbones. I am standing at the table in the kitchen in front of a bowl of food. I grabbed the spoon and was getting ready to take a bite when my grandmother comes over and slaps it out of my hand, yelling, "No," causing me to drop the spoon. Then, she takes the bowl to the back bedroom, into the master bedroom where my grandfather is. After he eats the food, she helps him to the master bathroom, where he becomes very sick. I am standing outside the bedroom door, watching. After they go into the bathroom, I sneak into the room and quietly peer around the open bathroom door. I wanted to see what was happening. My grandmother sees me and yells, "GET OUT!" I run out of the room and return to the living room.

As I was watching this event take place, I had an overwhelming feeling, a horrible thought, that my grandmother poisoned my grandfather. Why? This I didn't know. Shortly after this memory, I had another one.

I am in my grandmother's living room, wearing a blue dress, and I was sitting on top of my grandfather's lap while he was lying flat on his back. I was straddling him, sitting on top of his private area, and he was completely naked. I could see it was a bright and sunny day, as the curtains were pulled open, when suddenly, through the front door, walked in my grandmother. I get the feeling she was early. I felt she was working in the fields when she returned early. When she walked in, she was shocked at what she sees. She was angry. So very angry at what she was seeing. She rushed into the room, at the same time yelling in Hindi, while yanking me off him, pulling me away, then pushing me behind her, as she was still screaming and yelling at my grandfather.

At this memory, it seems to confirm feelings and memories I have always had, for as long as I could remember, but told no one. I was too afraid of not being believed.

The third and final memory took place after my grandfather died.

My grandmother was talking to my father, telling him, "He's still after her. I can hear him calling her name at night." My father brushes this aside as if she's crazy. Suddenly, they erupt into a screaming argument in Hindi. I am standing next to my grandmother, following her down the hall from the back bedroom to the front door. My father is standing outside the screened door, holding it open while they were still arguing. He says something, and then my grandmother slaps him real hard across the face. With this, my father shuts the door and leaves. I couldn't understand what they were saying and asked my grandmother, "Why did you slap daddy?" She waved me off as if I said nothing.

With these memories, I had to find out – I had to know if what I was seeing and feeling was true. I called my mother and asked her, "Did Bebe ever leave me alone with grandpa when she went to the fields?"

My mother said, "No, she would never leave you alone."

I then told her, "Well, she did. I remember her doing this."

After this, my mother couldn't really be sure, and later when I talked to my father, I asked him how my grandfather died since we were always told he died from a heart attack.

This is what my father said, "He picked up an animal that was dead on the road and ate it.

Because of this, it poisoned him."

What? What the hell! Why would he do that? I thought. This made no sense to me. I then said, "Why didn't he go to the hospital when he got sick?" I was getting the feeling my father was telling me a wild tale, with no true answers. I was shocked to learn that my grandfather died from poisoning. Although my father didn't know it at the time, but he had just confirmed my suspicions.

After that, I talked to my mother again a few days later, and told her what I remembered, along with my father's admission to how my grandfather died. She felt horrible and was very apologetic, and said, "I knew something wasn't right. You were so withdrawn. God, I am so sorry."

It was a relief for her to believe me. However, later, after my mother talked to my father, she then told me it wasn't true, and I misunderstood what happened. Now, they were making me out to be a crazy person, who was making up the things I was telling them.

With this, it only added to my already stressful life, causing my health to only worsen even further. Since I was no longer working, the little income I received came from unemployment, so I had to elicit my daughter's paycheck to help with the bills. I wasn't happy about it, but if we were to survive, I needed their help.

We were receiving food stamps, and I was forced to return one of our cars, and we were in danger of being evicted. I did the one thing I swore I would never do, I called my parent's and asked for their help. Not for me, as I knew they wouldn't help, but for the girls, who I knew they loved. This is what happened.

When I called my parents, I spoke to my mother and told her what was going on, but no matter how much I begged them to help, they flat out refused, In the background I could hear my father yell, "I don't give a fuck! Don't give her any money! Nothing! I don't care if they end up in the gutter! I am not giving her no money!" Well, that said it all, didn't it.

To this day, I have nothing to do with my family. For them to refuse to help me, they didn't only condemn me, they condemned their granddaughters as well. I believe, and still do, that family is family, regardless of circumstances. Family should be there for each other without expectations. I know this is not realistic, as most people think this way, *well if I help you, I expect you to return – to pay me back.* But if you can't, then what? You are hated and condemned as someone who cannot be trusted. When my daughters need something, without hesitation, I helped them without any expectations.

Well, we ended up in a hotel with four dogs after being evicted from the house we were renting, and this was only due to a friend helping us out. After a week, another friend offered us a house we could stay in, but it would only be for six months. This put all of us under a tremendous amount of stress. Not only for myself, but for my daughters as well. They were angry, so very angry, and I couldn't blame them. Sara ended up moving out the first chance she got, and Tiffany stayed, but she became very bitter towards me. I felt that she truly hated me for putting her and her sister in their current situation. Well, were they wrong? Yes and no.

After this happened, I started question my life existence. I began to believe that the reason I was born was to give birth to Sara and Tiffany, because they have a life – a destiny, and I was no longer needed. After all, they were women in their own right and were living on their own. I believed since they no longer needed me, there was no reason for me to remain. I wanted my suffering to end. I felt lost. I felt it was time. I felt it was time to move on. I was ready to give in and give up on my life. I was ready to let go.

Then, for some reason, I began praying, pleading with God, "Help me! I am alone! I am no longer needed! I feel unloved! I have no one! Yes, I have my daughters, but they cannot give me the love I need! They cannot cure the loneliness I feel! If you feel there is more for me in this world, then I beg of you, send me love!" At this point, I began crying. "Please! I don't want just any love, as it has not worked out for me…but send me one love…a great and true love! One, of a man who will love me for who I am, both within and without! A love, I will feel deep within my soul, piercing straight into my heart!" At the time I sent up this prayer, how could I have known the answer I would receive and in the way I would receive it.

Chapter 12

It was spring of 2011 when I was finally able to return to work. Unfortunately, it was not in the same profession I was working before my illness, as there weren't a lot of open positions in that field, nor in accounting. With this, I was forced to consider other industries, since by this time I needed to take whatever I could get. The job I ended up with was a booking agent at a travel agency. This was also the year I started thinking about returning to England. Was this a coincidence? I think not.

So why now, after all this time? This, I could not say. I hadn't thought about England since I left in 1993, now, all of a sudden, to feel a need, a desire, as if something or someone was pulling – pushing me to return. It made no sense. What or who it was, I didn't know. The only thing I knew, was I had to return. But how? Yes, that was a very good question, considering where I was financially. However, a small amount of these questions was answered when I went to the travel agencies job fair to apply for a position.

On the day of the job fair orientation, while I was waiting for a preliminary interview, I was watching the video that was playing about the company and their different locations they have around the world, and one of those locations happens to be in the United Kingdom. I was shocked to see this, especially since I've been feeling this need, this pull to return to England. Was this a coincidence, or was it more? How about I let you be the judge of that question.

After the preliminary interview, along with an over-the-phone interview, I received a job offer for one of the many positions they were hiring for. This was the time I started looking to find ways to move to the UK. With this plan, I decided to join a dating site. No, not for romance, but a place to get to know people, both male and female. For when I moved there, I would already have a small circle of friends. Yes, there were a few men I talked to – okay in truth, I was only talking to men. They seemed to be *possibilities*, if you know what I mean. Yeah, there were some who lied about who they were, or they ended up being scammers. Unbelievable, right? However, there was one who could have been a potential *relationship*. When we started chatting, there was an immediate – a mutual connection, and his name was Marc.

Marc and I spoke first via chat, then on the phone. He wanted to talk on facetime, but I didn't have that option. Then a day came when he stopped all communication, with no reason or explanation, he just ignored me. It left me wondering why and what happened? Was it something I did? I really hate it when men do this. It's very frustrating. Everything seemed to be going well, then boom, gone. I did eventually find out why: it was because I was in the United States, and he was in the United Kingdom. It was just that simple, and he wanted someone there. Well, hell, he could have told me that instead of just ignoring me. I would have understood; after all, I had no timeframe for moving there. Men!

Working for a travel agency had great benefits: discounts on cruise ships, hotels, car rentals, and flights. With this, I decided it was a good idea to make a trip back to England before I decided to move there. After all, it's been about twenty years since I left. So, in 2012 after I received my tax refund, I began planning my first trip back to England since I left in 1993.

While I was planning my trip, I had an idea of where I wanted to go – north of London and close to the place I left in 1993. So, I pulled up a map on my computer and found the location of RAF Mildenhall and began there. I felt I needed to look further north, and when I came to Manchester, I knew this was the place I needed to go. With the help of one of the men I met online, I found a great hotel that was right in the city center. My plan was to contact employment agencies, with the hope they could help me find a job. I thought it would be easier to do this in person versus thousands of miles away and across the ocean, over the phone.

While I was at work, I decided to check airline fares, and when I found one with a great price, I booked it for the end of April through the first week of May, as it was the only time I could take off from work, and before I even had my passport. So, to ensure I had my passport in time, I decided to pay for express service.

The interesting thing was, right before I took my trip to England, I had an unusual dream that seemed to take place around the Fourteenth or Fifteen hundreds, but I couldn't be sure. The dream – God, I will never forget that dream. It felt so real. Let me tell you what happened:

I see a man and a woman standing in an open clearing that's surrounded by what seems to be a forest, with a river running nearby. The man is caressing the woman's face, and the woman is looking down, or maybe her eyes are closed. I feel what they are feeling – love and passion. Their love is a powerful one, one I've never felt before, and there is something more…something is wrong. I can feel they are worried and concerned about something. I focus on the man. He is tall, with straight shoulder-length hair, and is wearing a long tunic and what seems to be tights. Then I turn my focus to the woman. She has dark long wavy hair that flows down and stops right at her lower back. Her gown is a simple one, that looks to be blue with white bell sleeves and a red sash – belt looped in the front.

As the man and woman are standing in the clearing in a loving embrace, there was suddenly a group of soldiers rushing down to them. Two soldiers grabbed the woman, snatching her right out of the man's arms. At the same time, two other soldiers grabbed the man and held him back, preventing him from helping the woman. Then the soldiers were carrying away the woman as she's reaching out for the man. With what I was feeling, I believe the man was her husband. She's seeking his help, but he is prevented from helping her, since the soldiers are holding him back. He feels helpless, not being able to help her. As the woman is being carried away, she's screaming at the top of her lungs for the man to help her, knowing he cannot. She yells, "I love you! I love you! I love you!" Once she's at the top of the hill, she is tossed in a carriage.

When I woke up, I was freaking out, feeling scared, just as the woman in my dream felt. It felt as if it happened to me, but it wasn't me, was it? It felt like it took forever for me to realize the dream wasn't real. I shook it off, since I needed to get ready for work, but at the back of my mind I was still wondering if it was real, at the same time, I was wondering how could it be? It was a different time, and it's impossible that the woman in my dream could be me, right? No matter the reason, whatever it was, it felt very real, and I felt the woman was me, and I wondered, *was this a past life memory?* How could I not? But why would I consider this was even a possibility? Was it even possible? Unfortunately, it was impossible to know.

After this dream, and with the emotions I felt from the woman, I began to rationalize what happened. After all, it happened to her, not me, right? But still, I felt what she felt

– with the fear she felt. From this – don't ask me how, but I knew these people were my connection to a life I lived in England, which explained my strong connection there.

You know, the funny thing about this, later I recalled another time when something strange and odd happened, of a possible past life memory. There too, I felt strong emotions from what the woman was feeling, and I wondered if that too was true? This happened during a time I was still married to Richard, and we were driving through the mountains and forest of upstate New York, on our way to take Sara and Tiffany to spend the summer with his father and stepmother, when I had this vision:

A woman is being chased – I feel that I am the woman. I cannot see who is chasing her, when next I saw a man, who I believe is her husband. He is partially lying in a large pool of water, and he's dead. The woman is so distraught, and I can feel her pain and the knowledge she cannot live without him. After she gives her husband a hug and kiss, she stands and runs to the edge of a cliff, and without stopping, she jumps and falls to her death – my death.

This vision left me stunned. It felt like I was watching a scene right out of a western movie. I didn't understand what happened, nor what I was seeing, but I felt it was me. How, I didn't know. From what I recall of their clothing, it seems the vision took place in the 1800s. You know what's funny about this, during the time I knew Frank, I had a dream he was my husband in the 1800s, and we were happy and very much in love. Was it possible the man in my vision was him? It could explain the powerful connection I felt with him. Could I be sure this was a past life memory, no, of course not.

It was D-day, and I was excited and nervous at the same time. It's been years since I've flown to Europe, and this time I was going alone. However, it turned out to be a great flight, and by the time we were flying over Manchester, I felt as if I was coming home, with a feeling of utter happiness. I have never felt such excitement and anticipation to land and get off a plane as I did that day. I don't recall feeling this way when I first went to England in the early 90s, as my excitement and anticipation then was to see Richard. Now, now it was so apparent – I was coming home.

By the time I was in the taxi heading for the hotel, it was a wonderful and sunny day, which was unusual for England. Once I arrived at the hotel and was talking to the desk clerk I said, "What a beautiful day."

"Ah yes, but before today, it was raining for two full weeks nonstop," the lady said in her Irish accent.

"Wow, really. Well, it looks like I brought the Arizona sun with me to Manchester." I joked, then we laughed.

The lady said, "I hope it will remain when you leave," and we laughed again.

"Your room won't be ready until two o'clock."

"Oh, well, if there is a place to put my bags, I will take a walk around the city center."

"Yes, I can lock your bags up in a storage room. There is a mall right down the way."

She pulled out a map and marked where we were, and which direction I should go in. The desk clerk locked up my bags in a storage room, and I took the map and headed out the door to explore Manchester City Center. In walking out of my hotel – no, on the drive to the hotel, I felt as if I had indeed come home. I felt peaceful, with a sense of freedom, something I've never felt before, not in my entire life.

Well, it took me forever to find the mall, because I went the wrong way, and even longer to get back to my hotel. I ended up waving down a taxi to take me back, which turned out to be only a few minutes away. I was closer than I realized.

By the time I returned to the hotel, I was exhausted. And once I settled into my room after my long walk, not to mention suffering from jetlag, I took a long-overdue nap. Once I woke up, I went down to the hotel restaurant and had dinner, then went to the bar and had a couple glasses of wine while talking to a gentleman who came to Manchester to attend the football game, is what they call soccer. Then I returned to my room to get some rest, since tomorrow was going to be a busy day, contacting employment agencies to see what my options were going to be in finding a job. Well, you can say it didn't go as I hoped. It was near to impossible to find a job with their strict guidelines. So, I decided to make good use of my time in Manchester and took the opportunity to reach out to Marc, to see if he'd be willing to meet with me. Well, let's just say, it didn't happen, and we never spoke again.

I had a great time in Manchester. I did and saw everything I could possibly see, including my first castle. Yes, even after spending four years in England, I never, not once saw a castle. The castle I found was one from a brochure the hotel had in their reception area. It was Skipton Castle, located in the village of Skipton. I took the train there, which allowed me to see some of England's beautiful countryside. I even met a wonderful old lady from Yorkshire, who said if I could manage it, I should make a visit to Yorkshire. Well, I never did get a chance, but I thought, *hey, if I move here, I'll have all the time in the world to visit Yorkshire.*

When it came time to return home, I found it to be very difficult for me. There was a feeling of sadness as if I was leaving a part of my soul behind. I didn't want to leave a place I found to be *home*. A place of peace and comfort. You know what was interesting, although the week I was in Manchester was beautiful spring weather, on the day I was leaving, the clouds covered over, and the rain began to fall once again as if the sunshine was going back with me. Or was there more to it? Was my soul so connected to this place that my sadness affected the weather? Or was there also a sadness in the Universe at my leaving? Something to think about, isn't it?

After I returned home, there was no question; I left a part of me behind, as I felt so lost. There was a sadness, a sense of loneliness, as if who I am remained in England. When I returned to work, I felt empty and lost. I was depressed, feeling that who I was and who I am was no longer a part of me. At that moment, I knew my life belonged in England. This I had no doubt.

<u>Verona, Italy</u>

What is this I am feeling? Marco thought, sitting in his office at his family business in Italy, when he felt a sharp burst of energy in his chest, directly in the center of his heart. This was a feeling he recognized, one he felt before. *When? Oh yes, in London.* Then he said aloud, "Is it possible? Can it be…she's here, in Italy? Or is she in England? How and why? I must know. I must talk to nõnna. I am sure she will know."

Without delay, Marco called his grandmother, with his need to know if Rebecca was in Italy, and at the same time, he was – *is it possible I will see her?* No, no more what-ifs. He needed to know, and his grandmother would have the answers, this he was sure of.

"Marco, you did feel her. She is not in Italy, but in England…oh…she's in Manchester. After all these years, she has finally returned, and she is close to where you live Marco, and," shaking her head, "And you are here. Mia-Mio."

"Manchester. What took her to Manchester? What can I do? I am here…what, am I to just jump on a plane and hope that this woman…and I…we will just bump into each other. The chan —"

Maria couldn't allow him to continue as he was. First, there was excitement at the possibility, but then there was a sudden change. Maria could feel Marco starting to panic, along with his frustration knowing there is nothing he can do. That there was no control of his own fate.

So, she cut him off and said, "Marco, I know you've had doubts. With what you are feeling, can you still deny the truth?"

Can I? Can I deny what I am feeling? Shaking his head, *no. But…* "Maybe what I felt is wrong. For me to believe this…if mother thought I was crazy before, and if she were to learn this, she surely will now."

Marco's mother hates his grandmother, and he never really understood why. But, if she knows what his grandmother can do, it can explain a great deal.

Nõnna knows things she shouldn't, and this, I am sure scares mother. Can I blame her? No. I wouldn't want nõnna to know things about me. Well, if she does, she never says. She loves me for who I am, no matter what wrong I may have done. Which is why Marco loves his grandmother more than anything. She loves him unconditionally. She puts no pressure on him, *except for this, this love. This woman.* Shaking his head, *can I blame her? No. I want this love she speaks of, but how can I believe in something I cannot see or feel.*

Maria only hears silence and feels Marco is deep in thought. She understands how hard it is for him to believe as she does, but he doesn't see and feel the things she does. *But he can.* She heard a voice say. Marco, just as Maria, was born into a family that's had strong powerful psychic abilities, going back hundreds of years. Although she knows the gifts are within him, as they have been passed down from family to family for centuries. If he does not believe and continues to doubt, he will never allow his gifts to surface and flourish as she knows they can.

Maria tries to help her nipõte see the truth, and says, "What you felt was not wrong, and you know this. You are just trying to find a way…you don't want to believe, because if you believe, you will feel…" Maria stops after realizing what he said, his concern for his mother. "Marco, your mother, why would she find you crazy? There is no need for her to know this. It has nothing to do with her," Maria said.

Bullocks, how am I to tell her. Marco sighed in resignation and tried to explain. "Well…there was a day she made me so angry, in telling me how the women I was dating…that I will never find love. How they are only interested in what I have, and they don't care about my heart. When I heard this, it made me so angry that I blurted out, "There is a woman who will love me for my heart, not for what I have! Nõnna told me so." I told her the story you told me, and you should have seen the look on her face. The look she gave me, it was the same look she's given you as if you are craz…oh, forgive me, nõnna…I am sorry," he said, realizing what he was about to say.

Maria lets out a small laugh, "Stop. There is no need. Your mother…it is who she is, Marco. There is no changing her."

"But I feel I have managed to make her hate you even more than she did before. I am sorry," Marco said with shame in his voice.

"Marco, do not worry yourself about what happened. It is done, and nothing more can be done about it. It didn't matter what you told your mother, and she has always hated me, even more after she realized there wasn't anything she could hide from me."

"Nõnna, I am so sorry. If it wasn't for you in my life…I don't know what would have happened to me. I sometimes wonder, would I have become as cold as her?"

"Marco, we cannot say. I am very proud of the man you have become. You are what Rebecca needs. You two will fit perfectly together. You will be as one."

"What am I to do then? She is in England…what can I do…there's —"

Maria cuts him off, "Marco…now is not the time for you to do anything. This is her time. Her time to remember. To know who and what she is. Remember what I told you when she would be moving to Arizona. There were things she had to do to prepare herself that will allow her to be ready. When you both connect, she will know and understand what it is. Remember what I said, when that time comes, your heart will tell you so."

"Well, since there isn't anything for me to do…now, nõnna, what I felt today…is this what you meant? Is my heart telling me she is ready?" Marco asked, with hope in his voice.

Maria doesn't answer Marco, but instead encourages him to figure the answer out for himself. "You tell me Marco? What does your heart tell you, then and now?"

"Hum…well…I don't…wait…I think I understand." *But do I really understand? Is my heart telling me she is real because she is close to where I can feel her? But wait…she is not that close. She's a country away.* Shaking his head, unsure what to think, but he's resigned to figure it out for himself.

"I think you do too. Wait…what about Jill, the woman you are seeing…is that her name?"

"Yes, and yes, her name is Jill. Well, I'm not sure…I will have to see what happens. I want to wait and be sure this is real. If this is the sign I've been waiting for, then Jill will be no more."

"If you are sure…then we shall wait for the next sign…or you will," Maria said, feeling pleased with the turn of confidence in Marco. She knows it's been hard for him to not be able to accept and believe what has been happening. He has become a man who needs to see and feel what's in front of him. To allow himself to release the possibility that not everything can be felt by hand, but through his heart and soul. This is not easy for Marco. However, she feels with her help he will.

"I am sure. Thank you, nõnna."

Right before Marco was about to hang up the phone, Maria receives a message from her guides. *Now is not the time for Marco to find Rebecca. Now is the time for Rebecca to learn, to remember who she is and who she was. When this happens, she will do something that will open the door to allow them to connect through their hearts and souls.*

To hear this, Maria feels overjoyed. Without realizing she spoke aloud, she says, "Thank you. May I share this with Marco?"

Marco was confused at what he heard his grandmother say, "Nõnna, are…you okay?" he gently asked.

Maria burst out laughing, realizing what she did, and says, "Oh yes, I am very well." *Yes, you may.* "Forgive me. I just received a message from my guides. Would you like to know what I learned?"

Marco let out a soft sigh, "Oh…am…if you wish to tell me, then I will listen," Marco said, hesitantly. *Guides?*

Shaking his head. *I still don't know if I believe this, but…*sighing again, he was resigned to hear what his grandmother had to say.

Maria heard the hesitation in Marco's voice and was unsure if she should tell him. "Marco, you sound unsure. If you are not sure, then…maybe it's best I do not."

For a moment, Marco panicked, then wondered why it bothered him so much that his grandmother didn't want to tell him. "Nõnna, please…I am sorry. I do, I want to know…it's jus —"

Maria stopped him. "Marco, there is no need. I understand you better than you think I do. If you truly wish to know, then I shall tell you," Maria said.

Letting out a sigh, *I do want to know…damn it to hell…I do.* "Yes, please."

Feeling pleased, Maria tells Marco what she learned from her guides. "Marco, now is not the time for you to meet. Now is the time for her to remember, to understand who she is…was. She will do something that will allow you both to connect through your hearts and souls," she said with glee.

God, tell me what I am to believe? Should I take this information and hold on to it as truth, Marco thought, but he is feeling confused.

Maria is waiting for Marco to decide what to believe, when she hears him say, "Oh…I see. Hum, do you know how long?"

"No. You will know when it's time. This cannot be rushed…there is a great deal you both must make amends for. You have felt her, a connection through your heart. This is where your power lies. When you and Rebecca are ready, this is when it will happen. Your heart and soul will tell you."

Feeling a bit peeved at what his grandmother said. "How can I rush something that hasn't even happened!" he said, in a harsh and angry voice, more than he intended. "I'm sorry. I know you mean well, but until something dramatic happens…let's just see."

"Oh…child," she laughs a little. "You will know…trust me."

"Very well, nõnna," he said with hesitation. He knows his grandmother means well, but after all this time, *what makes this time any different than others.* However, he was willing to see, to be open to what may or may not happen.

"Marco, I know you are unsure of this, but remember what you felt today when she arrived in England. Because my nipõte, you will feel it again."

"Okay, I will. I am sorry, nõnna, but I have another call. I must go. I love you. Ciao." Marco said as he rushed off the phone to answer his other call, and then later he will think about what his grandmother said.

Arizona

After returning home, I felt lost and sad, with a sense of loneliness, as if all of who I am was left behind in England. I suffered severe jetlag and ended up taking an extra day off from work to recuperate, and when I did return, this feeling did not abate. It actually seemed to increase, that who I am, and who I was, is back in England. In this, there was no doubt, with these feelings, I knew my life belonged in England, and I had to do everything in my power to make it happen.

After this acceptance, I started contacting companies that could help me prepare a proper UK resume (CV as they call it) and started searching and applying for jobs. In the time between my return from England and through the end of the year, it was decided, with all questions and doubts put aside. I knew I needed more information, and so I started researching how I could obtain a work visa. However, this turned out to be more difficult than I had originally thought. When I lived in England in the 90s it was easy, but now, apparently, they made a great deal of changes. It was no longer easy to get a simple work visa. You had to have a special skill and a company that was willing to sponsor you, and the skill had to be on their shortlist as a *need* that they were unable to fill from their own people. This was understandable, but at the same time, depressing.

I decided to check the UK shortlist, and I ended up finding a job in the accounting industry I felt I could do. It was simple enough; if I took a test and passed, I would receive a certification that would allow me to get a job. So, with this newfound hope, I went to the library and found math books I needed and started studying.

After being with the travel agency for about a year, I had a plan and began preparations for my next step. I needed to save as much money as possible, so renting my own place was no longer an option, and I decided to look for a roommate situation. This would allow me to leave when I needed to, and pay very little for rent and utilities, so I could save the money I needed. Unfortunately, this took longer than I planned, and I began to worry, and wondered, *was I ever going to find a place.* With 2012 quickly coming to an end, and I still haven't found a place to live, I began to worry. But then, right at the last minute, a coworker offered me a place at her house, and the rent was perfect.

During this time, a great many changes took place with my position at my job. I received a promotion, and I went from a regular travel agent to a flight specialist. A flight specialist is a person who's able to book flights outside of the normal system, same-day flights, cancellations, re-bookings, infants, and changes to the existing flight itinerary. With this new position came an increase in regular pay, along with more commission and bonuses, which allowed me to save the money I needed to move to England.

It's November 2012, and I decided after making multiple attempts to find a place to live in England online, it would be better for me to make another trip back to England so I could see these places in person. For some reason, I am not sure why, but I ended up reaching out to Marc, the one I was talking to online with in England, and I told him of my plans to move there next year. I knew in doing this, he would more than likely not respond or even agree to help me. So, you could imagine my surprise when I received a response to my message agreeing to help. He gave me three great places located in Cheshire to consider: Altrincham, Lymm, and Stockholm. With this information, I researched the three villages and decided it would either be Altrincham or Lymm.

Sometime after the new year of 2013, the coworker that offered me a place to stay – well, let's just say, the situation did not go well, as it turned out not to be the right place for me to stay. Luckily, I found another roommate from work and moved in with her in early March. Janet is her name, and she just returned from living in California, and has a house in Scottsdale. This was the ideal place for me to live, and right within the Kierland area, prime real estate. Not to mention, it was only a five-minute drive to work. I explained to Janet it would only be for a short time since I was moving to England, and she agreed to allow me to move in with her for the few months I needed.

Later I learned the skill I was studying for was no longer on the UK's shortage list. With this, I wasn't sure what I was going to do, and I had to figure out another option that would allow me to live and work in the UK, but what would that be? I didn't know, and I began to wonder, *now what am I going to do?* I went back to the internet and started looking at other possible options. I found an opportunity to help others by teaching them to speak English, and I thought, *I could do that. How hard could it be?* It's called TEFL (teaching English as a foreign language). They teach you how to teach English to those who are from a foreign country, or within a foreign country, like Italy, France, Spain, etc. I remember thinking, *why not England? Yes, it is an English-speaking country, but there are a lot of immigrants there who need to learn to speak English.* So, I researched the possibilities and found a school in London. In going to school and as a student, I would be allowed to work part-time. It seemed like the perfect choice. The student visa would allow me to live and work for twelve months, and in this time, I would be able to travel within the UK and see as much as I could on the weekends. In doing this, it would allow me time to figure out a more permanent solution.

Chapter 13

Later, after calculating the cost of the course, along with housing and food, I determined it was not feasible for me to attend school in London, so I went back to the internet and found a program that allows you to take the TEFL course online. It will allow me to obtain my certification here in Arizona before moving to England. I also learned some volunteer work would be required to gain experience before I would be able to apply for a position. I figured, if I couldn't work in England, then there was Italy and many other places I could work, since these are places I also plan on visiting.

So, I started searching for schools that would allow me to volunteer for at least three months. I knew with this, there would be no income, so before I go, I would need enough money to last for at least six months. To be sure, I decided to locate a UK attorney (solicitor), to see exactly what would be required, and what I learned: I would need to have one thousand pounds a week. After doing the math, and with what I already saved, plus what I will receive from my federal tax refund, this would be doable. After this new information, I became excited it was going to happen.

After I found an online TEFL course, I picked a date and registered. It was so easy. While I was waiting to start, I decided to look at some schools within the Cheshire area that I could volunteer at. I found a few and sent out emails asking if I could do some volunteer work, and I only received one reply that showed any interest.

I felt with the email communication it was difficult to give them a good feeling of who I am. So, I decided to return to England, even if it meant pushing back my moving date. I would also use this opportunity to look at some flats to rent for my six months stay. Once I had my date, I notified the school who was interested, along with a few others and asked if they would be willing to meet me in person.

<u>Verona, Italy</u>

Maria was wondering how Rebecca was doing, so she decided to look in on her, as she's done since she first connected with Rebecca when she was eight years old. It has been a year since Marco last felt Rebecca when she visited England, and before then, in the London pub in the nineties. Maria sits in her comfortable chair in her bedroom and begins to meditate, focusing on Rebecca's soul, allowing it to guide her and take her directly to where Rebecca is.

Once the connection was made, Maria leaves her body and travels the great distance to where Rebecca is, and to her surprise, she finds herself in a large open house with lots of windows, which allows in a great deal of light. Not a small dark room, as she's seen before, of what seemed to be a small trailer. She always wondered what made Rebecca go there, and now she was very pleased to see Rebecca in a much grander home, and Maria allows her soul to guide her to where she finds Rebecca in her bedroom, just off what appears to be the living area.

When Maria sees Rebecca, she is standing next to her bed in front of an open suitcase, packing. Maria wonders, *where is she going?* Maria looks around for the answers to her question but finds nothing. So, Maria decides she will watch Rebecca packing, hoping there will be something that will provide her with a clue to where Rebecca is going. *She's packing warm clothes. Where can she be going?* Maria noticed.

At this, Maria is jerked back to her body and decides to focus on Rebecca's energy, hoping this will provide her with the answers she is seeking. After what seemed a lifetime, Maria receives her answer, and her eyes snap open with utter excitement. *She's returning to England. It's time for her to remember.* Maria is full of joy and excitement after learning the time has finally come?

"Oh, mia mio. I must call Marco and tell him she is returning, and it's time for her to remember who she was – is. He will be so happy."

When Maria telephones Marco, she tries to contain her excitement but fails.

Marco heard his grandmother's excitement and wonders, *what could it be?*

"Marco, I have great news for you," Maria said.

Marco laughs, "I thought as much when I heard the excitement in your voice," he said. "So, tell me your good news then?"

Maria practically screams it over the phone, "She is coming! She is coming!"

Marco cannot recall when he heard his grandmother be so loud, when she usually speaks in such a delicate and soft voice.

Unable to help himself, he laughs again, "Who…who is coming?" he asked.

"Rebecca…the one you are to be with. Your one and only true love. The holder of your heart."

Marco stiffens at hearing Rebecca's name. In all these years he's heard her name, but never really believed Rebecca was her name, but one his grandmother made up, and he is not sure what to say or do. He's stunned at what he heard and is unable to conceive it to be true after all these years. Finally, after finding his voice, he says,

"What…" but stops, as he is unsure of what to say, but tries anyways, "What do you mean?" He finally asked.

"Marco, she's returning. Rebecca is returning. It's time. It's finally time for her to remember…to remember you," Maria said, in a softer and calmer voice.

Marco shakes his head. He doesn't know what to think or believe. "Nõnna, I know you mean well, but —"

Maria interrupts Marco, "Marco, I know it has been difficult for you to believe in what I've told you. Listen to your heart, and you will know what I say is true."

Marco wants to believe his grandmother, but can he really? "No, it's not possible. I feel nothing in my heart, so it cannot be true. How can you be sure?" Marco said, still unable to believe what his grandmother was telling him.

"Marco, I am very sure. From what I understand, since her visit last year, she's been feeling the need to move to England, and I believe it's because of you."

This is too much for Marco. Yes, deep down, he wants to believe his grandmother, but at the same time, there is too much of him that is telling him this is mad. "Oh nõnna…you know I love you, but I just can't do this…not now. Not anymore."

"She…what do you mean you can't do this now?" Maria said, with concern in her voice.

"Hum…how do I tell you this…I've…well…I've decided to consider marrying one of the women mother pushed my way. I am forty-five years old, and if I am going to have any life, a wife, maybe even a child, I must marry, and I must do it now. I cannot worry about a fantasy that won't happen. I'm sorry, nõnna," he said.

It's hard for Marco to say these words to his grandmother, and he knows what she says, and feels is felt deeply, but for Marco, he just cannot believe as she does.

"Oh Marco…no, you cannot do this now. Not when she is finally remembering…and returning. I know these last few years have been hard for you. Remember what happened last year when you felt Rebecca. Open your heart and soul, and you will know what I say is true. If you can wait, just a little longer?" Maria pleads with her nipõte. She knows if he marries this woman, he will never have the happiness he's longed for.

"Nõnna…I don't know. You said she's coming to England, but you don't know when. How long do you expect me to wait?" he said, feeling frustrated, then he says, "Oh nõnna…I don't know what I'm to do? I can't put my life on hold any longer for a woman that I may never meet."

"Marco…from what I saw, she was packing. Please wait a month. Can you do that for me before you do anything?"

Hesitant, but for his grandmother, Marco would practically do anything. "Alright…I guess…for you, I can do that. If after…will I have your approval?" he asked.

"Yes, you will have my love and approval. All I ever wanted was for you to be happy. If this woman you found makes you happy, I will be happy for you. I love you, Marco," she said as she thought, *ah, please God, don't allow him to marry this woman. Allow him to know and feel Rebecca is real and that she is coming.*

"Thank you, nõnna. I am home now. From what I can see, I have no plans to leave England right now. So, if she's coming, then I should feel what I felt last year, right?"

"Yes, Marco, you will. Listen to your heart. Open your heart and soul to receive her…her connection to you, to allow her heart and soul to connect with yours."

"If this is true, then I will feel her when she arrives. My heart has been open…well…maybe not so much…alright, I will try," he said with resignation.

"Thank you, Marco. I know it's hard. If you connect with her…what will you do?"

"I don't know. I guess…I will have to see how I feel. If…if this is true…if I…and I receive this sign, well…" shaking his head, *am I really going to do this…again?* "Let's just see. I don't want to say, not before I know. You understand, don't you?"

"I do understand. Thank you. I want this for you, Marco, so very much. It's what I'm meant to do. Thank you." There is so much more Maria wants to say, but she knows this must be Marco's decision. No matter how much she wants to push him, she knows she cannot.

"I must go now. I love you, nõnna."

"And I love you, Marco."

After Marco hangs up the phone with his grandmother, he thinks about what she said. Yes, he wants more than anything to have this be true. But how can he? After all, he made his decision to move forward with his life. Hasn't he waited long enough – twenty-five years to be exact. No, he will give the time he promised his grandmother, knowing nothing will come of it. Then he will marry the woman his mother chose for him. Is he happy about it? No. But he is tired of being alone.

Marco sets back in his chair, unable to get his grandmother's words out of his mind. For some reason, they will not leave him. He feels this pressure in his heart – it's fear. Fear it will be true. Fear it will not. How can he live like this, not knowing when it will be, having to always question, will this be the day? Marco wants more than anything to believe what his grandmother says, but if it is not true, the disappointment will be too much for him to bear. And yet, he cannot deny what happened last year either. With this, Marco places his hand over his heart as he remembers that feeling. *How can I believe this time?* Marco shoves these thoughts to the back of his mind and finishes his work at the office before returning home and retiring for the night.

He ignores the calls from Rachel, his fiancé, as he cannot bear to talk to her, not after talking with his grandmother. His arrangement – is what it is, an arrangement. As Marco is lying in bed, with his hands crossed behind his head, staring up at the ceiling, as he's thinking about what his grandmother said, and of the stories she's told him since he was a boy, and of his feelings and his dreams.

"I guess it can't hurt, but how do I do this?" he says aloud.

Marco remembers his grandmother telling him how he can speak to his guides, his guardian angels, and if he tries hard, he can get the answers he wants on his own. So, on this night, he decides to make an attempt, and to Marco's surprise, he hears a voice in his mind – *just focus your mind on your heart, and her heart. See her, and allow her in.* "Yes, you are right. Ballocks, now I am talking to myself." However, he does as the voice instructed and opens his heart and soul, and when he falls asleep, he dreams about Rebecca.

He is in a house standing next to a green wall looking at a painting, and when he looks down and to his right, he sees a woman with long dark wavy hair that flows down her back to her hips. She has small, slightly almond shape brown eyes, and a round face with a small nose and a small thin neck. She is a short nicely shaped – hourglass shaped woman, of about five foot three. There's a feeling in his heart, but not only in his heart, his body and mind were telling him, it's her. After everything his grandmother told him, he would never have imagined such an immediate connection, nor the feelings he would have for this woman. He told the woman, "I use to be lord of this estate." And after he said that, he thought, why did I say that? After a short time admiring the painting, they walk away together with a strong feeling of a deep connection between them. Marco felt this deep into his heart and soul. For Marco, he doesn't understand what this is.

Marco wakes with a start, "Oh my God, what was that? Is it possible? Is it really her? Is nõnna right? She really is coming, and soon. I must find out. I need to call nõnna."

Marco gets out of bed, takes his shower, and gets ready to start the day. After having his coffee and breakfast, he finally calls his grandmother before leaving for work.

"Good morning, nõnna. How are you feeling today? Are you alright?"

"Good morning, Marco. I am well. How are you?"

Marco hesitates a moment before he tells his grandmother what happened. "Well…I had a strange dream I need to talk to you about," Marco said, then describes his dream.

Maria smiles, *there is his proof,* she thought. "Marco, she is coming, as I have told you. The dream you had is the proof you've been looking for. The sign you've been waiting for. Did you have this dream after doing what I told you to do…opening your heart to hers?"

Marco felt resigned…*bloody hell, the woman is always right,* he thought, letting out a sigh. "Yes, nõnna, it did," he said, feeling like a fool. In all these years, his grandmother has told him about this love, this woman, but he has always refused to listen. *How could I believe of such a thing, since I never believed in such things before, but nõnna is right.* At these thoughts, he shakes his head.

As Marco was in deep thought, Maria was trying to get his attention and became concerned when there was no response,

"Marco! Are you still there!" she yells, then spat out a few unsavory words.

Marco, not realizing he was lost in thought, snapped out of it when he heard his grandmother yell at him over the phone and quickly said, "I am. I'm sorry. I was just thinking about…I'm sorry. Forgive me?"

At this, Maria laughs a little, "Marco, there is nothing for you to be sorry about. You have your answer. What will you do now?"

"Do…about wh…oh, you mean Rachel…God, I don't know." *What should I do?* he thought.

"Don't you?" Maria asked.

"Ah, yes," he sighed with a feeling of resignation. "Yes, nõnna, I think I know what I must do, but I think I will wait until after Rebecca arrives to determine how I feel. Can you give me that?"

Holding back another laughter, Maria says, "Marco, yes, of course I can. Marco, this place in your dream, do you know where it is?"

"No, I have never seen it before. Do you?"

"I believe I do, yes. And if you think about it, so do you."

"Ah…how, where? Nõnna, please tell me?"

Sighing, "It's the place I've told you about. The one you live nearby. You know the place. I've always found it interesting that you bought a house so close to it. Now I understand."

Ignoring the last thing his grandmother said, Marco decided to ask, "Do you mean Dunham Massey?"

"Yes, Marco I do. The place where you and Rebecca first found your love, as Robert and Elizabeth."

"So, what am I to do then, go to this place? If so, how will I know when the right time will be?"

"You will know. Your heart will tell you. My dear, follow your heart."

At this, Marco felt strange and frustrated, knowing he would do something he's never truly believed in. What is he going to do? What else can he do but believe. *Can I?* he thought.

"My heart…you really believe this?" he asked.

Maria smiles, "Yes, Marco I do."

"Alright then, I will give it a try."

"Your heart…you will see, and then you will know the truth. I love you, Marco."

My heart…to follow a heart that has failed me this far, he thought, but then says, "Alright. I love you too. Thank you, nõnna."

<u>Arizona</u>

From Marc's recommendation, I chose two villages in Cheshire, Altrincham and Lymm. After extensive research, I believed these two villages were perfect, since they were twenty miles from Manchester.

With my return trip, I will visit these villages, and the one I like the most, I will live in during my time in England. The one I really hope works out is the one I saw online, Lymm. It looked like a quaint village – old, a perfect English village. I was excited to visit them both and figure out which one would be the ideal one to live during my six-month stay. I determined years ago that the countryside is in my blood, and with the two villages being in the country, they were ideal for me.

In my search, I found a great B&B that was located between both villages. It's called Ash Farm. It's a two-hundred-year-old two-story cottage. In looking to see what else was around the area, to my wonderful surprise, I found Tatton Park, which was only a few miles away. I remember thinking, *oh wow. I can visit the place that was depicted in the movie Pride and Prejudice.* Pride and Prejudice was a story written by Jane Austin, who became one of my favorite authors. To another pleasant surprise, there was another castle within walking distance from the B&B, called Dunham Massey Castle, although it wasn't an actual castle per se. After seeing the pictures, I decided to visit this place as well. So, instead of only business, I was going to turn this into a mini vacation. Yay for me!

Here we go again. I had another dream right before my trip.

I was at an estate, where I didn't know, and as I was walking down a gravel path to the main – a very large house. It was large enough to be a castle, but it wasn't Tatton Park. Next, I find myself inside the castle, standing in front of a green wall looking at a large painting of a man. I believe he was Lord of this estate. I look over to my left, and there was a tall, dark-haired man wearing a black suit standing next to me. He was also looking at the painting and then says, "I am lord of this great estate. My family owns this castle." I look up at this man to see what he looks like, and he is a very tall man, but of course, I am only five feet three. He has a long face and strong jaw. He has a stretched heart shaped mouth, almond shape brown eyes, with a long nose and a long neck.

When I see his face, I feel a sense of familiarity, as if I know him. How, I cannot say, but there is an immediate connection with him, one I never felt before. As I am looking and talking to this man, I feel I am destined to be with him. Then, we walk away together —

This is when I wake up. It didn't just feel like a dream but a premonition. It's not like I have many to compare to, but it was the way I felt, along with a feeling I was going to meet this man when I return to England, either at Tatton Park or Dunham Massey Castle. I couldn't wait for my trip and was very excited at the possibility.

So once again, from April to May 2013, I made another trip to England. This time to save money, I took advantage of a friend's US Airways buddy pass. Well, I'll say this much, it isn't something I would choose again if I could avoid it. Because of the buddy pass, I could only board the flight if there was space available. My original flight out of Phoenix was at eleven fifty in the evening, but I did not get out until five-fifteen the next morning. It ended up being a very long and rough night, but at least I made it to my first destination, Charlotte, North Carolina.

Here came my first problem though; I couldn't get out of the airport, and if I didn't make it to Philadelphia in time to make my flight to Manchester, I wasn't going to make it there in time to check into my B&B. Then, one of the flight agents said I could take a flight to London, and from there, a train to Manchester, which is exactly what I did. There was no way I was going to allow this to cause a dent in my trip.

I made it to London, but not without encountering my first nightmare – a nightmare of a man that was sitting next to me. You see, I sat in the window seat, and when I needed to get out, the dumb ass would not move except to shift in his seat. Well, it served him right when my glass of water spilled on him. This is for his own arrogance. Then, the bastard coughed without covering his mouth – what an ass. Next, since I left my table down, the bastard decided to lay his head partially on mine, and I had a half of mind to force his ass up, but I didn't.

As we were reaching our destination, the sun was out, so I closed the two shades to keep the sun from blinding me. Again, the bastard reached over and forcefully raised the shade that was furthest from me – what an ass. By the time we landed, he jumped up, thinking he was going to race and beat the crowd to the door. Well, I laughed, because the dumb ass got stuck in the middle. It served him right. And no, landing in London did not give me the same filling as when I landed in Manchester.

After I was off the plane, I went to baggage claim, but once the last bags came out, mine was not there. Apparently, although the agent in Charlotte contacted Philadelphia to ensure my luggage arrived in London, they did not. However, the agents in London did everything they could to have my luggage sent to Manchester. I have to say, the employees with US Airways were wonderful. In this, I could not have had a better experience.

Before I boarded the train to Altrincham, I decided to get a bite to eat at the food court. After, I wanted to check out the shop directly across, to look for a mobile phone I can use while I was there, but after looking, I couldn't decide on one I liked. After asking for directions on how to get to the underground train, I was finally on my way to Altrincham.

Once I was settled on the train; finally, I was able to take a catnap. This was a good and bad thing. The good, I needed the sleep since I was up for over forty-eight hours. Bad, I missed the beauty of seeing the countryside as we headed north.

Chapter 14

<u>Manchester, England</u>

As the train was passing through Manchester towards Altrincham, again, I had that feeling of coming home. The feeling, as if my soul was – is tied – connected to this place, but how? I didn't know, nor did I discover the reason from my last visit. *Maybe this time, though,* I thought. To understand why my soul feels as if it's a part of this place, of a feeling of such love, welcoming me with a wanting, a giving of a gift. As if someone was saying, *your home – thank you for coming.* It's so hard to explain in words to what I felt. It was as if somehow, a part of my heart and soul was embedded deep in the crevice of this place and this land. I felt so many emotions flowing through me that it was hard to pick them apart. Here, I felt as if I belonged, that I am loved, I am welcomed, and I am home. Where, in the United States, even with my family in this life, I never felt this, ever. I felt that this is where I belong. That this is where I needed to be. This is where my heart and soul belongs.

It took twenty minutes by cab from the train station to the B&B – Ash Farms which is located in Little Bollington, right between Altrincham and Lymm. As we were driving up to Ash Farms Country House, it was magnificent. To be around the country's beautiful scenery, again, it felt like I was coming home. It was the same as I felt last year in Manchester, but here, the feeling intensified by ten folds. It was a long two days, and I was exhausted, so once I was taken to my room, which was at the top of the stairs and to the right. It had one of those old doors with the latch but also a new lock for extra security. The room had a double bed, a desk, TV, and a wardrobe. The only window in the room overlooked the back yard. It was a small garden with a picnic table and benches – it was beautiful. I didn't have a bathroom in my room, but my private bathroom was directly across from my room, and it was quite large, with a large soaking tub. It had everything you needed: toothpaste, toothbrush, shampoo and conditioner, and a bar of soap and a bath robe. This was good since I didn't have my luggage. Once I settled into my room, I took a little nap.

When I woke up a few hours later, I took a cab into Altrincham for dinner, but first, I needed to stop at a store to pick up a few items I needed since I didn't have my luggage, as I was forced to check my carry on. Across the street from the store was a restaurant called Frankie and Benny's. As you walk in the restaurant, one side is the dining room, and the other side is the bar. After being seated, I ordered my dinner, I don't recall exactly what I ordered, but it was delicious.

Towards the end of my meal, I started looking around and I remember thinking, *this place reminds me of Apple Bee's*, with all the pictures and memorabilia on the walls from time past. In looking around, I noticed a man standing behind the wall in the kitchen between the kitchen staff and servers. He was right at the window, and for some reason, I don't know why, but there was something about him, and I found I couldn't take my eyes off him – I felt drawn to him. He noticed me, and we just stared at each other, for how long, this I cannot say, and yes, he was a very handsome man. He was wearing a small black chef's hat, the ones that fit their head. He looked tall, I'd say about six feet maybe, or close to it. From what I could see from the hat, his hair looked to be dark, maybe black. Unknowing how long we were staring at each other, with our eyes locked together, when I finally snapped out of it, realizing what I was doing and turned away, feeling a little embarrassed. I looked around and wondered how many others in the restaurant noticed, but there weren't many around, so I could not say if anyone did.

However, the woman standing next to him, I have no doubt noticed. I remember thinking, *God, did anyone else notice. They must have; how could they not.* Then I felt this desperate need to get the hell out of there. I remember looking back at him, but he was no longer watching me, instead, he was busy working, but the woman standing next to him was. I felt strange, with an urgency to get the hell out of there. It was already a long day, and I needed to return to the B&B to get some more sleep. I didn't want to begin my first full day in Altrincham, still feeling exhausted. When I called for the waitress and asked for my check, the way she looked at me told me she definitely noticed. I also asked her for a phone so I could call a cab. I paid for my dinner and got the hell out of there as quickly as I possibly could.

Once I left the restaurant, I couldn't stop thinking about what happened, about him, and after I returned to my room, I was still unsure about what happened. Then suddenly, I remembered my dream, the one where I was going to meet someone on this trip, and wondered, *was he the one? No, it is not possible. The one I was to meet was at Dunham Massey Castle or Tatton Park, right.* So, with this, I brushed it off. This man I locked eyes with was not the one from my dream, and I decided to put it behind me.

With what happened at the restaurant still stuck in my mind, after a few days in Altrincham, I decided to return to the restaurant and see if *he* was still there, and what would happen on this second visit.

However, to my disappointment, he was not there, but I did run into this guy who helped me buy a GPS from

Tesco. Tesco is like our Sam's Club. He was in his early twenties and of African descent. He was a little taller than me, with a shaved head, and was with another man, a bit older than he was, who turned out to be his partner. His partner had short blond hair with a Scottish accent. We had a wonderful conversation and ended up becoming friends. I told him about what happened with the man on my first night in town, and he decided to ask one of the female waitresses about him. You see, he is a regular there and knew everyone who worked at the restaurant, but the man I saw he wasn't familiar with.

Well, when he returned, he told me what he learned. Apparently, the man I saw, this wasn't the restaurant he worked at, but that night he came in to cover for another employee. However, I did learn his name, it was Marco. Can you believe that. He informed me that Marco works at Frank and Benny's at their Stockport location and said, "You should go there."

I, of course wasn't sure, "What…no, I couldn't…how would it look."

Well, I decided to brush it aside. However, after not being able to get the guy off my mind, I decided to go to the restaurant where he works that Thursday. Yes, he was there, but I don't think he knew what to think when he saw me. There was a co-worker standing next to him, and they were talking while glancing in my direction. I have excellent peripheral vision, so when they looked at me, I would turn to look at him, they both quickly turned away. Then Marco disappeared into the back, and his co-worker was standing at the door near the kitchen, looking as if he was trying not to be noticed. He was peering out, and when I saw this, I laughed silently. It was so obvious of what he was doing.

There was another door closer to the dining room, and I noticed Marco standing at the window looking out to where I was sitting, and again, when I looked directly at him, he'd quickly turned away. It was so strange, so different from the man who maintained eye contact with me that first night I arrived, who was now acting shy. I was disappointed when nothing happened, so I left and put the whole thing behind me.

It turned out later, there was a reason I was drawn to this man – he looked like *him*, the man from my dreams.

Two days into my stay and after breakfast, I decided to venture out and explore my surroundings at my B&B – Ash Farm before my scheduled day. There is a small road in front, with a path leading to the right and another to the left, so I decided to take the path to the right first.

I walked a small way down the road before coming to a dirt path that turned into a cobblestone road with tall thick shrubs on each side. The path leads you down and through a tunnel with a small walking bridge. After going through the tunnel, then taking a right, a path takes you up to the walking bridge, to a bird-watching area. Following the main path, it takes you directly to the water canal and to a large open field. Later I learned if I continued this path, it would have taken me directly to the village of Lymm. The feeling I had – well, it was amazing. It felt right – perfect. After taking in the beauty of the place, I turned and headed back to the B&B to take the other path.

This path took me past two houses and a small bridge crossing River Bolin to a dirt path. To the right of the path was an open field with grazing cattle. However, this wasn't only a walking path but a road as well.

As I was walking the path, I recall a particular white cow that captured my attention. Now, what I am going to say next, I have no clear understanding, but it seemed to be watching me. It is strange I know, but it felt – well as if she knew me. What I was getting from her was as if she was welcoming me home. Yes, I know what you might be thinking, but it's true. It's hard to explain. It felt like I had come home.

Beyond the field was a large wall, which turned out to be the outer wall to Dunham Massey Castle. The closer I came to the outer wall, I felt I needed to slow my approach, as I was feeling something. It was a sense of familiarity about this place. It felt, well, as if I lived here before. That I belonged here. I looked back at the cow, and she was still watching me. I know what you might be thinking, and no, it's not that. There was more to this cow, as if it was more than just a cow. It was, well, as if the cow knew something I didn't.

I've learned since, cows are a connection to the earth and the spiritual realm, so maybe just maybe, it was trying to tell me something. Interesting, is it not.

As I continued my walk down the path, I turned to look to the field beyond Dunham Massey Castle, to the west. In doing this, the feeling of being home intensified. I felt the need to run, to run to my home, but where, and how? I knew I lived here before, but when? This I didn't know. These feelings I was having, they felt so right and so real. The urge to move here increased to one I never had before. There was no question, it was clear, I had to move here. So, I began to pray: *please God, help me find a way to move here, to this place, this area. I must move here. I have to move here. This is my home. I know this to be true. Please God, I beg of you.* In this pleading, I felt such a mix of emotions that I had tears threatening to surface.

You'd think after having these feelings my first reaction would be to go directly to the castle and see if these feelings intensified, but I didn't. I already had an appointment scheduled for that day; however, after what I was feeling, I was determined to make time to visit on another day.

I continued my walk to the end of the path, and as I was approaching the end, to the left – north of Dunham Massey Castle was a small forest with a narrow walking path. I looked down the path, thinking of taking it to see where it would take me, when something stopped me – fear, a tremendous and overwhelming amount of fear that stopped me right in my tracks. I felt if I took that path, something bad – that someone was down there waiting for me, wanting to harm me. I know it sounds crazy, but it's what I felt, and so I avoided the path and headed back to Ash Farm, so I could get ready to head to my appointment.

Cheshire, England – Marco

That same morning when Rebecca arrived in Cheshire, there was a feeling in Marco's chest – his heart. As he placed his hand over his heart, not understanding the pain, at least not at first.

What is happening? I've felt this before, but when, he thought. It has been a while since he felt this, and although he's tried hard to forget the feeling, there is no denying what it is – *wait! Is it possible…oh God, is it her? Is it because…is it…her? Is it true? Is it what nõnna said was going to happen…she's back?* This stunned Marco at the realization, causing his heart to jump a heartbeat or two before it accelerates with sudden excitement. *If so, how will I know where to find her?* Then he recalls what his grandmother told him, *Dunham Massey Castle!* he thought, but why did he think of that place? *But when and what day?*

In the middle of his thought, Marco's mother walks into his office. "Marco, I need you to go to Spain for business," she said.

Marco's mother is a strong woman of five foot seven with blond straight shoulder length hair, that's parted on the left side. She has a somewhat long face with slightly puffy cheeks, and a strong jaw – for a woman. She has large blue eyes and is elegantly dressed in a soft powder blue suit. Although on the back side, she can be a ruthless businesswoman.

Irritated at the sudden interruption, Marco says, "Mother, for what reason? When do I need to go?"

"There is a wonderful opportunity to obtain new business, and I need you to leave today. The person you need to meet with will only be there for a few more days. The quicker you go, the better."

Seriously? And after what I just felt. No! No, you don't mother. I will not go. "Mother, you cannot just spring these things on me and expect me to pick up and leave. I have a previous engagement."

Unperturbed by this, she says, waving her hand at him, "Cancel them. This is far more important."

"Who are you to decide what is more important? You are not in charge of this company!" Marco said between clenched teeth. His father was in charge, and under his father, it was him.

Marco's words angered his mother, "I am your mother! You will do what I ask?" she said, eyeing him as she did when he was a boy in trouble.

But Marco was no longer a boy in need of his mother's scolding. "Mother!" he said in a firm voice. "I am a grown man! You cannot make a business meeting for me without consulting me first!" Shaking his head, "I am sorry, but I cannot go!"

This angered his mother more than he knew. "Marco! You will go, and that's the end of it!"

Exacerbated, "Mother, I cannot go! I must stay here! If I go, I will miss out on a great opportunity that I've been waiting for a long time!" he said in his firmest voice, not looking at his mother, instead, he made himself busy by rustling with the papers on his desk.

Oh no, he doesn't. He will go. I will make sure of that, she thought but said, "Oh really, what is this so-called opportunity?"

"That is my business, not yours."

"Marco, whatever it is, if it has to do with the business, then it is my business."

Marco looked up at his mother. *She really believes this, doesn't she?* Resigned, he says, "It has nothing to do with the business. It's...never mind."

This secretiveness only angered his mother more. "Marco! What is going on? You cannot neglect your responsibilities with the company."

That was it. Marco was now angry at his mother's prying. "Mother! I am not neglecting my responsibilities! My personal life is none of your business!" *Ballocks, maybe I shouldn't have said that. But mother knows how to get under my skin.*

"Oh, this is personal, is it?" she said with her hands on her hip, mocking him. "It's a woman, isn't it? Have you not learned from your earlier relationships?"

"Leave it alone, mother! This has nothing to do with my earlier relationships. This is different. This is what I have been waiting...it's something I have to do!" Marco, realizing what he did, cursed himself under his breath.

Damn that woman! Will she not hurry up and die already! his mother thought. She's hated his grandmother ever since – she stopped as she realized, "Oh...no...Marco, it's not about this woman you've talked about? I thought you finally put that behind you, as a crazy idea your grandmother put in your head. Has your grandmother been feeding these crazy ideas again? Are you ever going to learn?"

Shit-shit-shit-shit! "Mother, you have no idea what you are talking about! Nõnna is not crazy! She is a good woman, and you need to watch what you say about her!" he said with a look that stopped his mother short.

However, Marco's mother would not relent on this, and she argued with him until he finally agreed to go to Spain. This, to just get her out of his office so she would leave him alone, but he would only agree to go for a couple of days, then he will return to find Rebecca.

Chapter 15

Dunham Massey Castle

It was Thursday when I went to see Dunham Massey Castle. I went through the back entrance, to the path lined with trees on both sides, within walking distance from Ash Farm. As I started down the path, I felt a sense of peace, again, feeling as if I've been here before – no, I lived here before, sometime long ago. The closer I came to the entrance, the stronger the feeling became. I had to walk up a few steps at the entrance, then down a few more steps to the ground on the other side, entering Dunham Massey.

With my first real look around, there was a sense of familiarity, again feeling *I am home,* with an immediate pull to a path directly to my right, in the direction taking you away from the estate to the open land and trees beyond the castle grounds. When I looked in that direction, there was a fear, a fear I did not understand or recognize. It wasn't that I felt something horrible was going to happen, but it was the unknown. It felt as if I wanted to run towards it. To run home. At that moment, I wasn't ready, not yet. I later learned that area is called Deer Park, and a few miles beyond was a place that use to be known as Watch Hill Castle, a castle that no longer exists, except for a few stones. I also learned there is a woodshed located in that direction as well.

After standing there for a few moments, with the pull to go in that direction so strong, I was unsure what to do. Eventually, I decided to turn away and walk in the direction that leads to the castle. As I was walking down the path, there was a building – a watermill. I stopped to look at it, and I felt there was something familiar about it, but what it was I didn't know. Further down, past the watermill next to the castle, was a small shop to purchase your tickets for the tour, along with souvenirs. Although they call it a castle, it's not an actual castle, but more of a manor.

After entering the castle, I didn't feel as I did on the grounds, except there was a type of presence. I wasn't sure what or who it was, and it seemed, well, it seemed as if whatever the presence was, was near me, as if it was following me, with a sense of familiarity, one I couldn't understand. As I continued with the castle tour, I noticed these feelings would come and go, depending on what part of the castle I was in.

When I entered the library – this place was more pronounced than the rest of the castle. This presence with me, or maybe it was another presence, whoever it was, was very strong there. For some reason though, to how or why, I didn't know, but it felt – I knew them. In the library, there was a man there to explain the history and stories of the room and the age of the books. When I glanced at the books on the shelves, there was this need, a feeling that I needed to go to those shelves. It was as if there was something there I needed to see. What it was I didn't know, nor was I allowed to go near the bookshelves. Due to their age and fragileness, they were blocked off to prevent people from touching them.

As I continued my tour, I entered the main living area, which is a long wide room with windows going across one side. This room is called the green room. The reason it's called a green room, is because of the green walls. Yes, it's the green room from my dream, and yes, there was a painting on the wall of a man who was Lord of this castle long ago. However, to my disappointment, there was no tall dark handsome man standing and staring at the painting as he was in my dream. I hoped and wished he was. Well, as we all know, dreams are mostly fantasy – what our deepest desires are, and they don't always come true. However, I have to admit, I wish this was the one that did.

I continued my tour, and when I entered the room they called the red room, again, I felt a presence, as if someone was watching me. It wasn't a bad feeling, but it felt as if I was being welcomed. With these feelings, I took out my phone and started taking pictures, hoping to capture whatever was in the room. Other times when I had these feelings, and after taking pictures, I'd capture something, so I was hopeful that I would as well this time. To my disappointment, there was nothing, but what I felt was too strong to ignore.

After leaving the red room, I was close to the end of my tour, and as I was standing on the second-floor hall peering out the window, I again felt there was something there, or maybe it was someone, since I felt as if I was being watched. I took out my phone and started taking pictures, and this time, to my wonderful surprise, I captured something. It was an orb, right on the outer wall across from the window. With excitement, I continued with my tour, then entered a room that overlooked the front of the castle, and again I felt something was there. So yep, I took more pictures, and yes, I caught another orb. There was definitely something going on here, what it was, I didn't know. Now, keep in mind, I didn't find this evidence until after I returned home and was going through the pictures I took.

<u>Spirits of Dunham</u>

"She's back. Look, she's back," said a female spirit.

"Who are you referring to?" said a male spirit.

"Look," the female spirit pointed at Rebecca, "She just entered the library." The man and the female spirit followed Rebecca into the library.

The male spirit looks at the woman in question, watching and studying her, to see if he can see what the other spirit saw. Finally, he does. He sees it as he penetrated Rebecca's outer skin and saw into her soul. *Yes, Isabelle is correct – it is indeed her. It's Elizabeth.* With this, the male spirit goes to Rebecca and stands next to her, as he watches and observes her with great interest.

The male spirit was Elizabeth Massey's uncle, Paul Massey, who died before Elizabeth was even born. When he was alive, he was a strong and powerful man – a warrior, a lord, and in life, he was a hard man as if he had no heart or soul. When he died, he didn't want to leave a place he loved, so he remained at the castle and forgot of the life he had, and in time when his heart eased and his soul was cleansed from the anger an hatred he had carried, he was given a choice to leave, although he felt he was no longer that harden warrior of his time, there was a purpose, a reason for him to remain. At the time, he didn't understand why, not until now.

Another spirit learns Elizabeth has returned, but he wasn't as happy as the other spirits were.

"Where is she? I want to see her!" he yelled. Without an answer, he moves around the other spirits that were blocking his view, and there she was, "There, there she is, that wretched witch! She has been reborn! Returned! How dare she! This woman, she even resembles Elizabeth!" He tries to go to her, to reach her, "She will pay for her decision…for what she did!"

Paul grabs John and holds him back. "Don't you go near her, John! As of now, she is under my protection!"

Paul said in a calm, yet powerful voice, no one would dare question.

But John Massey was not happy with this and yelled, "How dare you, Paul! How dare you interfere in my family affairs!"

"John, she is no longer your family! She is the daughter of the family of this time! You have been dead for almost five hundred years, and since, your anger has grown out of control."

"Well, I did swear vengeance on what happened to me, my wife, and my son!"

"John, I was there, and I saw everything that happened. You were at fault, more so than Elizabeth. You put your own daughter into the hands of a mad man."

"Don't speak to me of that time, as I remember it well! I remember what happened after we were killed! Why do you think I am so angry! Why I seek vengeance!"

He wakes, then rises from his body. He stands and looks out to the people around them. He turns to see his body hanging from the noose, along with the bodies of his wife and son. As he looks at his wife and son, then looks to the people, trying to understand what happened. Then his wife and son are there, standing next to him.

"What happened?" asked Baroness Massey.

"We are dead! Can you not see!" said Baron Massey, pointing to their lifeless bodies.

Suddenly, there is a large bright light forming in front of them.

"What is that?" asked John.

"I think...we need to go...walk into the light. Can you feel the love, the pull...the feeling of so much love?" said Baroness Massey.

"No!" Baron Massey yells, grabbing his wife's arm, "We cannot go! Look," pointing at their bodies, "What they did to us! They cannot get away with this! No! We are staying! We are going to make them all pay!" Baron Massey grabs his wife and son by their hands and pulls them, as he forces them to walk away from the bright light and their lifeless bodies.

Their anger festered beyond control, from that moment and through the centuries, with revenge being their only desire. Baron Massey and his family return to Dunham Massey, where they remain and watch everything around them move on, unable to do anything to stop it. When Baron Massey learned Robert returned as a Booth, instead of him going straight to purgatory, he was outraged, not understanding how this could be. For him to become Lord of Dunham Massey, Baron Massey wanted to strangle Robert. But he did not have the power, not yet. All he could do was watch him live the life that should have been his — feeding his anger — wanting his revenge, but powerless to take it.

"Paul, you cannot deny me my revenge!" said John through clenched teeth as he stared at Rebecca.

"John, you will not touch her or do anything to cause her pain. I will be with her…stay with her, to protect her from you or anyone else who wants to harm her. Do you understand me?" Paul grabs John's arm and yanks him back, making sure he understands what he said.

"Damn you, Paul! You've always had a soft heart for these people!" John is angry, but for now, he agrees to leave Elizabeth — Rebecca alone. *I will find a way! She will never find happiness!* he thought.

"Not always, John. Not always," he said with a heavy heart, although he no longer has a heart.

Rebecca

After leaving the main castle, I walked towards the gardens, and the closer I came to them, the feeling of *home* was stronger there, along with a feeling of familiarity. This was stronger and more powerful than when I first approached Dunham Massey Castle. Now, there was no doubt, I had some type of connection to this place. When and where, now, that was the question. Certain parts of the garden were stronger than others. I couldn't understand this; how can one part feel so familiar, and the other, nothing. I later learned the reason for why it felt so different. Not everything on the estate was from the same time period, as certain parts of the garden were newer. The parts of the garden I connected with were the oldest parts, but still, I did not know how old or when. However, later in my research, I learned the estate goes back to the eleven hundreds, maybe even further than that. How was I to learn which part was of what time period? Was there even a way to truly know? Questions I had, that even to this day I don't have the answers to. The only thing I was sure of, was I did live here, and I once called this place home.

In going out the way I came in, I again felt the pull to go down that path, the one that drew my attention when I first entered the property. Although I wanted to, I couldn't, not that day. Even if I wanted to venture down the path, it looked as it was about to rain, and I wanted to get back to the B&B before it did. Shortly after I returned to my room, it rained – down poured was more like it. I thought of returning to Dunham Massey castle before it was time to return home, but unfortunately, there just wasn't enough time.

It's Friday, and my last day in Cheshire, and the owners of Ash Farm suggested I go to Alderley Edge to visit the witch's caverns. This place is known for mystical going-on's – it's magical. The Wizard Walk and Witch's Caverns is a magical place, with a story going back hundreds of years, of a wizard living in one of the caves, with soldiers and white horses asleep on the cave floor. The story says: the sleeping soldiers are to wake when England is in great peril and once again in need of their help and leadership.

When I arrived, it was on a day the main office and shop were closed. It was disappointing, but there was nothing to be done about it. I wore short black pants with tall black boots with a small heel, with a maroon loose-fitted turtleneck sweater top. When I saw the rough terrain, it was apparent I was extremely overdressed, and I was definitely wearing the wrong shoes. Well, since I was there, I decided to walk the path anyways. I wanted to see if I could feel the magic the owners talked about. As I was walking, I felt – well, there was something, it was a feeling, but I wasn't sure what. As I continued walking along the wooden fence, there were large rocks on my left, with an opening – one of the cave entrances I assume, and standing near the entrance was a black raven, who seemed to be guarding the entrance, and there was something about the raven, as if it had some type of knowledge, a type of intelligence. I know it sounds strange, but it's how I saw it at the time.

As I was walking the path, there was a feeling, as if something or someone was there – watching me. I pulled out my phone and started taking pictures, wondering if I would capture anything. Then, I was suddenly pulled in the direction of the trees directly ahead of me, beyond the path I was on. I felt there was something out there, what, I didn't know. So, I took more pictures in that direction, hoping I would catch something.

As I continued down the path, it curved around to a slightly steep hill. It wouldn't have been a problem in better shoes, but heels with a slippery sole, even a little hill as it was, was dangerous. As I started down the hill, I flashed back to a time when I was a girl at camp. I was running down a small hill when I tripped and went tumbling down. Well, it was bad as a kid, but to take such a fall as a woman in her early forties – yeah, I don't think so.

However, there was no turning back, so I pulled back my shoulders and leaned back a little, and carefully started down the path, at the same time praying to God, asking for his protection to prevent me from falling. Suddenly I felt as if there was someone on each side of me, holding – supporting my upper arms, as they guided me down the path. But when I reached a place of safety, I felt the support dissipate.

Once I was off the path, I was thinking about what happened and how I felt – there was a feeling of unconditional love, along with a feeling that I was protected. On the main path heading back to the parking lot, I met an older lady and her German Sheppard dog – I am not sure why I remember this lady, but there was just something about her. Anyways, I stopped and talk to her, and we talked for about thirty minutes or so, then it was time that I head to my final appointment with a property agent to see a couple more flats.

Although my trip was over, I have to say it was a successful one. I made great progress, and I was now ready to return home to make the final preparations that will allow me to return in October and begin my six months to a year stay. In leaving England this time around, I felt different. It was a sense of security, a feeling of such peace and happiness, one I haven't felt in a long time, if ever. I found the perfect place, and if possible, I'll find a way to make it permanent. I have a plan, a purpose, and now a place. I left England filled with happiness and hope.

My flight home went a great deal better than my flight to London. Even if you can believe this, I sat next to a man – wait, wait for it, you are not going to believe it – yep, his name was Marc. Again, I know. Something was definitely going on. So, I started going over the number of men I met, just in this year alone whose name was Marc or Marco. The man I met online who assisted me in finding Cheshire, name was Marc. The man I had that moment within the restaurant, his name was Marco, and after returning home, one of my coworkers said there was a new employee in training, and his name was Marc, and he's British – she laughed. With the history between the Marc, I met online, the Marc and Marco in England, and now in training, I started wondering, *why am I meeting all these Marc's and Marco's.* To meet so many men with this name. Keep in mind, I didn't know or met any Marc's or Marco's in years. I know it's odd, as that is a very popular male name, but it's true. At least, as far as my memory goes. The reason for this now, I didn't know. However, it seemed to only get worse. As a booking agent, I talked to hundreds of people a day, and suddenly – it wasn't only first names, but last names that included the name Marc or Marco. It seemed as if someone was screaming at me to listen, as if they wanted me to know something. What it was, I didn't know, nor why? Not until a great deal later, when I learned that the universe was screaming at me to listen.

Manchester Airport

Marco did not leave on the day his mother wanted him to, but instead waited until the following morning, and when he woke up, he felt Rebecca. It was a strong and powerful feeling, and when he arrived at the airport, it seemed to intensify, and Marco wondered, *is she at the airport.*

No, she was not, but she was near.

She's here. She's back. I can't ignore this feeling. What do I do? What can I do? Do I stay, or do I go? he thought.

He wanted to stay, but he knows he must go. He has to honor his responsibilities in the commitment he's already made. Then he thinks about his grandmother, and *maybe she can tell me if Rebecca's here.* So, Marco calls his grandmother.

"Marco, she was there at the car rental, but she didn't stay long. This, what I believe is what you felt."

"What should I do? Do I stay and hope I will find her, or do I go and honor my obligations? But what if I don't have another opportunity?"

"Marco, you are right. You must go. Trust in God, in the power of the love you both have, that there will be another opportunity. Have faith Marco. Pray and ask God for his help."

"I'm scared —"

This is something Marco would never admit to anyone but his grandmother. With his grandmother, he could feel scared without judgment or look weak.

"— I don't want to lose her."

To hear this pleases Maria, but she would never say so. "Marco, you can never lose her. Your love is strong. It's a power so great...a gift given to you by God. This love, your love, has carried across time, waiting for the right time when you both are in a place to allow this love again. Have faith. Trust in yourself. In your heart and in her heart. She wants this. She feels one of the reasons she needs to move to England is there is a man, a love here waiting for her. The man is you. You are the man she is destined to be with. With this, she will not give up. Trust in your love."

"Can a love…this love you speak of…a love you said we had…is this love, that powerful…is — *what am I thinking, this can't be real…or is it?* "Nõnna, in what you say…is this really true?"

"Yes, Marco, it is all true. Everything I've told you is true. Your connection with Rebecca…what you are feeling…you know…you know what I say is true. Search your heart, and you will find the answers."

Chapter 16

<u>Arizona</u>

After I returned to work, I placed a picture I took at the Wizard Walk, the one from the trees, as the background on my monitor. When I saw the picture on the twenty-inch screen, I couldn't believe what I saw. There, in the tree line was an outline of a wizard. It was the same place I felt someone watching me. He was right there. He had a pointed hat and wearing a long robe that seemed to be tied at the waist with what looked like a piece of rope. He was bent over a bit, as if slouching, with his hand on his cane for support, and he had a long white beard. Needless to say, I was shocked, and I immediately called one of my coworkers over. I needed someone else to see if they could see what I was seeing. It took a bit, but after a few moments, they did, and to my relief, I knew it wasn't just me. It was a wizard, standing in the tree line, watching – me. What an amazing find, especially after reading about the legend.

Before I left Phoenix, I went to a local used bookstore to buy a book to read on the plane, but the story didn't draw me in, and I began to think I made a mistake in buying the book, and considered returning it to the bookstore.

It's funny, because the day I went to the bookstore, I walked by the section where the book was, but thought nothing of it. Yes, I glanced at it and thought *maybe*, then I'd shake my head and continued looking for a book. But no matter where I went, I kept returning to that section where that book was, and each time I would glance at it, then continued on to another section. The last time I stopped, I finally took the book down and looked at it.

Apparently, someone wanted me to look at the book and read what it was about.

It is a story that took place during the time King Henry V ruled England, and it was about a woman with great strength who endured many life challenges. It took place during the time of War of the Roses, and the name of the book is 'The Lady of the Rivers' by Philippa Gregory. My thoughts at the time were, *I am a woman of strength, who had…is still going through a great many challenges.* So, for me to read about a woman of strength, especially during those times felt inspiring. To me, it was a must-read, and so I bought the book.

A week after I returned home, and before I returned the book, I decided to give the book another go, and this time I was drawn into the storyline, and found I couldn't put it down. It was a good thing we were at our slower months, which allowed me to read in between calls.

What's strange though, something started to happen, something I could not explain. The story – well, part of the story, the characters, seemed familiar. Real familiar. It felt, well, okay, I know this is going to sound crazy, but it was as if somehow, the story related to *me*. How? I didn't know, but I did wonder, *could this be a past life connection*? I became addicted to the story, but not just the story, but the main character, Jacquetta of Luxembourg, who became a widow of Duke of Bedford, who also fell in love with the Duke's squire, Richard Woodville.

What was it about them? Well, their relationship was a forbidden one. The love felt between Jacquetta and Richard Woodville was a strong and powerful one, and something about it resonated with me and thus, pulled me in even deeper.

In reading this book, the idea of tarot cards and psychic abilities – let's just say, they intrigued me. However, there was also something familiar. Yeah, I know, crazy, right? The funny thing was, as I think back to my teens, I was fascinated with tarot cards and psychics. I wanted to know and understand this, but never pursued it. I guess it was the idea of what's out there with the past and future. I often wondered, *what does my future hold? Do I even have one? Who was I, and why am I here?* This last was my biggest questions, *why am I here? Why do I exist?* Who would think what those answers would give me a great deal later in my life? I was being drawn into a world I didn't understand, but there was this need to learn more, to find out exactly what was happening.

As I continued reading the book of these two characters, Jacquetta and Richard Woodville, who found a special bond, a connection, a love they never thought possible. At first, they shared their love in secret, until they were forced to reveal their relationship to the king, but only after they married in secret, thus preventing the king from forcing Jacquetta to remarry. In reading this, there was something very familiar about it. Deep down, I knew, somehow these two people had something to do with me, but how?

Suddenly, I started feeling that there was someone out there, a love so strong and powerful that I was meant to find – to connect with. Whoever he is, he is my one true love. The one I am bonded with, and I wondered how I knew this? Why was I feeling this way, *bonded?* What was that? Was that even possible? I believed there could be a true love, a soul mate for one person, but bonded? What did that mean? Is it possible to love someone so much with your heart and soul that it could be bonded to them? For what? Life or Eternity? Many questions I have no answers to, and how does one find out? Then I remembered, there was a person I've talked to in the past. Yes, it was from a psychic sight, but this woman proved to be the real deal, and I trusted her. I remembered her profile, how it mentioned how she practiced Wicca, along with her psychic abilities, so I said, *what the hell. It couldn't hurt.*

My hope was, she could help me understand what I was feeling, and maybe, just maybe, help me open a door that will allow me to connect with *him*. Who the *him* is, I didn't know? To find the one I was meant to be with, that I was bonded with. Maybe he's out there, waiting for me to finally discover the truth and connect with him. How did I know this? I don't know. I just did. It was a feeling deep inside me? Even this, I cannot explain.

I scheduled a time with this woman and when we spoke, I told her what was happening to me, and this is what she said, "There is a connection to this story, what exactly, this I cannot say."

I told her about the dream I had before I went to England. How I believed it might be a past life memory, along with my hopes and need to find my one true love.

She said, "Yes, I believe it was a past life memory. You have a connection to the place you visited in England. There is to be a love, and if you want, I can help you open your heart and soul to this."

What do you think I said? Duh, of course I said, "Yes-yes, please. What is it?"

"I will type it up and email it to you," she said.

And of course, I said, "Okay."

I waited anxiously for the email, and when it finally came, I didn't waste any time getting started.

Here's what the email said:

Make a list of what you want and what you are seeking for in your true love. Once you made this list, you want to think of those things when you do the following: Take a white candle and light it. Stare into the flame, and at the same time, you are to recite this: I deserve this love, and I am worth this love. Our love is true and will only belong to us. With my heart and soul, I provide this love, and I am open to receiving it. None should hinder nor prevent this true love.

These are the characteristics I listed: A true gentleman, romantic, faithful, classy, intelligent, playful, corky, sarcastic, and funny, financially secure, grounded, and down to earth.

After I performed the ritual, something amazing happened. I had a vision of a man; he was only wearing shorts and had dark wavy hair that sat just above his shoulders. He was looking up into the dark sky, and I felt he was looking at the moon and stars – seeking God. He was praying, asking for his help, to find the woman he seeks. His one true love. The love he is meant to be with. He seemed to be praying at the same time I was performing the ritual. It was as if, whatever was preventing us from connecting before, was lifted, allowing us to finally find each other – connecting our hearts and souls, bonding us as one.

<u>Cheshire, England</u>

At the exact time Rebecca performed the ritual, Marco felt it. It slammed into him – piercing his chest with a powerful energy, along with a burst of emotions that practically knocked him over.

Oh God, what just happened. Could it be? Is this what I was expecting when 'it' happened? But how do I know it's what I think it is? Marco is flabbergasted at the powerful sensation he felt that pierced the center of his heart. He was told he would know when it happened, but how could he be sure it is what he believes it to be? *No, with what just happened…it must be true. It has to be true. How can I deny it,* shaking his head, *no, not after what I just felt.*

The emotions were so powerful that he felt tears rising, as he thought, *it was her – Rebecca.* With Marco feeling these powerful emotions, as he was forcing back the tears he thought, *I'm a man. A man does not cry. This is ridiculous. God, is it truly her?* To Marco's shock, he received an answer to his question. One, he didn't realize he was asking to anyone but himself. *Yes.* That was all the voice said, but then Marco rationalized the voice as his own mind answering him. *Yes…you fool! Of course, I am going to say yes, because it's what I want to hear.* Then, there was more, *no, Marco, you are wrong. It is not you who is saying yes. It is us…we, who are of God.*

Marco felt as if he was going mad. "What…what is this? Who is this? I do not understand," he said aloud.

Marco was in his loft – his bedroom, standing by his bed, before he walks to stand in front of the window. He looks up to the night sky, trying to understand what or who the voice in is mind was, as he was sure it was not his own. Then, thinking it silly, he started laughing aloud, "Lord, I am going mad. I must be. It's the only rational explanation."

You are not going mad. We are here to help you and Rebecca, said the voice.

Marco froze when he heard the voice again. He feels as if he's going mad, then realizes there is only one person who can help him.

"Alright, I cannot do this. I need to call nõnna. She will know what is happening, and she will be able to explain it to me," he said.

Marco has never talked to his guides, which is what his grandmother calls them. Yes, he's spoken to God, but never, never has he received an answer outside his own voice – his thoughts.

What Marco is unaware of, those thoughts he thinks are his own, at times were his guides. Until they are sure the person is ready or open to hearing them, is when the guides come through. At first, it would be in your own voice, then when the time is right, it changes, depending on which guide chooses to speak to you. For Marco, now was the time when Marco and Rebecca's connection was made, thus allowing his guides to communicate in a more open manner.

"Marco! Oh, Marco, this is great news!" Maria said, feeling excited and happy about Marco's success. This is what she's been waiting for since Marco was born into her family. "You've done it! She's done it! This is what you've been waiting for! You can no longer doubt this!" Then in a softer voice, "You are not going mad. Those were your guides speaking to you. Don't fight it. Allow them to help you. That is what they are for."

Shaking his head, *no, this is mad. It's mad!* "I...I...don't understand," he said, sighing. "This has never happened to me before...why...why now?"

"You are asking that question when there is no need, as you already have your answer. It's because of Rebecca. This is the beginning, Marco."

"The beginning...more of this? How can I endure such emotions? No-no-no...this cannot be? If this happens at work, how would I look? How would I explain it?" he said, suddenly feeling panic.

"If you don't wish it, then ask them to only allow these emotions to happen when you are alone. Marco, this is your time. Allow it to happen. When you can, come here, and I will help and teach you what you need to know. What you are experiencing, I've already gone through it. You've always had this gift, Marco. A gift you've asked for. Now that Rebecca has opened the door…you are both connected now, as it should be."

Shaking his head again, "This is too much. I will have to think about this. I will come to Italy as soon as my schedule allows it."

When Marco ends his call with his grandmother, he sits on the edge of his bed and thinks about what happened, and how he feels about what his grandmother said. *Love, a very powerful love. It felt…as if I lost this powerful love, but now I've found it. A pain so strong, with a feeling as if my heart was being ripped out of my chest. Then there was a healing, a renewal as if what was once ripped apart was now restored. In this, this feeling in my heart, with the greatest power…this love. It felt like an overload of love, that is centuries lost…was being slammed into me all at once. Can this truly be?*

After this last thought, Marco finally falls asleep and dreams of Rebecca.

They are together near a tree by a lake. He has her in his arms, as he's looking down at her, feeling the love they feel for each other, along with a feeling of never wanting to let her go. They are so much in love, a love so strong and powerful – then, he is in the same place, but now, he's dressed in clothes from a different time, and there she is…no not her…yet…yes, it is her. He knows it is. He kisses her with a passion so strong, one he's never in his life has felt before. When he opens his eyes, it's not her of the past, but her of the now. He's kissing Rebecca. He feels himself leaving, as he is about to wake up, "Wait, what is your name? Please, please tell me?" As he is waking up, she says, "I am Rebecca." Rebecca. Her name is Rebecca.

Marco wakes up, he is stunned from his dream, and he is still feeling what he felt in his dream with a clear recollection of what happened. *Oh God, it's true.*

Marco wastes no time calling his grandmother. He needs to understand what just happened.

"Nõnna, how did you know her name is Rebecca?" Shaking his head. Yes, his grandmother has used the name Rebecca, but he had always thought she did that, instead of saying *her*, not because it was her true Christian name, but because it was easier to give her a name than say *her*, each time she spoke of Rebecca. Marco sits up in his bed, stunned at what he learned and how much his grandmother really knows. "What are you, nõnna?" This question, one he's never asked before, was now a question in his mind to who his grandmother is, for her to know such things.

<u>Arizona – May 2013</u>

After this connection and vision, something more happened. I began dreaming about him. It was practically daily, nightly, and at times, more than once a day through visions. I never knew when the visions would hit me, but when they did, they were so powerful I'd be consumed by them, weakening me to a state, that I would have to find something to support me if there was no place for me to sit down.

There were times when these strange sensations would come over me, where I would look straight ahead, with a blank stare as if I was having a daydream or was in deep thought. It didn't seem to matter where I was, or what I was doing. So, if someone were to see me, they would just think I was daydreaming. When in actuality, I was having visions – images of something or someone. At first, they weren't always clear, and sometimes – now how do I explain this. You know when you stare at something for a long time it starts to look blurry or foggy. You can see it, but it's not very clear. Other times, it was like a dark shadow, with a glimpse of clarity here and there, looking as if the object was right in front of me as if it was real. There was this feeling, as if something or someone was there. It was so strange. I knew something was happening, but I had no idea what it was.

After doing the ritual and reading the book, there was no doubt – I was sure more than ever there was something about these two characters, Jacquetta and Richard Woodville lives that had something to do with me. What it was, I didn't know. This became a constant question, without any answers. With this, I started having doubts about so many things. With the book, the ritual, along with the dreams and visions I was having of this man, I started to wonder if I was creating this out of my own wants and needs – a fantasy, because I couldn't believe this really was happening. How could I be sure?

It wasn't just of this century I was dreaming about, but of the life before – a past life, of the same two people. The man and the woman I dreamed about in the clearing before my trip to England, I was now dreaming of them near a lake in a forest, spending time together underneath a tree, then it changed to the man of this time, the man I believed I connected with the night I performed the ritual. However, in my dreams, he was older than I believed him to be, and during my waking hours, I had visions of a lake, a forest, and different ponds surrounded by forest trees, with one standing out, as if it was significant to me in some way.

These dreams and visions, they were like a quick picture show flashing before my eyes. However, the dreams were very clear, and I was able to recall them in complete detail, along with the emotions – feelings.

There was no question; when I dreamed about the past, the woman was me. How did I know? That's a very good question. But I have no good answer. It was just a feeling – a knowing that the woman was me. Now, for the man, that I wasn't sure of, but I believed – felt he was the man from my dreams, the one from this century. With everything that was happening to me, this man became very important to me, as I started to believe that I was destined to be with him. To rekindle a love so powerful – could it be my prayer was being answered? You'd think, all I had to do was reach out and pull it in, but nothing is ever that easy, is it. Not when you are playing with karma you both created from your past lives. We had to prove we deserved this, not only to ourselves, but to *them* as well.

The question was, why now and in this life? Was it because of my prayer to God? Or was it because of the ritual? Or was it both. Or is it more than that. There was no question I was guided to the book that awakened me, that which had been buried – concealed. In doing so, it pushed me to contact the person who could help me open my heart to his. It was the beginning of a knotted string, with the challenge of untangling those knots to reach my final goal, which was him.

The first knot was the job with the travel agency. The second knot was my trip to England in 2012. The third knot was my second trip to England in 2013. The fourth knot was the book. When I read the book and felt the connection, it led me to call the woman who gave me the ritual, which allowed me to open my heart to *him*, and of course the fifth knot, the ritual – and so on and so on, until it gets to the final knot – the end of the story. My story.

One thing I am certain of, is nothing happens without reason. Although we may not know what that reason is at the time. In time, eventually, the answer will reveal itself.

No, it may not be within the time we want, but in the time that God feels it's right. All we can do is be patient and wait, and I know that is the hardest thing to do. In knowing what I know now, I often wondered how my soul was calling out, begging to find this love. A love lost, but now in this time, was found once again. Oh, how the answer when discovered, will cause everyone to question what truly is out there…

There were so many questions without any answers. Why was I dreaming of the past, and why now? Was it because there was a connection between the man of this time, or was it with the man of that time, a time I'm still unsure of? I don't know. I didn't understand, but I had to find out. Too many questions with no answers. After a time, I started wondering, *would I ever find out?* Yes, I had to. Why else would I be dreaming or having visions of this man. Something in me was telling me when the time was right, I will know. It was a feeling deep inside, to the very fibers of my soul. Patients? For me, they were lacking, and I chose not to wait. So, I pushed and pushed. What a mistake that turned out to be.

Chapter 17

By the end of May, there was this compulsion to draw, a need to put the images I saw in my dreams and visions on paper. Why? I didn't know. I've never had an interest in the past to draw, nor did I care for it, but now I was drawing, and to my surprise, they were pretty good.

With everything I've been experiencing, the summer of 2013 became the worse summer I've had to date. I started suffering asthma attacks, and they came back with vengeance. At first, I didn't think much of it since asthma became a part of my life after being diagnosed in 2007. My last severe attack was when I was under tremendous amount of stress, but now, it made no sense, since I wasn't feeling stressed. On the contrary, I was happy and excited. I had plans to move to England for six months, so I didn't understand why this was happening. I tossed it aside, justifying it due to the Arizona summer months – it gets crazy hot here, and the air quality can be horrible – well, to me anyways. When it gets in the high hundreds along with the humidity, it can sometimes be ten times worse. Not to mention when it rains during these conditions, causing the air to be muggy, making it hard for a person like me to breathe, causing me to feel as if I am suffocating.

During these months, I would spend time in the lovely airconditioned indoors. If I did venture outdoors, it was directly to my car with air conditioning, and then once at my destination, after finding the closest parking space with the littlest walk to the indoors as possible, to the lovely airconditioned building.

At first, the asthma attacks were mild, then gradually they increased to a rougher, harder, more painful cough, to a full-blown asthma attack. These were the worse days of my life.

I know I should have started this sooner, but I wasn't much of a journal writer, so by the time I decided to record my dreams and visions, it was mid-June. Here is my first entry.

It was June 12, 2013, I'm standing outside an old shiny silver metal trailer that looks like one of those 1950 ones. You know, the ones with those large ribbits outlining the connection of metal to frame. I step inside the trailer and when I look around, I notice how much of a mess it's in, with a desperate need of cleaning and a great deal of repair.

Next, I find myself cleaning the trailer, with the need to bring it back to life and back to its former glory. As I am cleaning, something from the window caught my eye, and when I looked out, I saw a large, massive brick house that I hadn't notice before.

Suddenly, I am no longer in the trailer, but I am now standing outside the front door of the house. I open the door and walk in, and once inside, I found myself in a wide-open foyer with the walls of an elegant dark wood, with wainscoting.

Directly ahead of the front entrance is a long wide hallway, I felt this pull, with the need to walk down that hallway. As I was making my way down the hallway, I notice on each side of the walls were framed artwork – they were my artwork. What? How can this be? I thought. They're the drawing I did of the lakes, ponds, and trees. But instead of drawings, they were actual paintings, which I found odd. How can my drawing be here in the form of paintings? I thought.

Then I noticed straight ahead is a light coming from a cracked door. I slowly and quietly approached the door, and once I was there, I peer through the cracks and saw a man and woman lying on the bed laughing while being frisky. They look so happy and in love, and seeing this caused an ache in my heart, along with the feeling of jealousy, as I believed that woman should be me. To feel this way caused me great pain and sorrow, although I didn't understand why I was feeling this way.

As I watch the man, I can see him clearly. He has brown eyes with dark wavy hair, but when I look at the woman, because her back was to me I couldn't see her face. From what I could see, she has long dark wavy hair. Hum, it's similar to mine, I thought. I could feel the love they feel for each other, it seemed to flood the room, pouring out through the cracks, affecting anyone standing near, including me.

What I found strange, although I am standing there watching them, I should feel as if I am invading their privacy, but I don't. I felt comfortable as if I belonged. It felt right.

Next, I find myself outside. There is a section of grass, a type of courtyard, and the man and woman I saw in the bedroom are now dancing on the grassy courtyard. The man is wearing dark pants, with a white shirt, and the woman is wearing a short white flowery dress. Their dancing is a way for them to express their love for each other.

At this, I realize I am standing in a corner near the house, and it feels as if I am an observer, invisible to anyone around me, and they have no idea I am there. I look across the courtyard, beyond the floor of cobblestones to the window on the other side, and I see a man standing at the window, but I can't see what he's doing. However, as I see his sleeves are rolled up, it's possible he's doing dishes. He is wearing what appears to be a white dress shirt, and I find I cannot take my eyes off him. I begin to wonder who the man is. As I am observing this man, I notice the first two buttons of his shirt are undone, and from what I can see, he has a muscular chest, with broad shoulders. As I look up, he has dark wavy hair that comes just above his shoulders. He looks to be six feet tall or more. He is a very handsome man, and I could not help but stare at him in awe. I'm astonished by what I am seeing, when there is a feeling, a sense of familiarity, as if I know this man. But how? I thought. When suddenly he looks up, and in my direction – directly at me. It's as if he can see me, and I thought, can he see me? No, it's impossible. But still, he is looking directly at me as if he can see me, and then I realize, yes, oh God yes, he can see me. This caused me to panic, and I was startled by this realization. If felt as if I was a peeping tom that just got busted, but I was sure I'm invisible. This too was hard to explain, but the way he's looking at me, I have no doubt he can see me, and I am stunned, at the same time, fascinated.

I find that I cannot stop watching him, as he's watching me, in an unbreakable stare, and the look on his face is one of surprise. The way he is looking at me, it's as if he sees a ghost, and it feels as if he can see right through me. This is when I wake up.

I lie on my back staring at the ceiling wondering, "What was that? God, I can still feel what was happening in the dream with this man," I whispered. My heart was pounding as if it was about to burst through my chest. "There was something, something about him, something that touched my heart," and I wonder, "What does this all mean?"

This dream didn't make any sense to me. It was utterly confusing. I didn't understand it, nor what it meant. Though, there was something *special* about it. No matter what I did, I couldn't stop thinking about it – about him. Then that afternoon, is when it hit me, *oh my God!* I realized the man in the window – was the man I connected with the night I did the ritual. You see, later that morning before I went to work, I convinced myself I had that dream because I watched Dancing with the Stars the night before, even though there was this gnawing, a feeling, that there was more to the dream. And apparently, I was right, and this was just the beginning.

This need, as if I didn't have a choice, was forcing me to draw, since the images in my mind would not dissipate until I did. It felt as if something or someone was pushing me, and they were pushing me hard, with a feeling of uneasiness. There was this desperation, as if I didn't draw the images I was seeing it would be at great risk to more than myself.

There was no resisting the powerful compulsion. The first time this happened I was at home, sick after suffering a severe asthma attack, and the compulsion was so strong it forced me out of bed. I got dressed and drove to the store to purchase a drawing pad and pencils. Then once I returned home, I attempted to draw the image that's been plaguing my mind, of forest trees. To my own amazement, they turned out pretty good.

In this same month, I dreamed of a place that appears to have taken place somewhere between the 1400s or 1500s. How did I know this? It was based on the clothing the man and woman were wearing. I only remember bits and pieces of the dream, and it didn't make much sense. Here is the dream:

I was standing at a lake with a man. He was tall with dark hair. There was something familiar about him, but who he was, I didn't know.

I know this wasn't much, but unfortunately, it was all I could recall of the dream when I woke up. Although, I felt there was a great deal more I was missing.

Much later, after a great deal of thought, I realized the man in my dream, although different – now keep in mind it was only a feeling, but I believe the man in my dream was the man I connected with in this life.

Once the dreams started, they seemed to be coming in a rapid rate, one after the other. Here's another one that took place that same month.

I was in a room that appears to be in a castle. It's a small room with wooden floors, with a large, massive stone fireplace with a blue and gold coat of arms hanging above. There was a large rug situated in the center of the room, and on top of the rug sat a long thick wooden table.

To the back of the room and on the left, was a large window. The woman, I believe to be me, walked over to the window, and looks out to the night sky, to the shining stars and moon above. Then the woman looks down and sees the rocks and water below. I can feel how distraught she is. Something happened to her husband – he was killed. Then the woman was pacing back and forth in the room. I can feel what she is feeling – she doesn't know what to do. She stops for a moment and looks at the window, then returns to her pacing. There's this feeling that the king wants her. He wants her to be his wife. She feels confused and frustrated. There was no way she could marry the king since she was already married, but she felt she didn't have a choice. Then suddenly, she stopped pacing and went back to the window. She looked down, and then, as she was shaking, she climbed on the ledge. As she's standing on the ledge of the

window, she looks up to the sky and says, "Forgive me,"
then she jumps.

When I woke up, I was shaken by what just happened, and I was still feeling what she felt. Then it dawned on me —

"My recurring dream!" It was the one I had when I was a child. Every morning I would wake up after falling from a cliff, and right before hitting the rocks below. I thought, *how could this be?* As I was shaking my head, rubbing my hands over my face, trying to understand what happened. Then I thought, *oh my gosh, it wasn't a cliff, but a window.* I was stunned and wondered, *why was this happening to me, and why now? Could this be? Is it possible, this woman in my dream was me?* So many questions, with no answers.

These dreams I was having changed from flashes of bits and pieces to full detailed dreams. Not just of the past, but of the now. These dreams began to feel as if someone was trying to tell me something. What? I didn't know. You know when you have a dream, and most of the time you remember a small part of that dream, and you're lucky when you remember a dream in complete detail. But, although there is memory, you feel detached. In my dreams, there was no detachment. I felt everything as if they were still a part of me. It felt more like memories than a dream.

Although I suffered a few minor asthma attacks after returning from England, until one day while I was at work, I had my first full-blown attack.

My co-workers and supervisor heard me coughing, with that rough asthmatic cough, and my supervisor asked, "Rebecca, are you alright?"

I didn't want to make a big stink about it, so I said, "I should be fine. This happens. I will take my inhaler and in a few minutes I'll be fine."

Well, that ended up being wishful thinking. After taking my inhaler, unfortunately it didn't help.

So, my supervisor asked again, "Rebecca, do you want me to call the ambulance?"

God no! For what? For there to be a big scene, I thought, and then said, "No, give me a few more minutes. Sometimes it just takes a little longer."

Well, let's just say, that was a no go. I was not fine, and it didn't seem to get better, no matter what I did. It only continued to worsen, to the point I could no longer control the coughing. There was no doubt that I was having a full-blown asthmatic attack.

With concern in her voice, my supervisor again asked, "Rebecca, are you sure you don't want me to call an ambulance?"

At this, I knew there was no choice; I had to cave in. "Yes," coughing, "Okay," more coughing, "Fine. Call them." Now, I was completely out of control.

A few minutes later my supervisor returned and said, "They are on their way." By this time, I was coughing so bad I just nodded in understanding.

When the ambulance arrived, along with the EMTs from the fire department, to my relief, they entered through the doors that were located at the west side of the building and right behind where my desk was. So, there wasn't the big drama of the EMTs parading through the building for everyone to see. However, it didn't take long for word of mouth to spread, and quickly too.

After arriving at the hospital, I was given a breathing treatment and shortly after my breathing regulated, and I was released to go home. Unfortunately for me, this attack was the beginning of many more to come. There would be one here, one there, but not enough for me to be concerned with. However, it was also when the dreams became more consistent.

One day after leaving work from an asthma attack – feeling exhausted, I laid down to take a nap, and this is what I dreamed of:

I am in a small building, that seems to be a shop or a store. Again, I feel as if I am there, but only as an observer, invisible to everyone. Then I see a man – he's the same man from my dream I had the other night. He's leaning against a counter with his left arm resting on top, as he's talking to the woman standing behind the counter. He's wearing a dark red short sleeve polo shirt, with the first two buttons undone. His hair is loose and wavy, as he looked the night before. I pull my eyes from him, so I can look around the shop to figure out where I am. I feel there is something familiar about this place, but I don't know what. I turn back to look at the man, and as I am watching him, there's a feeling of familiarity, as if I know him, but how? I thought. I look around the small room again, trying to figure out where he and I are, and what this place is. Where am I? Then it hit me, it can't be, it appears to be the building...the place where you purchase a ticket to tour Dunham Massey Castle. Yes, that's it! He's there to purchase a ticket. But wait, how can I be sure? Looking around, I can't, but I feel I am correct. And I realize – I am standing somewhere off to the side, in a corner near the entrance. It feels as if I am actually there, but how can that be, as I know I'm not. This man captivates me, and I am unable to take my eyes off him. What is it? There is something, but I don't know what. There's just something so familiar about him. As I am watching him, a burst of energy seems to go from him to me, piercing deep into my heart – my soul. His eyes. His hair. His...body. He is...so handsome. Who is this man, I thought? Then suddenly, as if he feels it too, he turns and looks directly at me, as if he can see me. How is this possible? I thought. He has that look of surprise, as if he's looking at a ghost. It's – well, it's almost as if I can feel what he's feeling. I sense he feels it too – familiarity. There's something else; it's fear. I don't understand, as he too seems to know me. The way he's looking at me, and I wonder, does he know me? With the way he's watching me, it shakes me to my core. It's as if he can see right through me. I don't mean as if he is looking right through a spirit – ghost but is able to see deep into my soul.

When I wake up, I sit up in my bed, feeling so shaken by this dream, trying to understand what happened? *What is happening to me? What does this all mean?* More questions that I have no answers to, that left me lost to what to do? Although I felt lost and confused, I also felt excited, to the point I looked forward to going to sleep, with the anticipation of my next dream, in what it would reveal. It made going to sleep exciting – an adventure, with never knowing what to expect.

Every day I would go to work, but there would be only a few days where I'd be able to get through the day using my inhaler, then there were others, regardless of taking my inhaler, would have no effect, to the point it became useless.

I finally went to see my doctor and he placed me on a regular regiment, using medication along with my inhaler. With everything happening regarding my health, I feared my plans to move to England in October wasn't going to happen. However, I tried not to give up hope, no matter what was happening. I figured, once I made it through the summer months, I would be fine. Who knew how wrong I would be.

I knew once I was in England, I wouldn't have to worry about these asthma attacks. You see, during my time in England, I felt normal – great! I was able to walk everywhere without any issues with my breathing – no shortness of breath or chest pains. It was GREAT! It seemed there wasn't anything I couldn't do. The air – the weather, was so much better than Arizona. I felt free. Alive and healthy.

It's June 14, 2013 – I am on a plane sitting next to the window in a two-row section, when a blond female attendant walked over with a tall dark-haired man wearing a white dress shirt. When I looked up, I saw the attendant pointing to the seat next to mine, but I was not able to see his face as his back was towards me.

When he turned around to the seat he was being directed to, as he was still looking at the papers in his hands, but when he finally looked up and saw me sitting in the seat next to his, our eyes locked. I was amazed – it was him. He too looks surprised, and our eyes stayed locked, with what seem like eternity, when in actuality, it was only a few moments. When I finally turned away to look at the attendant, she was gone, and when I turned back to him, he was still staring at me. I am shocked to see him – this man as I thought, am I seeing what I'm seeing. This man…this is the man from my dreams. To feel what I am feeling, there was no denying it…he's the one I've been waiting for, the one from my dreams.

When words were spoken, he says, "It's you, isn't it?"

I felt stunned to hear these words, and I found I couldn't find my voice to respond. What was I going to say? Without taking my eyes off him, I finally found my voice and said, "Yes…it's you?"

After this, we just stared at each other, being unable to move. We both felt – there was a feeling of disbelief, that this was the way we were to meet.

I cannot say how long I was staring at him, when I finally noticed how handsome he is, more so than I'd recalled from my dreams. He's tall, of about six feet, and his body is beautiful – muscularly built. He has dark brown wavy hair and brown eyes, just as he did in my dreams, and I believe he found me beautiful.

This is when I woke up when my stupid alarm clock went off, it made me want to scream. Talk about bad timing, and I could still feel the intensity of what I was feeling in my dream.

When I was getting ready for work, I found it difficult to focus. My mind kept wandering back to that dream, to the man, and to how real it felt. In the way he looked at me – *was it love?* In the way he stood – tall and confident, along with the way he moved.

Two days later I returned to the dream and picked up right where I left off.

I'm back on the plane, and he's there sitting next to me. It seems I am picking up right where I left off. I feel pure and utter joy that warms my heart, and him, I feel an overwhelming amount of love radiating from him, as he is feeling the same love for me, as I am feeling for him. Finally, after all this time, we finally found each other, but to find each other in such a way – on a plane is baffling.

I rest my head against the back of my seat and close my eyes. Although my eyes are closed, I can feel his eyes on me – watching me, and I can feel what he is feeling, it's an overwhelming and powerful love. It feels as if it's flowing from him to me, of the purest love I have ever known, and I wonder, how can this be? Then I feel him holding my hand, and I open my eyes. Yep, he is definitely watching me. Oh God, the way he's looking at me...it seems as if his eyes...the emotions, seem to pierce deep into my soul. It's like a burst of electricity piercing deep into my heart, causing my body to shiver. I then wonder, how can someone in such a short time feel so much love for another? It's a feeling of complete happiness. I cannot believe I finally found him, this man sitting in front of me. How can he love me as much as I love him after just meeting? But I do. I love this man more than life itself.

He ends up being the one who breaks the silence and says, "You are so beautiful. I love watching you sleep."

At hearing this I thought, with him here by my side, how can one person feel the love and happiness I'm feeling for this man. I then move my head and placed it against his chest. As I do, he wraps his arm around me. He pulls me close and holds me tight against him. It's as if he's afraid of letting me go, because if he does, I will vanish, and once again be lost to him forever.

I understand what he's feeling, as I feel the same. I turn to look at him and stare into his eyes, and after a few moments he lowers his head, brushing his lips against mine, and kisses me with such tenderness. The kiss deepens to a strong passionate and powerful kiss, and I feel the heat of his love pouring into me, with a power I've never felt in my entire life.

There is something that is telling us, 'your bond is strong' and instinctively we know what each other is feeling; of a love so powerful it pierces deep into our souls, merging together to make us one – our souls that were once two, are now one, once again.

When he abruptly stops, I am left stunned and wanting. When he looks at me, he has a large smile on his face, and when we look around, we realize where we are – we are not alone, as we recall we are on a plane surrounded by hundreds of people. But for those few moments when he kissed me, it felt as if we were in our own little world, where only the two of us existed – our own little sanctuary. We both feel a surge of joy, to finally, after all this time, find each other, brings us great joy – happiness. We found our missing link – each other.

I woke up, and I was so angry! I didn't want to wake up and leave such a wonderful, amazing, and beautiful dream, especially after what I was feeling, what I still was feeling, and I wanted desperately to go back – to return to my dream and never leave. It seemed no matter how hard I tried, I could not. It was impossible, and I slammed my fist on my bed, I was outraged and frustrated! I felt it was too cruel to take me away from such a feeling – love, and I wanted to cry.

How could fate bring us together in such a way, to only tear us apart. To wake up from such a powerful dream, I was left – feeling desolate. I was desperate – no, I needed this love. Thinking back to the dream, it felt more as if I was in a semiconscious state, a very powerful daydream. Yes, you heard me correctly; this was a daydream. With this, there was no doubt something definitely was happening to me. I remember thinking, *God, I don't ever want these dreams to end.*

These dreams became a part of me, and I found myself longing for them. To feel what I felt in those dreams when I was with him, I felt I was leaving a part of my soul in those dreams. It was a promise of a possibility, and every day I wonder who this man was?

Chapter 18

At times, when I felt an asthma attack coming on, I'd take my inhaler, attempting to stop the attack before it worsens. Other times, when I felt weak and tired from the lack of oxygen, I would go into the quiet room during my lunch and breaks to lie down. The quiet room is a room set up for mothers who are still breastfeeding, or, in my case, if you are not feeling well, can go in and lie down on the sofa.

By the end of June, I was seeing my doctor on a weekly basis, and once again I was a regular visitor. The regiment I was already on to control my attacks wasn't working, and he tried to talk me into taking steroids again, but this I could not allow.

"If it isn't necessary, I prefer not to take steroids again."

To my relief, for the time being, he agreed but was very clear, "If the attacks continue to persist, I will have no choice but to put you on steroids."

By this time, in such a short time, so much was happening, and I needed to know – to find out exactly what that was, but I didn't know who or where I could turn to for answers. I became desperate, and wondered who I could talk to, and since there was no one I could think of that wouldn't think I was crazy, I decided to turn to the internet. You can find anything on the internet, right? Yes, there was a great deal on past life memories, dream interpretation, and reincarnation, but nothing I could find to explain what was happening to me. Was it that uncommon? If it wasn't, they were unknown. I began to wonder, was I a rarity? I was lost. Confused. Sad. So sad. I needed answers, and I had none. Was this man real, or was I making him up in my desperation to find love? My heart hurt. My soul hurt. My physical being was deteriorating. I was losing myself in these dreams and becoming severely depressed.

Then one day I came across a site about communicating with your spirit guides using a crystal pendulum. A pendulum can be anything really: a necklace, a simple chain, or you can buy one as I did. There are all sorts of designs; some shaped like a cone, a ball, a square – it really doesn't matter what shape it is, as long as the chain is long enough to allow it to swing.

The way it works, it uses your energy. As you know, every one of us produces energy, and if you can tap into that energy, you can communicate with spirits, or what they call your guides. For those of you who remember the Ouija Board, you use the pendulum in a similar fashion. What I learned, if you are going to use anything, is to use a crystal, since crystals hold energy – giving them power. However, it cannot always ensure communication. This is dependent on each person's energy. They can be ordered online, but it's best to hold the crystal in your hand so you will pick the best one, allowing it to tune to your energy. The one that vibrates the strongest is the one for you. If you are unable to find a store that sells one, and you have no choice but to order one online, then the one that resonates the strongest with you is the one you should buy. However, I wasn't so knowledgeable at the time.

After my research, I didn't want to wait, so after I found a mythical store, I hopped in my car and drove directly there. Once I arrived, I was amazed on how large the store was, with a large assortment of Spiritual and Wicca items. After browsing the store, I made my way to the counter where they kept the pendulums behind a glass case. With so many, I decided to ask the salesclerk for assistance.

"Excuse me," I said.

"Yes, how may I help you?"

"I am interested in buying a pendulum, but how do I pick the right one?"

She said, "To pick the right one is how the crystal feels when you hold it in your hand. Allow it to speak to you."

Speak to me. Really? I thought. So, I asked, "How do I know if it's speaking to me?"

She said, "You will know. Sometimes it will vibrate in your hand or start to warm, and this is how you know."

Well, I tried a few, and went with the one that felt right. I also bought a couple of white candles. Why, I don't know, but it felt right. Without delay, I took my items and went straight home. I had to see if this would really work and allow me to contact my spirit guides?

After I arrived home, I grabbed my laptop and went back to the internet, so I could learn how to use it. I know, I know, I should have asked the clerk at the store or looked for a book, but I didn't even think of it until after I arrived home, and come on, Google has everything. From what I learned, each person is different, and it may not work on my first try. However, to my lucky surprise, it did. It started swinging before I even started asking questions, as if it was ready and waiting – anxious to communicate with me, as I with it.

The internet said to test your pendulum by asking it simple questions, ones I already know the answer to. So, I asked aloud, "Which direction is yes?" Without delay, it swung forward and backward. Excited, I asked, "Which direction is no?" It swung left to right. I said, "Stop." I said this because I wanted to see if it would do so on command. Guess what? Yep, it stopped swinging and stood still.

At this point, I felt ready and began asking my questions.

"Am I in my bedroom?" It swung left to right, indicating no. *Hum…okay, that was good.* I continued with my test questions. "Do I have one or two daughters?" When I asked this question, I realized it wasn't a yes or no question, but before I could correct myself, it moved – swinging in a forward motion, as if it wanted me to move, so I did. I went to the coffee table in the living room, a short distance from the chair I was sitting on. On the table was an assortment of magazines. The pendulum stopped over the magazines, so I stopped. Then it started circling one of the magazines, and I felt the need to lower it, so I did. When I did, it narrowed on a number on the magazine. It was the number two. First, it circled over the number two before it stopped directly over it. My mouth dropped open. I couldn't believe it. It gave me my answer on its own. Well, that convinced me it really worked, better than I could possibly imagine. After this, I knew it was time to ask the real questions. The ones I've been seeking the answers to.

"Are there reasons behind the dreams and visions I've been having?" It swung forward and backward, indicating yes. "This man I'm dreaming about…is this a man I'm destined to be with?" It said yes.

At this, I felt stunned, and I had to stop, and for a few moments I held the pendulum in my hand. I didn't know what to think. My whole life, I have longed for such a love, a love so strong that no matter what, our love will endure. A man who will love me for me! For who I am inside, not for who I am on the outside. As we all know, the outside fades, but the inside doesn't. When I was ready, I continued with my questions.

"Are some of the dreams I'm having, are they from a different time?" It swung yes. "Are they a past life memory?" Yes. "My past life?" It said yes again. If you could feel the emotions swirling around inside of me, it would have knocked you off your feet. I was excited, happy, scared, shocked – there were so many feelings that it's hard to list them all.

After these first few questions and what happened with the number two, I decided to see if I can find a diagram to use with the pendulum, just like having a Ouija Board. There was no surprise to find the internet had a great deal of them. I chose the simplest one and printed it out. It was an A through Z, with the numbers zero through nine, with a yes and no. I tried to ask questions about the man, but it wouldn't answer.

After these first series of questions, I thought it was enough for the day, so I stopped. It would be several days later when I decided to use the pendulum again and ask questions regarding my past life. Although I'm Catholic, I wasn't always. My father is from India, and with the Hindu religion, they believe in reincarnation. This is the religion I grew up with. So, why am I Catholic? Well, that is a very good question. At the time, it was hard to say. I guess part of it was that Sara and Tiffany's father family is Catholic, and my mother was baptized Catholic. But I have to say, I think a part of why I did it was because every time I drove past our local Catholic Church, there was a feeling, a pulling, as if I needed to go into that church and become Catholic. It was as if someone or something was calling to me. When Sara and Tiffany were born, we didn't have them baptized, but when this happened, I thought, *maybe now is the time*. It was early 2000, and Sara and Tiffany were spending their summer with their grandmother Stella. I called Stella and asked if she'd be willing to talk to her priest and see if he would be willing to baptize the girls while they were there. She was more than happy to agree, and so the girls were baptized.

While the girls were going through their baptism, I decided to reach out to that Catholic Church and ask if I could become Catholic? They of course said yes. So, I also began my process, although mine took a great deal longer, and during Passover, I was baptized – purified. Now I am Catholic, as my daughters are.

Back to my questions on my past life, I first asked about my first life born on earth. Then from that one to my next, and so on. I have to say, the answers I received were interesting. However, there was no truthful way to verify. The one that captured my attention and shocked me the most, was the life from the 1500s. To the best I can say, they gave me a great deal of information. It was more than just dates but of names and places. A life I lived from the early 1500s to the mid-1500s, and this is what I learned: *I found a great love, but it was ripped from me. There was a king who wanted me, and he took me against my will, then I took my own life by jumping to my death.* At hearing this, I abruptly stopped, I couldn't believe what it was saying. I felt butterflies in my stomach as chills went down my body. The hairs on my arms were standing up. My dreams – the recent one, and the ones I had when I was about ten. At the time, I didn't know what to make of this, but now it made sense. Then I realized, *I have a time period. There was no more guessing; it was the* 1500s.

After taking time to process this information, I returned to the pendulum and dowsing chart and began asking questions about the man from my dreams. The one from this time – century.

"The man I've been dreaming about…who is he?" It was a slow process, as I had to write down each letter they went to, but this is what I learned: *he is the man from your past life, from the fifteen hundred's. He was your husband, your love from that time.*

I asked, "What is his name?" They spelled out Marco. *A name.* This is the second time they gave me this name. Then I asked, "Where does he live?" They spelled out Europe. *Of course,* I thought. My next question was, "Where in Europe?" Now, this answer blew me away – *in the place you visited recently.* I said, "WHAT!" At this, I was in utter shock. I didn't know what to think. This was the place I was planning on moving to.

I began to wonder what in God's name was happening. And I started questioning if this was real? I couldn't believe it. I had to know more. So, I continued with my questions.

"What else can you tell me about this man, Marco?" They said, *he has his own business. His family has money.* My mouth literally dropped open, and then I started to feel a tremendous amount of fear. I felt that I didn't deserve this man. Money, money has always scared me. I didn't know why, but it did. I had always considered myself a down-to-earth and simple woman. I didn't need much, nor do I now. I only required a simple house, car, and basic financial security. That was all that mattered to me. I was afraid to have too much money. Why? I didn't know. It's hard to say. Wealth puts you in a different category, a class of high society, of someone I am not. I needed to know more. So, I continued my questions.

Unfortunately, they wouldn't give me any further information about Marco, but it didn't keep me from trying. I needed to know, and this need turned to an obsession. There wasn't a day I didn't use the pendulum, and sometimes it was more than once a day.

When I think back to this time, it seemed that my asthma attacks increased, to the point I couldn't go a day without suffering an attack. What was interesting about this, most of my attacks happened at work. Then, once I left work and was at home, I seemed to be fine. I was breathing normally, and the coughing stopped. I remember thinking, *hum, if I'm fine at home, then something at work is affecting me. Something I don't recognize.* I figured since I was home, I might as well lay down and take a nap. When I did, I dreamed of this man.

I am walking down the main hall at work, heading to the bathroom, when I see a man with a group of executives. One of the men is a tall dark-haired man. It's him, I thought. When he notices me, he is as surprised as I am. I start to wonder, is this real or a dream? He can see me, as I can clearly see him. Then I thought, maybe this isn't a dream. When we passed each other in the hall, at the same time, we both turned back to look at each other. I realize then; it had to be him, and thought, yes, it's him, and he looks as if he's asking…thinking the same thing, yes, it's her.

Suddenly, he stops and asks, "What is your name? And what do you do for the company? If you don't mind me asking?"

I am ecstatic that he stopped to talk to me. I am nervous, but manage to say, "My name is Rebecca, and I work as a booking agent and flight specialist."

As we are talking, I feel – no, I know we both feel the same, a sense of familiarity. How did I know? I just did. It was a feeling in my heart – our hearts.

We both knew each other, but how? There was a look between us, and we just knew – I am the one he's been dreaming of, as he is the one I've been dreaming of. There was no doubt, somehow, we knew how we'd feel when we found each other. This, from what we felt in our dreams. It's a feeling in our chest – a pulling, a connection so deep; it was as if the hole that once existed in our hearts and souls, were now healed – whole once again. Of a piece we were unaware was missing. There was an energy of the purest love – God's love. Not just God's love, our love. A love that was ripped from us, leaving a hole we didn't know existed, until our hearts recognize one another, reuniting – a mergence of two hearts and souls, one, once again. A hole now filled with our love, along with our memories from a time past.

Then to my wonderful surprise, he asked me, "May I take you to dinner tonight?"

I was shocked, and I couldn't believe this was really happening. I, of course said, "Yes." I was feeling excited, scared, and nervous. I thought, is this really happening? Is this real? He is the man...the man from my dreams. This I had no doubt of. He has an accent, possibly European, but unlike anything I've heard before. However, I haven't heard every accent out there.

I woke up and wondered, is this a sign of what's to come? Or again, what I wish for? But I was feeling so very happy and excited, with a new-found hope of what's to come.

With this dream, in what was happening between us, it felt magical – miraculous, a blessing from God. *Can this be? And why me? Why now?* I thought. This, I cannot say. I felt God had a part in this. How? I didn't know, I just knew it to be true. With what's happening, how can I deny it, and I needed to find out, but how?

There were other times when I was sitting in the living room watching television when an overwhelming feeling would come over me, followed by a vision. I wasn't sure what to make of it. At first, I would brush them off as nothing more than daydreams. But there was a feeling deep inside, telling me they were so much more. I did try to find some kind of obvious explanation, but as they continued, it became harder and harder to disregard them as only daydreams. There was no doubt they were something more, but what? That was the question, that I had no answers to. Nor did I know anyone who could provide me with these answers. I was completely on my own.

One morning I woke up having difficulty breathing, so instead of taking the chance in going to work, I decided to stay home. While I was sitting in the living room watching television, I had a vision, with a need to draw what I saw. I quickly grabbed my pad and pencil and started drawing. I drew a lake surrounded by a vast number of trees. At first, I thought I was drawing the lake I'd envision from the book Lady of the Rivers. It wasn't as easy as drawing the trees and a forest, and I felt it had to be just right. Once I finished, it was perfect.

After I completed this image, I had a vision of another lake, and I drew this as well. It was also surrounded by a vast number of trees. Then a pond, and finally, a single tree. Geez, how many was I going to draw in one day. Well, it turned out there would be days I'd draw multiple pictures, and to my surprise, they all turned out great, just as I saw them in my mind. However, the tree, although it turned out the way I saw it, it was very difficult. I felt it had to be just right – perfect. You see, I had to draw each leaf in great detail, which took a great deal of time. And yes, it turned out just as I wanted it to.

These images, along with the need to draw were non-stop. Whether I saw the image in a dream or in a vision, I had to draw them no matter what I was doing. It felt like an obsession, as if they were too important to ignore.

One night when I was in my bedroom watching a show on Netflix, an image of the man I connected with popped into my mind, along with the compulsion to draw the image. So, I picked up my pad and pencil and started drawing. I remember my first attempts – well, let's just say I didn't do so well. Drawing trees and landscapes was a piece of cake compared to drawing an actual person. But no matter what, I felt the need – it had to be just right. It just had to be perfect. Well, it wasn't perfect, but it was better than I thought it would be.

I tried so hard to get the face right, but the nose and lips proved to be very difficult. His face turned out – well, hum, how can I say this – well, the best way I can explain it to you, to give you an idea, an image, is you know that movie, The Elephant Man with Cher, well – I know, horrible.

It seemed no matter how hard I tried to avoid drawing, I could not, as if I was not allowed to. That someone or something was pushing me. So, no matter how difficult or horrible it was, I had to complete the drawing. Yes, it was that important.

Chapter 19

Since that dream, I continued dreaming about us having a life together, and I began to wonder if these were premonitions, or again, a fantasy I've created. What type of dream? Allow me to share it with you.

I'm in a large dark house. It's dark because the wood inside is a dark cherry wood. It feels as if it's early morning, as the sun is not out yet, which explains why the house is so dark. I'm in a large kitchen, standing in front of a large stainless-steel stove. To the right of the stove is a large stainless-steel refrigerator, and it appears I am making pancakes. Then Marco walks in and sits at the island to the left of the stove. He's wearing a white t-shirt and is drinking coffee, and he looks as if he just woke up, as his hair is disheveled. I feel that this is his home – no, our home in Europe. Where and when, I don't know.

Then he asks, "Will you make me blueberry pancakes?"

I said, "Yes, of course I will."

Then he stands and walks over to stand behind me. He puts his arms around my waist, just as I was pouring the flour to make his blueberry pancakes. As I am pouring the blueberry mix in the pan, he leans down and starts kissing the back of my neck.

I raise my shoulders to shove him off, as I say, "You know, I love it when you do that, but not when I'm cooking. I'm likely to burn something." I smile, loving every minute of it, but say, "It's very difficult to concentrate with you kissing my neck."

He smiles and steps back as he says, "Okay-okay." Then he walks back and sets at the island and says, "I just cannot resist touching you."

I am still smiling. I love how affectionate he is towards me. Then I ask, "May I please have some money to send to my daughters?"

He says, "Rebecca, you don't need to ask me permission for money. If you need it, just take what you need. You know I trust you with everything I have."

I know what he says is true, but for me, it still didn't feel right. So, I say, "I know, but I feel I need to ask you before touching your money. All of this," waving my hand with the spatula to encompass the whole of the house, "Since I don't feel comfortable with it yet, as I'm still trying to get used to all of this. I know you trust me. It's…just so new to me. I promise one day I will get used to all of this. I just don't want you to think I'm with you because of your money."

He smiles and says, "You know I trust you. I know you are not with me because of my money. You are with me because you love me. I love how you are so concern about such small things. I have no fear, not with you, not ever. So please, do what you need, and if you feel you need to tell me first, then do so. I love you. You own my heart and soul."

To hear this warms my heart, and I say, "Thank you for understanding. I love you so very much, Marco."

He makes me feel so blessed to be in a relationship with him, in having complete trust and honesty between each other.

At this, I woke up. This dream, along with the others, they all felt so real, and I wonder how can I possibly deny what is happening?

Well, my asthma attacks continued to be a thorn in my side. There were days where they seemed to finally subside, allowing me to work and feel normal, until out of the blue, boom, and I'd suffer another attack. What was irritating about this, it seemed there wasn't anything I could do about it. I didn't believe there was anything around me to cause me to suffer such attacks, in what normally attributed to my attacks: stress, certain chemical smells, smoke, anxiety, along with feeling upset or angry. At the time these attacks hit me, I didn't feel any of these. There was no warning! And this aggravated me more than you know, which of course, did not help.

These asthma attacks became a weekly event, as did calling the ambulance, to the point I became well known – if there was an ambulance, you'd hear someone say, "Oh God, it's Rebecca. She's having another attack." However, it wasn't for me every time the ambulance was called. It was so bad though, that it became a running joke around the office. It was only when they noticed I was still sitting at my desk that it wasn't for me.

Jill would say, "Oh Rebecca, I saw the ambulance and thought, oh God, she had another attack.

I would look at her and say, "As you can see, I am fine. Geez…every time you see the ambulance, are you going to always think it's for me?"

"Well…yes, as most of the time it is," Jill said, then laughed, as did I.

"Oh great, what a reputation to have," I said, and we both laughed again.

This became an ongoing joke around the office until my situation turned serious. I continued going to my weekly doctor's appointment, and with the increase in attacks and with no sign of relief, my doctor decided it was time to put me on steroids. *NO!* Although I protested, it was unavoidable. The time had come.

He said, "It will be for only a week, so it shouldn't cause any major side effects."

The side effects would be weight gain if I was on them for a long period of time. Reluctantly, I agreed.

For a time, I did improve a great deal. Unfortunately, it was short-lived. A month after I stopped taking the steroids, the attacks started up again. But most of the time, I was at work when they hit me, and usually, it was when I was on the phone talking to a customer. When this happened, it was difficult to do my job. Since it is difficult to talk when I'm trying to control my breathing.

With the multitude of asthma attacks happening at work, I was forced to leave work and go home for the remainder of the day, and at times, it was the whole day. Since I practically used all my PTO (personal time off) when I went to England, I wasn't getting paid for the time I wasn't working. At the time, it didn't matter; since I was to move to England in October, there was no need for PTO. But when these attacks happened and I was forced to leave work, I was left with no choice, I had to dip into my savings, the money I needed to live in England for six months to a year. With all this, I began to fear it was not going to happen.

With everything that was happening, I was still using the pendulum to communicate with my guides. But for me, in my desperation, it wasn't enough. I remember reading in the book Lady of the Rivers about the practice of witchcraft, and for some reason, the idea intrigued me. So yes, I started dabbling in witchcraft – spells particularly. Nothing serious really: an abundance spell to assist me in getting more money, a wish spell, a spell to improve my health, and a spell to increase my abilities, and finally, a spell I hoped would help me find Marco. Either on or before my birthday, which was at the end of October. With this, I was still having dreams and visions, along with the need to draw them.

One day when I was home alone, as I was lying on my bed staring up at the ceiling, I started talking aloud to my guides. I figured why not? If it worked with the pendulum, why wouldn't it work without?

So, I asked, "When will I see this man, Marco, the one I've been dreaming about?" Now, I wasn't sure how I'd get the answer, and just when I believed it wasn't going to work, I heard these words in my mind. *He will come when the time is right and not before.*

When I heard this voice, at first, I wondered if it was me? Because it sounded like me, but it was hard to say. However, I thought, r*eally? Bloody hell. Well, that didn't tell me a whole lot, did it?*

Then, without me asking further, the voice went on to say, *there is a great deal of money on its way.*

Well, hell, I'll take that. This was great news. If true, then I just might have what I need to move to England, and in turn, allow my dreams to come true.

In my excitement, I heard, *now is the time for you to receive all you've wished for.* And I thought, *wow!* Then they said, *to have faith and believe. To have no doubts. No negative thinking. To only think positive. Believe in it, and it shall be.*

Wow! Now I know this was not me. These were not my thoughts.

This compulsion to draw, started to feel as if someone was nagging at me, pushing me, and refused to stop until I picked up my pad and pencil and drew the image I was receiving.

I remember one time when I attempted to draw without receiving what I believed to be inspiration – this was to know if I really could draw or if I was only able to draw when *they* wanted me to. And you know what I learned; it was not me. I only had the talent when I received inspiration to draw. I call it inspiration because I didn't know what else to call it.

Whoever or whatever it was, was giving me the image to draw. I remember a time when a strong sensation came over me, with the need to draw. When I put the pencil on the pad, my hand started moving – drawing on its own accord. I didn't feel as if I was doing the drawing, instead, it was someone else controlling my hands and arms, as if using my hand as its instrument, guiding me to draw what it wanted me to draw.

There were also times I received inspiration to draw without first being given an image in my mind. I wouldn't know what it would be until the image started to form on the paper. My hand and pencil moved fast, with no hesitation, and in minutes, it turned out to be a man. Once the outline of the image was there, then, and only then, did I receive the complete image in my mind, thus allowing me to complete the drawing on my own.

In time, I ended up drawing four images of who I believe to be Marco, then later learned the first drawing was Marco when he was in his early twenties, which is how he looked the night I did the ritual. The next was when he was in his thirties and finally in his forties. All the drawings were similar, but one. This was the third drawing, which was a great deal different. The fourth drawing was of a man in his forties, wearing a blue dress shirt with a blue and gray striped tie. His hair was short and professional-looking, with a bit of gray. I wondered what purpose it served to have these drawings, and ignoring them was not an option.

These drawings became constant – a daily thing. Although a few were of him – Marco, most were of lakes and trees. One was a church, and another was a cluster of clay buildings with an outdoor marketplace. I drew a standalone house surrounded by green fields, and yes, even a white picket fence wrapped around a small part of the house. The roof was made of clay and hay. It felt as if an unknown source was forcing my hand, wanting me to know and see, with a need for me to understand. What exactly, I did not know – not yet.

Whatever was happening to me, within a short time intensified. The dreaming and visions became nightly, even daily. It didn't matter if I was working or not. It didn't matter what I was doing, it would hit me. I did wonder why this was suddenly happening, and why now? I had no answers. What I did feel, there was something I needed to know, to understand, and this was *their* way of letting me know. Also, I felt it wasn't just happening to me, but to Marco as well. These past life dreams and the dreams of us now, were a way for them to connect us – to know each other.

You know what the scariest thing was, with everything happening, was how my feelings for him grew at a rapid rate. I say this because I wasn't just an observer in the dream and visions; I was also feeling what was happening, especially the dreams of the past. I remember wondering how this was possible. More questions I would not have answers to, not until a great deal later.

It's the morning of June 26, 2013 – *I am in a courthouse. Apparently, I am there to perform jury duty. However, now the courthouse is a place of study, where you learn to*

become a chef. Once I complete the program, I may choose where I would like to work anywhere in the world. Tiffany, my daughter was there, and she seemed to be very concerned for me. She doesn't want me to do this – to leave.

What I get from this, a feeling that she is trying to hold me back, not wanting me to leave and live out a lifetime dream. Next, I am in Italy thinking of this man I was to meet – Marco. I'm wondering where he was and when I might find him. Suddenly, there was an Italian man standing in the restaurant wearing a white t-shirt, blue jeans, and was wearing an apron, and he was sweeping the floors. He was a tall and handsome man. I knew this, even though I couldn't see his face.

Then there was an older man, also Italian, and he was the owner and chef of the restaurant. When he walked through the front entrance, he came directly to me. He has a balding hairline and is shorter than the handsome man. After introducing himself to me, apparently, he noticed me watching the handsome man, then guided me over to introduce the young man to me as his son.

I woke up. I felt this dream was a message, that the man I am looking for is Italian, possibly from Italy.

<u>Verona, Italy</u>

Marco is in Italy to see his grandmother. After what happened – after what he saw when he looked out his kitchen window, and again when he was at Dunham Massey Castle's shop to purchase a tour ticket to tour the castle, while talking to the woman behind the counter, asking her questions about the history of the place, when he turned and saw her – Rebecca. Both times she looked as if she was a ghost, a spirit, and he wondered, *is she dead?* For some reason, this question scared him in a way he couldn't explain.

If she is the one, and he believes she is. But, if she's dead, it's over. If this were true, he knew he would never have the love his grandmother had always told him about. He had to know if what he saw and believed to be true, was. He knew, no matter what he believes, his grandmother would know the truth. For she knew things, this he could not deny, that proved to be true.

In the two days Marco spent with his grandmother, with what he learned, he still felt lost. He has no understanding. How could he. For Marco, this was too bizarre, and beyond his comprehension. *A soul connection? A reincarnation...gifts?* he thought, in remembering what his grandmother told him. These gifts his grandmother told him about, he apparently has. *How is that possible?*

He asked his grandmother, "Nõnna, I am Catholic, and so are you. How can you believe in such a thing when our faith does not?"

"Marco, we cannot control the faith we are born into. Yes, we are Catholic, and Catholics do not believe in such things as psychic abilities, but when I learned I had these gifts, I too, was confused and afraid. I felt something bad was happening to me; that evil was at hand. I couldn't go to my mother and father and tell them what was happening, because if I did, they would have sent me to our priest, believing the devil had hold of me. As I grew, so did my knowledge and my abilities. At first, I went to our library to try to find information that would help me. Here too, I had to be careful. I had to make sure no matter what I was doing would go unnoticed. It could not get back to my family. It was hard, too difficult at times. Then, one day I came across a gypsy – she recognized something in me. As I was coming out the library's front doors, she pulled me aside and asked me to follow her back to her home. She said it was important that she speak to me. I hesitated at first, but then a voice in my mind said, *go, Maria, she has the answers you seek. She is safe.* So, I went. I followed her to an open clearing, far from anyone and away from prying eyes. There was a silver trailer I followed her into. It wasn't much, as it was very small. It had a bed, an area to sit, and a small window. She pointed to the bench near the window and asked me to sit. Once I took the seat on the bench, she sat on the bed across from me.

The gypsy reached over and took Maria's hands, then turned her palms up and said, "I want to look at the lines in your hands," she asked, and Maria nodded yes. "They tell many stories. It shows you are a wise woman…well, you will be. Very wise and very powerful. You have gifts beyond what you could possibly imagine.

You feel you've wronged someone, and you've waited a long time for this life you chose to be born into. There is a need to make right the wrong you did." The woman looked up, "You are aware of your gifts, aren't you?" The gypsy said as she looked directly into Maria's eyes.

Maria nodded yes, as she said in a quiet whisper, "Yes."

The gypsy returns her eyes to Maria's hands. "You have nothing to fear. Your gifts are from God. They are the ones you've asked for, to allow you to do what you feel you need to do. You are only in the beginning of your power. In time, it will grow, and you will become a very powerful psychic and a wise woman."

At this, Maria asked a question, "What did I do? Can you see that?" Maria asked as she kept glancing from her hands to the woman.

Without looking at Maria, the gypsy said, "You hurt someone in a past life. In this life, you will have a chance to make right the wrong you felt you did then. God is with you. Don't fear this. This is a gift, a gift from God." At this, the gypsy looked up at Maria again. "If you like, I can help you. Come to me every week, and I will help you understand your gifts. Help you to focus, to meditate, and speak to your guides, who are of God. With this, you can succeed in your quest, to right the wrong you feel you did."

Stunned, Maria is unsure what to make of this. "I don't know…my family?" Maria was engulfed with fear at this question.

The gypsy, still holding Maria's hands, gave them a gentle squeeze, "Child, do not worry about your family. They do not need to know. Can you manage to come to me, this day, every week?" The gypsy asked but still noticed the hesitation on Maria's face. So, the gypsy asked, "Do you want to know and understand your gifts?"

Maria bites her bottom lip, looking down at her hands, wondering what to do. Then slowly and quietly says, "Yes, I will. I need to do this. I must do this. I have no one else to talk to. Can you help me? Tell me…tell me of this past life, of this wrong you say I did?" she asked with hope in her voice.

The gypsy smiled, "Yes, and a great deal more. You are to become a powerful psychic, a gifted woman, beyond many out there. You will have a nipõte, who is one of those you feel you wronged in that life. But, not now, not yet. There is much to do before we go there. Come back to me next week, on this day, at this time. Yes?"

Maria said, "Yes…oh, will this cost me anything? How much? I don't have much money." Although Maria's family is one of the wealthiest families in the village, they do not allow her to carry much money on her, only what she needs for school.

"Oh, child. What I do for you. What I will give you will give me a great reward. I am not going to charge you. What I do, is a gift from me to you."

Maria hugs the gypsy and says, "Thank you! Thank you so much!" Then, she realized she never asked the gypsy her name. "Wait, what is your name?"

"You may call me, Bell."

"Thank you, Bell. I will be back next week, today." Maria left the gypsy with a feeling of hope. Relieved to know she will finally understand what's been happening to her. Just to know she is not going mad is a relief. A great weight off her shoulders she didn't realize she'd been carrying.

Maria smiles at the memory. Who knew, years later when she was a woman with her own family, her mother told her she was glad she did not end up with the curse – gift their family had through the centuries. Maria was shocked, then explained to her mother what happen when she was a girl, and her mother told her of the history of their family's ability – gifts

"Marco, it was frightening to be…to live in a strong Catholic family…it was very difficult. She helped me Marco, as I am trying to help you. If you can open your heart and soul…not only your heart and soul but your mind as well. I can help you understand. Can you do this?"

Marco doesn't know what to think. His grandmother has been his rock, the one who's been there for him more than his own mother. She's never lied to him, nor has she made up stories. She's always been straightforward, telling him the complete truth. This, he knows. But what his grandmother asks of him, how can he see and feel – believe in what she says, and yet, *how can I not.*

"Alright, nõnna, I will try. I cannot promise, but I am willing to try."

Maria gives Marco a hug, "I am so pleased. Thank you, Marco. Shall we begin?" Marco nods yes. "First, you must sit and relax your entire mind and body. This is called meditation. Once you reached that meditative state with your mind and body relaxed, it will open your mind, allowing you to hear your guides. They are there to help you. What they speak is of God."

"Nõnna, do you remember…after that night in London, what I did, and what I did shortly after when I couldn't sleep? When I was so worried and feeling ashamed for what I did, by blowing my chance to meet her…Rebecca. Back home in my small cottage, unable to sleep, I decided to go outside and stand out in the early morning cold," he said, as his mind wanders back to that night.

It was a beautiful night, not a cloud was in the sky, and the moon and stars were shining bright, brighter than Marco has ever seen before. The moon was so large that it appeared low in the sky, so low it was if, if you reached your hand out, you can touch it.

As Marco stared into the moon and stars around, he tried to see beyond, needing to seek the heavens above, in his search – in his need to find God – to speak to God.

At this, Marco returned to the present and said, "I needed to speak to God, to find a way to make right the wrong I did. I wanted him to help me…to give me another chance. When nothing happened, I figured God refused to answer my prayer. No matter how much I pleaded with him, expressing my feelings, I felt since he didn't answer my prayer, it was decided that he found me undeserving of this love you told me about," Marco said with shame and sadness in his voice. He lowers his head, unable to look at his grandmother. "Because of my mistake, but maybe," he raised his head, with hope in his eyes, "It wasn't the right time. Maybe now is the time." *Now I sound mad. This is maddening.* Feeling frustrated, "Oh, I don't know nõnna. Maybe I'm just trying to justify what happened."

Maria could feel Marco's anguish and pain. He doesn't understand, nor does he believe in what she's told him. This, she cannot blame him for. For Marco, only proof will do.

"Marco, there are times we pray to God, and he does not answer our prayers. These reasons…God may not answer your prayer, either because he feels what you are asking for is not in your best interest, or maybe it's not the right time. When the time is right, this is when he will answer your prayer. But now, Marco, he must feel now is the right time to answer your prayer. This is good, very good news Marco. Speak to him, he will answer you. If you like, I will help you speak to God by speaking with your guides," she said, then had a thought, *dare I...* "Marco, there is another thing I can teach you, help you do if you would be interested?"

Marco listened to what his grandmother said, in a way, it made sense. *It can't hurt to try.* "What could that be?"

"I…well…I can help you…astral project. Do you know what that means?" Maria asked, shaking her head. *No, of course he doesn't.* "No, you probably don't."

Marco, of course has no idea but says nothing. He only shrugs his shoulders.

Maria explains, "Well, what astral projection is…you can, your soul can leave your body and travel to where your heart desires."

Marco's eyes widen; *she is truly mad. She cannot mean what she says.* Marco gives his grandmother a questionable eye, "Nõnna, that is not possible."

"Oh Marco, anything is possible. If you are willing, I can help you. You can travel…you can see Rebecca." Maria can see Marco's hesitation, with the questionable look in his eyes. "Marco, research this on that computer of yours, and you will see what I say is true. When you are ready, I will teach you…show you how to travel…to see Rebecca."

"Alright. I will think on it and research this astral projection." He could barely spit out the words. Then said, "If I'm willing, and do this…" *I am mad to even consider this*… "I will let you know," he finally said.

"That is all I can ask for, Marco. Now, are you ready to learn how to meditate?"

Hesitantly, Marcos says, "Y-e-e-s…I guess so."

Chapter 20

<u>Arizona</u>

Never did I have such vivid dreams. Vivid dreams with feelings – feeling of what the people felt in my dream. And ones that lingered for days, years after. As we all know, there are times when we wake from a dream with a sensation, a lingering feeling. Such as a scary dream, when you still feel the fear you felt in the dream – a nightmare.

I would later learn these dreams, where I felt invisible, were me astral projecting. How? I didn't know. From this, I learned if two people have a strong enough connection – a bond, a commitment so powerful, one soul can call to the other, but only if both souls are ready. Did he even know he was calling to me in his need to find me, to see me, in his need to be with me? No, I don't think so.

My asthma attacks were back with vengeance, to the point and without choice, my doctor put me back on steroids, but a thirty-day regiment instead of a week. Needless to say, I was not pleased.

Since I was back on steroids, along with a multitude of other medications I was taking, there came a day while I was at work, I was sitting in my chair with my back towards my desk, when I found myself staring down at the floor, unable to move or talk. I heard a familiar female voice calling to me —

"Rebecca. Rebecca." I wasn't sure who it was.

It seemed no matter how hard I tried; I couldn't move or speak. She finally approached me when I didn't answer her. That's when she realized there was something seriously wrong with me, and Jill yelled out, "We need to call 911!"

At this, my supervisor came over and tried to speak to me, and when I didn't respond, she authorized the other person to call 911.

"Call 911. Rebecca is not responding! Can someone get her daughter Tiffany! She works in the cafeteria!"

By the time my daughter arrived, the EMTs were already there assessing the situation. When my daughter saw me, she became very concerned – worried, as she didn't know what was happening. It scared her to see her mother in the condition I was in. She started crying out of fear of what was happening to me.

One of the EMTs asked, "Can you tell me what is happening?"

I tried to move my lips, but they wouldn't move no matter how hard I tried.

Then I heard someone say, "She can't speak." It turned out to be one of the EMTs. Then they started discussing between themselves what they needed to do. "Let's get her blood pressure and measure her oxygen."

"Can someone tell us what happened?" asked one of the other EMTs.

"We don't know. But she has asthma…she's been suffering from asthma attacks," said Jill.

"Is she having a stroke?" asked the EMT, to the one taking my vital signs.

At this question, I could see my daughter, and there were tears in her eyes. She was so scared of what was happening to me.

I wanted so bad to tell them what was wrong…just say something, so I tried to speak, "I…don't…know…what's wrong…" That was it. That was all I could manage to say at the time. But I refused to give up, and kept trying to force out the words until Finally I could speak. I told them what was happening; in my recent asthma attacks, along with the medication I've been taking.

Not being able to determine what was wrong, they placed me on the gurney and wheeled me out of the building in front of everyone. They put me in the ambulance and took me to the hospital. Once I was at the hospital, they ran a series of tests, but the doctors couldn't find anything wrong with me. They came to the determination; it might have been due to the combination of medication I was taking.

With everything that's been happening and with prior events, I decided to put in my paperwork for FMLA (Family Medical Leave Act), to ensure my job would be secure. It couldn't be more obvious that this became an ongoing problem. With the amount of work lost, there was no doubt I would have lost my job if not for FMLA.

You see, the company is on a point base system: you get one point for each day you miss work. Once you reach seven or more points, you are either suspended and/or terminated. With the multitude of asthma attacks I was having, they caused me to lose a great deal of work. There was no doubt, I would have been terminated. FMLA protected me and saved my job.

After this, I decided I wouldn't go into work if I wasn't feeling well. I didn't want to risk something happening and again have the ambulance called. So, when I was tired of lying in bed, I would spend my time in the living room watching television until I started feeling weak, and then I would go to my room to get some rest. However, I found this to be difficult since my mind was filled with this man. This man whose name I believe is Marco. It seemed as if I could see him, standing right in front of me. Then there was a feeling he's coming to Arizona. How did I know this? Let me try to explain.

It's that feeling you get when you feel afraid, but instead of fear, it's a wonderful feeling, with a tingling sensation, like static electricity going through my body, causing the hairs on my arms and the back of my neck to stand up, giving me a chill from head to toe. With a tightness in my chest, but not a painful one. It feels as if someone has their hand around my heart, caressing and filling it with warmth and love – happiness, that is felt directly in the center of my heart.

Or, you know that feeling when you first fall in love. It's similar but ten times stronger. It's as if I was touched by the hand of God. With his hand cupping my heart, filling it with a surge of his warmth and love. Not only piercing my heart, but it was flowing through my body. In this feeling, you want – no, you need to close your eyes, wanting to savor this wonderful feeling. It's a purity of the greatest love, causing your body to weaken, and lose all control. Your strength being taken from you, as if you are going to collapse – pass out. This is the best and only way for me to explain how I feel when I get these feelings.

One day, while I was at work, I felt that somehow – somehow, Marco had a connection to the company I was working for. What it was, I didn't know. I wondered what it might be, and at the same time, I wanted to know what was happening to me. Was it something I was creating, or was it because it was something I desperately wanted. Something I wanted my whole life, of a wish, a desire, to find that special someone, that special love. I didn't know. I wanted it so much, and desperately wanted it to be real – true. But how could I not help but question the truth of it.

I started thinking, wondering, had something like this ever happened before? In this question, I started searching the internet but found nothing close to what was happening to me. You know, even now, as I write these words, it's mind-blowing on how much and how quickly these things happened, and shortly after my return from Cheshire, England. At the time, I didn't put too much thought into it, but now, how could I not. The hardest thing was, there was no one I trusted enough to talk to about this, in what was happening to me. I felt lost and confused. There were so many times I wanted to cry, hoping once I was done, everything would be alright, and I would go back to normal. However, this never happened. Normal? How did I know my life from this would never be normal again?

I was alone, forced to endure this on my own. However, now, all these years later, in what happened, in what I experienced then, was truly miraculous.

With the increase in asthma attacks at work, I began staying home more and more, to a point it would be the entire week. When I returned to work, it would only last a few hours before I ended up suffering an attack and was forced to leave work. These asthma attacks were kicking my ass, and I was at a loss of what to do. It seemed no matter what I did; nothing was working. My doctor tried so many different things, from changing my medication to placing me on a breathing treatment, along with a thirty-day steroid regimen. But no matter what I did, nothing was working.

With the amount of work I was missing, I made a large dent in my savings, to the point there was no way I was going to England in October. My dream, my dream was over. With this, I became depressed. I kept asking myself, *why does this keep happening to me? And why now?* With the attacks, dreams, and visions, I felt lost, and my depression became severe. I was in desperate need of answers. But where was I going to get them.

I was at home lying on my bed resting and I couldn't stop thinking of him – Marco, when I had a vision of him. He was standing in what I believe to be his bedroom. However, it looked more like a loft with a bed than an actual bedroom. He was standing next to his bed talking on the phone, and I hear him say, *I must go to Arizona. She…I know she's in Arizona, and I must go and find her.* I was shocked, "How is this possible?" I said aloud. But it felt right – true.

It would be a week later when that feeling, that sensation came over me again, telling me he was here. I knew it. I just knew it was true. I felt him arrive in Arizona. But, at the same time, I started questioning whether he really was, or was it my want – my need for him to be here. To be true. My thoughts were running ragged. *Is he really here in Arizona? If so, why hasn't he found me?* But then I'd think, *silly, if he just arrived, how would he have time to find you.* We had this connection, one that let us know when we were in the same place. Was this our way of knowing each other, so when we were close by, or when we found each other, we would know it to be true? This, as of yet, I did not know. But something said it felt right.

Enough was enough! I needed answers, and I needed them now! And there was only one way I knew how to get them, was through my guides, in using the pendulum. I wanted – no, I needed to know if they could help. As soon as I grabbed the pendulum and placed my first finger and thumb to the top of the chain, without hesitation, it immediately began to move, and it moved at a rapid rate. I asked it to stop, and it did. I placed the alphabet template I found online on the table in front of me and began asking my questions.

"Can you help me find Marco?" It swung forward and backward, indicating *yes*, then it spelled out, *we can...wait.* At this, it paused, then started circling until it finally spelled out *yes.* Then to my surprise, it spelled out, *he wants to meet you. He's willing to arrange a place of your choosing. He said he's been trying to find you since he arrived in Arizona.*

I was stunned at this realization and said, "Really?" Then quickly asked, "Is that possible?"

The pendulum spelled out, *yes, it's possible with our help.*

I felt a surge of excitement at the possibility. Finally, I would be able to meet Marco, and so I asked, "How do I know this will work?"

It spelled out, *you have to trust us and what you feel. It will tell you the truth.*

To be honest, I didn't understand what they meant by *what you feel*, but decided to give it a go and so I asked, "Where does he want to meet?"

It said, *wait, we will ask.* I thought, *'we', who are we? There is more than one?* Interesting, right.

In the few moments I was waiting for the answer, the pendulum was continually moving in a circular motion, and then the answer came, *right now he is in Phoenix. He wants to know if you will meet him somewhere in Phoenix.*

Well, that was impossible. And I said, "I would, but right now it's not a good time for me to travel that far. Ask him if he'd meet me in North Scottsdale."

They said, *we will ask him...wait.* Within a few moments I received my answer, *he will meet you wherever you choose.*

At this, I had butterflies racing through my stomach. Now, I was stuck having to figure out where in Scottsdale we can meet. The only place I could think of was —

"I don't know…see if he knows about Starbucks. And if he would be willing to meet me at a location near me? Or would he prefer somewhere else?"

They said, *he will meet you wherever you wish, but we will ask. Wait.*

And so, I waited for my answer. As I was waiting, I was trying to think of another place, but with the summer heat, I couldn't think of a place that would work. It had to be indoors.

The pendulum started moving, indicating they had my answer. *He says he is familiar with Starbucks and will meet you there.*

At this, I became really excited and said, "Okay, great." *Yes.*

After the conversation with my guides, I sat there wondering if this was really possible. Was this really happening?

The Starbucks we agreed to meet later that afternoon was the one closest to me, at Kierland Mall. Although I arranged to meet Marco, there was still more I wanted to know first. So, I asked my guides, "May I ask you more questions about Marco?" It moved in the direction for yes. "What type of work does he do?"

They said, *Computer Engineer and Financial Advisor.*

I was shocked to receive this information and said, "Really?"

Of course, they said, *yes.*

"Wow." Was all I could say. Then I asked, "Is he Italian?"

They said, *yes,* but also added, *but only part. He is also English and Spanish.*

I was amazed by these answers. "Can you tell me his last name?"

At this, they tried to spell out a name, but it wasn't coming across very well. I'd get a Z and then other letters that made no sense. So, I determined it wasn't meant for me to know at the time.

However, this did not deter me from asking more questions. "Does he have a great deal of money?"

I wasn't sure why I needed to ask this question, but at the time, it felt necessary. Maybe it was because of the two careers he was in. No, it was more than that, that I was sure of.

I received my answer, and it was a *yes.* At this answer, I was suddenly engulfed with fear, along with thoughts, *how is this possible? Can I do this? The dream I had told me he had money. But that was only a dream, right? Do I want to know how much?*

Apparently, I did because the next question I asked was, "Is he very wealthy?" It swung with swift speed in the direction indicating *yes.*

I thought, *oh God. Do I dare ask further questions? No, I think it's best I do not know.* And so, I did not inquire any further with this question.

After all of this, we agreed to meet at Starbucks, if he wasn't there, I would not push it. The money thing really freaked me out, and I felt if I failed to meet this man, whose name I was told is Marco, then I would wash my hands clean and walk away before it even started.

The day came to meet Marco, but when I went to Starbucks there was no Marco. I did attempt to meet him several more times, and right when I was about to give up, a feeling came over me that I needed to try this one more time, and if it didn't happen this time, I was done.

Later that afternoon, I went to Starbucks and waited and waited, but there was no Marco. He never showed up. I felt a sense of relief, at the same time, disappointment – hurt, and I was upset. Then to my surprise, I was angry. And I mean, I was really angry. "How dare he!" I yelled in the air while driving back home.

After returning home, I went to my bedroom and began to wonder: why? Why wasn't I happy? After all, I wasn't happy to learn of his financial status, as I felt fear in learning he was wealthy. Maybe there was more to it than money. It was him. Our connection – a soul bond.

After taking a few moments to calm down, I grabbed the pendulum and began asking questions to *why*. And this is what I learned: apparently, he was very busy with work. You see, for Marco to remain in Arizona for a few months, he had to establish a legitimate business, a reason to remain, some in computer engineering, and some with his family business. In this, he was working on establishing new business in Arizona. In doing this, it will allow him to return over and over again.

My guides assured me that he would let me know as soon as he could arrange the time, and we will attempt another meeting. Did I believe this? Yes and no. It made sense, but still? No, I had no doubt he was in Arizona. How could I, after what I felt. You see, there were times while I was out running errands I'd get this certain feeling, the one I've mentioned before, telling me he was somewhere close. Where, that I didn't know.

The times I was spending at home was becoming more and more regular, than the time I was spending at work. My health hadn't changed; it actually worsened. Therefore, it was making it difficult for me to do my job. In my time at home, when I wasn't resting, I continued using my pendulum, wanting – no needing, more information about Marco.

With the amount of research I was doing on the internet, in looking for ways to increase my abilities – I know what you are thinking – however, my reason was – well, I was desperate. In doing this – if my abilities were stronger, then maybe I could bring us together sooner. I know it's insane. I was becoming craze with what was happening to me, and I didn't know what else to do.

What I did find was something I never in my life believed I'd do – again. I started looking at sites about witchcraft. Yes, witchcraft – again. Although, I still didn't understand what I was doing, it didn't stop me for dabbling in it. Yes, I could have contacted that one person who assisted me in connecting with Marco, who's into Wicca, but I was afraid to ask her. Afraid of what she would say, because deep down, I knew exactly what she would say, and I didn't want to hear it. And she would have been right, as it proved to be a big mistake. The little I learned online about witchcraft wasn't nearly enough to prevent – I didn't understand what I was doing.

Lesson: never dabble in something you have no idea what you are dealing with, because I promise you, you will not like what will happen.

What I learned, is there is white and black magic. White magic spells are used for good, and black magic spells, well, are of course, used for bad. I figured, *well, I will only use white magic, not black.* That was simple enough, right? Wrong. With the multitude of websites I found and the variety of different spells each website had. Again, I chose the abundance spell to increase money. I chose this because of the amount of money I lost from not working. With the lack of PTO, I had nothing to cover the time lost due to the asthma attacks I suffered. I was pulling more and more money from my savings, so I could cover my rent and expenses, at the same time, taking away all hope – my dream. There was desperation, the need to replenish what I lost. I remember thinking, *what could it hurt to try, right.* Wrong.

However, the abundance spell wasn't the only spell I found. There were so many different possibilities, in the assortment of spells, along with potions, I felt could help improve my health. At this point, I was so desperate, and I was willing to try anything. Besides the abundance spell, I also found one that could bring me what I want. During all of this, the dreams and visions I was having never stopped.

It's early July 2013 – There's black all around me. Then suddenly, I see a small circle of light barely piercing through the darkness. It seemed to flash a few times before growing larger and larger. Now, I am in a pure white place, as if there are clouds all around me. As I am looking around, trying to understand where I am, I suddenly see Jesus. He's walking towards me. I am surprised, not understanding what's happening or what to think. As he's approaching me, he looks very sad, along with a look of disappointment.

When he reaches me he says, "God is upset with you. You didn't give him a chance to help you."

Next, there was another man approaching – it's my husband.

Jesus tells us, "Evil is at hand, and your souls have been cursed. There is nothing I can do since you took your own lives." Next, we were standing near a large mirror, but it's a window with what looks to be swirling water. As we are standing near this window, Jesus says, "This is where you will enter to be reborn. If your love is true, you will find each other in your next lives. There is one thing I can do for you. I can give you the gift of sight and knowledge. With this gift, it will allow you to find each other if your hearts are true.

I woke up. How do I explain what I felt after that dream? It's hard to put into words. The only thing I can say, it felt – real. This, I have no doubt of. Again, the question came up, *why am I dreaming of a past life and now an afterlife?* What was the reason, and why now? At the time, I didn't know. The only thing I could say, there was a knowing – a feeling that I will learn the truth in time.

In the continuous use of the pendulum, I opened a doorway without realizing it, and allowed in a negative spirit. At first, he acted as my guides did. However, as time went on, that changed. This entity was playing with me. It took advantage of my weakened state, my desperation. It knew what I wanted, and it preyed on it. This entity, who claimed to be a new guide, managed to convince me, this man I believed to be Marco was not. That his actual name was Edward. This guide told me, if I wished it, I could speak directly to Edward, and he to me without the assistance of our guides.

Note: When you dabble in things you know little about, it can cause you to open a doorway, a doorway you have no business in opening. A doorway to other realms, allowing any spirit/entity into your space. Remember, we have free will, so unless you are aware of this and know what to do to protect yourself and your space, you are open to anything that's out there. Your *guides* cannot help you, as they are only to watch and guide you. It's *your* choice.

In what I was doing, I was wide open to whoever and whatever was willing to help me. Well, it gave me the *illusion* that it was helping me. Which I did not realize at the time.

When the pendulum spelled the name Edward, the man I knew as Marco's true name, apparently Edward was directly communicating with me. I did have doubts at first, but after speaking to him, I pushed that doubt aside. For one who is desperate, it wasn't impossible to believe.

However, I did continue to ask questions, to how this was possible. "How can I be speaking to Edward, since I know he's still alive?" Then I thought, *or did something –* as quickly as that thought entered my mind, I quickly shook it off. I needed to know the answer to this question. I had to be sure.

The one who claimed to be Edward, spelled out, *with the help of our spirit guides and God, is how it's possible.* When he said this, I realized, *wait a minute, didn't they say I could speak to Edward without the use of our guides?* And with this thought, I was truly confused.

Without actually speaking these words, I received a message. *I am so happy to finally be speaking with you now that we are connected. And soon, with our communication, we will find each other.* That is what the pendulum spelled out, of what Edward said.

With this, I felt even more confused, so I asked, "Wait. I thought you said…without the help of our guide, how is that possible? Then I decided to ask, "Okay, if you are him, are you currently in Arizona?"

With this question, Edward did clarify. *What I meant when I said our guides don't need to help, is that I can speak to you, versus them relaying to you what I am saying. Yes, I am in Arizona, and I would like us to meet. Will you be willing to meet with me?*

"What!" *Is it possible?* I thought, then excitement shot through my body, and I repeated the words in my mind, *did I want to meet? Duh...yeah! What a stupid question. Of*

*course, I did. How could that even be a question.   Isn't
that what we've been trying to do.*

"Oh, I understand. Yes, of course, I want to meet. Isn't
that what we've been trying to do? Of course, Just tell me
where and when, and I will be there?" I said, then waited
anxiously for his answer.

And when his answer came, he said, *yes, I know, and I
am sorry it hasn't worked out, but this time will be
different. Where do we want to meet? That is a good
question. What part of town are you in again?* he asked.

"I am in North Scottsdale. Are you still in Phoenix?"

He said, *no, I am also in Scottsdale.*

I couldn't believe this, and so I said, "Really? Wow,
you are so close. How about Starbucks at the Kierland
Mall? Do you know where it is?"

He said, *yes, I think so.*

"Okay, great. How about seven tonight?"

He said, *alright, I will be there.*

I was thrilled and excited. I said, "Okay, great, I will
see you there." Then our conversation ended.

Finally, we were going to meet. Yes! I know how it
seems, and you are right. I did feel like a child, a teenager,
who was going on her first date. Sometimes I wonder about
myself as I shake my head at my own child-like behavior.

It amazed me to have a conversation using a pendulum
with someone who's still alive. Never in a million years
could I have thought this was possible. How can I deny it
though? It was happening. I went to Starbucks and waited
for Edward to show up for two hours, but he never did. I
went home completely disappointed, feeling like a fool.

*How could I be so stupid to trust something I cannot
see or hear. I am a fool,* I thought on my way home. I was
so desperate to find this man from my visions and my
dreams that I was willing to believe in anything. In this, I

became angry. I was so very angry. Partially because I was hurt, but more so because I put too much into words through a pendulum.

I wanted to blame someone, but I had no one to blame but myself. I allowed words I received from a pendulum to drive me. At this, I felt that I was in no doubt going mad. And so, it caused me to doubt the validity of what was happening. I started wondering, if it was due to the amount of asthma attacks, with the lack of oxygen, I was becoming chemically unbalanced. My mind was playing tricks on me. It was so strange, I kept trying to wrap my mind around what was happening; as I thought, *the pendulum moved to the letters on their own accord, spelling out what was said. It was an actual conversation. Wasn't it? How can I doubt this to be true? Then, how can I not? Then what about…he never showed up. What does that mean?*

Once I returned home, I went to my room and grabbed the pendulum. Just as I was about to use it, I stopped. I hesitated. Did I want the answer? Would I trust the answers I will receive? Will it be an answer I am looking for, or will it be the truth? What else was I going to do? I needed answers, and this was the only way I knew of getting them. Yes, I was afraid of what the answer might be. I did question who I was talking to. But there was no resisting it. I had to know – to understand.

I needed to know what happened? Why didn't he show up? I wondered, was I even talking to him? And so, I asked my first question, "Why didn't he show up?" I decided to call this Edward *him* because I wasn't sure who I was talking to or if I could trust it. But I needed something now. Later…later I could think and decide what is the truth.

This is the answer I received, *you were talking to Edward, and he did go to meet you, but you were not there.*

I was flabbergasted at this answer, *I wasn't there? Really?* "How can that be? You saw me." If I am speaking to my guides, then of course, they knew I was there. "You know I was there. You are my guides, are you not? You know and see everything I do," I said.

And this is what they said, *this is not us telling you this, this comes from Edward.*

At this answer, I stopped them from continuing and said, "Wait! Why are my guides speaking to me and not Edward?"

They said, *we are speaking to you because you are angry, and with this, your energy is negative. Now is not the right time.*

Okay, maybe this was true. I was angry.

Then they said, *he wants to speak to you. Will you speak to him?*

Now, this was an interesting question, *do I want to speak to him? No, but what the hell. Maybe the ass can explain a few things.* Hesitant, I said, "I don't know if I should. As my guides, what do you think I should do?"

After a moment of stillness, they finally answered, *you should speak to him. Give him a chance to explain.*

I thought, *hum, okay, maybe they are right.* So, I said, "Very well, connect me to him then." You notice I am still not calling him by name.

As I was waiting while the pendulum did that circling thing, my thoughts were, *what is this? What is happening? Is this really happening, or am I a fool?* I wondered, was my desperation in this man so great I was willing to believe in anything? I am afraid I have to say yes, yes I was.

When it stopped circling, it said, *he is ready. Are you?*

I said, "Yes, go ahead and connect us."

I know what you must be thinking, is it possible to have this type of conversation? Well, it must be. How else could you explain the pendulum moving to each letter spelling out the words. I know I wasn't moving it, that I was sure of. I was barely holding the top of the chain, so there was no influence on my part. Some words they were attempting to spell out, I had no idea what they were going to be, until they completed the word. However, was it possible? Yes, anything was possible.

After the pendulum circled a few seconds, slowly it spelled out, *Rebecca, are you there?*

I felt nervous for some reason, as if I was on my first date. Of course, I knew better, but it was strange, that I can tell you. I said, "Yes, Edward, I am here." By this point, I was a great deal calmer. But that didn't last very long because next thing I knew it, I was lashing out at him. "What happened to you? You didn't show up? Why?" I said. I was pissed. More so because I felt like a fool for believing in such a thing.

He said, *I did. I am still here waiting for you. You are the one who didn't show up.*

It was only a pendulum moving, but I felt – I picked up he was angry. Very angry and irritated with me.

I thought, *seriously!*

So, of course, I lashed out at him, "I did show up! I waited for you for over two hours! You were the one who did not show up! How can you say you are still there when you never showed up!" *Bastard!* I thought.

Then he said, *I'm sorry. But I am here waiting for you. I must have come to the wrong place.*

Unbelievable, right? *What do you think? Seriously?* I thought, then said, "Where are you exactly?"

He said, *I am at the mall.*

My thoughts, *at the mall? You have got to be kidding me.* Then I thought, *wait...what mall?* "What mall, because you were not at Kierland Mall?" I asked.

And this is what he said, *the one at Camelback and Scottsdale Road.*

"Seriously!" I said aloud to myself, then to him I said, "Are you serious? That is nowhere close to Kierland Mall. They are in completely different directions."

Yes, it was possible he mixed up the two, but did I not say Kierland Mall? I am sure I did. Fashion Square mall was never mentioned.

Here is what he said, *I am sorry. I went to the one closest to me, thinking it was the mall you were referring to.*

I thought, *yeah, right.* But I allowed him to continue.

When you mentioned the mall, this one is down from where I am staying. I am in North Scottsdale. Didn't you say you are in North Scottsdale?

I rolled my eyes and said, "The one you are at is the Fashion Square Mall. What hotel are you staying at?"

He said, *I am at the Scottsdale Resort, on Scottsdale Road. Do you know of it?*

At this, I pulled out my computer and googled the hotel. To my surprise, it's where he said it was, and it was close to Fashion Square Mall. So, I began to think, *maybe it was a mistake,* and said in a much calmer voice, "Yes, I do." I explained where exactly Kierland Mall is located.

"Well, you needed to go further north on Scottsdale Road, towards Greenway Hayden Road. This is where Kierland Mall is located, on the west side of Scottsdale Road."

He said, *I am sorry, Rebecca. I should have asked for more information. Can we try again?*

I said, "Edward, I don't know. Let me think on it, okay." No, I was not ready to try again. I needed to wrap my mind around all of this – in what was happening. Did I really believe this was happening? I couldn't be sure.

Then he said, *okay, I understand.*

And I said, "Thank you. I must go now." As I was anxious to be done with this.

His last words were, *okay, goodbye.*

"Bye," was my final word.

With what happened, it was enough to set me back for a while. However, I did attempt to meet Edward a few more times, and all my attempts came to nothing. I became discouraged and felt this was never going to happen. More than once while I was driving, I'd get that overwhelming feeling, *he* was somewhere nearby. Where, I didn't know. I started wondering, *can I even trust what I'm feeling?* This, I didn't know either.

As I continued using the pendulum, something different started happening – it was behaving strangely. When I asked a question, it attempted to spell out the answer, but it seemed confused instead of any word that made sense. It looked as if it would spell one word, but then it would do that circle thing and attempt to spell out another word. Then it started swinging right to the left, which was the sign for no. Then back into a circular motion, as if it was confused. It was the strangest thing I saw. So, I googled, *issues with the use of a pendulum,* and I learned if you use a pendulum too much without cleansing it, it can kill the energy, causing it to be confused in its answers.

To cleanse a pendulum or any crystal, you can place it over burning incense or in water with sea salt. What I also learned, at times, crystals need to be recharged. To do this, it is to place them in direct sunlight. Once I cleansed my crystal/pendulum and recharged it, I started using it again. It seemed to be working fine at first, until it started having issues again, in acting confused. I didn't understand why, and decided to cleanse it after each use.

In this time, very unusual things started to happen. For instance, not understanding why, when the pendulum started spinning at high speed, like a helicopter propeller. It would spend so fast that at times it would fly right out of my hand. It was the strangest thing. After this happened a few times, I decided it was time to take it back to the store where I bought it from, since I couldn't find anything about this online.

When I entered the store, I went straight to the lady behind the counter and asked, "Have you heard or seen a pendulum spin in a helicopter spin?"

She said, "No," as she looked at me in utter confusion.

So, I decided to show her. I pulled my pendulum out of my purse, and to my wonderful surprise, it started spinning. And it did, as it did at home. It spun so fast that it flew right out of my hand. The lady behind the counter was astonished to see this. Unfortunately, she had no answers for why it happened.

The only answer she could give me was, "Your energy must be strong."

Since I was so inexperienced, I accepted her answer.

Chapter 21

I continued to communicate with Edward with the assistance of our guides. When I dreamed of him – Edward, who I used to believe to be Marco – yes, you noticed that I am again using Edward's name. Well, I believed it was true – and when I asked him of what I learned about him in my dream – I did this to confirm what I was dreaming was real. At times he'd confirm the dream was real, and other times he'd say they were not.

Some of my dreams felt like messages, as if they were trying to provide me with information of our past life, and what the connection with this man was. There were many times when I questioned the truth of what Edward was telling me about the dreams he denied, when I felt sure they were true. The problem with this, I didn't have any proof. It was only a feeling that the dreams were the truth.

The interesting thing about this, shortly after telling Edward, the dreams and visions seemed to stop. Or, shall I say, they were strange, as they made no sense. Allow me to explain by sharing one of my dreams:

I'm outdoors – it feels as if I'm somewhere in England. I can't explain why – it's not what I see but what I feel. I am outdoors, sitting at a counter, like the ones you see in a bar, and I was having dinner. What I was eating, that I couldn't see. As I was eating though, there was this feeling I needed to turn around and look behind me.

When I do, on the other side of the street, I see a man walking in a white t-shirt and jeans. He has dark hair, and he seems handsome, although I can't see his face. So, I disregard this man – he is none of my business, and I turn my attention back to my meal. However, what I felt earlier would not leave me, and the need to turn around again was profound – I needed to look at him again. There was something – something about him I could not understand.

When I do, this time I can clearly see his face – he looks so sad, lost, and confused. He looks as if he's lost. If feels as if he's searching for something or someone he's lost. I'm staring at this man – somehow, I know he cannot see me. I can't explain it. It's just a feeling. To me, it's as if we are in two different places. A place where I can see him, but he cannot see me, as if there is an invisible veil shading me, preventing him from seeing me. What's strange, he's walking alone down an empty street, except for a few parked cars on both sides of the street. The street appears to be – deserted.

As I am watching him, I feel so sad, and I wanted to – wish I can help him find what he lost. Just as I was about to stand and go to him, I find myself on a boxcar bus. There is a couple next to me talking about what they were going to do when they get off the bus. They are going to the ski slopes. Suddenly the bus comes to a stop, and people start piling off the bus. When it comes to my turn, I look down to watch where I was stepping, and notice I am wearing platform heels – I never wear platform heels, but as I take the last step off the bus and start walking away, my right heel brakes. However, it didn't seem like a big deal, since I just popped it right back on, snapping it back in place.

I woke up and felt this overwhelming feeling about this man, of something I couldn't quite explain, sorrow, fear, pain, and love.

<u>Cheshire, England</u>

Marco felt confused – it was gone. *Why?* He doesn't understand what happened to the connection he had with Rebecca, since their connection was a strong and powerful one, allowing him to see and feel her when he dreamed about her. But now, those visions and dreams seemed to have abruptly stopped. And now, the dreams he does have are of him feeling sad, confused, and lost. It's as if he's searching, trying to find Rebecca, but failing. He wonders what's happen to her, where is she, and where has she gone. *What happened to Rebecca...to our connection?*

Aloud he says, "What happened? Why was our connection severed? Did something happen to her? Is she okay? God forbid, nothing serious has happened to Rebecca. I need to know. I need to find out. I must call nõnna…she might be able to tell me if anything happened to her. If she is okay. Maybe she will know what happened to our connection."

Marco called his grandmother and explained what's been – or better yet, what's hasn't been happening.

Maria's gifts are strong, so when Marco told her of what's been happening, it took her no time at all to connect with Rebecca, and then explains to Marco what she sees.

"There's a blockage that's preventing you from connecting with Rebecca. I don't know why —"

But before Maria could say another word, Marco interrupts her. "Is she okay? It's nothing serious," he said, swallowing a lump in his throat. "Has something happened to her?" he asked, with worry and fear in his voice.

Maria hears this and quickly reassures Marco, "She is safe, Marco. But she has been very ill. It's not clear what exactly she is suffering right now, but they don't want you to give up on her. Whatever it is, it's up to you to find out. They want to see how strong your will is to be with Rebecca. Marco, do you believe the love between you, is it strong enough…to save her." This last, Maria wasn't sure why she said it, but when she did, she heard Marco gasp.

"Save her! Strong enough! For what?" he said, in a voice louder than he intended.

"To fight for her. To not give up on her…on both of you. To prove to them that your heart and soul are open to the love you are meant to have. That you are dedicated to finding her."

"How am I to fight for her? My heart…you know, it's —" *what is it? What can I say? Is my heart in it?* After a few moments, he says, "What am I to do?"

"Marco, when the time is right, you will know. You must be open to hearing their message. It may come to you through a dream, a vision, or even a voice in your mind. Your guides are telling you what you need to do."

"How…I've never…very well," he said, resigned. What was he to say?

"I have faith in you, Marco. This is your time for both of you to be together. Don't give up, Marco, not now."

"Faith?" *Do I have faith? Can I do what she says?* Resigned, he says, "Yes, thank you, nõnna. I love you. Goodbye."

"I love you too, Marco. Ciao."

<u>Arizona</u>

It's around noon on Sunday, and I am doing my laundry when I am suddenly hit with a vision. *It's him. I see him standing at a window. The closer I look; I am able to see out the window to the large city beyond. It looks and feels as if it's New York City. Then, I'm looking around the room, it's dark, and the only light in the room is coming from the window. I look back at him, but I can't see his face, only the view of his back, as it appears that I am standing behind him. Even though I can't see his face, I feel it's him.*

I feel the reason I am here is because he is thinking about me, wondering where I am and how he can find me. I feel as if I can feel what he is feeling, and I am able to hear and see what he's thinking about. He's wondering if my face is as he's seen it in his dreams and visions. To see a face and not have any idea of who I am, and he wonders how he can find me from this.

Next, he's sitting on the sofa that's situated in front of the window where he was standing earlier. As I am looking around the room, it looks and feels like a hotel, maybe a suite. I say this because it has a living room and a kitchen, and I don't see a bed.

"It's you," I said telepathically.

He is surprised, "What? How is this possible?" he asked.

"I have no idea, but it's happening. Do you feel it?"

"Yes. How are you?" he asked.

"I am well. I am just in the middle of doing my laundry. What are you doing? I saw you standing at a window. Are you in New York?" I asked.

"You can see me?" he asked, then said, "Yes, I am in New York City on business. You are doing laundry," he said, but it wasn't really a question.

I laugh a little, "Yes. So, what I saw is right. You are in New York," I said with surprise.

This time he laughed. "I'm sorry. I am surprised and unsure what to do. It has been so long since…this has never happened before. Do you know why that is?"

"I do not. Before it happened, I felt you thinking about me; as I was thinking about you, maybe that is why it happened. I love that it is happening, are you?"

"Yes, I was thinking about you, wondering how I would be able to find you. I am confused…tell me about yourself?"

"What do you want to know? I will tell you whatever you like to know."

But I did not get a reply. I believe this was because we were not allowed to ask such questions, so they cut off our communication. We are only allowed to communicate what our guides allow, and if we try to say something they don't think we are ready for, they will cut off communication.

Not only was the vision a powerful one, but it was also amazing how we were able to communicate telepathically with each other. I didn't know how this could be possible, or even if it actually happened, but I believed it did with the way I felt.

I know what you are thinking. This is what happened when Edward spoke to me. But – how can I explain this. I just…knew it was different. How I felt was different. I felt so much love flowing through my heart, it had to be real.

Later that same day, not too long after the first vision, I had another one:

I am in a bridal store – apparently, I am there to purchase my wedding dress. I want to find a nice dress, one I love and will be perfect for me, but affordable. I feel afraid, because I don't want to spend a great deal of money – his money. It's not my money I'm using to buy the dress, but his. I am sitting on a sofa in a viewing room, and I tell the lady who is assisting me about my limited budget. What's funny, this place reminds me of the one that's seen on television, but I'm not positive.

Next, Marco is at the front counter talking to the clerk. I am unaware he is even there, and I hear him say to the clerk, "No matter what she says, there is no limit. She is to have the dress she wants – loves. Do not allow her to know or see the price. Just allow her to try on whatever gown she wants. I want her to find the right one. The one she loves."

Now, I am in a house, where, I don't know. I'm on the phone talking to my roommate Janet, "Will you come to England? I'd like you to be a part of my wedding party...I'm getting married!" I yelled with excitement.

"What!" she said, smiling from ear to ear.

I said, "Yes. I know, can you believe it. If you don't mind, will you help me style my hair?"

She was so happy for me and agreed to do my hair.

I am feeling so happy – blessed to finally find someone who truly and absolutely, without any doubt or hesitation, loves me. I have never felt happier, as I did in that moment, not in my entire life.

I can't recall exactly when, whether it was days or weeks later – I was in my bedroom dressed in a nightgown, sitting crossed leg using my pendulum to talk to Edward, when something strange happened. There was a voice that was not mine – it was Edward, he was speaking to me in my mind. It was the same words the pendulum was spelling out. How did I know it was Edward? Well, he told me of course, along with the fact he could see me. How did I know this? Ah, well, allow me to explain. The strap to my nightgown slipped off my shoulder and as I was adjusting it, I heard, *leave it, I like it like that.*

I stopped, shocked at what I heard. I was speaking aloud but in a soft whisper so I would not be heard by my roommate. "What? What do you mean?"

I can see you. Didn't you just fix the strap on your nightgown?

"What? How…you can see me? How?" This startled me. My nightgown was skimpy and revealing. My hair was up in a bun, as it always was when I'm going to bed.

Yes, I can see you. Because I can.

"If this is true, then stop looking at me. I am not dressed."

I know, and I like it.

I became self-conscious, so I grabbed my robe and put it on. Then I heard, *don't do that.*

And I said, "I'm not going to sit here half naked if you really can see me."

He said, *oh, come on, please?*

"No, Edward! Now stop it!"

Alright, fine, he said.

And then I said, "Let's test you and see if you really can see me. What am I doing right now?" At this point, I had my drawing spread out on my bed looking at them.

You are looking at your drawings. You just pointed to a picture you drew of my house.

"Oh my God, you really can see me, can't you?"

Yes, isn't it great?

"No."

This went on all night and into the wee early hours of the next morning. Right about 5:00 a.m., he tells me, *I want to be with you, to marry you. Why should we wait? Haven't we waited long enough?*

"Are you crazy! We haven't even met in person yet, and you want to run off and get married? You don't even know where I live."

Sure, I do. I can see you remember. I can see where you live. You live in a house, and you have a red car parked in the driveway next to a blue car. There's a tree surrounded by rocks in the front of the house. There's a gate on the right side of the house to the backyard, which also leads to the front door. Am I right?

Are you kidding me! I was shocked. I couldn't believe it. "You really can see me and know where I live, can't you?"

Yes, I told you I could. Now, does this convince you? Will you now allow me to pick you up and take you to Las Vegas, where we can get married?

Seriously? I thought, at the same time I remember thinking, *what in the world am I going to do? Is this even possible? Is this really happening, or am I going mad?* It was determined, I was going mad, but I decided to say, "I don't know. Do you want to go to Las Vegas and get married? No one even knows what's happening or that you exist. How would I explain such a thing? My daughters, how could they possibly understand their mother running off to get married?" I said, then thought, *I can hear the girls now, geez, didn't know mom was even seeing anyone, let alone get married.* How can doing something like this make any sense? It didn't, and so I said, "No, it's not possible. I can't. I won't —"

Edward interrupted me. *Rebecca, do you love me?* he asked.

Do I love him? Seriously? I thought. "I don't know. How can I? I can't deny, with everything happening, there are…I have feelings for you, but…I don't know you. You don't know me."

Then he said, *it doesn't have to make sense. You and me…this is a miracle sent from God. Do you believe that? For us to have this, could have only come from God. God wants us to be together, which is why he has allowed me to find you, and to communicate with you in this way.*

Okay, some of what he said made sense. Still, this was mad. However, I continued to talk to him, and allowed him to convince me to go with him, because I wanted to know if what he says was true, and when he showed up at my door, I would finally meet him. See that he is real – that this is real. So, after our conversation I started getting ready for his arrival. I know what you are thinking, but keep reading and the answer will be revealed.

I waited an hour when I realized – knew he wasn't coming. *Again, I was a fool.* At this point, I'd had enough of his games, in the *let's meet*, but nothing ever happens. I felt like an idiot. A foolish idiot. Was I that desperate for love, in wanting so desperately to believe this man was real, that I allowed myself to be sucked into this fantasy, in thinking, I was truly talking to the man from my dreams. I began to wonder *did I do this? Did I create this man out of my wants and desire, to find love? To be and feel loved?*

At this point, I was fueled with anger. I grabbed my pendulum and demanded to speak to Edward. Once we were connected, as upset as I was, I lashed out. "Where are you? You never showed up! I am done! I am not doing this anymore!"

He said, *Rebecca, I am very sorry for this. I am not going to be able to make it.*

"Sorry!" *What the fuck!* "You are disappointing me once again!" I yelled aloud. Then, to humor myself, since by this point the only thing I could do was laugh at the ridiculousness of the situation.

Then I said, "Oh, why can't you make it this time?" I asked sarcastically. "What's your excuse now?"

Well, I am not there where you are. I am in heaven.

My mouth dropped open. I couldn't believe what he just said. I was shocked and was engulfed in fear, as my heart dropped into my stomach. I did not expect this answer, but when I heard this, I remember thinking, *God, tell me this isn't true? Did something happen to him on his way to my house, and now…he is dead.* The last was hard to utter the words, let alone think them. In this, I dropped the pendulum. I didn't want to know anymore. I was too afraid.

After gathering myself, I picked up the pendulum and asked what I so desperately needed to know – to understand. "What do you mean you are in heaven? How can that be?"

He said, *I am not alive. I am in heaven.*

I couldn't believe this. I didn't want to believe it. *What in God's name is happening?* I thought. Needless to say, I freaked out. *How can this be happening?* "No, this cannot be. How can this be? What is happening? I don't understand." Then, it hit me, *oh God,* "Who the hell are you? Why are you doing this to me?" I demanded. I knew. Somehow, I just knew, but I didn't want to believe it.

He said, *I am a spirit who doesn't want you to find this man, or find love, as you don't deserve to have love.* Now, the voice that was once calm and kind was now one of hatred – evil.

To acknowledge this, I was suddenly engulfed with fear. But I took a few moments and a few deep breaths, and after letting them out, I said, "Are you serious! What the hell are you! What the hell do you want!" I yelled.

The answer I received was not one I expected. It shocked the hell out of me.

I want you to join me in heaven. Will you come and join ?

I completely freaked out at hearing this. "NO! GET OUT NOW!" I couldn't believe this was happening to me. I started thinking, *of course, you do. You've watched those paranormal shows? How stupid could you have been?* I should have seen this coming. I was so blinded by my desire to find this man who I was dreaming about. In what I was doing, I ended up opening a door and allowed this unknown entity, and a very negative one at that, in. This entity had an agenda, and it was – he wanted me weak and vulnerable, and he succeeded. This entity wanted me dead, and I was determined not to let it win, and I was going to take back my life. I wasn't going to allow this entity to have me – to win, so I fought back.

By now, my roommate was at work, so I was home alone. At the top of my lungs I yelled, "LEAVE! GET OUT-OF-MY-HOUSE! YOU-ARE-NOT-WELCOME-HERE! LEAVE! NOW!" Unfortunately, this did not work. The *thing* just laughed at me. I could hear its evil laughter in my mind. I started to worry, wondering *how to get rid of a negative entity/spirit.* And this, I didn't know. But I had to find out.

After this event, my health declined rapidly. No matter how hard I tried, I couldn't go to work. I started thinking about committing suicide. I was feeling so depressed; lost, alone, unwanted, and unloved. I just wanted my life here to be over. I started to feel I didn't deserve to be in this world anymore. With this, I started thinking of ways I could take my own life. I thought of crashing my car into a building or a pole while going at high speed. I thought about taking sleeping pills, with the hope I would just fall asleep in my bed, and when I awoke, I'd be in heaven, if that's even where I'd end up. *He*, this Edward, took away my power, and now he was trying to destroy my spirit, which is what he wanted. In his success in destroying my spirit, this entity was thriving by taking away my will to live. All this, because I didn't understand what I was doing, in my need to protect myself, before using a pendulum or dabbling in witchcraft. Because of my inexperience, I opened a doorway to a world, one I couldn't fathom.

I started wondering – going back to when all this began, was this man I was dreaming and having visions of, was he even real. How could I be sure? When I started communicating with Edward, the dreams and visions had practically stopped. The ones I did have, were of him feeling sadness, confusion, and loss. Were these messages, warnings, that something was wrong. My connection to him seemed to have stopped, and I believed he felt it too, which explains the odd dreams I was having of him searching for me, because he lost our connection.

This also explains why the pendulum acted confused. It was, what I believe, was trying to prevent the entity from speaking to me. But, because of the lack of knowledge I had, I didn't understand what was happening, and in turn, I opened a doorway and welcomed *it* in, and in doing this, gave it permission.

There was nothing my guides could do, with free will and all. All they could do was try to warn me. Try to help me see what was happening. Due to my inexperience, I didn't see or understand this, and therefore, turned over my power to this entity, and in doing so, allowed *it* to block my true connection with the man I was dreaming about. The man my guides first told me of, the man they said the name was Marco. The entity wanted me to believe what he said, so I would give up on *him – Marco,* love – everything, including life.

Spirit Realm

Rebecca's guides have been watching over her throughout her whole life. Watching her go through her struggles – seeing and feeling her pain, heartbreak, and now, her loss in faith, not just in herself, but in life. As needed, Jesus would add more guides to help Rebecca down her chosen path, and in this path, lead her to the love she seeks. In a short time, Rebecca has already made it through a great deal from which she's suffered a hard and unloving life. This, to take her down the path she was always meant to be. With what happened with the negative entity/spirit, it made her feel lost and confused. It forced her to lose her will, in this, forcing her to make wrong decisions. Now that Rebecca is thinking about ending her life, this, her guides cannot allow to happen – not this time.

"What are we going to do? This spirit, a family from her past…he is so angry. He does not want her to succeed in this life. What should we do? What can we do?" asked Victoria.

"All we can do is watch. She opened herself to this spirit, and if she allows this spirit to manipulate her, there is nothing we can do. All we can do is keep trying to get through to her and help her see what is happening. She receives our messages, but then this spirit comes and tells her different, or prevents our messages from getting through," said Angela.

"If we are not allowed to help her…this spirit will take her off the path she is meant to go down. Now, he is trying to push her into taking her own life. We cannot allow this. This is not what Jesus wants," said Victoria.

"Yes, I know. Jesus said, if her life is in danger, to call on him," said Angela.

"Look. Look what's happening. She is so unhappy and depressed. She is talking about ending her life. I think it's time to call Jesus?" said Victoria.

"No, we cannot…not yet," said Angela.

At this, Jesus comes to check on Rebecca. "Hello, Victoria and Angela, how is Rebecca doing?"

Relieved to see Jesus, Victoria tells him what's been happening. "She's not doing well. She's allowed a negative spirit…an old family member from her life as Elizabeth…he is playing on her want and need to find love. To find Marco. Now, after what recently happened, her thoughts…she's thinking of taking her life."

"This, we cannot allow. Let me consult with God and see what we can do," said Jesus.

Rebecca

As I laid in bed, considering how I was going to take my life, suddenly, there was a strong and powerful voice that yelled, "STOP! STOP IT NOW!" with a roar, and I was sure the room shook. But, with this, for some reason, I immediately snapped out of my state of confusion, and the feeling of desperation, and the need to take my life. I began to fight. I fought with such power I didn't know I had, and regained control of myself once again. Once I did, I attacked and started yelling at this spirit.

"God is with me! I feel him! You have no power over me! I will not fall to your will! God will not allow it! God, I seek your help, your strength, to help me defeat this entity and dispel him from my house and from my existence. Leave! Get out! You are not welcome here!"

After this, there was a sense – a brief moment of relief, but unfortunately, it was not over. Not yet.

The Spirit Realm

Within moments of leaving, Jesus returned, "Everything will be alright. God decided to intervene himself. His voice was strong and powerful…he also sent her his love and strength. With this, she's fighting back."

They were all pleased and rejoiced in God's intervention.

"If we can get her back on track, Rebecca will have the love she's longed for. The love she's forgotten," said Joseph.

"The love from the life before," said Angela.

"Now is her time to remember, learn, and understand," said Victoria.

"This will be hard for her, but it's something she must go through to ensure what happened then will not be repeated. After her visit to Cheshire and going to Dunham Massey Castle, allowed her and Marco's spirits to connect, and Maria is essential to helping Marco and Rebecca, but not in the way she believes," said Jesus. "Continue to help Rebecca in remembering her life as Elizabeth. What she learns will cause her great pain, but it's one she needs to go through if she is to understand what she must do. If she is to have the love she seeks. There is someone we have in mind to help Rebecca, but this will not be for a while," Jesus said, then he asked, "How is the connection going between Marco and Rebecca? Are you still helping them connect in their dreams and of their past lives together?" he asked.

"Yes, we ensured this continued, even with the spirit's influence. Marco can feel something is not right, but he does not know what exactly is happening," said Victoria.

"This too will be difficult for Rebecca, as we already know. We must continue to allow them to connect through their dreams and visions. Continue encouraging her to draw by allowing the memory of Elizabeth's gift to draw to come through, for it to continue to inspire Rebecca. In the images she sees will trigger her memory, causing her to relive what happened to Elizabeth, and help her learn who Marco is," Jesus said, then inquired on Marco. "How are Marco's memories going?"

"He is resisting. But we feel with his grandmother's help, he is opening himself up to his gifts. We have sent him dreams of his past life as Robert, to help him remember their life together as Robert and Elizabeth. The love they shared and still can share. At first, he can feel and believe there is something to them, until he starts to use his mind to rationalize it instead of listening to his heart. When this happens, he brushes them aside as nothing more than mere dreams. A part of him wants to be open to what is happening, to believe, but that technical mind of his keeps getting in the way, telling him it's not possible. Although Maria is spiritual and has been trying to help him…once he's away from her, he returns to his technical thinking," said Victoria.

"Don't stop. Keep helping Marco remember through his dreams, and eventually, with Maria's help, he will learn the truth. It will also guide him back to the place in France, where he took his life as Robert," Jesus said. "For now, continue doing what you have been doing, in helping Rebecca and Marco connect through their dreams, allowing them to remember their past life as Robert and Elizabeth. They must remember their love, when it first flourished, and why it was lost. For Rebecca, with what's happened in her life, these memories will help to heal her soul. To forgive those who hurt her and herself. Most of all, Rebecca and Marco must understand what led to their tragedy as Robert and Elizabeth, so they do not repeat it again.

Rebecca

After what happened with the entity, and what I believed to be God's intervention, as I think back to that night, it felt as if the entity was trying to enter my mind, in order to destroy my soul. There is no other way I could describe what happened. Although that night I had a moment of relief, when I woke up in the morning, I heard *his* voice again, but this time I ignored him, and I grabbed my laptop to research ways to protect myself.

I did find a few protection prayers and chose the one – if you call on Archangel Michael to help you, he will. So, that night when I laid down to sleep, I again heard, but not only hear, I felt the entity trying to reenter my soul. First, I called for God's help, then right after, I called for Archangel Michael to help me. I repeated it over and over again in my mind, *help me, Archangel Michael, help me. Protect me from this entity.* In doing this, something happened. What I felt was as if a battle was taking place. I wanted to open my eyes to see what was happening, but I was too afraid, so I kept them closed. However, even though my eyes were closed, I could see flashes of white light. I tried to open my eyes at this, but no matter how hard I tried, I could not. It seemed as if a great deal of time had passed before I finally succumbed to sleep.

Note: An entity, or what you can call a spirit, can feed on your fear, therefore, empowering them. Instead of fear, get angry, and stand your ground and mean it. In doing this, you take away their power.

Chapter 22

<u>Cheshire, England</u>

"Why is this happening?" Marco said aloud, after waking up. He is still not dreaming of Rebecca. He begins to wonder if there's something wrong with him. "It seems nothing I do is allowing me to connect with Rebecca. Have I lost her? I need to know. I need to find out, and the only way I know is to call nõnna and ask her what she knows, if anything." Marco said, speaking to nothing but the air above his bed. "I know she said I will receive a message, but nothing has happened. I've received nothing. Is it because I am not open enough for this message to come through? I must see if she can help me."

Maria was in her kitchen when an overwhelming feeling about Marco hit her. It was a feeling of desperation. A desperate need for her help. With this, Maria takes a few moments to focus on Marco, to see if she can tap into what's happening to him. When she receives what she is looking for, she waits, ready for Marco's call.

When Maria received Marco's call, she says, "Ciao Marco. How are you this morning?"

"Good morning, nõnna. I am not doing so well. I need your help. I don't know what to do," Marco said to his grandmother. "I keep waiting for this message you said I am supposed to receive, to tell me what I am to do, but I have received nothing. Is there something I'm doing wrong? I don't know how to explain this…I fear…I am losing her. How can this be happening? Is there something I'm doing wrong? For our souls to connect in the way they did, has allowed me to remember and feel the love we once had…I can't lose her," he said with desperation and sorrow in his voice. "Please, nõnna, help me?" Marco said, pleading with his grandmother. The desperation he felt since he's been closed off from Rebecca is driving him mad. Then he thinks, *is this my fault?* Then to his grandmother he says, "Maybe it's me. I am the one that is closed off." Shaking his head, he then says, "I just don't know. Maybe I'm just not recognizing it. It's my fault why our connection has been lost?"

Maria's heart breaks for her nipõte. "Marco, I am sorry for what you are going through. What is happening is not yours or Rebecca's fault. Your fear is what's preventing you from hearing and understanding their message. This, along with doubting yourself. Because of this, they've asked me to help you. To tell you what you need to do. Marco, what I've learned may cause you great pain. Are you ready to hear what I have to say? If so, then after, you will need to do what they tell you to do. In doing this, will bring you back together again."

"Yes, nõnna, anything. Please tell me, I must know?" Marco said, with a sound of relief in his voice to what his grandmother told him.

"In Rebecca's desperation to find you, she's done something…she opened a door and allowed a spirit who wishes her harm to come in. This spirit is someone from her past, your past. A family member who can't seem to be able to let go of what you both did in that life. This spirit is very angry that you are both connected in this life. He does not want either of you to find each other and have the love and happiness you once had. Marco, Rebecca is so new to this, she does not understand what's happening to her. With what she's been feeling from the dreams and visions, of your past life, and of you in this life, it made her desperate to find you. This spirit made her believe she had you, and then when she learned she was deceived, she was lost.

Because of this spirit, she's not sure if you are real anymore.

To know you are out there and to not know what to do…she has no one, unlike you…you have me. There is no one for her to talked to, who can help her understand what is happening. This, this is what forced her to seek answers in other ways. Instead of finding her answers, she instead opened the door to a world she does not understand. This spirit saw this and played on her vulnerability. It was its opportunity to take advantage of her by convincing her she was talking to you. It gave her hope, only for him to take it away from her, where now, she questions if you truly exist. She questions her dreams and visions, of the feelings she has, as her own creation, or one the spirit created for her. She thinks everything was all in her mind, what she calls a mountain of lies.

The spirit did this to convince Rebecca she is going mad. In this, it sent her into a deep depression, and because of this, the spirit is trying to push her over the edge, to force her to take her own life," Maria said, but before she could go on, she could hear Marco gasped at the last thing she said, but Maria refused to stop, she had to continue. Marco needed to know it all. "In what she's been through, from the time you both connected, of the memories of her life before, has caused her to suffer greatly, by affecting her health —" Maria heard Marco gasp again, but ignored him and went on. "Do not concern yourself, and this is a good thing, not a bad one. Rebecca needs to free herself from the pain and suffering she suffered in that life. With the decline in her health and what she's been doing, it weakened her enough to allow this spirit in."

As Marco listened to what his grandmother was saying, he was shocked at what he heard, and in this, he was engulfed with fear. It left him lost to what to do. *If I can help…God, please, I will do anything for Rebecca.* "Nõnna, what can I do? I can't allow her to go through this alone. How can I help her?" Marco asked as he thought, *please God, I can't lose her, not now.*

"Marco, your love from that time was very strong and powerful. A love like no other. You need to tap into that love and use the power of your love, the love embedded in your soul, both of your souls, a memory that is beginning to reawaken."

"Nõnna, how can I do this? If I couldn't hear the message before because of my fears, how am I to now, to do what they ask of me, in what is needed to save Rebecca?"

"Marco, you're stronger than you realize. Your fear comes from many things. In questioning yourself on what you did then is wrong. It doesn't matter what you did or didn't do, but what you do now. To believe, you must open your heart and soul to the truth. To the love you shared from a life long ago. Rebecca has her own road to follow, just as you do. For you, you have me, as she has no one. Even with me, you doubt…you doubted this. Since you've connected with Rebecca, you can no longer, can you? Although, I know you try. You must allow this connection to open once again. To allow the power of your love, which is embedded in your soul, to surface. Now, you need to tap into that power. In doing this, you will pull her out from what's been happening to her. The power of your love will bring her to you and into your arms —"

Maria stopped when she received a sudden message from her guides. One that she needs to relay to Marco.

"Marco, they are telling me you must go to the lake. The lake where you first discovered your love from that life. The lake there still holds the power and the energy of your love. There, you can tap into that power. You must stand as close to the lake without stepping into the water. Close your eyes and open your heart and soul to allow the energy…the power of your love to flow through you. Do not force it, just allow it to happen. At the same time, reach out to her, and attempt to connect your soul to hers. In doing so, you will pull her out and away from this spirit that's trying to harm her. Your love…the power of your love…a love given to you from God…this love will push through the barrier blocking you from her. You will free her and bring her to you. In doing this, will strengthen your love and your connection to her, and she to you. You can do this, Marco. You have the power within you. You've always had," Maria said.

"Nõnna, do you really think I can do this?" he said, then hesitantly, "Nõnna, I…I believe…I think…I understand," Marco said. *But do I? Do I really understand?* "This love you speak of…I think I've felt this power in my dreams. It's hard for me to explain or understand it, even now, as I speak the words. But, since Rebecca and I connected…there's just something…oh, I don't know how to explain this. All I know is I will do whatever it takes. I cannot lose her, not now."

"Marco, your love for her has always been there. Your love is a strong and powerful love, an eternal love. If you believe in that love, then you will succeed. I love you very much, and I want this for you. I always have. Once this is done, and all is well, you must come to Italy. I think it's time to tell you everything about your past lives together and my connection to you both."

"I will nõnna, I promise. Thank you for everything. I love you very much."

After Marco arrives at the lake, he feels an immediate connection, an energy so powerful – love, surrounding him.

This feels familiar, but how? he thought as he was shaking his head, *it doesn't matter.* Marco closes his eyes and opens his heart and soul to allow this energy – the power of their love, that is still embedded in this place, *their lake* from long ago. At the same time, he prays to God, *God, please help me open my heart and soul, and allow me to do what needs to be done, so I may protect Rebecca and return her to me.* Within seconds of Marco's prayer, a power so strong slams into his chest, opening that place that has been closed, and allows the love to emerge from where it's been hiding. A force so powerful he's at a loss to what's happening. No matter, he takes that power and focuses all its energy on Rebecca.

In this, he pulls an image from his mind of Rebecca, one from his dreams and visions. With her image strong in his mind, he takes that energy – the power within him, and forces it out, allowing him to pierce the barrier that's been placed between them. For just a moment, he could feel the spirit that's possessing and affecting Rebecca.

There are three flashes of white light – then he finds himself standing face to face with Rebecca, there at the lake, where he's standing now. Without hesitation, Marco pulls Rebecca into his arms and holds her tight, afraid of letting her go, thus losing her forever. *You will not lose her. You are destined to be together. This is your time,* said a voice in his mind. A miracle, to have this moment together, in each other's arms.

"Oh God, I can't believe I have you here in my arms. I don't want to ever let you go. I want you to know and feel the love I have for you. I was worried and concerned for you. I love you. I was so worried about you. If you ever need me, just think of me, and God will bring you and me here, to this place, our lake, where I will be waiting for you. In this place, you will be protected and safe. All you have to do is close your eyes when you need my strength and protection, and I will be here at this lake – our lake. This is our safe-haven, our sanctuary, given to us by God."

At this, Marco suddenly feels Rebecca being torn away from him, and he reaches for her, as he calls out to her, "Remember, this is our sanctuary, our safe haven, where you will be protected." Then Rebecca was gone.

Rebecca

When I woke up the next morning, I still seemed to be in a semi-dream state. I say this, because as I was waking up, I could still hear the voice of the man I was standing with near a lake. When I hear his voice, I realize, *It's his voice – Marco's voice.* It was Marco, the man from my dreams. We were standing at the edge of the lake, standing face to face, as he's telling me, *"This lake is our sanctuary. Our safe-haven. Our place to be together."* Then I heard him say, *"I was worried and concerned for you. I love you."* At this, I thought later, *love me? Did he really say I love you?* What I felt from this, is that he knew what happened. As I became more and more awake, I realized there was this feeling, as if he couldn't reach me before, but now, here in this place, this lake, he was finally able to reconnect with me, and I with him, and at a time I needed him the most.

After I was fully awake, I wasn't sure if what happened and what I heard was real. Did I actually have a conversation with Marco in a semi-conscious state, or was it another one of the spirits deceptions? How did I know this was real – truth? The one thing I knew for sure, it felt real – right. It was peaceful. The air wasn't thick as it was before. The heaviness I felt with the spirit was no longer there. It was light, clean, and clear – refreshing. No, it didn't feel like a deception. It felt real.

After taking a few moments to go over what happened, I finally decided to get out of bed and get ready for work. Once I arrived at work and was waiting for a call, I couldn't stop thinking about that morning, in what happened, not once did it leave me. I kept hearing his voice, repeating those words over and over again. It wasn't the spirit that called itself Edward, but a different voice. A protective voice, telling me, *yes, this is true. This is real.* "God, can it be?" I whispered so no one around me could hear.

The following morning it happened again. I woke up in a semi-conscious dream state, as I was still in a conversation with Marco. *"This lake is our sanctuary. Our safe-haven. Our place to be together. I love you."* We were together again, and for some reason, I could only remember the part right before I woke up. With this dream, it left me with a feeling of a love so powerful, of a love so great, a love that is greater than anything I've ever felt or known in my entire life. It feels me with great happiness to have him, Marco, back in my life. Our connection was back, and in this renewed connection, there was a small electrical current coursing through my body, sending chills from head to toe.

Again, to my amazement, I went to work a second day in a row. For me, that in itself was a miracle, and I could feel Marco throughout the day. It was different though. It wasn't anything like I felt before with Edward. What I felt was strong and powerful, that at times, it was difficult to focus or concentrate on anything else but him, which made it very difficult to do my job. It's one thing to have this happen at home, but to have this happen at work – well, let's just say, work is not the place for it.

The visions were back and stronger than ever before. To have them would cause me to lose complete control of my entire body, leaving me weak in the knees. So much so, no matter what I was doing or where I was at, I was forced to sit down or grab hold of something close to steady myself. At times when this happened, I found myself staring off into space, to the vision I was receiving. Once it was over, I'd return to normal.

In this, I found my confidence begin to return. I knew this man I was dreaming about, and with our return connection, was indeed real. Whatever it was that caused me to lose my confidence – those of greater power wanted me to know he was real. With God's help, our dreams were our connection, a way for us to be together. It allowed us to touch and feel each other. A way to communicate, since we couldn't in real life, but not of personal things, name, work, or where we live. No, it wasn't anything like that, but proof to each other we were real.

Although I couldn't remember much of my dream, it was those last few words, *"This lake is our sanctuary. Our safe-haven. Our place to be together. I love you."* I'd hear upon waking up that left me breathless, a reminder that what I was experiencing was real. There was no doubt; we were destined to meet. When? That, I did not know. The only thing I could determine, it would happen when God deems us ready.

It was several days later, and I found I could not stop thinking about those dreams, of what happened in them, or the words of concern, worry, and most of all, love. It was as if they were a part of me. This, from a man I don't know, and yet I do. When our first connection started, and then our communication, then to see and be with each other every night after that spiritual fight, he helped me, he saved my life, and became my protector. There was no doubt, all of this was a miracle. This was all done to show me, and I believe him as well, a confirmation that we were real. That our connection was real.

No, I couldn't remember everything about these dreams, but there was this feeling within me, telling me they are real. But for some reason, I wasn't allowed to remember the dream in full, but what they allowed me to remember. How could I be sure? I couldn't. It just was. It was – faith.

How can I explain what I was feeling in a way you will understand? Have you ever felt there was something wrong? You know, that feeling in the pit of your stomach, only to learn you were right. There was something in you, an unknown source that alerted you something was wrong. Have you ever had that feeling as if someone was watching you? When that prickling on the back of your neck happens, you stop to look around and find someone watching you. It's what some women call *women's intuition*. It's your instinct, an alarm bell going off. Now, take those feelings and imagine how it's like for me, intensified ten times stronger than normal, flowing through my body with a rush of powerful emotions, slamming into me like a locomotive.

It seemed once our blockage was lifted, in our reconnection, the feelings I felt for Marco intensified – escalated to unprofound proportions. It didn't matter where I was when these feelings hit me. When they did, they hit me hard. It felt as if I could feel him inside of me, and all around me, and I believe he felt the same. I knew when he was thinking about me, as he knew when I was thinking about him. It was a continuous sensation that never seems to let up.

With these feelings growing, at times, I believed he was in the building where I worked. Yes, that's how strong they were. I remember thinking, *how can this be?* These feelings were too powerful to ignore, so I would stand up half expecting to see him, and if I didn't, I would think he was somewhere in the building or possibly somewhere nearby. It was hard to say.

The times I looked around and found nothing, that he was nowhere I could see, no, he wasn't there, and I felt disappointed. But it didn't matter that I couldn't see him, what I felt was too powerful to ignore, he was somewhere nearby, whether in the building or within the vicinity. When this would happen, I would remember that dream I had of him touring the building. In this, what I was feeling, only grew stronger, and I had to know. I had to be sure. I had to see for myself if it was possible, and I wondered if my dream was coming true?

I left my desk and walked slowly towards the hallway where I saw Marco in my dream. I had to know if it was possible my dream was coming true. I'd like to say, *yes it did*, but I am afraid, to my disappointment, it did not. With this, I wondered why these feelings were so strong, that I believed he was there.

I could not deny these feelings, nor could I understand them. What I was feeling was nothing to what I felt with Edward. Everything seemed to change that morning after I had the fight with the entity. The dream with him at the lake. I felt there was something more about that lake, something of a greater power residing there, that was unbeknownst to me. So, it didn't matter that I didn't see him; I knew without a doubt he was close. Where? Now, that was the question, wasn't it?

<u>Verona, Italy</u>

"Marco, come sit next to me," Maria said as she padded the seat next her hers on the log. "Do you remember when I brought you here when you were but a boy? I told you about the story of a pure and powerful love you had in a past life. Where you were known as Robert?"

With a crooked smile, Marco answered, "Yes, nõnna," he said sarcastically. His grandmother was relentless in telling him this story. "The one you continued telling me about every year since."

"Don't mock your nõnna. Listen to what I have to say. There is much you do not know, and it's time you did," she said, then began to tell the story, as she did when she would read him a bedtime story. "A long time ago —"

Marco raised his eyebrow and said, "Really, nõnna. A long time ago?" he said with laughter.

Maria practically smacked him in the arm and said, "Shh, now listen." Marco only smiled but did as his grandmother said. "When you were Robert, you fell in love with Elizabeth, who you know now as Rebecca, and it was her sister who pushed you two together. Both families arranged for Robert to marry Elizabeth's sister Grace, and in doing this, they would merge both families together, so they would strengthen their power, wealth, and status within the land. This land was already under the power of Robert's family. Grace, her sister, had no interest in marrying Robert, and it didn't matter that it was a prearranged marriage before Robert and Grace's births.

The only thing Grace cared about was reading her books. She would fantasize about a life in traveling the world, not worrying or caring about honor or family obligation. She wanted to travel, and in her travels, she hoped she would also find her one true love. Grace knew what she wanted and what she was looking for, and it wasn't where she lived. So, when she noticed Robert and Elizabeth had a great deal in common, she hatched a plan and begged her sister to spend time with Robert, so she didn't have to. In this, she hoped Robert and Elizabeth would fall in love, and she believed when this happened their families would release her and Robert from the agreement, then allow Robert to marry Elizabeth in her place. In doing this, it would leave her free to live out her dream.

Well, her plan worked, but not in the way she hoped. Both families were so determined to make the marriage happen between Grace and Robert, that when they found out, they forbid Robert and Elizabeth from being together. No matter what, Robert and Grace were to marry. Robert and Elizabeth's love was one of the greatest loves to be known, even greater than the famous Romeo and Juliet. It was so powerful, they refused to listen to their families and continued their relationship in secret. After a time, before it was too late, both decided to take matters into their own hands, and went outside of Cheshire and married. They felt that if they were married their families would have to accept their relationship. However, this did not work as they hoped.

Elizabeth and Robert's family disowned them when they learned what they did. However, because Robert was the eldest son, heir to the family title and estate, he could not be completely cut off. His father ordered him out of their home, which was Bramhall Manor, and to never return until after his death. After a time, Robert and Elizabeth did manage to be happy. Yes, it was hard for Robert and Elizabeth to not have their family, but they had their love for each other, and they believed this was enough, until that love was taken from them when Elizabeth was ripped from Robert's arms, kidnapped, and taken to be with the French King. Until one day, when the king's preacher wanted Elizabeth, he did things without the king being aware. In kidnapping Elizabeth, he forced her to France. He deceived her by telling her she was to marry the king. However, the king only wanted Elizabeth as a mistress, one of many —"

While Marco was listening to this story, he felt something – a sense of familiarity – *is it possible. This is me…there is something very familiar…but —*

"— When Elizabeth refused, they hatched a plan, by telling her Robert was killed in his attempt to rescue her. Elizabeth was so hurt…it destroyed her. With her family not wanting her, and the man she loved, the only love she'd ever known was dead, she couldn't live with herself, and so she jumped from the window to the rocks below. Robert was her heart and soul. When Robert learned what happened and why, he couldn't live without Elizabeth, and so he also took his own life, by piercing his heart with a dagger —"

At this, Robert automatically moved his hand to the birthmark directly over his heart. Maria noticed this, but said nothing. "They both believed they would be together in death, or if reborn, would find each other in their next lives and renew their love.

"Marco, I know what you are thinking. How do I know this?"

Not really. I am thinking about the birthmark over my heart. "Well, yes, I do."

"I know this because I was the sister. I was Grace. It was my fault Elizabeth and Robert died, as well as my mother, father, and brother…they too were killed by Robert's father. At the time, he was the law of the land, and someone had to pay for the death of his eldest son and my…Grace's family was the easiest by using the terms in their agreement. This is why I believe you were born into my family. It's a chance for me to make right the wrong I did to you, Elizabeth…Rebecca, and my family. Not only that, but to help bring you and Rebecca together, to allow your love to have the chance in this life it didn't have then. I must do this before I die. I must bring you both together, so you can have the life you were not allowed then. This was my choice, my purpose, to return to this time in this life. God granted me this request, and he gave me the gifts I have to allow me to remember, so I can help you and Rebecca," she said as she placed her hand on Marco's cheek.

Marco tried to take what he heard in, but this was too much. He didn't know what to think. Then he realized, with recent events, how could he not. "Nõnna, I know you believe you are at fault, but how could you be? Whatever happened then does not have anything to do with you now," Marco said.

Shaking her head, as she said, "It is my fault. I made sure…I pushed them together, hoping they would fall in love. In doing so, I caused the death of all my family. Marco, what happened then…you cannot make the same mistakes you did then. You have to do what's right by not rushing into anything."

"Nõnna, how can I allow what happened from a life long ago to affect me now," shaking his head, "No, one has nothing to do with the other."

Maria grabs Marco's hand, "Marco, but it does. You went against your family, ignoring what needed to be done, as did I. Because of this, this one decision destroyed everyone involved. You cannot make the same mistakes you made then. Marco, the place where you took your own life still stands. Go there and see this place and allow yourself to remember. Allow yourself to relive what happened. Maybe doing this will help you remember," she said as she laid her hand where she knows Marco's birthmark is and what it represents.

At his grandmother's touch, he knows she's referring to his birthmark. *It has something to do with this.* "Nõnna, what do you know about my birthmark?"

"Marco, I cannot tell you. You need to learn the meaning for yourself when you return to the place in France."

Marco was unsure what to think. For so long, he's had a technical mind, and there was no belief in life after death or of rebirth. If you lived your life right, then you go to heaven. That is the Catholic belief. Marco had resigned long ago; this would not be his fate when he left this world. To hear his grandmother talk about reincarnation, a fully dedicated Catholic woman shocks him. Can he believe what she tells him? This, he just doesn't know. He wants to. He really does, but —

"What place…where?" he finally asked.

"It's a place in France, in Loire Valley, to be exact. There is a château there where you took your life…I cannot tell you more. It is up to you to find this place."

"What…you want me to go there and see if I can remember what happened…in taking my own life. You want me to see, and possibly feel this?" To ask this question shocked Marco. *Why would I ask such a question, let alone believe it to be possible?*

"Marco, you must, if you are to understand. I do not know if you will feel, but...promise me, you will go?"

Marco lets out a breath, sighing, "I don't know, nõnna…this is too much," he says, shaking his head. Then turns away, unable to look at his grandmother. "You want me to believe in something…I don't know if I can." He turns back to look at his grandmother and sees the desperation on her face. *Whatever it is, she believes this.* "Alright, nõnna, I will go."

Maria lets out her breath and hugs her nipõte with relief. "Thank you, Marco…you will see I am telling you the truth."

<u>Arizona</u>

With what's been happening, the visions and dreams growing stronger to an unbelievable intensity, that I started seeing things in real-time. It was a day at work when I was sitting waiting for a call, and I had a vision of Marco. He was sitting at a desk. Although it wasn't very clear, I knew it was him.

From what I could see of this office, it was small. There were electronics and cords everywhere. Then I realized it wasn't an office, but a server room, and from the feeling I was getting, it wasn't a place in Europe, but here in Arizona. As I was watching him, I could feel his energy, and I knew he was aware of me watching him. These feelings were overpowering – they were consuming me as if they were taking over my mind and body.

Then the phone rang, and just like that, the connection was severed. When this happened, it was heartbreaking. A pain, as if I lost him. I did for a brief moment wonder if this was true, or was it the entity? As quickly as the thought entered my mind, I thought, *no!* And quickly dismissed it. This, I had no doubts of since it felt different. It felt – right. What I felt was a love so powerful, it could only be true. I started wondering, *if I can feel him, can he feel me?* Then I thought, *a miracle. This is true. A blessing from God.*

With all this, my past life memories increased, as if there was a desperation for me to remember. To know and understand what happened. I was drawing daily; it was a need, no, an obsession, to draw the images in my mind. And it didn't matter how hard I tried to ignore them; these images I was getting would not go away. It was as if a force was pushing me to draw, and if I refused or tried to ignore them, the feelings would intensify, to a point I felt I was practically going mad.

Along with the visions of a life before, I didn't just see the images; I could feel everything she felt. It was as if I was reliving it all over again, the good and the bad. I had a powerful love, with a passion stronger than I ever felt or believed was possible. A sister, a much-beloved sister, who was my best friend. A secret that caused great anger and pain to all of us, mine, and his family together. I could see and feel everything. The emotions, they took me over, and with it, my strength. There were times I'd start crying, an uncontrollable crying, as if I, myself, had suffered this great loss.

With this, the dreams, the visions – memories, caused me to suffer severe anxiety, and with this, an increase in asthma attacks. I felt I was losing my mind and myself.

One of the few days I managed to go to work, I suffered a severe asthma attack. Although my daughter was working, she was unable to drive me to the hospital. So, there was no choice; my supervisor had to call 911. After I was at the hospital and in one of their private rooms that had a long glass sliding door, and after the doctors ran a series of tests to determine what was causing my multitude of attacks, I was lying in bed waiting, just watching the people pass by the glass door, and when I looked away, then back again, I was shocked at what I saw.

It was Marco. I was sure of it. He was slowly walking past my door as he was looking inside. It was as if he was looking for something – for me. He appeared – he looked as if he was a ghost. He was looking right at me. I could see what he was wearing: a yellow dress shirt with dark, possibly black pants. I could feel his concern – he was worried about me. He knew what happened to me, and somehow, someway, he was there. Well, his spirit was there checking on me. He wanted to make sure I was alright. It not only shocked me, but I was surprised he was able to do what he did. It made me feel happy and wonderful that he cared enough to look in on me. I don't know how he did it, but he did. Maybe it was our connection, the power of this love we seemed to have, as well as his concern for me. It was all so overwhelming. I wondered, *was it possible that he felt my pain and anxiety so much so, it allowed his spirit to leave his body and seek me out.*

After getting home from the hospital, I felt great and normal again. On the following day, I decided to stay home from work after the previous day's event. However, when I returned to work, it was all so strange, how at times, I would believe all was well, then boom, right out of the blue, I'd suffer a severe attack that would force me to leave work and go home. And as always, after getting home, it seemed to stop, and I'd feel normal. Was there something I wasn't aware of that was causing these attacks? If so, how? Or was it something more? Something that was completely out of my control. And when I laid down to rest – sleep, I'd dream, or times when I would lie on my bed, I would have deep and powerful visions. It felt as if someone was trying to tell me something, but what?

Saturday night, or shall I say Saturday morning, when I woke up, I felt tremendous joy. I dreamed about him – Marco. Well, at least I think I did. Okay, let me explain. I was asleep, and as I was surfacing from a deep sleep to a more semi-conscious state of sleeping – this is hard to explain. In a way, it felt like a dream, or was it my own wants and desires. The only thing I knew for sure was that it felt very real.

Before I woke up at a normal hour, I woke at three-thirty in the morning, and I knew without a doubt I was with Marco. And when I finally woke up at my normal time, I could only remember bits and pieces of the dream. Here's what I remembered: *We are at the lake, our lake. We are standing face to face holding each other as we are expressing our love. Next, we are sitting on a bench facing the lake, and Marco has his arm around me, with my head resting against his shoulder.* That was it, but what I felt when I awoke from the dream, it had to be real.

I was having this dream every night, but every morning I'd wake up, I'd only remember bits and pieces of the dream, to the point, it became normal – a regular part of my waking morning routine, and after waking up, I went about my day as normal. Once I was home, later that evening, after it was dark outside, I found I needed to go to the store. As I was going to my car, I noticed how full and large the moon was. It was so bright in the sky that it looked powerful. It felt as it was sending strong and powerful energy directly at me. For a long while, I couldn't take my eyes off it, and it took all my strength to pull my eyes away, so I could get in my car and start for the store.

As I was driving, I had this overwhelming feeling, as I did when I was about to have a vision. But this vision wasn't like the others. It was an extremely powerful vision. No, not a vision, but an actual memory. I say this because it felt different, not at all the same as the other visions I had.

The vision was during the time Marco and I spent together in our dreams, at our lake. Here is what I saw: *We are together at our lake, enjoying our time together, filled with so much love and passion that one could feel for another. This is our place, where we can come and be together, here in our dreams. This is our sanctuary. A place we can be together, so we can communicate, to feel and to touch. This allows us to express our love – the love we felt for each other then and feel for each other now.*

Since 'they' cannot allow us to be together in physical form, at least not yet, they have given us this gift, allowing us to be together here, in this place, our lake, where we can learn and get to know each other. This, because it's not our time to be together in the physical world. Because of this, we were not allowed to remember. Not yet.

What we feel – although we are not allowed to remember, for us, it doesn't matter, because we can be together, each and every night, here in our dreams, where we can have what we cannot have in real life. Here, at our lake, our sanctuary, a place that is protected and safe. The place where we first found our love, a powerful love that was a gift given to us by God.

While the vision was happening, I arrived at the store and parked in the parking lot, waiting for the vision – the memory to be over. In this memory, I could feel everything we felt in our dream. It was a love so powerful that was old and new, of a time lost and a time anew. After the memory was over, I couldn't move. I was too stunned at what I saw and what I was feeling. The emotion was so great; it brought me great joy and sadness. Then suddenly, I realized I wasn't the only one who experienced this memory; Marco did as well.

After finally getting control of my emotions and the beautiful memory given to me, I went into the store and purchased the items I needed, then headed home. On my way home, I couldn't stop thinking about what happened. *A miracle* was the only word that made sense at the time, a precious and wonderful gift from God. I could feel what Marco was feeling, as it was what I was feeling. Our love never died. It can never die. The power of our love connected our souls, bonding them for eternity. It survived;

to carry through time, waiting until the time we were both ready to remember our love, and allow it to bring us back together, allowing us to love once again.

Everything that was happening seemed to be telling me; when you find a love, a love so powerful, a true soul to soul connection, it's a merger of two souls, making you one, and this love doesn't end when you die. It carries on, waiting until the right time when you are reunited in your next life. This, when both souls are shown to be ready. A signal is sent out when this happens, piercing both hearts and souls, reconnecting them, making them one once again. Once your souls make this commitment, it's for eternity. Time is not a factor, as time does not exist.

They knew this was what we needed, to prove to us that we are real. Our love is real. I am real. He is real. We were given this time that allowed us to see and touch each other, to solidify what's been happening as truth. We were given the gift to step through a window, to a time and place, allowing our souls to merge, opening our hearts to this love. It allowed us to rediscover the love we lost all those years ago. In our dreams, there is no doubt, but outside, in the real world, we question, wondering, is this real? Is what I'm feeling real, or is it a fantasy? But there's something, something we cannot explain, a knowing that is felt in our hearts and souls, telling us it's real. Our hearts hold the greatest power, stronger than our brain – so you must listen to your heart. It is truth.

What's happening is beyond our brain's comprehension. A powerful force beyond what we know and believe on earth. A power, when ready, opens all knowledge from a life lived before. It's like a sewn-in DNA, but instead of our blood, it's a DNA of our souls. All the knowledge from our previous lives waiting for when we need it. In turn, we are opening to reveal the knowledge we need, alerting our body, the shell that now holds the soul, of all the knowledge from previous lives. This, some belief, is known as an old soul. I have lived many, many lives, as most of us have. God designed each and every one of us, waiting for the right time before allowing your soul to reveal its truth. Your truth. My truth.

In this, as I was driving home, it was as if I could feel the power of the moon, and with it, I felt the need to pray. To plead with God, to allow what we've had in our dreams to be in our physical lives.

"God, this gift you've given me…us," I started saying, with an overwhelming amount of emotions. At the same time, with a feeling of desperation. "I beg you; please allow us to have this. Not just in our dreams, but here, in our physical lives. To feel what I felt in those dreams…oh God, I beg of you. Plead with you. Please, allow this." I repeated this over and over again, and at the same time, I was glancing up at the moon until I finally arrived home. Once I was out of my car, I stood in the driveway and stared up at the moon, and once again, I pleaded with God to allow what we had in our dreams to be real, here in our physical world.

Chapter 23

Okay, I think it's time to get into the strange and unusual things that were happening. I say strange and unusual, because it was not like me to do these things, and I didn't know or understand where they were coming from.

One day, when I was unable to go into work, I was in the kitchen fixing something to eat, when words popped into my head. And when I tried to speak them aloud, instead of them coming out in words, they came out in song. Keep in mind, I am a horrible singer. What was funny about this happening, was for the first time in my life, I was happy. And after this first experience, I'd find myself humming throughout the day, and wondered why this was happening to me now. I couldn't remember a time I was happier than I was at that moment.

With my health issues, and barely able to work, I didn't feel so happy, but it seemed I was. Or was it my soul that was happy. It was hard to understand, and I still didn't have any answers. Whatever it was, it was bringing me great joy. I wondered what it was. Was it the fact that there was this love out there waiting for me? But not just any love, a strong and powerful love? Or was there more to it?

These songs I was singing, or at times humming, were some I recognize, and others – the words, I didn't recognize. The words, they felt as if they were related to Marco, and these words I never wanted to ever forget, so I wrote them down, and now I will share them with you.

Oh God, I have been searching for so long – for my love, the one who will complete me. To be everything he wants me to be. A love, for each other, loving with all our hearts and souls. Kissing, feeling, and loving each other for all time. Taking us through time and space, caring us beyond death. Loving each other for eternity. God, where is my love – bring him to me, please.

And here's another: *I wonder where my love is. Who he is? What he is, and what he's doing. Where is he, oh – I wonder where my love is. Could he be near me? Has he seen me? Does he know me? Has he heard and felt me, as I have heard and felt him? My love, who could he be. Does he think of me? Hope for me? Wanting me? Praying for me, as I have been praying for him. Oh – my love, please find me, love me, hold me, never let me go. Where is he? Oh God, please, bring him – bring my love to me. Bring him soon, as I am here waiting.*

It's funny, these songs remind me of the way Bards of the time told stories. Is this why they came to me in the way they did, or is there another reason. However, the power of these words was as if my soul was trying to tell me something – alerting me, by whispering these messages in my mind, a need for me to know and understand. It was as if there was a greater power saying, *listen, it's your heart speaking the truth.* However, that happy moment ended up being short lived. You'd think I would have embraced what was happening, but there was a part of me that refused to believe it was real, and often wondered, *how is this possible?*

I am standing outdoors, and I am dressed in a long cream yellow gown, that flows down past my feet, with long bell sleeves. There is a man on a horse – I am very angry, and I am yelling at him, "Go away! I will not go with you! If the king is so captivated by my beauty, then I shall cut my face, and make myself ugly!" As I put the knife to my face, and as I was about to cut, the man jumped off his horse and

grabs the knife from my hand, stopping me from cutting my face.

I woke up and said aloud, "What the hell was that!" I felt anger and fear from my dream, and I was still feeling them, as if I, myself, experienced this event. "What in God's name is happening to me?" There was no doubt, after this dream, I was freaked out.

It seemed no matter what I did, I could not prevent these asthma attacks from happening, and nothing seemed to help. To those I worked with, and who knew me well, became alarmed with what was happening to me.

I remember my supervisor saying, "Rebecca, we are very worried about you. I feel…we feel, there is more going on than just your asthma. There must be more causing your attacks."

I explained, "The doctor's ran series of test, and couldn't find anything out of the ordinary."

However, the day came that proved my supervisor was right.

That was a day I will never forget. It will be embedded in my memory for all time. It was on a day I managed to go into work, and I was on a call when I started having chest pains. At first, the pain was minor, like heartburn, but then it quickly worsened, to where I had to put the person I was on the phone with on hold. The pain had escalated to the point I could hardly talk. Automatically I put my hand on my chest rubbing it, as if that was going to do anything to help. But in mere seconds, the pain increased tremendously.

At that moment my supervisor walked by and noticed something was wrong, so she asked, "Rebecca, what's wrong?"

I tried to tell her, but it was difficult to speak. I managed to get a few words out in between the pain, "My…chest…hurts," I managed to say.

Without another word, my supervisor pushed me in my chair to her desk. With the new company policy – this, I believe was due to the multitude of EMT's that had been called to the office. So, before she could call 911, my supervisor had to call our human resource department to obtain permission first. However, just in the short distance from my desk to hers, the pain in my chest increased to unbelievable proportions, to ten times what it started off to be. It became a sharp stabbing pain. After my supervisor spoke to the 911 operator, she turned to hang up the phone, and when she turned back to me, she noticed I was sweating perversely. The shocked look on her face told me it wasn't good. Apparently, the 911 operator asked if I was sweating? At the time, I was not.

It seemed like seconds after my supervisor hung up the phone when she noticed sweat pouring down my face, as if someone had dumped a cup of water over my head. It was later when I learned that severe sweating is a sign of a possible heart attack. By the time the EMTs arrived, I wasn't just in pain, I was screaming in pain. When they asked me their series of questions, I was unable to talk. My supervisor gave the EMTs as much information as she could.

Then one of the EMTs asked, "Can you stand?"

The only thing I could do was shake my head no. With their help, I was placed on a gurney, and as I was being wheeled out, with the pain being intolerable, there was no holding it in, and I was screaming all the way out of the door and into the ambulance.

Once I was in the ambulance and we started off for the hospital, the EMT in the back with me was monitoring my vital signs, and something apparently registered on the machine that I was having a heart attack, and as he was shoving chewable aspirin in my mouth, he was telling me, "You need to chew these," he said with great urgency. He also signaled the driver, who turned the sirens on, and the worried look on his face concerned me.

Next, him and the driver were discussing which hospital they should take me to. The driver said, "I'm going to take her to Thompson Peak Hospital."

The other said, "No, we need to take her to the Mayo Hospital."

The driver said, "Thompson Peak is closer. Are you sure?"

The other said, "Yes. I think it's the best one."

Without further conversation they took me to the Mayo Hospital. During their conversation I was freaking out, never in my life have I been in an ambulance with the sirens going. Mind you, I have been in many by this point. So, this told me my situation was very great. The Mayo Hospital was the best place, since they specialize in heart attacks.

With everything that's happened in my life, not once was I put in such a position. As soon as I was wheeled into the emergency room, the emergency staff quickly acted. It was a scene right out of a movie or a television show. I don't know how many hospital staff were working on me, but I seemed to be surrounded by them. They were doing everything they could to get to the root of the problem. They tried asking me questions, as they were hooking me up to machines and jabbing me with needles. In my state of condition, I couldn't respond, but I could hear someone calling out orders.

One woman who was right next to me said, "She's breaking out with hives!"

The one giving orders said, "Quick, give her Benadryl!"

The woman than said, "I will have to put it in her shoulder."

With everything happening, I finally lost consciousness. Either from the pain, or the multitude of medication they were giving me, possibly both.

When I did finally wake up, the pain was completely gone and they allowed me to sit up, and then asked, "Are you hungry? Would you like something to eat?"

I said, "Yes." By this point I was starved.

Then another person – a doctor came in and said, "We are going to admit you."

I was shocked. I could only look at her for a few moments before I nodded with understanding. Shortly after, another doctor came in and said, "We don't know what happen, but we don't believe it was a heart attack. To be sure, we want to run a series of test, so we are admitting you. We want to take the necessary precautions." Again, I nodded in understanding.

After my first night in the hospital, and after they ran their first, second, and third series of test, it was determined I did not have a heart attack. What they did find, was a severely diseased gallbladder, one that was close to being cancerous. A surgeon eventually came into my room and explained what they found, and what they felt needed to be done.

"As you know, we did a series of test, and in these tests, it was determined you did not have a heart attack, but instead we found that you have a severely diseased gallbladder that is close to being cancerous."

You can imagine how I felt when I heard this. One, it was a relief to know I didn't suffer a heart attack. Two, to learn I had a severely disease gallbladder, one that could turn into cancer – *shit,* is what I thought.

The surgeon went on to say, "Now, you can wait, and have it removed later, but we feel since you are already here, we'd like to perform the surgery to have it removed. We feel this is not something you should put off."

I nodded in understanding. I wasn't sure what to think, but if it was that dangerous, then yes, they should remove it.

The doctor continued, "I want to operate right away. The chances of waiting…allowing it to fester…there is too much of a high risk of it becoming cancerous. There is a panel of doctors who have been discussing your case, and before we do anything, they want to run further test just to be sure you didn't have a heart attack."

I told the doctor, "Do whatever you need to do."

It was two days later when it was decided I would be undergoing surgery. Then there were further discussions, and it was postponed until mid-morning on that Saturday. During this time, I was only allowed to drink water until around dinner time, when I was notified that the surgery wouldn't be that day, only then I was finally allowed to eat.

When the day finally arrived, instead of the first surgeon who initially spoke to me, it was a woman doctor who came into my room to inform me of the counsel's final decision.

She said, "Tomorrow morning we are going to take you down for surgery, however, we may need to perform two surgeries. The first one will be to remove the diseased gallbladder, and the second one will be to check for any loose stones. There is no way to know if there will be any loose stones until they get inside and have a look around after removing your gallbladder."

I said, "Okay, do whatever needs to be done." If it was that bad, I wanted the blasted thing out of me.

After the doctor explained what they planned on doing, I was given consent forms to sign. However, I thought I signed two consent forms, but as it turned out, I only signed one. The first surgery was a success, but to be safe, they wanted to perform the second surgery. Since I only signed the one consent form, they were forced to contact my daughter Tiffany for next of kin authorization. Apparently, it took several attempts before they finally reached my daughter and obtained verbal permission.

With the surgery, I didn't feel there was any point for my daughters to miss work only to sit in the lobby waiting for my surgery to be over, which obviously proved to be an error. While they were waiting to reach my daughter, I started coming out of anesthesia and the doctor explained they needed to perform the second surgery and were waiting to reach my daughter for authorization. I figured since I was awake, I could give them the authorization they needed.

I was barely alert and slurring my words when I said, "Go ahead, I'm good."

My roommate Janet was there to see how I was doing, and she too tried to give permission. "I can authorize it," she said.

I said, "Yeah, she can."

The doctor of course said, "You can't approve the second surgery because you are not family," and just ignored me.

They finally reached Tiffany, and she gave them authorization to perform the second surgery. Everything ended up going well, and there were no lingering stones left behind.

After my surgery, it was a couple of days later when the doctor released me to go home. I cannot tell you how grateful I was. I was never so happy to leave a place as I was to leave the hospital. A week in the hospital was more than enough for me. Since my stomach was swollen after surgery, and seeing how they had to cut my clothes off, it left me only with my pants, which would not fit over my swollen stomach. I called Tiffany and asked her to run by my house to pick up a bra, then to go to a Department Store to buy me a cheap oversize shirt and a pair of large sweatpants so I would have something to wear home.

Once I was home, I asked Tiffany, "Would you mind staying with me. Just until after I take a shower. I don't feel very steady, and I don't want to take a chance of becoming dizzy and fall in the tub."

She said, "Yeah, okay."

I took a nice long shower, and after I was clean and relaxed, Tiffany agreed to make me something to eat before she left. Once Tiffany left, I crawled into bed and went to sleep.

It was another week at home before I was able to return to work. I was still weak and in some pain, but with a warm cloth over my incisions it gave me some relief.

On my first day back, my co-workers and boss were pleased to see me back and were relieved that I was alright.

There was no doubt, in the dramatic improvement of my health – asthma attacks, was due to a severely diseased gallbladder. What was interesting about this, when I googled what the symptoms were for a bad/diseased gallbladder, I didn't have any of the symptoms, except for the severe chest pains, which I took as asthma related.

With the number of times I visited my doctor, along with the multitude trips to the hospital, not once, especially at the hospital, did anyone consider there was more going on with me than having an asthma attack. Although there were things happening that made no sense, there was not one who requested further test. However, with all this, after time, things seemed to get back to normal.

After everything that happened, I was given an opportunity to make some extra money at work, in collections of all places. It wasn't in the way I've done in the past, as this job took little effort. I just had to call the customers who booked a car rental, because instead of their credit card being charged, the rental car company charged the travel agencies credit card instead. This was a great opportunity, and I was pleased and grateful to be one of the few chosen for this job.

We were given a percentage of commission for each payment we collected. Needless to say, I did very well. I made three thousand dollars on top of my regular pay. I pretty much made a small amount of what I lost from my savings. Unfortunately, it was not enough, as it was too late to go to   England.

It was funny, when I was feeling disappointed in not being able to go to England, my supervisor reminded me there are reasons things happen, or should I say, don't happen. If I was in England when this happened the cost would have been astronomical, as I didn't consider the need for international medical insurance. It wasn't even a thought in my mind. But after what happened, I've since decided before I attempt another move to England, I will be sure to buy international medical insurance.

You know how they say, *things happen during the time when you are undergoing surgery*. Well, this must have happened to me, because at the time, it was the only thing that explains what happened after. Around the time I was doing collections, words were forming in my mind, to the point I needed to write them down. Now, keep in mind, I never cared, nor was I a good writer. Shoot, I didn't even like reading until this same year. But believe it or not, I was a horrible writer. I couldn't write if my life depended on it. But now – now when the words formed in my mind, I would type them in the opened word document I kept open on my desktop, and to my shock and surprise, the words were good. Really good. Before I knew it, I was writing a story – a book. Me? What a laugh. But no, it was true, I was writing a book.

My very first book I read was Pillars of the Earth, by Ken Follett. This was given to me by my roommate Janet. You see, I felt the need to broaden my mind by reading. I talked to Janet about this, thus, she gave me Pillars of the Earth to read. I looked at her as if she was crazy. The book was huge. It was about a thousand pages.

I said, "Really? For my first book."

Janet said, "It's really good.

Well, I gave it a try, and she was right, because as soon as I started reading the book, I was immediately drawn in, and found it difficult to put it down. I read it with every free second I had. It is a great book. Who'd think, this one book would lead me to read a great many more books. I had no idea by not reading, how much I was missing. Not to mention, if I hadn't started reading, I would never have read Lady of the Rivers, which put me on the path I'm on now. Amazing, isn't it.

I remember one day when I attempted to wright without receiving what I call *inspiration*. I did this to test my theory, and yep, I was not wrong, I was a horrible writer. I went as far as trying to pick something out of the blue to write, versus what *they* gave me – inspired me to write. I gave a friend the part I wrote from inspiration, and the part I attempted to write without, and she looked at me, and was astonished how difference the two were. It was obvious, I wasn't doing the writing.

As I continued to write this story, there was a need, an urgency, that I needed to tell *their* story, no, my story. It's strange to say this, as I know it is not my story, but at the time, it is how I felt. It was a fierce urgency and one I've never known before. The lives of these two young people were buried – forgotten for all time, to never be remembered, until now. A life, a love, lost due to a decision they made, in going against all their families, by marrying.

With everything happening all at once, I was still attempting to record all the dreams and visions that were coming in rapid rate, here are a couple.

I am in an office – it looks to be a place I work at. At this office I meet a man, and we are in the beginning stages of getting to know each other, and I felt a very strong connection to him. Then, there is a blond woman, she says to me, "You need to know, there is something not right about him. It isn't good." I looked at her, but I wasn't sure what to think. Then I looked at him, as I question the validity of what she said, and without verifying the truth of her words, I started wondering about the man. I didn't want to believe her, but instead of talking to the man, or asking other's that know him, I ended up listening to this woman, and I cut off all contact and communication with him. Why? I don't know. I felt sad, since I believed this was a man I could care about very much.

And so, I began avoiding him. I no longer wanted anything to do with him. Although, I didn't give him an explanation to why, he seemed to understand. After this, every now and then when I looked at him, and when we made eye contact, he looked so sad – hurt. I hurt him. To think this broke my heart. Without another thought, I went to him. I had to. I had to know. I had to be sure he was alright.

When I approached him and put my hand on his shoulder, he didn't do or say anything. He only looked at me. Then after a few moments he said, "I don't understand why you did this? Why you walked away from me? From something I felt was good." At first, I didn't know what to say. What could I say? I could clearly see how much pain he was in. How much I...hurt him. It was breaking my heart. As I continued to look at him, I noticed there was something not right about him, he looked as if he was using or taking something. Maybe drugs, but I couldn't be sure.

Suddenly, without understanding why, there was something in me that felt such horror and regret to what I did to him. I deserted him, and without explanation or proof to what was said to me. At that moment, I realized how wrong I was. The blond woman was wrong. She deceived me. But why? This, I did not understand, and I knew I should never have listened or believed her. He did – does, care about me. He really cares about me. In this realization, and with the way he looked, my heart sank. I began to feel so afraid and scared. I had this feeling, if I didn't act now, something horrible was going to happen to him, and I would lose him forever.

Without further thought, I immediately reached for him and turned him around, so that he was facing me. I placed my arms around him, and pulled him close to me, with the need to comfort him. Then I said, "Forgive me! I am so sorry! You mean so much to me! I also felt the connection. A strong and powerful connection! I...I...love you!" Tears were running down my face. My heart was hurting so much for what I did to him, and I realized how much I needed him to know and understand how important he was to me. "I want you in my life! I made a grave mistake in listening to this woman...this blond woman! She told me things...she deceived me!" Feeling ashamed, "I allowed her to deceive me. I am so sorry. I don't know why I listened to her, but...I am sorry! Please forgive me! I had no idea how much you cared about me!" I pleaded with him, desperate for his understanding. I was feeling so much pain and regret in my actions towards him. "I should never have listened to her. I should have come to you first and told you what she said and allow you to...I'm sorry!" What was I to do or say? How could I make it right?

Next, we were together, and everything was fine – perfect, even after what happened. We are together. I seem to be standing in a large house, which appears to be a mansion, with a grand staircase. It is wide at the bottom and narrows at the top. I feel that I am there to meet his family, and that this is his family's home. This is where we start to plan our lives together. Then the phone rings and it's my ex-husband. He says, "Danger is coming. You need to get somewhere safe." After hearing this, I see a large dark cloud in the sky moving towards my grandmother's house where my daughters are living. I immediately call them, "You need to hide! Get somewhere safe! Somewhere no one will find you!" Then the dark clouds turned into soldiers. They were marching towards my grandmother's house – to my daughters. I am scared and didn't know what to do, or how to help them. How can I save them? My daughters are in danger of being hurt – killed.

I woke up with the fear still coursing through me. This practically scared the living shit out of me. It was strange, because although I had no name for the man, it was clear after the dream it was Marco.

This is the dream I had following the dream above.

I am in a village. A very small village that is out in the middle of nowhere, surrounded by trees – a forest. People are running everywhere, trying to escape from impending death. There are these creatures – they are small, maybe three feet tall. They are very thin with sharp teeth – what they were, I don't know, but they are trying to kill everyone. A few of us run into a building, into what looks to be a throne room of sorts. It looks like an old Greek throne room, with a large chair, with marble columns surrounding it. We are standing, huddled together, afraid of being killed by these creatures. We came here deciding to stand together as one, so we could fight these creatures by combining our strength, and with great effort, we defeated these creatures and chased them away. Once the creatures were gone, we were finally able to relax, with a feeling of relief. We were free from danger. When suddenly, standing in front of us at the entrance was a tiger. Still high on adrenaline, we attacked the tiger, and it was me who ended up cutting the tigers head off, and it rolled a few feet away.

As his head sat several feet from his body, he was still alive and his head – his mouth – he was talking to me. I look at him, shocked, "How can this be?" I asked.

Then he says, "I am your protector. I was sent to protect you. To keep you safe from those creatures."

I fall on my knees in front of his face, looking into his eyes, horrified at what I did. My actions killed an innocent. One, who was sent to protect me. What could I say? Nothing, there was nothing I could say except, "I am sorry! So very sorry!" Then I slumped forward with my face in my hands. I am crying, feeling so ashamed for what I did.

Then he says, "Don't worry yourself. You did not know. You did what you had to do, to save yourself. I was trying to tell you, but you were too afraid. You reacted out of instinct and fear. After what happened with those creatures, you could do no other."

I look at him, astonished at his compassion, his forgiveness – I was crying and so upset that I killed an innocent. My protector. Then, I noticed a scar on the right side of his face. It started above his eye, going down to the side of his mouth. And this is when I woke up.

This dream really affected me, even to this very day. I didn't know what to think. I still don't. What was the meaning of this dream? What was it trying to tell me? These were questions, even to this very day, I am unsure of the answer. I set here staring off into space, trying to understand what this dream was trying to tell me then, and today, and I think I have a possible answer. Or maybe, a semblance of an understanding. Fear. It takes away our rational thinking. It cripples us, causing us to lose all understanding of what is right and what is wrong. Even if the answer is right in front of us. Think before you react. See with more than just your eyes and your fears. Dissect it. Open your heart and soul to the truth.

It seemed like a lifetime ago since my trip to Cheshire, England. You would think up to this point it was enough, in what I was going through since my visit to Cheshire, but it wasn't. With the dreams coming in a rapid rate, I became lost, and I didn't know what to do. Then, out of the blue, my health started declining again. No, it wasn't as severe as it was, and work wasn't being as affected as it was before, but it was enough to question what was happening? What was the cause? In this, along with feeling lost, I started feeling depressed, and I didn't know what to do.

In this, I allowed myself to fall apart, and I didn't care about how I looked. I stopped fixing my hair, but instead, I would put it up in a bun and stopped putting makeup on. The clothes I chose to wear were easy and without thought. It also didn't help since my surgery; I was still unable to fit into most of my clothes. I did think this was the cause, but it wasn't. At least, not all of it.

It was time I sought help, but from who and where. I took a chance, I decided to call a phycologist I went to years ago to see if she could possibly help me. I remember thinking, *who can I go to…a phycologist? If so, how do I tell them what's been happening to me without telling them the full truth.* I didn't want them to think I was losing my mind, and in turn have me committed. What else was I going to do? I had to see a phycologist. So, I decided to contact the woman who helped me before, when I learned I was molested by my grandfather. So, I called and scheduled my first appointment.

This dream happened around November of 2013. *I am in a house with a woman I know from work, and it appears to be the holiday season. I notice the house is a mess, and there are other people living there as well, but I don't know who they are. For some reason, I seem to be sad, unhappy, and miserable. I don't feel like celebrating Christmas, so I leave.*

Next, I find myself back in the house, and suddenly there's an earth quick, which causes the roof to cave in. Then, there's a man in the house. I'm not sure who he is, but I feel he is dangerous. There's a dog, a sweet dog that's playing around this man. This man is a very large and strong man, and he seems to really hate me. I am sleeping on the sofa when this man attacks me and tries to rape me. I try desperately to fight, to force him off me but he is too strong, then the other people who live at the house return. I say, "There was a man here trying to rape me!" They looked around the house, but the man was no longer there. He seemed to have vanished, and they look at me as if I am crazy. Then I woke up.

Again, another dream that didn't make any sense. If these dreams were trying to tell me something, what it was, I had no idea – at the time.

I started receiving more and more information regarding my past life. Memories that were resurfacing through dreams, and at times, through visions. This need to write this book became even stronger than ever before. I needed to tell their story. I started receiving names of Elizabeth and Robert, but I didn't understand what this meant. I began to wonder, were these their names? But it was hard to say. The funny thing about this, at the time when I was thinking of names, to name Tiffany if she was a girl. One of them, which I wrote in her baby book was Elizabeth. Was this the start of what was to come? That, I couldn't say. I wasn't just remembering a past life with disconnection of all feelings, but with complete connection, feeling everything that happened to me – to *her*. The good and the bad. This, I wish on no one. To live such heartache, tragedy, was – well – painful. Disturbing. A complete tragedy.

In all this, there could be no doubt, I was the woman from my dreams and visions, and I felt everything she felt. No matter how much I may have wanted the dreams to stop, they did not. Instead, they became a part of me for all time. Her – Elizabeth's love for Robert, her family, along with her sorrow, how can one person endure so much. I wasn't only dealing with my current life issues, but also my past life issues. There was no wonder I was still suffering from asthma attacks, since one of my biggest triggers is emotions, stress, anxiety, etc.

I was sitting on one of the chairs in the living room as I was writing my book – when I first started, I was handwriting the story, then later I would transfer it to the computer – when the worse of all memories surfaced. Her rape. In this life I've never been raped. To feel such a tragedy of a traumatic experience, a rape – her rape. A rape, from hundreds of years ago – it didn't feel as if it was hundreds of years ago, but of the here and now. As if it was happening to me, right then, on that very day. When this happened, I started crying – bawling uncontrollably. At this, I was never so glad to be home alone. How was I to explain my emotional breakdown to Janet. Even through all of this, I tried to write everything I saw and felt, but it proved to be too difficult. I had to stop, and I threw down the pad and pen and allowed the emotions to take me over, and I cried until I couldn't cry anymore.

When I thought I was in a better place, I attempted to write the horrible tragedy she – I suffered. With this, I knew I needed help, and I needed it right away. I had to know what was happening to me. These dreams and visions I was having, were they what I believe, from a life before – were they real? Or were they something else? I needed these questions answered, but how? I thought about going to a past life regressionist, and wondered, *how do I find one, and a good one. The right one? What would it cost? Would it be too expensive?* No matter what I had to know. Whatever it was, I had to find out, and I must tell their story. To me, it felt as if their lives, of who they were, in the love they shared, were erased – forgotten, as if they never existed. So now, in this life it was time – it was up to me to tell their story.

I did question if remembering a life before, in reliving *her* life, a life that was full of love, pain, and sorrow, were the reason why my asthma attacks increased. There was no doubt, these memories were causing me to be an emotional wreck. But it wasn't only asthma attacks, it was also from extreme anxiety, which is also a trigger for asthma. To the point, I ended up taking antianxiety medication, along with antidepressants.

I am hoping this appointment with the phycologist will give me some of these answers, but if not, then I will need to seek out a past life regressionist.

Chapter 24

Since I determined I needed help, I had yet to find it. Yes, I have an appointment with a phycologist, but she cannot help me with past life memories, so I was still in need of help, and there was no question, I could not put it off any longer. I had to find help, and I had to find it now. The problem was, where, and who could I go to that wouldn't think I was crazy. Around this time, I sought out books that might give me answers, and one of the books I found was by Dr. Brian Weiss, who specializes in past life regression, and I thought, *that is what I need, a past life regressionist.* But where do I find one. I couldn't seek out Dr. Brian Weiss, but there had to be someone in Arizona, right?

Well, it's the day of my first therapy appointment, and after the initial greeting, I told the phycologist about my plans to move to England, and what happened when I returned. I explained to her about the asthma attacks, and then about my gallbladder. The sadness I felt knowing my plans to move to England were no more. However, I chose not to tell her of the other things, of the past life I was remembering. How does one bring something like that up? This went on for the first few visits, until I finally decided to tell her about my drawings. I explained how drawing had become a calming experience – relaxing. That at first, I was drawing trees, lakes, ponds, and in some cases, people.

I said to the phycologist, Denise, "I am not sure why I'm suddenly drawing, and to my surprise, they are good. I never had an interest in drawing before, nor did I care to. Even if I tried, as I did when the girls were little, it was horrible. I couldn't draw even if my life depended on it."

She seemed to be interested in what I was telling her, and so she asked, "Can you bring them in on your next appointment? I would really like to see these drawings."

You have no idea how pleased I was to hear this, and at the same time I was nervous for her to see them. But of course, I agreed.

The following week when I showed up for my appointment, I showed her my drawings, and I was surprised to what Denise said. "Could these drawings be from a past life memory?"

I looked at her with utter shock by her question. I didn't expect that from her as a phycologist. However, I was relieved that she asked the question, and I let out a breath and said, "Yes…I think they are. I have thought about going to a past life regressionist so I could further explore these memories I've been having."

Denise again surprised me on what she said next, "There's no need. I can put you under a trance."

I was shocked, yet ecstatic. I felt great! To finally have someone and in the professional field no less, who was willing to help me find the answers I've been seeking, was a huge relief.

I said, "Really?" I was astonished and surprised.

Denise said, "Do you want to give it a try on your next visit?"

Did I? Of course, I did, so I said, "Yes, very much."

It was a huge weight off my shoulders to know there was someone who believed in me and was willing to help me. I did worry, that I will learn the dreams didn't mean anything. That instead, I would learn they were my own creation – an illusion. My own fantasy. I had to ask. I needed to know, and so I asked her the question. "So…you don't think…I'm crazy?"

To my wonderful relief she said, "No. Not at all. I believe in past lives. There are many who can recall certain past life memories and events. I am not just a phycologist…I also believe in spirituality. I am open to the possibilities there's more out there then just science. I believe in spirit guides, angels, and more. We will work on this on your next visit. We will find out what's actually going on here," she said, still looking at my drawings.

As I was leaving Denise's office, I felt as if a huge weight had been lifted off my shoulders. You have no idea what that felt like, to know the person I am seeking help from was open to the possibilities of what was happening to me. I felt that I could finally breathe. I didn't have to find a way to explain what's been happening to me without revealing the truth. I could be completely open and honest with her, without feeling the fear of being labeled *crazy*, along with the fear of being locked up.

Well, it's the day I am to go under a trance, which is another word used for hypnosis. I am going to have my first past life regression. I was excited, yet, at the same time, I was nervous. I didn't know what to expect, so Denise explained what she would be doing, after we went through the normal questions.

"How are you?" Denise asked.

"I am doing well, but I am very nervous."

"There is nothing to be nervous about. I will explain everything before we get started. How did your week go? Was there anything new that's happened?"

"My asthma attacks don't seem to be getting any better. However, on a good note, I am able to work more than I have been."

Denise said, "That's good you are able to work, but…I want to ask you something."

I said, "Yeah, okay."

"Do you think these asthma attacks you are having could have anything to do with this past life you are remembering?"

I said, "I don't know. I never thought about it before." Well, as you know that wasn't exactly true. When she asked the question, I had forgotten I'd even thought of it. Yes, I thought it was possible, but then – well, I brushed it off.

"Well, we will figure it out. What I am going to do is help you relax your body. So, I'd like you to close your eyes and take a deep breath, in through your nose, then blow it out slowly through your mouth."

As I was breathing in and out, she was speaking softly, helping to gradually ease me into a deep hypnotic state. To both of our surprise, it didn't take long.

Denise began to ask a series of questions. "What do you see? Where are you?"

During this, I felt so relaxed. I felt at peace. Calm. After a few moments, I started seeing shadows, images that were trying to appear. Then, I found myself in a room, a room I was familiar with. A room from my dreams.

I said, "I am in a castle…a room. I am upset. Very upset. I am pacing, rubbing my hands together, not knowing what to do. I was just told my husband is dead…killed, trying to save me."

Then suddenly, I was no longer Rebecca, but *her*, the woman from my dreams, she was the one speaking.

"No…how could this happen? What am I to do? I can't do this. Not this. Not here and not with this man…this king. I have to. I must…God, please help me. Tell me what to do? How can I live with such a man…a man who killed my love, my husband? I cannot live without him. I have no one," I said – she said. There was such sadness in my voice. And yes, I was clearly aware of everything that was happening.

Denise asked, "What are you doing?"

Without answering her question, I – she continued, "I have to. I have no choice." She was standing at the window looking out to the moon and stars in the sky, then down to the water and rocks below. When she says, "How can I do this? It's a sin to take one's life, but I can't live like this…without him. I am so afraid. I have no choice…I must do this. To live without him, is too painful." I climb to the edge of the window and look down to the rocks below, then up to the sky – to God. "God, please forgive me?" Then she jumped. When this happened, I snapped out of the trance and found myself feeling very weak and confused to what happened. So, I asked, "What happened?"

"You jumped. When you did, you snapped out of the trance."

"Oh my God…it's true. It's really true. These dreams…they are from a past life. My past life. I jumped?"

I felt so stunned at what happened. What was shocking and amazing, was that I was able to feel everything she was feeling when she took her life.

Denise asked, "What do you think about what happened?"

"Oh my God, I can't believe this is true," I said, still stunned from what I've learned. "This told me more of why I took my own life. They killed my husband, the man I loved with all my heart. I felt I had no other choice. I couldn't live with what happened." At this revelation, still feeling stunned and shocked, I needed to know and understand more of this past life I was remembering? Of who I was.

Then Denise said, "Yes, and during this memory you were different. You sounded different. As if you were not yourself, but this person you use to be in your past life. Do you want to try again?"

Try again, really. That was a ridiculous question, of course I wanted to try again, and again. So, without hesitation, I said, "Yes. Very much so. I need to understand and know why this is happening, and why it's happening now."

We scheduled my next appointment for another regression. Finally, I was getting answers, and I felt and thought, *I am not crazy*. With this, I hoped that finally I would understand why this was happening. At this, I did start to wonder, *were my asthma attacks related to this?* I didn't know for sure, but I hoped to find out in the coming weeks.

Even through all this, the dreams never stopped, even in my waken state, with names continuously repeating themselves in my mind. The names were Robert and Elizabeth. I know these names came up in my dreams before, but I couldn't be sure, and I'd hope to find out for sure in one of my regressions.

It was my second regression, and we went through the process of putting me under, and once I was there, I could only see utter darkness. I wasn't sure what was happening or where I was. Then, after a few moments, I could see flashes of light, and then I heard a voice calling my name, "Elizabeth – Elizabeth." *Elizabeth is my name,* I thought. This is the first time I learned my name from the past life. As the light became brighter, I was suddenly in a white place of pure white, as if I was surrounded by clouds. There was a man who looked to be Jesus. He was there to meet me after my death, and he was sad because I took my life.

He said, "Elizabeth, God is very angry with you."

I asked, "Where is Robert, my love, is he here?" As I was looking around and behind the man I believe to be Jesus, thinking he would be here waiting for me, but he wasn't.

"Robert will join us shortly," he said. This was also when I learned the name of the man from my dreams, my – Elizabeth's husband. "Why is he not here? He should be here already."

"Elizabeth, you are the first to arrive. But he will be here soon. I am very disappointed in you – in taking your own life. God is very angry with you. You asked for his help, but you did not allow him time to help you. With incorrect information, you took your life. A life given to you by God. To take your life and before your time, has angered God. I am sad…you chose to take your life, before allowing God to help you." Jesus – to see the sadness and disappointment – I could feel Elizabeth's pain and her regret.

Robert finally arrived. Once he was standing by my side, Jesus guided us to a window, which looked like swirling water. "I have something horrible to tell you. Evil is at hand. With evils help…they are working to prevent your souls from ever meeting in your next lives. I did all I could to fight this, but I failed, since you both took your own lives. For this, I am prevented from helping you. There is nothing I can do," he said with sadness. "If your love is strong enough you will find each other in your next lives. I could not stop this. What I can do, is give you a gift, the gift of sight and knowledge before you're sent back to be reborn. This gift will assist you in finding each other. Elizabeth, I have always been with you, and I always will be. Believe and trust in me, and all will be well."

Robert and Elizabeth walked through the window of rebirth, and when this happened, it broke the trance. This regression was very intense. To learn what happened – it also confirmed the dream I had before. It also gave me more insight to what my dream did not. It gave me names.

You know what was really weird? After these two regressions, it seemed my asthma attacks were getting better. I started to think, *was this past life I was remembering the cause?* When I thought back to when this started, it was after I returned from England. I had first thought it was due to the summer heat, but now – what if? After visiting Dunham Massey Castle there was this strong feeling of a life I lived before. It had to be there. Still, I couldn't be sure.

To try to find these answers, I decided to google Dunham Massey and see if I can find an area that matches the drawings I did. I felt, If I was correct, I will find a match. To my shock and surprise, I did. The drawing of the lake and the tree, I found to be in Deer Park, which is called Smithy Pond, and the forest trees I drew, were similar to the trees that were still remaining. Not too far from Dunham Massey, I found where Watch Hill Castle was located and the river the flows by it, along with the area the drawing I did of an open clearing. I couldn't believe it; it blew my mind.

On my next regression, Denise told me she thought it was time to find out why I was suffering from these asthma attacks. So instead of a past life regression, we were going to do a current life, one focused on when the asthma attacks first started for me, which was during the time I was dating John.

When I arrived at Denise's office, thinking we were going to attempt another past life regression, and this time I wanted to use my phone to record it, so I could playback what happens, in the way I sounded. However, since we were focusing on my current life, I decided not to record it, what was the point. Boy, how wrong I was. It turned out to be a big mistake.

We began with the normal relaxing, with breathing in through the nose and out through the mouth exercise. Then Denise began her questions, "What do you see?"

"I'm with John, and we are at a church celebrating the Fourth of July. The dust was thick in the air from everyone walking around. As we were leaving, I started coughing. It was a very hard and painful cough. After we arrived at his house, he ran inside and when he returned, he had his inhaler in his hand. He helped me into the house, and after I sat down, he instructed me on how to use his inhaler. Within a few moments, I felt immediate relief. My throat was raw, and it was difficult to talk."

"What else is happening?" Denise asked.

However, I didn't answer her right away. From what she told me later, there was a small silence before she received my response.

And then my answer came – no, it was not an answer. "What am I going to do? Who can I tell? There is no one, no one I can tell," I said. However, although I could hear myself talking, it wasn't my voice. I felt I was there, but wasn't. There was something – someone – else.

"Who am I speaking to?" Denise asked. "This is not Rebecca, is it?"

There was no answer, but *she* continued as if Denise never asked a question. "I am so scared. I don't know what to do, or who to tell. There is no one who can help me. No one I can tell. I don't know what to do." I could hear the sadness and the pain in her voice. She spoke so soft and sounded so young.

Trying to reassure the girl, Denise said, "Everything is going to be alright. You are safe. You have a new life," realizing the girl was more than likely Elizabeth from my past life. "You are now Rebecca, and she is going to do everything to make sure you and she are alright. She is going to tell your story, so everyone will know what happened to you," she said, then asked, "Elizabeth, is that your name?"

At this question, I did – she responded. "Yes. I don't know what to do. I am all alone with this."

Denise said, "You are alright. You are safe."

Then, just like that, the trance broke. When I woke up from this, I knew and was able to feel what was happening. It felt as if I was there, but not. I heard a voice, which was not mine. Denise told me it was Elizabeth. That something from my regression triggered her to appear. I wondered how this was possible. Denise told me that each time I went under and regressed to my past life, my voice changed. It was a softer, delicate, younger voice. I could not believe this happened. And of course, this was the time I chose not to record it. I decided from that moment on, no matter what, I was going to record each and every regression. With this, it left me looking forward to learning what happens next.

In the next couple of days after Elizabeth's appearance, I kept hearing a voice. It was a soft and sweet voice, a young voice. It was telling me, "There is something there. There is something there." As she was telling me this, I believe she was also showing me the place where the *something is*, which was the tree and a lake, the one from my dreams and visions. There was this urgency in her voice, as if it was a life-or-death situation, if I didn't go and find what was there.

On my next appointment, I told Denise about this, but she decided to discuss other things first before we went right into a regression. Denise told me about a client of hers who went to see a psychic who does past life readings. Her client gave her the recorded CD of her session to listen to.

Denise said, "She seems really good. If you're interested, I can see if my client will give me the name and number of the psychic."

Would I be interested? Are you kidding me, of course I was, and said, "Yes, please?"

Well, she did get the information, and without delay, I called and made my first appointment.

Although Denise has been helpful, for some reason I still felt I needed to see a professional regressionist. Why, I didn't know. There was just this need I had to try a professional. What I expected, was nothing to what I received. You can say, I had a huge shock. Let me explain.

The person I went to, he started with my current life – my childhood. He wanted me to go back to my earliest memory I had of my childhood. My earliest memory was when I was two years old. From that memory, he gradually worked his way up through the years until we reached age ten, and then nothing. I could tell by his voice that this baffled him. How could someone not have any memory at age ten. It was true though, I have little to no memory of that time in my life, and now this proved it. After several attempts in trying to bring those memories to the surface, failed, suddenly, there was a flash of light, and I found myself in an office – a conference room —

I am sitting at a long oval table with a little girl, and that little girl was me! It was me, at age ten. She was sitting at the head of the table, and I was in the chair to the right of her, and I was the same age as I was at the time of this aggression, forty-three.

Directly in front of me is a wall of windows, and through those windows, with the sunlight shining through, you could see a courtyard. I am sitting there talking to her, telling her, "Everything is going to be okay. Look at me, I am you. I am living proof of that. If I survived, so can you. Don't give up. Be strong, and know you are loved. God is with you. Jesus is with you. They are always protecting you. There will be many challenges you will endure. Life won't be easy, and you will suffer great pain, and love will be hard to find." Then, I place my hand over hers, "But trust in yourself, in me, as I am you, at age forty-three. I never thought I would get to this point, but I have. I...we have two beautiful daughters. Trust in God, he will help you. You will survive. Yes, there will be hard times, with pain and sorrow. In going through this, it will make you a stronger and an independent woman."

After this, I snapped out of the regression. I felt overwhelmed by what happened, with a multitude of emotions coursing through me. Most of all, I was shocked. I knew what and how this happened. I Looked at the person who assisted me, he was looking at me with such confusion. He didn't understand what happened. All I said was, "I remember. Oh my God, I can't believe what just happened. This was a memory, of what Jesus did for me." I kept saying this over, and over again.

Even after I left, leaving the man confused to what happened. This didn't matter. What mattered was I finally understood that Jesus had always been there watching over me. Protecting me. They knew what I went through then, and what I was still to go through. And there was only one person who could help me – her. This is why my memories were blocked, because Jesus blocked them after I attempted to take my life. By bringing us together then, me as a child, and me as an adult, he knew I would be the only one who could help her – me. I know, this is so confusing, so you could imagine what it was like when it happened.

Which is why that time of my childhood was lost. It was I – I was the only one who could help save her – save me. I, I was the one to convince her – I saved my own life. It was me who convinced myself that life was worth living. It was shocking, I know. But now, now I knew, there was a purpose. A reason for me to be born. Although, she didn't know it yet, she would in time. When she did – I would find a great love. After this, I could feel God's love flowing through me as tears threaten to surface, but I forced them back. It was me – me! I was the one who saved me! I couldn't stop repeating this, it was shocking to discover something so extraordinary as this. I was amazed, astonished, shocked, and surprised. I had no idea this was even possible. Yet – it was.

This explained so much, to why I couldn't remember that part of my childhood, and why I never attempted to take my life again. It was me. I kept saying this all the way home, still reeling from the shock, of a wonderful gift bestowed to me by Jesus. Now, I know and understand why I couldn't remember, as it hadn't occurred yet. The purpose wasn't to remember, but to feel and know everything would be alright. And who best to hear it from, then myself. What a wonderful, glorious gift.

It wouldn't be until a few years later when I would learn time moves simultaneously. Going from past to present, and future. And, I don't mean of our current life, but of all our lives. As the past is occurring, our present is proceeding, as well as our future. Amazing isn't it.

<u>Verona, Italy</u>

Ever since Maria connected with Rebecca, she's checked in on her every now and then, wondering how she was doing, especially after what happened with the spirit. When she looks in on her, she is pleased to find Rebecca is doing well. And to her wonderful surprise, Rebecca found a woman with strong psychic abilities that could help her. Maria feels this woman can also help her reach Rebecca. For Maria to know there is someone who can help Rebecca understand what's been happening to her, can help her learn the truth.

"When the time is right, I will go to her, and let her know I am there," Maria said aloud. Just then, Maria hears a knock on her front door, and when she opens it, to her wonderful surprise, it's Marco.

"Marco, what a wonderful surprise, and just at the right time." She reached for Marco and pulled him in for a hug. Then guides him to the living room so they can talk. "I have much to tell you. Sit-sit." Waving to the sofa, then she says, "Why did you not call and tell me you were coming?"

With everything that's happened, Marco desperately needed to talk to his grandmother. Yes, he could have called, but to be honest, he missed his grandmother and wanted to surprise her. For as long as he could remember, she has always brought him comfort when he needed it, or when he felt lost as he does now. He felt it was best to just hop on a plane and fly directly to Italy.

"Nõnna, you look so happy…good news then?" *Could it be about Rebecca? Oh, please let it be.* "I didn't call because I wanted to surprise you.

Smiling, she said, "Yes. Very good news. She's doing very well Marco. Much better than she was," she answered the question he did not ask. "Well, I always love your surprise visits," placing her hand over his. Then, she quickly changed the subject, "Are you going to your mothers for Christmas?"

"Yes, I am. I am sorry I cannot spend Christmas with you," he said, feeling true regret.

His mother hated his grandmother. Why? That, he never understood. He knew it had something to do when his mother met his grandmother when she was dating his father. That is all he knows. If it was up to him, he'd rather spend Christmas with his grandmother. He hated leaving her alone, and with this, shame washed over Marco's face.

Maria saw Marco's sadness and felt his shame. To her, in the way his mother feels, it no longer matters. She understands his mother, more than his mother prefers. For Marco's mother to know Maria has the ability to know her secrets, has always scared her.

Maria waved her hand in a dismissive jester, then said, "I understand Marco. But if you are truly honest with yourself, if it was possible, you would return to Arizona right now?" Maria said, as she placed her hand over his, then said, "Hold hope in your heart. There is a good chance you will see Rebecca on Christmas, and at the place you stay when you are in Arizona."

Marco looked at his grandmother and wondered how he could go to Arizona, since he was spending Christmas with his mother. "Really? How can you know this?" he asked. Since he was old enough to understand, he's known his grandmother knew things others did not. She was a well-respected woman, and at times, she was known to be a wise woman.

For a long moment, Marco could only stare at his grandmother, as he thought, *how can this be? Mother is always adamant, that family be together on Christmas, except for those times I've insisted on spending Christmas with nõnna, the times I had business in Italy during Christmas.* When he did, he'd insist on remaining, so he could spend Christmas with her. *What could possibly pull me back to Arizona…to Rebecca?* Marco smiles at his grandmother, "It's called the Princess. The Fairmont Princess, nõnna."

"Oh, yes-yes. The Princess, thank you."

Then he tries to say, "but —" is all he manages to say, before his grandmother interrupts him.

Maria smiles at Marco, she sees the uncertainty in his eyes and says, "Yes, you are to be with your mother, as she will not understand if you were to leave during the Holiday. But," she said, as she takes his hand in hers, "You will return to Arizona. And when you do, you will see her. This I know," Maria said as she gave Marco's hands a shake. "This I see. Trust me, and you will see I tell the truth. No Marco, your mother will never understand…you know this. There will be too many questions…questions you cannot answer."

Closing his eyes, he felt so confused. Yes, he wanted to follow his heart, as it was telling him he needed to return to Arizona. Feeling lost, he decided to ask his grandmother. "What am I to do then?"

"Do nothing different. Do what you need to do. Spend Christmas with your mother, your sister and family. Then, when you can, go back to Arizona, and once you are there, I will do what I can to help you and Rebecca meet."

Marco gives his grandmother a hug, then says, "Okay nõnna."

Chapter 25

<u>Arizona</u>

My next therapy appointment was December 17, 2013, and we attempted another regression, and this one I recorded. So, what you will read is a detailed account of what happened.

As always, we started out with me closing my eyes, breathing in and out, until Denise was sure I was ready, then she asked, "What do you see?"

After a few moments, I said, "I don't know where I am."

"Okay, just take your time."

There was a short silence before I spoke again. "Just darkness."

"Trust that your guides will take you to the right place."

Shortly after she said this, I was at a lake. "I'm…standing, looking out at the lake."

"Are you by yourself?"

"Yes. Somebody's coming. It's Robert. He's here. I am so happy to see him. He's scared because our family won't accept our relationship."

"They don't understand," Denise said.

"No, they don't get it. I don't understand. I don't understand. It wasn't our intension. But sometimes things happen…that aren't intended," I said with sadness. "I just don't understand why they can't accept us. Robert is so angry…how his family cannot accept…we both don't understand why it matters. Why it's such a big deal. Why can't they just accept us. I am feeling so much pain and fear. They have forbidden us to…ever be together again…to see each other. But it's impossible. It's impossible. It just cannot be. With the way we feel…we just…we cannot. We cannot obey that request. We just can't. When we aren't together, it's too painful. For us to cease, to ever be together…we can't. That would just kill us both. So, we've agreed to see each other regardless of our families wishes. But we must be very secret about it. Very quiet, and very careful, they never find out.

"You don't want to dishonor them. Disobey them, but —"

"No!" I said firmly. "But they are asking too much of us. We are of the same family…if we were together, we would still be together in the same family. Why does it matter? Robert supposed to marry my sister…so what. If he marries me, isn't it the same?" Shaking my head, "But, it's not the same. Because I am not the eldest daughter. I don't get this…I don't get it. Maybe…I'm just too young to understand." At this, there was great sadness in my voice. "Or maybe, my heart is just in the way of understanding."

"What does your sister want?" asked Denise.

"She doesn't want him. She knows how we feel about each other."

"Okay, she's in support."

"Yes, but she also knows she can't go against her family. Our family. Our father's wishes. Our mother's wishes. She's the eldest, he's the eldest son of his family, they are to marry, to join both families…we didn't have a male line, and the only way to secure our family fortune, title, and status, is to marry with another family, with status and title, to maintain everything."

"And that's Robert's fear?"

"Yes, their family is very powerful…very wealthy. They own most of the land, as we use to own most of the land," I said in a voice of shock and surprise, that the question was even asked. "We used to own what they own.

Now, they own most of it. So, we must merge…but…won't our marriage still merge the two families? Apparently not," I said abruptly, with a touch of anger in my voice. "I don't get it," I said with sadness. "Robert doesn't understand," I said in a straight unfeeling tone. "Maybe we just don't want to understand," my voice softens, with a feeling of sorrow.

At this, Denise noticed the difference in my voice. I was no longer Rebecca, but —

"Who are you?" Denise asked

"I am Elizabeth."

"Hum…and you feel alone?"

"Yes. I feel alone. I have my sister though. She supports me. I can talk to her…but, I still must be careful. Our families, our parents, can never find out. Robert's father was so angry. You don't go against your parent's wishes. You must honor them. Respect them. Do as they ask. That is God's will as well, to honor your family. Your parents. But, they ask too much of us. How can they force us apart? Force him to marry someone else? How is it fair? For anybody to go against my family, his family…there's only one way, but we can't think of that now. We're hoping to find another way. We don't know what to do. All we know, is we cannot stop seeing each other. We refuse."

"Yeah."

"To do that…we can't. Being apart is too hard. I can't imagine, neither can Robert."

"Have you been with Robert before this life?"

"I don't know. We feel like we've been together forever. We feel this…our gift is a blessing from God. No one can feel the kind of love we feel. Most people marry out of convenience. For our love, it's unthinkable."

"Yeah. You're supposed to be together."

"We know we are supposed to be together. We are going to try…try to see if our family will change their minds. In the meantime, continue seeing each other in secret. We'll always come here, to the lake, which we found to be our place. Our happiness. Now, so far away from my family home and his. No one will see us, unless they come out this way, and hardly anyone ever comes out this way."

"Where are you?"

"I'm at Dunham Massey…my family owns…our family use to own this, but they don't own it anymore. Something changed. Yeah-yeah, something changed. Someone else owns Dunham Massey…our family doesn't own it anymore."

"So, you…your family needs this connection."

"Yes. We lost our line years ago…the Massey's before us, lost our line and ownership of Dunham Massey…I get the name Booth…Booths. Booths. There's more I think…the Booths…now, I understand. My family…so angry…they want…they need to merge…his family is so powerful, and stronger than ours, because our line ended. We don't have that power…as we did before. We used to own everything here, until the line died."

"They don't want anything to mess it up?"

"They need control again. They need power. They don't like being…towards the bottom. They are still very well. But, they are not as strong and powerful as they use to be. Robert's family is more powerful now. They own most of it, along with the Booths. They've become more powerful. My family cannot accept that Dunham Massey is no longer their home. Their property. Even though it has been rooted away from them. They feel the only way to get it back, is to merge with Robert's family…gain the power and strength…huh…oh…wow…now I understand more…stupid…it doesn't make since…all this power, wealth, property, and status, have anything to do with love." In this, I sound like a child. "Why can't our love still be there, along with the power. Why does it have to be my sister…married to Robert? I don't understand. Can they still have the power and status without him marrying her. She doesn't want to marry him," she said this, with utter sadness.

"She wants you to be happy."

"Yeah. She doesn't want to be married to a man who doesn't love her, and who loves me. She wants us to be together. But, she knows, she can't go against our family…our parents. They are too insistent on this happening. It must be the eldest of his family, and the eldest of our family, which is her. It's not fair. We deserve to be together. How can they tear us apart, knowing how much we care and love each other? They don't care about that stuff. Love has nothing to do with it. No one marries for love. They marry for status, wealth, to better themselves and their standing. So, we will go against them for as long as we can.

What do I do…you don't go against your family," she said, with confusion in her voice. "But, how can I let him go? How can I see him with my sister? It will destroy me. It will destroy him. How can we be together if that happens? We will not be allowed. We've got to do something, but what? He doesn't know what."

In this, I am only an observer, as I am watching Elizabeth and Robert together, at the same time I was trying to explain what was happening as it was taking place.

"We are trying not to think about that anymore…trying to focus on each other and see what happens. But we must be careful. Our family gathers quite often, and when that happens, we must be careful. We cannot show that we are still in a relationship. We must make them believe we are doing what they asked of us. Robert and I are so upset.

"You are put in a position, to not make a good choice?"

"Well, it's not fair," she said, with a slight anger in her voice.

"You have to listen to your heart. I know it's right within me."

"How can such a love we feel, that was given to us by God, be destroyed."

"It's not going to be destroyed. The love will live."

"It will be destroyed, if Robert has to marry my sister," she said firmly and with sadness.

"He'll still love you."

When Elizabeth answers, she becomes defiant, "It won't be the same! We will never be able to touch each other, feel each other, ever again!"

"Yes, you can."

"Once you are married, it's a sin to be with anybody else," she said this in a calmer voice.

"You believe that?"

"Oh yeah, it's a sin," she said, with shock in her voice that someone would believe different.

"God put you two together."

"God put us together, but our families, they have a different belief."

"But God doesn't put people together, then call it a sin."

"No, but if Robert was married, then it would be a sin for us to be together. It would be a full sin. You're not to be with someone who is married…can't…that's against God's will. We must find a way we can be together, where they cannot break us apart. But how do we do this without going against their wishes? We must wait and be patient…and wait…and hope, that God will find a way for us to be together. We believe in that."

"You are already married."

"Were together now."

"You are already married, in your souls."

At this, her voice changes, to a sound of great joy, "Yeah. Our souls are connected in such a way, our hearts…we feel this bond. When were not together, it's almost like our souls are ripped from our bodies, and when were together again, it feels as if we are complete…as one…hmm."

"The minute you think of each other, you are together."

"Hmm, yes."

"Distant doesn't create separation."

"No, distance doesn't. But, when we are actually together…there's a difference. There's a completion."

"Of course."

"Togetherness, a bond, the security," she said.

"What do you think God wants you to know right now?"

"We deserve to be together."

"God wants you to know, that you are, and always will be."

"But it's hard. We…I got…our families."

"It's very hard."

"We don't know what to do. We must honor our families, our parents, and their wishes. But, at the same time we must honor what we feel in our hearts. The bond, the connection we feel. How can we honor both!" Again, Elizabeth suddenly becomes upset. "It's impossible! It's impossible! We can't honor both," she says, as her voice calms again, "But what do we do? Go against our families, and do what's best for what we feel is in our hearts? We must wait…wait and pray. Pray to God, that he will grant us a way."

"Right."

With confidence, she says, "He will grant us an answer. We must be patient and wait.

"Patience? God is the answer."

"Yes. In the meantime, we will meet in secrecy, here at our place, near the lake."

"There's nothing else you can do?"

"No, nothing. But when we are together, we have sworn to put our sorrow and any feelings we have about it behind us. This is our place of happiness. Our security. This, where we consider our sanctuary. Where we can wrap ourselves around each other and forget everything that's happening outside of this place. Our families…anything else…it's just about us, nobody else," she said, with what sounds like a child's giggle, but filled with so much happiness and joy.

"It's a good idea."

"It's just our place, protected by God. No one can invade this place. And no one can take away the happiness we feel here. We swore to each other when we meet at this place…this is our place. Our time together, to be with each other, and express each other's feelings. Forgetting anything else outside this place. We are only to be one hundred percent fully and purely happy. Happy, with just each other, and the love we feel. Our bond and connection…nothing else in this land will matter. To us, that is our agreement with each other, and we have accepted that, and the happiness that we feel…it's, so easy to do." Again, there's a childlike giggle of joy. "Forget about everything, as if no one else exists, anywhere around us. It's just the two of us, alone…alone in this land. No one else surrounding us for miles and miles. It's our place. This is our sanctuary. This, only us…where we shall be, and God should know of."

"Elizabeth, doesn't God approve of this?"

"We feel he does."

"I think so."

"We can only explain that our hearts…feel the way we do…the love we feel, could only have come from God himself. How else can we feel so strongly about each other?"

"This is a sacred place."

"Very sacred…hmm."

"And so, you decided, no matter what happens in this time, and in future lifetimes, you will be together."

"Oh yes. We have already agreed to that…we already know our souls are bonded for life. We feel that they…we've been given this gift from the heavens…that they've allowed us to feel this kind of love for each other. That no one…anywhere, can feel for each other. For some reason, we have been blessed with each other, even though our families don't see it. We do, and we must honor the gift God has given us. We're going to continue to be together, and hope that God will find a way out for us, because he could not have put us together, just to have us ripped apart."

"That's right."

"We believe that, fully and completely. So, we have placed our lives in his hands, and wait for the outcome."

"So, in your eyes, that feeling of safety and security, where you can call on him when you need it. A good thing to memorize."

"I don't ever want to leave this place…so hard, when the time comes to leave and go home."

"Yeah."

"Feels like my heart is ripping in two, when we have to part and pretend like nothing's happening. That is a great pain we feel every day. Every day."

"And no one knows you're here."

"No one. Not even my sister. This is our place…we have determined…this is only our secret, between each other. No one should ever know." Short laughter. "Robert's doing something. He's digging a hole near the tree…I'm asking him, why he's digging a whole near the tree. He says, I shall see in a moment. He wants me to take off my bracelet. I ask him why. He just says take it off and let me have it. So, I remove my bracelet and give it to him. He has a ring on his hand…he removes the ring. He has a cloth he's wrapping them in. He's placing them in the hole near the tree. I ask why…why is he…why are you doing this?" She burst out with laughter, as she's suddenly filled with great joy. "He says…no matter what happens, a part of us will always belong to this place. Something from both of us, will always be here forever." At this, I become emotional, with tears threatening to surface. "No matter what happens," she says, as she's struggling with her words. "This is our spot for eternity. There will always be something of us here, near the tree, our special spot…underneath the spot, where Robert carved our initials when he was being foolish one day. He looks at me like he just got an idea, but he wants to wait and contemplate it first. He will let me know tomorrow. He has to be sure before he tells me…he doesn't want to excite me until he is sure."

"So, he's coming there tomorrow?"

"We come here every day. We make sure one way or another. No matter what, we come back here every day and spend time together. We can never go a day without seeing each other," she said with more laughter. "He says…this feels kind of weird…but," I said letting out a breath, "If God truly brought us together, to be…that, even if something were to happen to us, and our lives ends here in this time…that if we are to be born in another life, we shall ask God to allow us to remember that…we will come back to this lake, to this place," she said, with great emotions, as she struggles with her words. "And this spot and remember what we placed here…to remind us, this is a love we shared before, and it will continue, in many lives after. We will remember that spot, and we will find a way to remember to dig up that spot, so we can reveal what he's placed there, and to know this was us. This is us, from before."

"Beautiful."

"He is so amazing, so romantic. He believes in such things…that we will continue…that our love will continue, even after our death. It will carry on, to all our next lives…because our love was a gift from God, so only…God will not allow this love to be destroyed, no matter what life were in. It gives me such hope."

"So, Elizabeth, will you talk again?"

"Hum-hum."

"So, let's do that again."

"It's time for us to leave. It's getting late. We have to go home."

"Okay."

At this, I returned to normal.

"I hope you got that?" Denise asked.

"Oh wow…yes, I did. It's still recording. Now I know what's buried there, and why it was so important for me to know."

After coming out of this trance, Denise told me when I was talking about the bracelet, I was rubbing my own wrist, as if the bracelet was there.

"The client I told you who went to a psychic, well she gave me permission to give you her name and number. I believe she can help you understand your drawings and give you more information about your past life."

"Oh, thank you. It would be great to have more answers," I said, pleased at the possibility.

"Here's her number. Give her a call and let me know how it goes. I would be curious to what she has to say."

"Okay, thanks. Yeah sure."

Later when I listened to the recording, it was so strange to hear myself, I sounded so young, like a child. I find it interesting of her words, they were not of the sixteenth century, but words I understood. I wondered why. What I believe, is my guides help to translate into our language now. What was interesting in what happened, in the way I felt – the emotions, the laughter, there was so much feeling of love and happiness in her voice – my voice. It blew my mind. This really happened. This was me. My life, in a time long ago. I had a great love, a love that seemed to go – last beyond time. Now I understood. Now I know why I was having these dreams. Drawing these pictures, and dreaming of this man, then and now. He is Robert, and I was Elizabeth. Now is our time to remember and renew our love. What a wonderful miracle. A true and great gift.

Chapter 26

<u>Jonee the medium</u>

It was the day of the reading, and I was very nervous, at the same time excited. I didn't know what to expect. Her name is Jonee Scibienski, and she does her readings at her house. As I reached the end of the cul-de-sac, to the right was a large two-story blue house.

As I was full of nerves, I walked up the few steps to her front door and rang the doorbell. When she opened the door, she was an older woman, of five feet and five inches tall, and she was pleasant and welcoming.

"Hello, come on in. My name is Jonee," she said, motioning her hand towards a corner at the end of her living room, "This way, and watch your step," pointing to a small step into the formal living room. "If I don't say something, it seems someone always falls or stumbles."

As nervous as I was, I could only say, "Thank you, I'm Rebecca."

"Welcome, come this way. It's just around the corner."

Once we were in the corner; it's a small space she created as her office with a partition separating the living room from this space. Directly in front of the partition is her desk and two chairs with a small table situated in front of the desk, and a book shelve with an assortment of angels, fairies, dragons, and other nick knacks that were gifts from friends and some of her clients. There is a laptop on the desk, she uses to record the readings. Behind her, and to my right, is another table situated in front of the window that's covered with blue drapes, along with another computer. The living room and her space is done in blue. To the side wall, just right of me, and near the door into her kitchen is another tall table. On it is a variety of different decorations: masks, angels, fairies, and more.

She motioned to one of the chairs in front of the desk, "Have a seat. There is a pen and paper if you would like to take notes," pointing to the table next to the chair.

She began to explain what she'd be doing. "I will record your reading, and you will have the only copy of the reading, along with the only memory of the reading. The reason for that, is so I don't go insane with everybody else's stuff. You need to know that, so you are sure to ask me all the questions during this session. What I am going to do is contact your guides. Are you aware what guides are?"

I said, as I was looking around, "Yes."

"Good, because I am dealing with them, and they will tell me everything. They will sensor nothing. They won't show us anything you can't handle, unless you ask, okay. Feel free to ask questions at any point, they won't get me off track. Just be sure you want to hear the answers."

"I do. I want to know all the answers. I think they know that already," I said with a slight smile.

"Now…first, they are going to look over your body, to see if there are any areas you need to pay close attention to. Then, they will go into what's currently going on in your life, in what changes you might consider making, and finally, they will take me into your potential future. Now, when I say potential, you were given free will at birth, that allows you to change anything I give you today. That is why you are given the information. But, keep in mind, that will empower you to mess good things up, not just change the bad ones."

"Right." Was all I could say. This was all too bazar. I've been to psychics before, but nothing like this.

"Now, I'm going to be quiet for about a minute, then I am going to say a prayer out loud, using your full birth name, which you will have to tell me. This is the name on your birth certificate. Once this is done, they will tell me everything. So, I need your full birth name?"

"Rebecca Jane Dahli."

There was a little laughter, then she started rubbing her hands together, as she went silent for a few moments. When she spoke again, it was a prayer. "I ask God if he would have his shield of love and truth around Rebecca Jane Dahli, so Gods love and truth, and only God's love and truth will exist between Rebecca Jane Dahli and myself. I allow the masters, teachers, and loved ones, of Rebecca Jane Dahli to channel through me, out of whatever realm to say what they wish. I ask permission of the lords of the Akashic Records, so that I may look into the records and remove whatever information I am allowed. Okay lots of stuff around you. Okay now, do you still have issues with your mom?"

"Huh…yeah." Wow. That's good, since I've had issues with my mother for as long as I could remember.

"That's coming through," her hands clap, then she asked, "She's still alive?"

"Yes."

"So, you are going to have to deal with them, one way or another. They have to be dealt with, because you know, as well as I know, she doesn't have a lot longer to be here, okay…and the worse that would happen in the mist of her dying, all this stuff will come up…okay."

"Hum," nodding.

"There is a man standing behind you."

Okay, that was weird. As I said, "Oh." I wondered who it could be, but said nothing.

"He's not talking to me, but I can feel a lot of love from him. Did you ever have a miscarriage?"

Wahoo, okay, she is good. Slowly, I said, "Yeah."

"Yeah, there is a child too."

"Oh," I said, feeling shocked.

"Okay, you see that occasionally. Okay. It doesn't always mean anything, just a lot of love surrounding that. Okay. I feel like…physically, you have a lot of things you are going to have to watch…your hips bother me, and your lower back, a lot. I am a little worried about your heart, and I think that's because…more figuratively, than literally. But figuratively, can become literal. I feel like, you've been emotionally abused most of your life." At this, I am nodding my head through pretty much most of what she was saying. She hit the nail on the head.

"The thing that bothers me the most about it, is that you accept it so easily, okay. I think, part of this, is past life guilt, alright. Whatever…we can go into the past life if you want?" I nodded. "But the guides are saying, whatever you did in this life, in the past of this life, in the past of other lives, is done. All you can do is do the best you can in this one. But somehow, I want to constantly say I'm sorry-I'm-sorry-I'm sorry around you. Do you do that a lot?"

"Yeah." I am stunned and wowed by her accuracy.

"Okay, so you need to be really conscious of all the times you do that. I would keep a log, so that you could really look at…are you just mouthing those words out of guilt, or was there something really to be sorry for? And if there is, then just say *I'm sorry* then let it go. Because if you did something, you can't fix it, it's done. All you can do is choose not to do it that way again."

I said, "That's when…I think is why I've been having a lot of past live memories and dreams…I've gone…to have hypnosis, and recently I've gone to someone who does past life regression. I've been dreaming a lot about it ever since."

"Okay, which life?"

"It was the life around the renaissance period I think…medieval."

"That's the one I am getting."

"Yeah," I said with surprise.

"You were female, right?"

"Yeah."

"It's the one I'm getting. It was an interesting life. I don't know how much you got into it, but it was a life you were incredibly. You were duplicitous…where, depending upon who you were talking with, you would act whatever way they wanted…as you were manipulating all kinds of things around the background, okay. And that's why you feel so guilty, because a lot of what you did in that life had huge repercussions on other people. Some of those repercussions were literally death."

"Oh." This stunned me. I wasn't sure what to think or feel, but the one thing I was feeling at the time, was fear.

"And it was all because you had such a need, to feel like you had some kind of control in your life…and what you have to understand, women back then had zero control. So, you did it by manipulation. Okay. Women were not supposed to enjoy anything. They were supposed to sew and pray a lot and produce lots and lots and lots of children," she said.

"Can I ask a question?" I finally said.

"Uh-huh."

"Did…hum…the dream I've had constantly…then, when I had the regression…it really made sense…hum…I took my own life in that life," I said, but I wasn't sure what I was really asking, but I had to know if I took my own life, with the dreams and then after the regression of what I learned, when I jumped from the window.

"Yes, you did."

"Yeah…and believing this king killed my husband. But it didn't happen. But he told me because he wanted me. My…but…I believe my husband took his life, after he realized I took my life."

"Okay, first of all, yes, you did kill yourself. But I would argue, it was a lot less about you feeling bad, as it was about control again. You are not going to control me. You are not going to wreck my life. You didn't think what it would do to anybody else."

"Right-right, that's exactly right. Because I was…what am I going to do? I don't want to be in this position."

That is what I believed, from the little information I received. Who knew, how much more there was to be.

"So, the hell with it."

"Like this…right…and that's exactly what it was…because I can't live like this. I wanted to be with this love. I want to be with…I don't want to be in this situation. I can't do this…then when they said…when he died, it was…almost an easy decision…because…well…I had no reason."

"It was a giant cop out."

"Right." She was not wrong about this. Taking one's life is a cop out. But, when you feel as she…I felt, what was left? This life was becoming a part of me, as if that life was merging with this one. This was scary, very scary.

"Pretty much on your part."

When Jonee said this, it hurt. Although, it was a different life, it still hurt…it still was me. The one thing I grew to know, Jonee is blunt, she doesn't sugar coat anything, nor should she.

"Right-right," I said feeling somewhat defeated.

"Because there were children…there were other people that depended on you," she said.

I thought, *children? What? I didn't feel there were any children, but were there? Oh God, no…tell me this isn't so.* At this realization, my heart sank. It could explain why I was so protective of my daughters.

"You wrecked the entirety of your family life there. In this life, you've got to get past it. It is a past life situation, but things you have to learn about this, is that there is a balance between self-centeredness and constant guilt.

"Hum." Is all I said. I didn't get it, nor did I understand any of this – at the time.

"They are the same end of the spectrum. Because, when we are feeling guilty…when we are down all the time, we are always thinking about ourselves."

"Hum-hum." There was no denying what she said. I felt this way, even in this life.

"So, you have to be saying to yourself, *none of this matters now*, okay. What matters now is you figuring out what gives me pleasure…not from a selfish thing, but from a thing making your life work, so the people around you don't have the concerns they have, and you don't have the concerns with them…do you have a daughter?"

It's amazing how she jumps from topic to another in the blink of an eye.

"I have two daughters," I said.

"I thought so. One of your daughters is becoming way too much like you."

I smile, as I know exactly who she is talking about. "Hum…Sara."

"A lot of guilt and stuff…I don't like…your lesson has to do with guilt and selfishness, okay. You have to let go of the guilt. But that doesn't mean you have to become selfish again. It just means you have to find a balance between selfishness and selflessness, okay. In this life, to keep the peace and the power at bay. You don't want to lord over those. In that life, it was all about power…are you divorced?"

"Hum-hum." There was no doubt, she is good.

"But he's still around you?"

"Hum…well —" I tried to say, I was not sure exactly what she meant.

As if she knew where I was going, she said, "He's not in the physical area, but he tries to be."

"Yeah."

"He's still around you…when I say that…he's still in your aura."

"Oh." Was all I said. Geez, I had no idea someone can be in your aura, even if they are not physically in your life. If so, geez, no wonder why I hated him so. I can't rid myself of him.

"Which means, you two aren't done. Now of course, you have kids, so that makes it harder to be done. But you're not completely emotionally done either. Which means, he can hurt you, over and over."

Well, there you go, you can say she hit the nail on the head.

"Yes, I still have a lot of anger." A lot, there was more than a lot. I hated the man with every fiber in me – yeah, there was no doubt, he still affected me.

"Yeah, so that's obviously something that would help you a lot. If you can work through that…hum…what's his birthday?"

"May 13, 1965."

She did something with the information, then returned with, "He wants everything the way he wants it. He has a vision of what his life is to be, and everybody has to conform. So, I'd say, you're living out part of your past life. Within that life you had two people controlling you; a father, and another man who controlled you, that you fought against every chance you got, by being duplicitous, alright. In this life, everything you try to do…in that way, it's going to get…you in trouble. It won't work. It will only make him more…angry and more stuck. Okay. Plus, the fact…I don't know what he expected you to be. I really don't. But *you're not a part of this* could be the typical thing that women do. You know men do it too, but women do it much worse. Where we pretend to be something were not. When were in love, okay.

So, I call that false advertising, okay. So, who he married, was this sweet submissive, happy go lucky…aren't you the most wonderful thing, that ever walked…person."

Boy she got that right. I was so innocent and inexperienced.

"Then after a few years, especially after you had the twins, it was like wait-wait-wait, I got all this other stuff, and you're not participating, like I need you to do in this. But you see, he never told you he would in his scenario. He was going to be the man, and you would still adore him, and the kids would be secondary. But that would be very-very difficult, with one child.

Damn, she was good. Even as I am typing this from my recording…she hit it, right on the head. Feeling stunned, all I could say was, "Hum-hum."

"But twins, it would be impossible. So, he really feels like you ripped him off."

"Hum." *Ass! I am not surprised, as he made it clear he did not want the responsibility.*

"Okay, this saying someone told me years ago, *anger and resentment is though you've taken poison, and expect the other person to die.* So, all the feelings your having…some of these are connected to the past life, and I can't tell you who he was in that past life. Simply because I am invading his privacy then…I won't do that. But I can say, he was one of the main players, okay. That indicates you owe him, somehow."

Fuck that! What?

"So, the only way I can see…in dealing with you owing somebody, is for you to begin…not allow the games to continue. So, you have to stop reacting. So, what you do, is say to him *we made an unfortunate choice when we were young*, but that shouldn't be, *we spend the rest of our lives resenting each other, for an unfortunate choice. Especially because we have two beautiful girls who was not part of this choice. How can we make this work well for all of us?* Now, I'm not telling you to back off all the time, because that doesn't work. But I am telling you to understand that for him, when everything went south, it was as if somebody ripped his world in a million pieces again. So, if you can, understand why he reacts the way he does."

How can the bastard have everything revolve around him? Poor him. It seems to always be about him. Ugg, there was no doubt, I had issues.

"Is because he's so afraid of all the ways you can still hurt him."

Me hurt him, really?

"Then maybe you can stop and breathe and say, *what fear button am I hitting right now*? Okay. Whenever somebody needs absolute control, it's because they have an immense fear of something. So, he fears that you can continue to hurt him."

Again, me hurt him, really…what the fuck! I did not understand this at the time.

"You fear…he can continue to hurt you. *There was no question about that.* "So, both of you are reacting. He gets frustrated very easily and gets determined. You get frustrated very easily and feel hyper-hyper sensitive." *Well,*

I can't argue with that. "You easily hurt…so you close down, and it makes him more frustrated, because he doesn't know how to deal with you, when you aren't communicating. And then you don't communicate, and it makes him want something worse, so it becomes this vicious cycle that indirectly…your daughters are in the middle of. You are here to learn how to stand your ground, and to be independent, without being a bitch." Even now, I laugh at this part…well, I didn't then. "This year, has been pretty difficult at times…wasn't it?"

That's putting it mildly. "Hum-hum."

"Well, it should start getting better. However, you need to understand this year was directly connected to a period seven years ago. So, you need to look at what was going on in your life seven years ago, and fourteen years ago. Because, if you haven't finished it, or cleaned it up, then this is going to hit you again in another seven years, and be harder…when did you get divorced?"

"99," I said.

"So, that was fourteen years ago. So, it was the first year of your divorce…trying to get your bearing again?"

"Oh yes, there was a lot of issues with everything…seven years ago was around the time I had my first asthma attack, and now I have severe asthma problems, this year included. Then, I had my gallbladder removed."

"Okay, but you understand what asthma means don't you?"

"Yeah…well yeah, to a point."

"It means, rethink things. One, you don't feel safe."

Okay, so I didn't have a clue, but said, "Yeah."

"Okay. Two, at times you feel overwhelmingly smothered by everything."

"Hum-hum." Yep, can't deny that.

"And the third thing, it means…is, you don't trust."

"Yes." That, she was one hundred percent correct.

"Okay," she said.

"That's exactly right," I said.

"How you can work on this, is to surrender yourself to God. You were in the 1500s, were with the king. You had three times to make amends but failed."

"I have a question about my life in the 1500s…was I cursed after my death in that life?"

"No."

Confused by this answer, as I was so sure I was. I again asked, "I was not cursed?"

"No. There is no such thing as curses."

I was surprised to hear this, but said, "Okay good," I said with hesitation though.

"Let me explain what I mean by that. God does not judge. Does not condemn. Does not cause anything, okay. God loves us and wants us to be happy. Your soul directs that. What happens is, you are forced to come back and experience similar circumstances. It's not a curse…it's karma."

Oh, okay, that made sense. "Now, did I take my life in all my lives?"

"At least three primary."

"I've been dreaming of a man in this life, someone I feel I am to connect with." Here we go. It was time to find out about this man. The man I believe to be Marco.

"Not yet. They are saying, you have to be ready."

"And they know I'm not ready now, right?"

"No, you're not ready. Not even close."

"Even if I want to, I'm not?" At this, I was trying to get more than just *no you are not*, as I felt I needed more.

"No, you're not. So, this is going to take work…and what they are saying is work on yourself. Work on making your life a good one. One, that someone else will want to share. And when you have it, at that point, that is when you will meet him. If you are working towards meeting him, you will never meet him…it's the opposite you have to do."

Yeah well, that was a lot easier to be said, then to actually do.

"Remember, you are here to figure out who you are. So, work on you, in getting your life going. Do what you need to do, to be happy…poof, he will be there."

"And they are not going to tell me when that's going to happen, are they?"

"Absolutely not! It's up to you. If they were to say six years, let's say, and I'm…there not saying that…then you will get all depressed and say I can't wait six years. And if they were to say three months, then all you do is spend your time looking for somebody…it doesn't work that way."

"It could be tomorrow, and I would not even know it. I can sense that," I said. It was true. I felt that it will be a day I would least expect it to happen. As she said, *poof, and it will happen.*

"Yeah, you could miss him completely because you're looking. So just let go," she said.

But it wasn't as easy as that. I said, "Yeah, I know, and I've been having these weird dreams. I'm trying…to surrender myself to Gods will, and let go, but this past life keeps coming up, and the dreams —"

"They are trying to make you clear it all out."

"Yeah, I'm being told something…trying to learn something. I have to figure this all out."

"Part of what you are here to learn, is who are you? Not who were you. Who are you, and what do you want, and how do you make the steps to begin the process to have it.

And I'm talking about your life…what are you doing for a living?"

"I'm doing sales right now."

"Do you like it?"

"To a point, yeah."

"Because, if you don't, you need to find the other thing that helps define you. It doesn't have to be a job. It could be something you do that you love. But you have got to have a whole series of definitions in place first."

"Hum, okay."

"Okay, we are at the end of your hour. Do you have any further questions before we wrap up?"

"No, I don't think so."

This is where she ended the recording and handed me the CD. During this, I did ask her about using a pendulum, and she didn't see any harm, but told me it was important to shield myself with God's white light first, and if at any time there is an entity/spirit trying to come through that are not my guides, she told me to ask for Gods white light and to use a white candle. A white candle is a protection against unwanted spirits.

After I left, and on my way home I went over what she said, and what I was going to do.

With everything I learned during my therapy sessions, I began to understand a great many things; why I suffered from anxiety and certain fears. One in particular, was the fear of heights. Although I feared heights, it wasn't to the extent that I couldn't take the stairs or fly on a plane. These things didn't scare me. But, if I were to be on or near the edge of a cliff, or even standing looking over a banister to the bottom below. Or, when I was driving up or coming down a mountain, I couldn't drive on the side of the road with the drop off. And it didn't matter if I was in the fast or slow lane, so I am sure I pissed off a lot of drivers. I couldn't drive fast, if I had the feeling of falling, or feeling as if I was going to fall.

If I took a ramp that crossed on the highway; as long as I kept my eyes straight on the road and drove slowly then I was okay. Since after I learned what I learned about taking my life, my fears are gone. I can stand at the edge of a cliff, drive through a mountain, or the freeway ramps without fear. To think, a tragedy from a past life could truly affect me in this life.

Chapter 27

I took the information Jonee gave me about using the pendulum and purchased a new one. This one I cleansed and charged in the sun. I lit white candles before each use, and asked for Gods white light to surround me, protecting me from unwanted spirits and negative energy.

I'd say, "May I speak to my spirit guides?" The pendulum moved up and down, indicating yes. "Am I speaking to my spirit guides?" Again, the pendulum moved, indicating yes. After this, I proceeded with my questions.

"This man I believe to be Marco, is this his true name?" It swung *yes*. "When the entity was causing me problems, did I ever actually communicate with Marco with your assistance?" It said, *no*. "Is Marco still in Arizona?" *No*, it swung, then it spelled out, *he's back in England.* "I've been feeling that Marco is staying at the Fairmont Princess. Is this true?" *Yes.* "Did he purchase a condo there?" *Yes.* "Did he do this because he knows I live in Scottsdale?" *Yes.* Then it spelled out, *but also for business.*

It was amazing with what was happening. Still, could I trust the answers I was getting even though I am using the protection I was told to have. Was it possible? I continued with my questions.

"For business. What type of business?" They said, *wine.* "Really? Will this information be confirmed by Jonee when I see her again?" *Yes.*

And it was. Anytime I was unsure of the information I was getting, I would see Jonee, and she would confirm the information I received was accurate, which gave me the confidence I needed.

After this line of questions, I decided to do some research, I wanted to see if it was possible for someone to purchase a condo at the Fairmont Princess, and to my surprise, it was. I continued having conversations with my guides, but not as often as I use to. I became cautious to the amount of time I was using the pendulum, but with Jonee's help, I was becoming more and more confident.

With my conversations with my guides, along with the dreams I was having, I learned Elizabeth and Robert married on Christmas Day. When I learned this, it was as if a light bulb went off, and I thought, *that's why I love Christmas, and why I had always hoped...wished, to marry on Christmas, even after my divorce, if I were to ever marry again.* For as long as I could remember, Christmas had always been my favorite time of the year. My favorite holiday.

Although I loved this holiday, it was also the time I felt the saddest. I would become depressed, with a sense of loss, as if there was something missing. What it was, at the time, I did not know. But later, when I learned it was love, but not just any love, a one true, soul-to-soul love, it blew my mind. What's funny, after going through what I went through, in reliving this life as Elizabeth, I am still waiting to meet Marco. We are approaching Christmas; I don't feel as I once did. Christmas is no longer as special as it once was. Is this because of what I now know? Or is it more?

After this, my life started taking on a whole new meaning. I started feeling better, and I even started losing weight. I started putting myself back to where I was before all this started. It was a few days before Christmas, and I was at work feeling great, better than I had in a long time. I was walking through the small galley kitchen area, that consist of a small refrigerator, sink, and a coffee machine, when I was hit with a powerful vision:

I can see Marco. He's with his mother, in what looks like a house. I hear him say to her, "I must return to the states, and right away."

His mother was not happy about this, and said, "No! You cannot go! It's Christmas, and you must spend it with your family."

He then said, "I'm sorry, but it's not possible. There is something I must do, and I must go now."

His mother ended up convincing him to stay for Christmas Eve dinner before he left, which he agreed.

After this, I felt he was coming back to Arizona, because of me. Later that night, I felt I needed to go to the Fairmont Princess on Christmas night. I usually go every year – they do a spectacular Christmas event, but I've never been on Christmas night before.

My roommate was having her family over for Christmas dinner, and my daughters had other plans, so it was just me. By Christmas, I had lost all the weight I gained from surgery and dressed in black pants with a white top and a red cover up, and I went to the Princess around seven o'clock. I walked around looking at all the Christmas displays, ending back at the main entrance. I decided to stop at the Starbucks located on the property and bought my hot Americano. Then found a seat outside and watched the light show along with the other people around me. There was a couple – the man bent down on one knee and proposed. It was such a sight to see. I remember thinking, *that's never happened to me.*

It was getting close to nine o'clock and nothing had happened. But just as I was about to give up, I heard a voice in my mind say, *wait. Do not leave.* So, I waited another thirty minutes, but still nothing. Again, I was about to leave, and again I heard the voice say *wait.* This time, it wasn't just wait, it said, *walk towards the ice-skating rink.* I wasn't sure why, but I did as it said. As I was walking down the path to the ice rink, I saw this man, but I couldn't clearly see his face. He was tall, with loose wavy hair. He was wearing a T-shirt and jeans. The T-shirt looked to have a British flag on it. He seemed to be looking in my direction, as I was looking at him, trying to see his face, but the light was shining directly in my eyes, and I wasn't able to.

As soon as I walked past him, I felt something in my chest, it was the feeling I knew I would feel, telling me it was him. However, I was not allowed to do anything. I had to wait. He had to be the one to make the first move. No matter how hard I wanted to turn my head and look back, to see what he was doing, it felt, as if I was prevented from doing so. It wasn't until I reached the skating rink and stood next to a pole, when I was finally able to turn around. I wondered if he was there, following me, hoping to find an opportunity to speak to me. To my disappointment, he was not. I was disappointed, but then later, after thinking about it, I felt pleased, because I saw him, and knew no matter what my doubts were, he is indeed real. This was my proof.

After I returned home and was relaxing in my room, I felt this need to draw a picture, a picture of the man I saw. As I began drawing, it felt as if it wasn't me drawing, but someone was using me as an instrument, helping me to draw. When the picture was done, I could not believe what I saw. This was the man, the man I saw in my dreams and visions. The man I was destined to meet. This picture was the best picture out all the ones I drew. What I felt when I saw the completed image, it was again, that deep feeling in my chest, telling me it was him. It was a confirmation, that I did see him – Marco. I was so happy to have a drawing of what he truly looked like.

After this night, with no further doubts he was real, I became excited, and started preparing for what was to come. Although I felt secure – sure it was real, to be safe, after everything that's happened, I thought it was best to see Jonee, and let her confirm what happened.

<u>Marco – Lorie Valley, France – January 2014</u>

Marco went to France to visit his family's and his grandmother's vineyard. As he went to the normal places when he visits Lorie Valley, there was one chateau that seemed to stop him in his tracks. When he turned to look at it, there was something familiar about it. *How could I have not noticed this place before? And why is it now affecting me so?* he thought.

Marco had no choice, he had to go into the chateau. It was calling to him, so much so, he could not resist it. As he entered the main entrance, he was immediately taken back, to the familiarity of the place, as if he's been there before. He toured the chateau, although he felt there was something familiar about the chateau, it wasn't anything that begged to understand. Then, he walked into the study, and it hit him like a ton of bricks. If he hadn't caught it, he would have collapsed in front of everyone. *What in God's name is happening to me?* His chest, the spot over his heart – his birthmark began to throb with a burning sensation.

Marco automatically put his hand over his birthmark that was directly over his heart. Then images of a time long ago flashed through his mind. This room, a man – a man he seemed to recognize – *how is this possible?* he wondered. More flashes of other men, then the man again – he was hurt and in pain. Not a wound, but pain of the heart. *He lost someone…his love,* Marco thought. Then, *how could I know that. No, it's not possible.*

After everyone else left the room, Marco found himself alone. He walked to the window, and as he was standing there looking out, it felt familiar, as if he's done this before. But as far as Marco knew, he's never been to this chateau before. *Is it possible, I visited this place when I was a child, and just don't remember?* he thought.

After a few moments at the window, he walked to the fireplace, and as he stood there, he had flashes of a man from another time. He could see, hear, and feel everything.

"She's dead, no, this cannot be." The man said." The other man that was with him, he too was familiar to Marco. A man he hated. He was surprised he could feel the anger and hate this man created in him. Who is this man? Marco thought. Then, he saw the other man, the one upset, lashed out at the older man. *"No! You are lying. Tell me, you have proof? Show me her body?" The other man only smiled, and said, "Lord Robert, I do not have the body, as it was tossed in the water to float out to sea to be shark food." The man said, then produced a necklace. "But I have this as proof of her death." Robert took the necklace and slumped in a chair.* Marco could feel the pain, the sorrow this Robert was feeling. Next, Marco saw the man who he heard called Robert standing at the fireplace with a dagger in his hand, and after a few moments, he struck it into his chest, falling to the floor directly in front of the fireplace and heard the man whisper, *"Elizabeth —"*

Marco grabbed his chest, shocked at what he just experienced. He rushed out of the room and out of the chateau to the street outside.

Rebecca

"NO! No, I cannot do this. I cannot see this. No, not now. Please. This is too much for me." As I am begging, pleading not to have to experience this, I was being shown an image as I was feeling what he was feeling – Robert standing at the fireplace when he struck a knife into his chest and fell to his death, and with his last breath he whispered, *Elizabeth,* and he was gone.

I was in my car driving home from a doctor's appointment when this vision hit me. Although I tried hard to fight it, I felt I was being forced to see – to experience what Robert experienced when he took his life. It was the most difficult vision – feeling, more so than experiencing Elizabeth's rape. I was bawling my eyes out and had to pull the car over, and just allow the experience – the feeling to wash over me until it subsided.

After I returned home, I wasn't done with what happened – I was being pushed – forced to draw what I saw. I fought it, I begged to not be forced to draw the scene of Robert's lifeless body, but it didn't matter; I was made to do this. I felt that I had to know and feel what my – Elizabeth's actions did, in the pain she caused, in turn, the death of Robert. I think I sat there after the drawing was done crying until I couldn't cry anymore. It was the most horrific thing I have ever experienced in my life.

"No, this cannot be happening," Marco whispered, shaking his head, trying to rid himself of the image he saw, and what he felt. Marco wasted no time, he called his grandmother, knowing she would have the answers.

Maria was in her garden tending to her flowers when her phone rang. She stopped what she was doing and removed her gloves before she answered her phone. "Hello?"

"Nõnna, I must speak with you."

"What's wrong Marco, you sound upset."

"Nõnna, I am in France, and I passed a chateau…there was something familiar about it, so I went inside, and in this one room, something happened —" Marco paused, and took a deep breath.

Maria said, "You remembered, didn't you?"

"Nõnna...yes...well, something happened. I could see a young man and an older man. The older man was telling the younger man his wife was dead. Then I saw the younger man take his life...a dagger right in the heart. Nõnna, I didn't only see it, I felt it...all. I know you know what it is, so please, tell me?"

Sighing, "Marco, you remembered when Robert learned of his wife's death, and you taking your own life because you couldn't leave with the guilt that you failed Elizabeth."

Shaking his head, "No. Nõnna, this cannot be true...real."

"Marco, but it is. You need to go back and remember it all. Then once you have returned home, go to Bramhall Manor where your family lived during that time. There you will remember everything."

"What?" Shaking his head, "No! How can I go back and remember more...to feel...no-no-no! I won't."

"Marco, it won't be as it was there. It will be good and happy memories."

"I will think on it. I need a drink," Marco said, as he saw a pub. "Nõnna, I am going to go and have a drink and try to clear my head."

"Marco —" Maria stopped what she was going to say. She knew it would do no good, and Marco needed to decompress. "Marco, I understand, but don't drink too much. I love you, and if you need me, I will be here for you."

"Thank you, Nõnna. I will call you later." Then he hung up the phone.

<u>Arizona - 2014</u>

In the two weeks I waited to see Jonee, something amazing happened. My roommate was in the hospital, and while I was home alone watching television, there was this – that sensation, but it was ten times stronger than it was before, but before I could do anything about it, Janet called and asked me to come to the hospital to watch a show on television, we usually watched at home.

After returning home, what I felt before I left intensified. There was this need to talk to my guides. I turned off everything in the living room and went to my bedroom. I grabbed my laptop, as this turned out to be a great way of communicating with my guides using the alpha keys. Once I was ready, my guides told me that Marco wanted to speak to me. I was shocked, but not because he wanted to speak to me, but because he could with the assistance of our guides. I stopped the pendulum. I didn't know what to think. I remembered how this happened with Edward, and I wasn't sure if I could trust it. But this time, there was something different. My chest – my heart was telling me it was real. True.

I asked my guides how this could be? They told me it was because he was open and ready. He was at his grandmothers, and she was helping him. With what they said, the feeling in my chest only increased. I said, "Okay, I am ready. Go ahead and connect us."

When we spoke, it was like I was speaking to him through instant messenger. We had an actual conversation.

"Rebecca, are you there?"

"I am here Marco. Is it really you?"

"Yes, it is really me."

"How is this possible?"

"From what my grandmother says, it's through the assistance of our guides."

"I cannot believe this is really happening."

"It is love, it's really happening."

"Was it you I saw at the Princess on Christmas night?"

"Yes, it was me."

"Why didn't you approach me? I was waiting…hoping you would."

"I am sorry. I was too afraid. I was afraid I would approach you, and it would not be you."

"I can understand that. I am not sure I would have done differently if I was in your place."

This conversation when on for about an hour, and he confirmed his side of things, and I confirmed my side of things, and it matched. It was the most amazing conversation and feeling I have ever experienced in my life, and I never wanted this feeling to go away.

Finally, it was the day of my appointment with Jonee, and I told her what happened, and the conversation I had with Marco. She confirmed the connection and conversation we had was true, that it really happened. You can imagine my shock to learn this. She confirmed everything that happened on Christmas, However, at this point, there was nothing I could do but wait. It was up to Marco, he had to be the one to approach me. She also told me – well, she confirmed that I will be returning to the Fairmont Princess. When, this she could not say.

Ever since the first communication happened with Marco, we continued to communicate in this way, with the help of our guides and his grandmother. Although it was so easy to provide each other with the information we needed to contact each other, we were not allowed. Trust me, we tried – hard. I remember saying, "Call me, my phone number is 602-555-0101." I'd ask him to repeat it back to me to make sure he received it correctly.

He would say, "Yes, I have it, it's 602-555-1214."

I'd say, "No, it's 602-555-0101."

He'd say, "Yes, okay, I have it. I will call you now."

I said, "Okay, I am waiting."

I waited and waited, and no call ever came through. So, I asked, "Did you call me?"

He said, "Yes, but you did not answer."

I said, "I did not receive a call."

He said, "I am not sure what happened, but I tried calling you."

I then asked him to wait, and I asked to speak to my guides who confirmed we were not allowed to exchange this information. So, I in turn explained this to Marco, and we didn't try again, at least not right away.

At the end of January, I received a request to speak to my guides. So, I grabbed my pendulum and my laptop and began speaking to my guides.

"You need to go to the Fairmont Princess on the first Saturday of February, and you need to wear red."

"Why do I need to go to the Fairmont Princess?"

"Marco's grandmother is going to arrange for Marco to be there so you two will meet."

I was shocked. I couldn't believe it. I said, "What? Is that possible?"

"Yes. When you go, you must wear red. All red."

"Why red?"

"His grandmother is going to tell him to look for a woman wearing all red with dark long hair, and that you will be with a blond woman, and you will be at the bar."

"What…okay, I can wear red. I have a red dress. A blond woman…what blond woman?"

"You must invite your roommate Janet *to go with you."*

This was odd to me, but I said, "I am not sure if this is a place she will want to go."

"She will go with you, if she believes you are meeting someone."

"So, I am to tell her I am going on a blind date, and I would need a wing man – woman?"

"Yes. She will go."

Well, I did as my guides asked, and to my surprise, Janet agreed to go with me.

It was the first Saturday of February, and I was returning to the Fairmont Princess. I wore my red dress with the matching cover and my black boots. We sat at the outside bar and waited. We arrived at seven in the evening, but by ten nothing happened.

Janet asked, "Where's this man you are supposed to meet?"

"I don't know. He was supposed to be here by now."

"Why don't you text him."

I looked at her, I didn't know what to do. Janet didn't know what was happening. She would never understand. So, how can I text a man I didn't have his number for. I had to think quick, so I said, "Okay, yeah, you are right. I will text him now." I pretended to send a text and waited for a response. But after ten minutes, after not receiving a response I said, "I guess he is standing me up."

Just then, a couple of men walked over to us, and we started talking, and we forgot about my *so-called date*, to my relief. Then, right around eleven or after, I saw a man standing off to the left side of the bar, leaning against the metal railing watching me. He wore brown and cream combo looking silk top with brown pants. He was staring at us – me. He looked angry, so I turned away, thinking it wasn't Marco, since that angry look made me feel as if I was invading his space. Later, I notice him walk away, going down the steps on the other side. I never did meet Marco that night, but I was sure the man I saw was him. I wouldn't know for sure until I met with Jonee again.

The next morning, I contacted Jonee and arranged to meet with her the following Saturday, and when I met with Jonee, without giving her too much information on what happened, she was able to confirm it was him. His anger was because I was talking to two men, and he couldn't figure out how to speak to me without looking mad – crazy. I understood this and couldn't blame him for it. I probably would have done the same thing.

With work, things seem to be going well. Yes, I still had my occasional asthma attacks, but I was able to get through my shift with little loss of work. During this, I continued with my drawings, from the dreams and visions I was having, and at times, I would speak to Marco. I even connected with Maria, Marco's grandmother. She'd been watching me ever since she knew I existed. It was a wonder to know this woman was there and cared about me, as if I was one of her own. What she went through to help me and Marco, still blows my mind. She's been astral projecting herself, so she could travel and see me.

On one of these occasions, when I felt her with me, I also felt Marco. At one point, I felt his hand brush my face along with feeling his and her love. It was a wonderful and glorious feeling. With Maria's help, along with our guides, Marco and I agreed to meet the first Saturday of March at the Scottsdale Quarter, near the water fountains. I was so excited. It was finally going to happen, this I had no doubt, until the day of our meeting, and again, to my disappointment, he was a no show.

When Marco did not show, I reached out to my spirit guides to find out what happened. "Why didn't Marco show up?"

"We are sorry Rebecca. There was a problem with the tire on the car that was taking him there. They had to turn around and return to the Princess."

"Oh, I am sorry there was an issue. Can we try again?"

But instead of my guides responding, it was another spirit that communicated with me.

He said, *"Hello Rebecca. I am sorry, but you cannot meet with Marco. I will not allow it."*

Shocked and surprised, I said, "What…why? Who are you? I know you are not my spirit guides."

"I am Adam, and because you do not deserve to have this love."

I was shocked. I didn't know what to think, then something strange happened. My pendulum started circling uncontrollably, as it did when Edward started talking to me, so I became concerned. And just when I was going to put the pendulum down to cleanse it and light my white candles, it spelled out this, *Rebecca, this is Paul, I am here to protect you. Adam will not harm you.* He went on to explain who he was, that he is a spirit, a family member of Elizabeth's, but he would not explain who Adam was, and so I believed Adam was a lost spirit who needed help. Since I've learned so much about spirituality, and in this, I learned I can help a lost spirit move on, so I decided to give it a try. So, instead of getting angry, I sent him love, and expressed that I wanted to help him. He seemed sincere, and I believed I helped him, but I would later find out I did not.

When I saw Jonee again, she explained that Adam was blocking Marco and I, preventing us from communicating, and if we did, we wouldn't receive everything. He did this, in order to prevent us from meeting. From being together. Jonee explained this spirit – Adam was a family member from my past life as Elizabeth. In order to free myself from this spirit, I needed to speak to him, and resolve the issues that still existed between us.

Because of Adam, my health started to decrease again. So, one night while I was taking a shower, feeling depressed, I could hear Adam in my mind mocking me. At this, I had enough, and when I finished taking a shower and was dressed, it was time I had it out with Adam.

I sat on my bed and crossed my legs, then I began talking to Adam. "Adam, I know who you are. Or at least I believe I do." I paused, taking a moment to collect my thoughts. "I tried to help you move on when you started bothering me, but you refused. At first, I thought you were just a stray spirit lost, not knowing what to do or wanting to leave. It wasn't until after I spoke to a woman I know, who told me you were a spirit…a family member from my life as Elizabeth. Please, tell me who you are, and let's talk about what happened?"

Well, at first, I received a reluctant answer. There was great anger there. I did learn Adam was Elizabeth's father, and there were two others, Elizabeth's mother, and brother. They refused to move on, because they wanted to make sure I didn't have the happiness they felt I did not deserve. I explained to them what happened; the rape, kidnapping – everything. They told me what happened to them – what Lord Davenport did to them. I was heartbroken by this, but in the end, we forgave each other, and they finally passed to the other side. It was over. They were finally at peace. What was sad, I learned who Edward was, he was Robert's brother. I am not sure why he was so angry with me, to where he felt he had to deceive me in this way, nor do I know to this very day.

For me, it was the beginning. I suffered so much pain and sorrow from what happened. From what I did. It was my fault - my family – Elizabeth's family died. How could I forgive myself for that? My health once again declined, and finances was worse than ever. I started working from home, but in doing this, I gave up on life. I once again became severely depressed.

With what was going on with my roommate, and my issues, it was time for me to move out. I found a small studio apartment, and there, everything changed.

Chapter 28

<u>August 2014</u>

I moved into my small apartment, and I am still working from home. So much has been going on, that I didn't know what to do. I have been meditating on a regular basis, and I continue to communicate with Marco, but it felt as if it wasn't going anywhere. Maria, Marco's grandmother's health had deteriorated rapidly, but regardless, she increased her visits with me, in her attempts to help Marco and I find each other.

At times, more than I'd like, I can feel Marco's pain. In feeling his sorrow and pain, along with what I was going through, it sent me spiraling out of control, and into complete and utter depression. My health was again out of control, and I felt lost, I wasn't just dealing with my issues, but Marco's as well, not to mention the desperation in Maria trying to bring Marco and I together. I needed help so I decided to go to Jonee's channeling.

What is Jonee's channeling? Allow me to explain. Jonee, after several visits told me about a channeling she has every first Friday of the month, and she thought it would be a good idea for me to join, but for a long time I decided not to attend, as I really wasn't sure if I wanted to attend a channeling. Who would I want to come through? Well, Jonee's channeling is not what you might think. Jonee doesn't channel your loved ones as you might believe, but she channels these being that are called Equinoxx, which are of the light, connected to the source of all power – God. You can ask any question you want, so long it does not invade someone else's privacy. So, you know how you can go to a psychic, and they will tell you whatever you want to know regardless of someone's free will – privacy. This is unlike anything like that. You are communicating with beings – entities who are in direct contact with the source – God.

I went to Jonee's channeling, and I asked about Marco – if Maria had a message for me. What I was told, was that I needed to go to the Fairmont Princess at the end of August, to the outside bar, but not at the bar itself, to the seats near the water fountain. I wasn't sure of this, since at the end of August it's still very hot in Arizona. However, they said that Maria was going to do what she can to get Marco to go there. They didn't think it would work, but I should still go, if anything, I can have a good time.

Well, I went, and he didn't show up. It was hard for me to try once again to meet Marco, to only have it fail. These were more than I could handle, and all it managed to do was send me further into depression, to the point, I contemplated on taking my life – again. This time, I had strong prescription sleeping pills in my hand, and I was trying to decide if I was going to take them or not. Each time I brought them to my mouth, a voice in my head kept saying *no-no*. After hearing no-no several times with a force pushing to put away the pills, I put them away and went to bed. Although I did not take them, I was lost all the same. By this time, I had stopped working due to my health, and was barely surviving.

For a long time, I disappeared, away from everyone or anything. I wanted my solitude, as I needed time to think. To think of what I was going to do with everything that has happened, and everything that didn't happen. Who did I want to be? The person waiting for a man I have never met, waiting for him to decide to come into my life – something I have no control of. Or, do I want to fight and take my life back, and become my own person once again?

Well, it would be several months before I finally kicked my depression and decided it was time to make a change in my life. I was taking my life back.

January 2015

I decided it was time to leave the travel agency and go back into accounting. I knew it was a risk, but the only way to obtain current experience was to start out in temp jobs. In this decision, I would no longer be required to be on the phone eight hours a day. And to my amazement, my health improved. I was making it through a nine-hour day, every day for months. When one contract ended, another one started. I did this throughout the year 2015.

In August, the time came to move out of the apartment, and go back to being a roommate. Through a referral, I found a great place in Mesa, Arizona. During my time there was great. I worked a few temp jobs, and I believe the longest I went without work was thirty days. Thank God for my roommate being so understanding, since I bounced around a few times during my time with her, until I found a great job, that would become permanent.

Marco and I, for a short time, continued communicating. I know what you are thinking, but it turned out to be more difficult that I first believed. He kept reaching out to me, I believe due to his grandmother's persistence, in her death bed wish. And what could I do, turn away from a man who was grieving. No, this I could not do. I just couldn't.

Shortly after, Marco's grandmother Maria passed away. However, before she did, she was sending me information, in what seem to be in rapid rate. In doing this, it caused her health to decline rapidly, until she finally succumbed to her illness and passed away. I remember this day, as it was the day I felt tremendous sorrow, and knew she was no longer of this world. I also felt Marco's pain, and I knew with the passing of his grandmother he would need time to grieve, and therefore, I decided to let him go. It was the hardest thing I had to do, but I knew without his grandmother, he would go back to believing what we have was not real. With this, I had to cut myself off from him. I couldn't live through his pain, not again.

This was also a time something amazing happened. I was sitting on the sofa watching TV when I felt a vision coming on, so I took a few moments and allowed it to come through. To my shocking surprise, it was Elizabeth. I could see her sitting in a chair near the window where she jumped to her death. She was sitting there staring out, feeling sorrow and regret for what she did, so I reached out and spoke to her in my mind.

"Elizabeth, there is no need to feel so sad. I am here. I am you. I am Rebecca, and I am well."

"I did it. I hurt everyone. I killed Robert, and I killed my family. Because of what I did…it's all my fault," she said in her soft, delicate voice.

"There is nothing you can do now. You need to move on – forgive yourself. Robert has been reborn in this life with me. Your family has moved on, and they are now at peace. It is time for you to also be at peace. You did what you felt you had to do. Let it go. Forgive yourself as your family has forgiven you."

Whatever did it; I felt Elizabeth's ego finally moved on, and was now at peace. I learned a great deal later that your ego and spirit are not the same. Although your spirit – soul moves on, your ego can remain – stranded in the life you suffered if you feel regret.

Later on, in this same year, I met a man online that I connected with. There was something about him, a sense of familiarity as if I knew him before. And I knew he felt it as well. I would like to say everything worked out, but it didn't. The best thing that came from this time, I started writing my book, *The Power of Love,* again? I did a complete rewrite and was pleased with the final draft.

By July 2016, after finally moving on, with the knowledge Marco and I were not meant to be together in this life, along with the knowledge our souls were bonded, connected for eternity. With this knowledge, I knew we would find each other, maybe not in life, but in death. I felt comfort with that, and after meeting this other man, I knew I could move forward and love again.

In all this, about six months into the year 2016, I couldn't forget about Marco, and when I started book two, this book, my story, I reconnected with Marco again. And this time, it was different, it was more powerful than it was before, and once again, I found myself needing to return to Cheshire, England, so I decided, this time I will seek help in finding Marco, by hiring a private detective.

<u>December 2016</u>

I just received a call from Mr. Davenport, the private detective I hired. He found Marco. I was shocked. I couldn't believe it. There was no doubt he was real.

"Ms. Daniels, I have to say, I am amazed at what I discovered based on your information, of the man you wanted me to find, to prove to you is real. Well, he is. He is as real as you and I. His grandmother owned the vineyard in Italy, but it was sold off in parts years ago, and recently, the final part where this man – Marco's grandmother lived was also sold.

He lives in Cheshire, England, as you suspected, and his family has their own vineyard in France. I have here in front of me his name, number, and address. If you would like them, meet me at my office tomorrow morning at eight and I will give everything I discovered.

I have to say Ms. Daniels, I didn't expect to find anything. In the way you obtain the information, I have to say…it has opened my mind to the possibility there is more out there."

Needless to say, I was shocked. I couldn't believe it. But did I want the information? I decided to think on that until the following morning.

On the following morning I called Mr. Davenport. "I have to say Mr. Davenport, I am shocked and relieved. I half expected you wouldn't find anything, and to know you did, relieves me a great deal. I will be at your office tomorrow at eight," I said, then ended the call.

The following morning, I met with Mr. Davenport, and said, "Mr. Davenport, I thought a great deal about this, and at first, I was going to decline to receive the information, but then again, I decided I needed to, and I will choose to open it or not."

"Ms. Daniels, I can understand what you mean. It is a great deal for me to comprehend what happened, and to accept how you came about the information you provided me. Here is the information," he handed me a large envelope. "Inside you will find his full name, address, family history, and a photograph of the man himself. I wish you luck in whatever you decide to do with the information."

I took the envelope with care, and held it against my chest and said, "Mr. Davenport, thank you very much for your help." Then I turned and left his office. Without opening the envelope, I decided it was time to return to Cheshire, and to the lake. There, I would decide to open the envelope if I chose to. So, I planned my trip for the end of April to the first week of May 2017.

Well, I am back in Cheshire, and I'm returning to Dunham Massey, and this time, I am finally going to the lake. On this trip, I decided to meet with an archeologist, who explained to me the history of the castle and lands around, and how the particular lake – our lake, was smaller, but through the years it has grown to cover a great deal of the land than it used to be. To learn this, I knew the bracelet and ring were now under water, and irretrievable.

I decided on the following morning to return to the lake alone, and I had the owner of the bed and breakfast at Ash Farms make me a picnic lunch with sandwiches and white wine, and I brought a blanket. When I arrived, I stood facing the lake near *the tree*. I felt the energy, the power of this place, it was amazing. The love I felt, was like a strong wind forcing its way into my body and into my heart.

I was wearing a yellow flowered summer dress, and I was sitting on the blanket only a few feet from the lake, admiring the lake and surrounding trees while I was drinking my wine. I could feel the calm and the peace of this place, the energy of the love we once had – we once shared.

After a time, I decided to pull out the envelope of the information about Marco. I decided this was the perfect place to open it, but only made it to the photograph, which I stared at with awe. I couldn't believe it, he looks just like the drawing I did of the man I saw at the Fairmont Princess on Christmas night in 2013. After a short time, I sat the photo down and stared out to the lake.

As I was taking in this wonderful and miraculous place, I felt something strong and powerful in my chest, as I had before. This time, it was different, stronger. Then I heard a noise, with a need to look to my right – there, there he was – Marco. He looked just like the man in the photograph and in my drawing. I couldn't believe it. He was there, walking towards me with purpose in his step, as if he knew I was going to be there. He was wearing black slacks, a blue dress shirt, and his hair was dark and wavy – more handsome than I ever could have imagine.

With a sudden unsureness, I turned away to look at the lake. When I did look back at him, he was right there, standing looking down at me. I couldn't move, all I could do was stare up at him, believing this wasn't real. Thinking, that at any moment he would vanish right before my eyes once he was upon me, and it would be nothing but a lovely, beautiful daydream, a fantasy when —

"Hello, how are you? My name is Marco, what's yours?"

Feeling shocked, I wasn't sure the words in my head would come out of my mouth. I took a deep breath and said, "R-r-Rebecca is my name…pleased to meet you…Marco, is it?"

"Yes. What brings you here to the lake?"

"Well…after meeting with an archeologist yesterday, I wanted to come back, wanting to absorb the feeling of this place…a place…a magical place." After I said this, I turned to look back at the lake, and when I did, it was as if I was seeing a different time. Then remembering he was still there, I turned to him and said, "Sorry…I know this must sound crazy…but there is something very special about this place. Do you feel it?"

"No…no not at all. And yes, I know exactly what you mean. I feel it too. I've dreamed of this place," he said looking out to the lake, "Of a time long ago. Of a special woman…a love…I'm sorry," shaking his head, "Now I'm the one sounding crazy."

"No-no, not at all…I get what you are saying. I too…had dreams of this place…of this love…from long ago."

"Then it is…I'm sorry…I might sound crazy if I am wrong…but —"

"You are not wrong. It is me Marco, Rebecca…the one you've been dreaming about. The one you connected with and was speaking to all this time."

At this, I stand up, and Marco reaches out to lend me a helping hand. When I was steady, he pulled me into his arms and said, "I have waited so long for this day to come. Now, for it to finally be here…God —"

No more words were said, he kissed me with such passion – I can feel his love for me, and I knew he could feel my love for him.

During this, flashes of our life before as Robert and Elizabeth, here at this lake, were in an embrace and kissing. I could feel the love, the passion they felt. It was so powerful. Then, there were more flashes, another young girl, another family, it was Grace, my sister. It was both our family. Our wedding, the pain of our family's anger…and our pain. Our loss. It was all there, in our kiss. The door between our two worlds opened, making us now one. I was Elizabeth, and I am Rebecca. We were now one and the same. I could remember my life as Elizabeth, of the past in complete detail, and I wondered if Marco felt the same.

Once he broke our kiss, as I was looking in his eyes, I knew he did. "You saw it too? You remember, didn't you?

He said, "Yes Rebecca I did. Will you…will you marry me?"

I was shocked, and yet I wasn't. Finally, there was nothing keeping us from being together, and so of course, I said, "Oh Marco…yes…God yes I will marry you."

It is winter, and the snow is covering the ground, and I am standing outside a small quaint church. It was early evening, as there was a little light left in the sky from the sun sitting in the horizon. I am standing facing the church, and I see candlelight flickering in the windows. As I slowly enter the church, I notice how small and cozy it is. The candlelight was the only light in the church, a beautiful romantic atmosphere. I see Marco standing at the front of the church with the priest next to him. I look over to the left, and there are my daughters. I am happy, excited, nervous, and scared. Never in a million years did I believe I would be getting married again, let alone to a man who is my heart and soul, and to have my daughters there, looking as if they were very happy for me, warmed my heart.

As I start down the aisle towards Marco, just the sight of him sent a rush of joy, love, and happiness through my body. I felt fully and completely blessed. When I reached Marco, he took my hands in his, and brought me close, so were standing face to face, staring into each other's eyes. Neither of us being able to look away, feeling the love we have for each other, as it flows from him to me, like a warm blanket wrapping itself around us – embracing us, making us one once again.

We both are fighting back tears that are threating to escape. Our love – to marry, will complete us. Our marriage will bond us for eternity. To never part, ever again. The end to our story.

<u>Spiritual Realm</u>

Maria is at the well of light between the spiritual realm and Earth, watching the happy union of her nipõte and Rebecca getting married. All she wanted – wish for is now complete. She can now rest, having fulfilled her destiny, in bringing

Marco and Rebecca back together. "Bellissimo. I love you both." Then she sends Marco and Rebecca her love.

The End

Acknowledgements

Joan Scibienski is a true Psychic for over 30 years and was a great help to certain part of my book. To know more about Joan please visit her websites listed below and her books, The Ariana Series and You Were Born Psychic. Published by Flint Hills Publishing.

Joan L Scibienski
Ariana Series.

Joan L Scibienski
You Were Born Psychic

Please check out her website.
www.intuitivedirections.net
www.channelingeq.com

Acknowledgements

Kathleen Donaghy is licensed psychologist who was a big help in the psychological part of this book.

Please visit her website.
www.heartcenteredpsychology.com/welcome